THE STONE BREAKERS

THE STONE BREAKERS

EMMANUEL DONGALA

TRANSLATED BY
SARA HANABURGH

SCHAFFNER PRESS
TUCSON, ARIZONA

Ain't I a woman?

SOJOURNER TRUTH, 1851.

to my mother

ONE

YOU WAKE UP in the morning and you already know that this is just another day. That the day about to begin will be identical to yesterday, to the day before, and to the day before that. You want to linger a little longer in bed, steal a few extra minutes from this day already ticking away, so you can rest your aching body a bit longer, especially your left arm which is still sore from the vibrations of the sledgehammer that you use every day to strike the hard stone. But you have to get up. God did not make this night longer for you.

The three children are still asleep, two boys and a girl. The two boys share a mattress rolled out over a piece of plywood on the living room floor. The girl sleeps with you. You took her in a little over a year ago after her mother, your younger sister, passed away. Died of AIDS. A wrongful death. She could hardly believe it when she realized that all her symptoms pointed to AIDS: shingles, weight loss, diarrhea and the tuberculosis cough.

When she received her test results and told you that they were conclusive, that she was sick with AIDS, suddenly you were terrified, then overcome with a violent rage against her husband and with good reason.

Your sister Tamara had never had a blood transfusion and the few times her bouts of malaria did not respond to chloroquine tablets, and they had to give her artemisinin-based combination therapy injections, she had always used single-use needles. Besides, you were sure that your beloved little sister whom you had taken care of your whole life had always been faithful to her husband and that he was probably the first man she'd had sex with. How did you know? Big sister instinct! So that man who became her husband was the only one who could have infected her. Your indignation toward him intensified each time you saw him sit down at her bedside, all affectionate, attentive, wiping her forehead now and then with his handkerchief, stroking her hair, speaking lovingly to her. The hypocrite! By shattering a life in full bloom like that, the man was nothing more than a murderer because, in addition to taking away a sister's life and depriving a child of a mother, he was also killing the only intellectual in the family. Sad to say, but in Africa it's not only AIDS and malaria that kill, marriage does too.

Incapable of keeping your suspicions and anger to yourself, you decided to confront your sister and reveal the horrid truth about the man she continued to love. You sat on the edge of her bed, held her hand in yours and unleashed the string of insults that escaped from your mouth as she sat there motionless, looking at you with eyes that seemed enormous on her emaciated face. When you finally stopped talking, a faint smile formed on her lips. Her voice weakened by her illness, she said to you:

"Méré, I may be the one who infected him, who knows? We didn't get tested before we got married. Now, we're both HIV-positive and I've developed AIDS first. Is it because my defenses are weaker than his or because I've been infected for longer, I mean well before him? Who knows! So, it's no use accusing him."

Then, she closed her eyes, fatigued by the effort. You felt lost, and for a moment your beliefs shaken. You quickly came to terms with the fact that the illness had dulled your poor sister's critical faculties. You will always blame that man for her illness. But put it out of your mind for now. You have to prepare for the day ahead.

It is not time yet to wake the little one. First, you have to perform your morning rituals to prepare your body for the day ahead. You begin with your trip to the latrines. A hole enclosed with some corrugated iron sheets to protect the intimacy of its user. You are greeted by the odor, which is stronger than the Crésyl disinfectant you often use to spray the place. A woman has to squat. You do so without fearing that a cockroach might scurry across your buttocks or thigh, because you know that like mosquitos they hide from the daylight.

You're done. Next, you go to wash up with cold water. Warm water is good at night; it relaxes your achy carcass dirty with sweat at the end of a hard day of physical labor and makes it easier to sleep. In the morning you need cold water because it perks you up. You take a bucket and go to get water from the barrel you have placed just below the awning to collect rainwater. In the rainy season, that is what you use for all your activities: bathing, washing dishes, clothes.

You feel better after washing up. Now you have to attend to the children. You wake up the two older ones, two boys aged twelve and nine. You tell them to go wash their faces. To brush their teeth with the water, not from the barrel, but from the demijohn which is the potable water you buy for twenty-five francs a bucket. You remind them not to waste it, to take just enough to fill their cups. Grumbling, they get out of bed but speed up pronto when you raise your hand as if you are getting ready to give them a whack if they don't get a move on, because today you have to arrive at the quarry earlier than usual. For the little one, you need warm water. You are happy you bought a gas cooker that works with butane gas bottles. No more wood and charcoal fires with their cinders and irritating smoke that burns your eyes and poisons your lungs. You put the water on.

Now you can wake up the little one. Her name is Lyra. She is eighteen months old. You watch her for a moment as she sleeps so innocently. Then, in one spontaneous affectionate gesture, you swoop her up and hug her in your arms. You took her in thirteen months ago, the same day your sister died… But stop thinking about that. You have shed enough tears for your little sis. . .

You are going to test the water that you put on the gas cooker. The temperature is just right for washing the child.

It is time to feed them, fill their stomachs so they will be able to last until evening. You send the older one to buy frit-ters, a baguette and a few retail sugar-cubes while you prepare a cornmeal porridge. When everything is ready, you all start eating. They have the porridge with the fritters. You yourself have a strong tea with slices of buttered bread. It does not stave off your hunger for hours like eating a portion of boiled and pounded plantains or like warm *foufou* does, but at least it pre-vents you from having that sensation caused by an empty stom-ach, like you are floating above the ground.

While you are all eating, you turn on the radio. It plays a central role in your daily life. Your sister is the one who instilled this habit in you, listening to the radio in the morning during breakfast. She had just returned from studying abroad in New Zealand and still lived with you. The first thing she did when she got up in the morning was turn the dial on her radio. You would tease her about her obsession, and one morning she had retorted enigmatically: "When the Apocalypse comes, you'll be caught naked or wearing nothing but your underwear, whereas I will already be dressed and ready to flee." In any case, even if listening to the news every morning did not change anything in your day-to-day misery, at least you would be aware of what was happening in the world.

You have all finished breakfast. It is time to send the two boys off to school; luckily for you the school is not far, barely a ten-minute walk. You give the usual advice, for the older one to watch over his little brother, for both of them to look be-fore crossing the street, again for the older one to look in on his brother during recess and for both not to hang around and come straight home as soon as class finishes. Backpacks on, they're off.

You get the wicker basket and you fill it with provisions

for the workday: water in a two-liter plastic container, a bunch of four bananas, some grilled peanuts and slices of boiled cassava.

Everything is ready.

"… Tanzanian albinos are living in fear. Several have been assaulted over the past weeks.

Their attackers kill them and use their victim's body parts, such as their hair, arms, legs, genitals, even their blood, to make potions which, they guarantee, will make their clients rich and bring them eternal youth. Gold miners say that pouring an albino's blood into a mine makes nuggets spurt out without having to dig in the earth while fishermen maintain that baiting the waters of a river or lake with an arm or leg cut off of an albino's body makes you catch big fish stuffed with gold. The Tanzanian president has ordered that strong measures be taken against all those involved in the murders.

TRAGEDY IN NIGERIA: A Manchester United fan killed four people as his minibus sped through a group of Barcelona supporters after the English club's defeat in the finals of the League champions.

The incident occurred in the city of Ogbo Wednesday evening after Barça's 2-0 win. "The driver passed next to the group then made a U-turn and drove speeding into them," said a police spokesperson. All across Africa, soccer amateurs follow very closely the European teams who recruit some of the best players on the continent. Last month, a Kenyan fan from the Arsenal team hung himself after his team's defeat at the semi-finals of the Champions League."

You turn off the radio. And now, you're off to the quarry.

Quarry, by the way, is a big fancy word to refer to that large area along the river that is scattered with large stones and rocks. This season, when the water is low, is the best time of the year because it is easier to find stone. It is when large sandstone boulders which had previously been submerged under the water, become exposed after the water levels recede and are scattered across the riverbed. These rocks, when broken into large slabs, then crushed, are the ones used to make the gravel that is found in any type of construction work that uses stone.

On the way, you take the usual detour to drop off Lyra at Auntie Turia's. You are lucky because Auntie looks after the little one all day whereas some women working at the quarry have to take their kids with them, like Batatou with her twins. Lyra is always happy to see her great aunt.

Within a second of taking the little one in her arms Auntie gets right into it, interrogating you:

"Is it true, Méré, that you've decided to refuse to sell your bags of gravel for ten thousand francs?'

"Yes, Auntie, that's the decision we all came to unanimously, but you never know. Today is crucial, we're going to find out if we're strong enough not to give in."

"Just don't get caught up in politics, my child. Politics is no good. It killed your uncle."

"Don't worry, we simply want to sell our merchandise at a reasonable price. All right, I've got to get going!"

TWO

YOU TAKE THE basket off your head and hold it by the handles. This way, you can swing your arms and walk faster. You are eager to get to the quarry before the first trucks of buyers so that you can inform them of the decision you all made unanimously yesterday. You have been chosen to be spokesperson and, even if you were compelled and forced to accept this function, you must not disappoint those who have placed their trust in you. But you can't manage to get Auntie Turia's concerns off your mind. You tell yourself that she is wrong and you feel reassured, thinking your decision has nothing to do with politics. You are simply fighting for your daily bread. For that matter, were it not for those various billboards at the traffic circles displaying the President of the Republic in a jacket and tie, in sportswear running the marathon or in nursing scrubs administering polio vaccines to children, his wife by his side or a trowel in his hand as he lay the foundation stone of a school or hospital, on a tractor breaking ground to build a new road, on a sailboat in a skipper's outfit.... Without all those billboards, you would have never even recognized his face. Your sole concern was to figure out the fastest way you could cut enough stone to make the money you so urgently needed. You had not planned on demanding a new price; it had imposed itself, little by little, almost by stealth.

At one point, when you heard on the radio that the government was building a world-class airport in the north of the country, you were indifferent, as you were to most of the news broadcast on national radio. At any rate, if even ten percent of what it regularly reported doing was actually achieved, this country would be a paradise on earth today, leaving Switzerland, the USA and Japan far behind. Since your sister's death, the only news that would interest you in the least would have been a report on the development of an effective AIDS vaccine, or on what would allow you to regularly pay your rent.

The news about the airport had not really interested you until the day you learned that the construction of the airstrip and its pharaonic buildings required a colossal amount of gravel that the factory could not provide, and that given this huge demand, the contractors who supplied the airport construction with the stone they bought from you had doubled the delivery price for their customers. At first this news had delighted you for one simple reason: half of the area zoned to build the airport was marshland with no rocky surface, which meant that all of the stone would come from your region, buyers would be lining up for your merchandise and before you could even fill your bags, they would already be bought, and each bag bought would allow you to get out of this stone nightmare quicker.

But then, little by little, as you listened to the news on the radio, you started to question the whole thing. Every day, the radio would inform you that the price of oil had increased, then decreased, then increased even more than it had decreased. When it soared like that, a lot of money landed in the coffers of the state, a major oil producer like others had their diamonds. Just by observing the lifestyle of politicians and their families, you knew money was pouring into the country as plentifully as the rain came down in the wet season, especially since your ex-husband— who could not afford the used car you had bought together, and could barely pay the rent without your contribution—had acquired two cars since you separated, including a Japanese SUV for his little girlfriend who would taunt you incessantly from behind the wheel whenever she saw you walking under the sun. In the span of six months, he had managed to build a villa, where he was currently living with that bitch. Or rather, she was the second since you had left him. In the meantime, he had become a member of parliament, elected after the electoral commission had eliminated his opponent on the pretext that he, the opposition candidate favored in the second round, had violated electoral law because he was distributing leaflets two hours after the end of the campaign! Where was this sudden opulence coming from, if it was not, one, that he was head of the party of the president, and two, that oil money was also pouring into his pocket? Besides, for you, stone was your oil, and you were no idiot. You knew that two plus two was four: if money was pouring into the country, there was no reason why you should not collect a few drops in your purse as well.

This simple reasoning was so satisfying to you that the following day you shared it with another woman who worked at the quarry—just to chat, nothing more.

She liked what she heard. She told another, who told another, and so on. Then, four or five days ago, all the women working in the quarry held an impromptu meeting where they decided that they would refuse to sell the bags they toiled to fill for ten thousand CFA francs each and to raise the price to fifteen thousand. Then, they all agreed to ask you to be their spokesperson, their representative to the buyers. You refused. And yesterday they brought up the issue again.

You asked them why they wanted you, when there were older women among them, women who had been breaking stones for several years, who had more experience, whereas you had only been there for four weeks and you had no intention of staying any more than eight, the time it would take to get you through this temporary rough financial patch. You pronounced their names one by one, showing your respect for them by addressing those who were old enough to be your mother as Mama or Mâ and as Yâ for those who were just old enough to be an older sister: Mama Moyalo, for example, could represent you because not only can she transfix a police officer with her gaze, but also, since she is from Mossaka, she can wield the Lingala language like no other. Or Mâ Bileko from Boko—in her day, she was a businesswoman, so she knows how to negotiate. And

Yâ Moukiétou, the elder sister from Mayalama village, whose authority became undisputed when she knocked out a man whom she suspected of trying to grope her on a bus. But there were also those who were younger than you: Batatou, mother of triplets, one of whom died during childbirth. Bilala, whose family had banished her from her village and whose own children had accused her of being a witch and all but burned her. Laurentine Paka from Hinda, the coquette among you, who never ceases to amaze you by always carrying a book from the "Adoras" collection, those romance novels published in Côte d'Ivoire. Iyissou from Sibiti, the taciturn woman who can sit and break stones for hours without looking at anyone or making a sound because, as everyone knows, she has never quite been herself since the Presidential Guard's soldiers ripped her son out of her arms, threw him into a tarped truck, and disappeared forever with the child, a handsome eighteen-year-old boy. And think of Anne-Marie Ossolo, the urbanite, who came to the quarry five days after you, not at all shy, a very beautiful woman despite the scar that cuts across the right side of her face... But to no avail. They all wanted it to be you because you went to school for a while, you could read, you could write, and you spoke French well.

Most of these women were illiterate or had very little schooling. You seemed a bit bizarre to them because it was not often that a girl who had completed high school ended up breaking stones on the riverbanks. They were unaware that the country was overflowing with unemployed graduates. They did not know for instance that Léonie Abena, a former high school friend of yours, despite having a degree in psychology, was currently selling palm nuts, bananas, and grilled peanuts in the city's central market to survive; or that Olakouara, your neighbor's son, with a master's in physics and unemployed since graduation, was selling cassava flour and single cigarettes at night in his parent's yard in hopes of gathering enough money to buy fake papers that would allow him to finally leave the country for Europe or America. No, they did not know. You tried everything to get yourself out of this situation, to refuse.

You told them the truth, that in fact, although you had made it through high school, you never passed the college entrance exams, but they just took that as modesty. You had insisted, persisted, saying that going to school did not mean that you were the most competent, that you had the necessary leadership skills and knew how to talk to people and how to negotiate. But you were ready to help, to write whatever needed to be written in French. But all in vain. They had complete trust in you. Their sincerity was disarming. You felt that you had to accept. But you said that accepting did not mean that you were the leader, just the spokesperson. They applauded and some of them took you in their arms and embraced you tightly. To conclude, they reconfirmed unanimously that the new selling price for one bag of gravel will be fifteen thousand francs. When you thought everything was done, Mama Moyalo raised her hand to say that she did not agree. In Africa, we always bargain, she said; we have to start by setting the price at twenty thousand francs to eventually come down to the final price of fifteen thousand. If we immediately reveal that we want fifteen thousand francs, we will end up at thirteen thousand or even eleven thousand francs after negotiations. Smart—this grande dame from Mossaka! You had not thought about that. Obviously, everyone agreed and applauded. Each finally took her place by her large block of stone to start the hard day's work.

But all that was yesterday, and today is a new day. Perhaps it had done everyone good to sleep on it, as they say, and the women had changed their minds. Then Auntie Turia would not have to worry about you anymore. With this reassuring thought, you start to pick up the pace.

THREE

YOU HAVE WALKED so quickly that today you're the first to arrive at the quarry, whereas you are usually among the last. Only Iyissou is already there, taciturn as usual; she nods her head slightly to let you know that she heard you say hello and is acknowledging your greeting. It is not long, though, before the others arrive. And you can tell, they have not changed their minds, because each of them reminds you not to forget that you have agreed to be their spokeswoman. It is as if a new solidarity has emerged among you. You can feel it in the way you address one other, in the slight knowing smiles indicating the awareness each of you has of the importance of what is going to happen today, in your gestures and in what is unspoken, all of which speaks more loudly than what is said. In spite of it all though, you sense a bit of anxiousness lingering around the quarry in contrast to yesterday's enthusiastic, almost swaggering attitude. But it is time to get to work. You each take your place in front of your large slab of stone and start banging and waiting.

•

The first trucks arrive mid-afternoon to buy the bags that are already filled. Before, they would only buy by the cubic meter and a cubic meter is ten bags. Since it took three and a half to four weeks to break a cubic meter of gravel, many of you spent days, even weeks, without receiving any money because you did not have ten full bags. But, for the last two weeks, the trucks have been coming almost every day and their clients buying by the bag, too impatient now to wait for a cubic meter.

Not so long ago, after several days without seeing a single truck, it was a scramble when one appeared on the horizon after all those days of famine when not a cent had landed in your purses. Every woman for herself. To be the first to get to the buyer who had come with his driver. He would climb down, his shoulder bag stuffed with bills. Arrogant, he would look you up and down as you squawked around him like chickens, each trying to be the first to offer him your merchandise.

He would ignore you and, strutting around like a cowboy, walk around the bags you had carefully lined up, kicking them here and there, turning some over just because they were not full, and yelling out threats. You would watch him do this without batting an eye because any sign of protest could mean another day without selling anything.

But since the construction of the new airport had caused a bulimic demand for stone, the world was upside down: the buyers would now fight over a bag, each of them claiming that he had been the first to reserve it. Once, two of them had even come to blows. That incident had heightened your awareness of the fierce competition between them to make a profit, and it made you understand the importance they attributed to your bags of gravel.

Today, they show up four at a time, in dump trucks. They stop in the powdery sandstone's ochre dust. The buyers climb down and head over to the bags. Contrary to the usual, none of you rushes over. They are surprised for a moment by your lack of urgency then pretend they didn't notice and begin their routine drama—going over toward the bags and pretending to inspect them carefully, even though you know that for a week now they have not been so fussy. But today you are not begging. Quite the opposite.

Since you are all acting so indifferently toward their drama, one of them loses his patience and comes over to your bags. A week and a half's worth of work. He taps them with his foot and, satisfied, starts opening his money bag to count out his bills. "Just a minute," you say to him, "not so fast! As of today, each bag is twenty thousand francs." The guy thinks it is a joke. "Listen, lady, don't waste my time." He takes out his bills anyway and starts counting. "I'm not joking. I said twenty thousand francs," you say again. "Are you crazy or what? Who would buy your bag of stones for twenty thousand francs? OK, too bad for you. You can go eat your stones if you want to," he says scornfully and heads over to another. "The new price is twenty thousand francs," you hear another woman's voice rise up addressing another buyer. The same price, consistently the same price, uttered by so many women's voices. The buyers finally understand it is no laughing matter and start to take you seriously. They do not know what to do. They walk over to where they can talk about it amongst themselves.

You all act as though they did not even exist, and you continue to bang the sandstone slabs with your hammers. They come back and taunt you, tapping on their money bags stuffed with bills, because they know that they have money, and you don't. They threaten you and warn you that from now on, they will go elsewhere to find stone and that they will never come back to your quarry unless you bring the price back to ten thousand francs a bag because, "Ladies, you have got to know that you're not the only ones selling stone; there are others elsewhere as well." Then, they head back to their trucks, still strutting like John Wayne, all confident and domineering, slam their doors, start their engines and speed away.

After they leave, the women all get up, come over to you and form a circle around you; you congratulate each other and swear you'll hold out until they give in. But you have to get back to work. Each of you goes back to your pile of stones and starts banging again.

•

In order to procure the stone slabs to crush, more massive boulders have to be broken up. You do not know why, but this work is reserved almost exclusively for men. When the quarry women spotted a boulder that interested them, they would pay a man to do the job. He would place rubber tires underneath the rocky mass and burn them; and the rock would crack under the heat. Tires were a better source of heat than wood. Then the man would stick an iron rod in the crack and hammer on the rod with a sledgehammer until the boulder burst into several large slabs. All you had to do then was haul them over to your spot.

Now you are at your spot, beneath the tropical sun. To avoid getting burnt to a crisp, you have built a makeshift sunshade for yourself by spreading a pagne over intertwined palm fronds held up by bamboo poles stuck into the ground. You select a good-sized slab and you start hammering away. Occasionally, the rock does not absorb the shock and the hammer bounces back, its impact sending vibrations through your arm and spine. You bang and you bang. What was once a large stone slab is now nothing but a scattered heap of medium-sized rocks. Then the hardest part starts, and the most dangerous too: turning those blocks into gravel, the deeply coveted end product. It requires sustained attention. A single moment of inattention or fatigue, and hello accidents. Your first days were particularly difficult. You did not know how to hold the hammer, from which angle to strike the stone, and so your hammer came bouncing back much more frequently than actually crushing the rock. Once, it landed on your right index finger after bouncing back. You howled from the pain. Luckily, nothing was broken, but your swollen finger had left you in agony for several days. The pain was worse than a festering wound, and you had to use your middle finger instead. But that was what it was to learn the trade. Now, after four weeks, you were used to it. You knew where to position your fingers so that any blow to them would already be absorbed. Your only fear was the unforeseeable, like those shards of stone which, depending on the direction they flew, could get you in the face, at best injuring you, at worst, taking an eye out.

You are a lefty, so you hold the slabs that you are going to crush with your right hand and you work the hammer with your left. You secure the hard rock between your legs and continue hammering. The temperature never gets below 90 degrees Fahrenheit. You are sweating but you cannot go bare-chested like a man because you are a woman. You pick up your plastic canteen and pour a little water into your cup. You drink a little to whet your throat and you splash your face with the rest, but it does not refresh you much because it is tepid. You put the cup and can away and raise your eyes to look beyond your small area. As if in a prison camp, about fifteen women are hammering stone like you, some to feed their children and send them to school, some to take care of a mother or a husband who is ill, some to simply survive, or some, like you, to make much-needed money as quickly as possible. How many more hours, how many more days will it take to achieve this?

In a passing moment of distress, your mind starts to wander, and you tell yourself that perhaps it is your own fault that you are here now. You should have accepted your fate, respected the customs of your society and not rebelled so dramatically. You would now be the wife of a member of parliament, and you would be the one driving around in that Japanese SUV instead of that child who insults you every time she sees you. But, gun-shy after what had happened to your sister, you could not let yourself get killed foolishly by a husband.

In the third month of your sister's illness, he had become increasingly impatient with you, constantly blaming you for having sacrificed him—him and your marriage—for her. It is true that you were spending a lot of time with Tamara, but how could you not have? What did he think? That you would abandon your sister just because your husband's meal wouldn't be ready, or his shirt would not be ironed when he got home? Or that you would be in the mood to make love every evening? In six months-time, you no longer recognized the man you had been with for twelve years. He had started spending a lot of time in front of the mirror before going out, and he who, like you, had never cared much about his clothes, had started buying designer brands. He had even splurged on a pair of English John Lobb shoes while you were withdrawing from your sav-

ings to pay for your sister's care. Not only did you not understand why he was acting that way, but you especially wondered
where he had suddenly found all that money. Then, he started
coming home late, and sometimes just stayed out all night. Despite all of that, you were not too upset; your main concern was
your sister's condition and her suffering, which you felt in your
soul and in your flesh as if it were your own.

After Tamara's death, you went back to being the woman
that you were before: attentive to him, his meals hot and ready
when he got home, his shirts ironed, exactly everything a good
wife was supposed to be. But he did not change; he was incapable of breaking the habit. And then there was the night he
came back at two in the morning, stinking of beer, and wanted
to make love. All you could think of was your sister. You did
not know whose company the guy had been in the previous
two nights when he came home just as late as tonight, and you
got scared. You refused to open your legs to him. But after he
insisted and started to raise his voice, being a good wife, you
asked him, if he really wanted it, to use a condom. "What?!" He
shrieked, shocked and indignant. "And how long is this going to
go on?" "Until the day a test proves that you are HIV-negative,"
you replied. You did not have a specific reason to suspect him of
any infidelity but, traumatized by your sister's experience, you
did not have the resilience to trust a man who came home at
two A.M. reeking of alcohol. He got angry, screaming that you
were his wife, that you should obey him instead of shirking your
conjugal duty with fanciful excuses. You told him that he would
have to respect you if he wanted you to respect him, that his
conduct was despicable and irresponsible for a married man and
father of two children. You asked him what he would have done
if you were the one coming home at an ungodly hour, with a
belly full of beer. He yelled back that he was the man and that
you should know your place. Too easy. You looked at that being
who was supposed to be your life companion, a seemingly educated man who had sworn before the civil authorities and before
God to be faithful to you and who was now using the convenient
excuse that all of our men waved in our faces to justify them-

selves each time they failed to uphold their commitments, the so-called tradition: they may be Christian or Muslim yet fetishist, be monogamous officially yet polygamous with women married traditionally, be proponents of democracy but a democracy weakened by being labelled "African style." Always the bogus excuse of African exceptionalism. It made you nauseous. The grimace of disgust on your face aroused him and he wanted to take you by force. You kneed him where it counts, and he started howling in pain. Feeling humiliated, for the first time in your marriage he started to hit you first with his fists, then with his feet; and, surprised by the suddenness and brutality of the assault, you stumbled and fell. You could not stop him because he was stronger than you. Finally, you managed to get away and lock yourself in the children's room. They, not understanding at all what was happening, started crying, trembling with fear as the sounds of furious banging rattled their bedroom door.

You left early in the morning. You could not go to the police. You could not go to the court of law because husbands were always right in this country. Traditional law was stronger than the law of the State. You could only go to your family.

You arrived at the crack of dawn at your Aunt Turia's, your mother's oldest sister. She started screaming and wailing when she saw your split lips, your black and blue eyes. She prepared some warm water, compresses, ointments. You began to explain to her what had happened. Though not everything, because how does one tell their elder mother that they had demanded that their husband wear a condom? She lectured you endlessly as she applied pressure to the compresses on your bruises. If he had hit you, it was because you had behaved badly. You must have disobeyed him. A husband, like a chief, should be respected. Again, this mantra of tradition. And she, a Christian, added that, according to the Scriptures, a wife must submit to her husband. But she had forgotten that in those same Scriptures it was written that one should not commit adultery. It would seem that in this country, the exception prevails once again: the principle of the Ten Commandments only applies to women. At the end of her sermon, she suggested taking you back home to him; she was ready to ask his forgiveness for you if you didn't have the courage to do it, or, rather, if you were too proud to do it. You understood that she had understood nothing. Not only because she had enjoyed a happy, ideal marriage with a remarkable and loveable man—who, unfortunately, was killed during the riots that had followed the last presidential elections—but because she was of another generation, the generation of the Latin Mass where, eyes closed, you would kneel in faith before the priest, oblivious to the fact that in his gibberish what he was actually saying to you was: "Close your eyes so I can dupe you." Thank God, yours is the generation of women with open eyes!

Your aunt kept on talking, but her voice became a mere murmur, no longer penetrating the walls of your thoughts, which had returned to your husband. Heeding your parents' advice, and that of your society, you had renounced equality in marriage, which was what had actually connected you at the beginning of your relationship to become the ideal wife, as tradition would want. So, you did not understand why he thought that he had to go looking elsewhere. You were still young, barely in your early thirties. Your name, Méréana, means that you are beautiful; that is what your mother used to tell you while she braided your hair when you were a little girl. You gave up your last name, Pahua, to take the name of this undeserving being. And hadn't you done everything right? The food had always been ready when he came home, because wasn't the saying that the quickest way to a man's heart is through his stomach? Never once had he complained that one of your meals was too salty, nor that the rice was not cooked enough or that the cassava flour porridge, the *foufou*, that you kneaded in a kettle wedged between your feet, was not firm enough. You had always washed and ironed his clothes, done the dishes, maintained the house properly. And you always followed his recommendations even when it meant you lost out. You had even sacrificed your future by dropping out of school when your second child was born so that he could continue his studies in order to later assume his traditional role as head of the family. What more could one ask of a woman? Ah, making love? There too, he could not complain. Besides, you had given him two children, two handsome boys. The most beautiful woman in the world can only give what she has; you had given everything you had. But that had not stopped him from wandering elsewhere, and you were told to accept it because you were a woman! Because you were in his house. He no longer saw your intelligence, or your beauty. All you were there for now was to perform your duty. He was forgetting, however, that other men attracted by your looks and by your charm swarmed around you, and if you had been irresponsible and promiscuous like him...

•

The heat burning your legs suddenly brings you back to the reality of the quarry. The sun has changed position. It has shifted with the passing hours and no longer falls directly on your makeshift sunshade. So, you have to reconstruct the shaded area by realigning the pagne and a few palm fronds. You take the opportunity to go empty your bladder behind the tall grass that borders the river, where you can have a little privacy. You kick your feet a few times up in the air to stimulate the blood circulation in your legs, numb from being immobile, and you clench and open your fists several times to relax your fingers.

When you return to get back to work, you hear one of Batatou's babies crying. You let their mother know that you still have water in your canteen in case the baby is crying from thirst. She tells you it is not thirst that she's crying from, but hunger. She takes a large breast out from underneath her top, positions it into the child's mouth and the latter starts sucking voraciously. Tatou means "three" in her language and, since she had given birth to triplets, she came to adopt the name Batatou, "she who has three," even though the third was stillborn. You return to your spot and you get back to crushing those big slabs that, now, you refuse to offer for less than fifteen thousand francs a bag. You take a slab, and you hold it with your right hand while your left raises the hammer to bang it. You bang and you bang. After a minute, you have the impression that your arm has detached from your body and thoughts and that it is moving on its own, mechanically. Like a machine. Nevertheless, from time to time, you do stop to breathe. Even a horse stops to breathe.

Finally, it is time to go home. You have to leave the quarry before it gets too late; you do not want to be on the road when night falls. But, more importantly, your children are coming home from school, and you do not want to leave them home alone for too long. Normally, you work from eight in the morning to four in the afternoon, but that depends on how you feel each day. Sometimes you only last six hours instead of your usual eight, because you are so exhausted. That is why you have a secret admiration for Yâ Moukiétou, who performs nine hours of hard labor every day. No wonder she has the arms of a weightlifter.

One last time, you go over the instructions for the next day: offer each bag at twenty thousand francs so that in the end you can negotiate down and settle on your lowest price of fifteen thousand francs. Once again entrusted with your role as spokesperson, you return to your spot and start gathering your things.

FOUR

THIS MORNING, when you get up, you have a feeling that this day is not just another day and is going to be different. Anxious and excited at the same time, you will not rest for a second until you reach the quarry. You rush through your morning routine as fast as you can, and you hurry the children to finish their breakfast quickly.

"A young boy guilty of having written a love letter to a young girl from a different caste has been beaten, paraded, head shaved, through the city streets then thrown under a train in the state of Bihar in India. According to the police, Manish Kumar, fifteen years old, had been kidnapped by members of a rival caste while on his way to school. One man has been arrested and a police officer suspended.

The Vatican is denouncing the devastating effects of the pill on the environment. According to the President of the International Federation of Catholic Medical Associations, Pedro José Maria Simon Castellvi, environmental pollution caused by the pill is due to the release of tons of hormones into nature through the urine of the women who take them. The author also asserts that Catholic scientists have sufficient data to substantiate the claim that environmental pollution caused by the pill has resulted in substantial masculine infertility, as constant decrease in the number of sperm in Western men indicates.

The release of the film A Woman in Berlin has sparked controversy in Europe. The film breaks a taboo by evoking for the first time the mass rapes committed by the Russians in 1945. Historians cite one hundred thousand rapes committed in Berlin between April and September 1945, and in all two million German girls and women between the ages of eight and eighty who were raped on the Soviet front. The controversy is around..."

You turn off the radio and, anxious again, your mind returns to the quarry.

Was it really a good strategy refusing to sell your bags yesterday? You suddenly feel a heavy responsibility since you are the one who came up with the idea. Based on your quick mental calculation, you figure that if the vendors refuse to buy your stones for another week, you will all be in trouble because you will not last that long. You yourself could scrape by for five days, maybe six, but Batatou with her twins couldn't make it for more than two. She has one full bag right now that she could have sold yesterday if you had not all decided to refuse. Since she barely fills a bag and a half every two weeks, that means it has already been a while since she has sold anything, and she has nothing left to provide for her children's basic needs. So, when the eighth day comes, and you are all completely broke, you will be willing to sell off your bags maybe even at half price. You panic at the thought of this. As soon as you send the two children to school, you hurry to your Aunt's to drop off Lyra and then hustle to the quarry.

Surprisingly, without having planned it, all of the women have arrived early this morning. They gather around you, their chosen spokesperson. You do not know why, but your presence seems to comfort them. As if to reassure one another, they reaffirm their commitment to sell at fifteen thousand francs a bag—excuse me—to first ask for twenty thousand francs. You could not muster the courage to share the doubts that crossed your mind this morning as you listened to the radio. And you watch them as they disperse across the quarry, each taking her position in front of the large slab that she will break today or the small pile of stones that she had broken the day before. All of you hanging on to the hope that the buyers' trucks would appear at any moment.

But the time passed. After reaching its zenith, the sun began to set on the other side of the sky. You all rearranged your pagnes or cardboard boxes to restructure the shaded area protecting you. Those who were thirsty drank the water they had brought, those who had babies breastfed or fed them. Then everyone returned to their stones, pretending to ignore the fact that something was missing from their daily routine: the familiar sounds of diesel engines, the acrid odor of their gas fumes, the ochre dust stirred up by their tires, the men shouting, their bags stuffed with bank notes. In an hour or two, you will be packing up to go home, with not a cent in your purse for the second day in a row.

You feel you can no longer keep quiet and go on like this, disappointing your friends in a world where so many lies give rise to so much false hope. You cannot do it anymore. You must speak the truth.

You get up, go over to Mâ Bileko and call the others. They come and gather around you, puzzled looks on their faces. You get straight to the point and tell them that you are beginning to doubt your strategy, that perhaps those people were not bluffing, perhaps they would go elsewhere for their stones, then you would risk being without money if you did not sell them over the next three or four days, your children would starve and, finally, you say that it is not too late to back out, that you could increase the price up to only, say, twelve thousand francs, as opposed to fifteen

As you speak, you feel as though many of them are thinking exactly what you just said because, unfortunately, harsh reality often shatters dreams.

Laurentine Paka has understood and is trying to absorb the shock of your declaration of surrender. She proposes giving two weeks' notice, during which time you would all continue selling at the current price of ten thousand francs but while negotiating with the buyers, rather than just stopping outright like you had done. This less aggressive approach would certainly allow you to get an additional two thousand francs, perhaps even three. Retracting your word does not mean that you are breaking it. If everyone agrees, she continues, you, their spokeswoman, could contact the truck drivers and explain that it was all just a simple misunderstanding and that they were welcome to come back to the quarry.

She finishes speaking and waits for their reactions. "Alright," says Bileko, "but you know, we're only women, so they may not take us seriously. Despite all the talk about gender equality, believe me, in this country we may be able to do things without men, but we cannot do anything against them. I know what I'm talking about. We have to find a man to team up with our spokeswoman. Or those of you who have a husband could ask him to come support us."

You look at Bileko. If, amongst all of you there is one person who does not deserve to be here doing this hard labor, it's her. She was rich back in her day; she even had employees working for her.

All of a sudden, Moukiétou's voice rises up. She gestures wildly with her right arm, her biceps like a bodybuilder's, from machete wielding and axe swinging when she used to cut firewood and now from hammering away at stone slabs. "I do not want any men getting involved," she says passionately. "Who's to say they aren't going to betray us and side with the merchants so they can make a few bucks. Besides, about the men some of the women here are married to: why aren't they here, breaking stone? Want me to tell you why? They just wait around, sitting on their asses, for you to bring them money so they can go spend it on their mistresses. I do not trust any man. They may have balls between their legs, but they're not so ballsy!"

Yâ Moukiétou always contributed very lucidly to discussions and decision making as long as she could first spew her hatred of men often with very colorful language. She always ended with that same final sentence, with few variations, implying that she was speaking from experience. In any case, you could not get any more man-hating than her! Nobody knew if the legend that surrounded her was true; still, the women at the quarry used to tell that: she used to sell her firewood at a market and, one day, she left early and caught her husband with his pants down, lying on top of her fifteen-year-old little sister who struggled desperately beneath him as he grunted like a pig. Moukiétou did not scream. She simply went into the kitchen and grabbed the large pestle which she'd used the day before to crush hot peppers and, driven by her violent rage, struck him with it. It was after that incident that she migrated to the city and became a stonebreaker, far away from her village and her woodpiles. Some say that the blow had shattered the man's skull and that he died instantly. Others say it was quite a different story: that she was calm and focused like a predatory animal, and that she did not hit him right away. She called him out, and when he turned around, she deliberately aimed at his pelvis, went straight for the testicles, which were instantly reduced to a pulp. Who knows what really happened! Since then, any man whom she suspected of fixing his gaze on her was in danger. "We cannot back down," she continued, after she had released her venomous outrage toward men. "But darn it all, don't we know how to bargain anymore? Even kids know how to do it. We start with a price we know is outrageous, but we have a second price in mind that we're willing to settle on, perhaps even a third. Either way, we know our lowest price beforehand. Ours is fifteen thousand! No way we're selling at ten thousand. Yesterday we told them twenty thousand francs, that's very good. They did not hesitate to double their prices at the airport construction site! Sugar, milk, flour, everything has increased, but we have been selling at the same price for at least three years..."

A baby's cry interrupts Moukiétou's speech. One of Batatou's little ones has started crying. Everyone looks at the mother as she reaches her hand into her top and pulls out a breast which she tries to shove it into the child's mouth. You all know that the child is crying because he is starving, and you know that his mother has not eaten much either since yesterday evening. She did not sell anything yesterday, and she won't sell anything today. Moukiétou was a widow. Her husband was killed by a random drunk while rioters looted after the presidential elections. Only the strength of maternal love kept her coming back day after day to this quarry where the work resembled that of a labor camp. You can already guess what she is going to say when she raises her left hand to speak, holding her breast firmly in her toddler's mouth with her right. You know just by seeing the starving look on that child's face, because, between saving one's offspring and your ideal of equity—a fair wage for the fruit of your labor—a mother's choice is quickly made. You forgive her in advance for accusing you of getting them all involved in this reckless venture; or for accusing you—whose ex-husband had become a politician—of not knowing that those traders claiming to be businessmen and their sponsors all had political umbrellas which, for some of them, were provided by the President of the Republic himself or at least by his close relatives. The example of your husband, an incompetent whose wheeling and dealing eventually got him elected to parliament, should have taught you. Yes, I understand you, Batatou. Go ahead, let your anger explode!

You are surprised. She is not angry. She speaks calmly, almost apologetically. "Don't think that just because I'm a single mother with two small children that I have it rougher than you. It's true, I did not eat much last night, but rest assured, I still have enough porridge for the children, a little rice and some foufou to last a few days. I don't know if we're going to win or lose or if we've made a mistake standing up to those men. I don't know. I also don't know what we're supposed to do. But I will say this: I accept whatever you propose. If you think that we need to continue refusing to sell our bags for ten thousand francs, I agree; if you think however, that we should drop the idea, I also accept, because I trust you all. When the children start to suffer, when I am truly backed into a corner and there is not a single grain of rice or a cube of sugar at home, then I will come to you and say: My sisters, I have held out for as long as I could, but I cannot do it any longer. I'm sorry, but I cannot continue this fight with you anymore; I'm giving up. Then, I will be ready to sell my bag for half price. But, for now, I am with you!"

You are all surprised that those words came from the one you considered to be the weakest link of the resistance. Those words in your support, uttered simply and sincerely, destroy the justification you just gave for giving up. Those words strengthen everyone's resolve.

Anne-Marie Ossolo raises her hand. What is she going to say, after such a moving plea? You give her the floor.

"I don't have any children," she says, "so my situation may not be as tragic as Batatou's, but for me it is no less dramatic. I am two months behind on my rent, and the landlord is threatening to evict me if I don't give him at least one month's advance out of the two I already owe; and he wants it by the end of the month—that's less than ten days from now. Where will I go? Out on the streets? And... and..." she hesitates for a moment, she who is usually never shy for a penny, then discloses, "I owe a trader from Mali two *pagnes*, a Dutch wax print and a Bazin fabric. If I don't also give him an advance by the end of the month, he is going to show up at my door when the cock crows, and the whole neighborhood will be woken up to come out and see me being insulted, threatened, and humiliated. I would rather commit suicide than live with such shame. Despite all of that, I will say that I'm with you because I truly need the money and, just like Batatou, I'm ready to see this through to the end."

You do not know why, but you are proud of her. A girl born and raised in the country's capital, who has seen it all, and who certainly knew all the tips and tricks to survive there. Outside the city, she's dead. What the hell is she doing here breaking stones?

In any case, if Laurentine Paka is the most coquettish, Ossolo is absolutely the most beautiful. The beauty of a woman is often based on the usual criteria, or even clichés, but it was different with Anne-Marie Ossolo. She had a unique aesthetic: silky black skin, full lips slightly upturned that gave her smile a provocative look, and naturally thick hair which she styled effortlessly in long braids with no need for extensions or artificial mesh, or simply pulled back and tied up with an elastic band in a ponytail that fell behind her neck. Her slightly prominent cheekbones gave a mysterious Eastern look to her almond shaped eyes which she could fill with a languishing gaze at will. It was the kind of unusual beauty that would make you pray, if you were a woman, that her path would not cross that of the man you have set your sights on, and if you were a man, would make you stare wide-eyed and pinch yourself three times to make sure you were not dreaming. But where did she get that horrible scar that zigzags across her temple and right cheek, ruining the otherwise perfect symmetry of her face? And again, what is she doing here breaking stones, this girl who, you have no doubt, can easily get what she wants through other means. But what you find most surprising is what she has just revealed. Two months behind on rent? We have all had that happen. But in debt for two high end pagnes? That's nearly a hundred thousand francs! She must have had means before landing at this place, because what trader, especially a West African, would sell merchandise on credit to a client he knew was penniless? On the other hand, everyone has their own life secret and besides, how many of them know yours? Misfortune had led you all here by chance, that was enough to bring you together.

"Thank you Batatou, thank you Anne-Marie," you say, rising again. We all agree now that what we are asking is not excessive."

"Yes," Bilala can't help but interrupt you, "especially when you think of the price of oil." "It's true, the price of oil has increased again," you add, to show that you listen to the radio, therefore you are well informed. But Bilala replies that she is not talking about barrels of oil; anyway, she doesn't even know what that means, a barrel of oil. She is talking about the price of a liter of kerosene that she buys at the pump for her hurricane lamp.

"Gravel is our oil!" young Mouanda shouts out, carried away, forgetting that she had supported your earlier proposal, which was to retreat. Everyone bursts out laughing and applauds when Mama Moyalo asks, half serious, half joking, in her impeccable Lingala, if prostitutes from the former Zaire could increase the price of a trick from three hundred to five hundred francs, why couldn't you also increase the price of your work? You start laughing too, overcome by a sudden cheerfulness which makes you all forget your precarious situation for a moment. Not for long though, because Mama Asselam brings you back to reality when she says you absolutely have to give Batatou's children something to eat. The latter protests saying she does not want a handout and that for now she can still feed her children.

"It's not about a handout or charity," Mama Asselam interrupts her, "those children are being sacrificed so we can remain a united front, so we have a duty toward them." Before Batatou can even reply, Laurentine Paka is passing around a plastic cup, which fills up quickly with coins.

To show that your spontaneous revolt is now an organized movement, Laurentine does not give the cup directly to Batatou, she hands it to you instead. You are the designated spokeswoman, and everyone expects that from now on, any action taken should have your approval. You spread out a headscarf on the ground, pour the coins out and start counting them. Two thousand fifteen francs in denominations of five-, ten-, twenty-five-and one hundred-franc coins. Incredible. Few of you spend even a thousand francs a day. You are happy. You are all happy. You put the coins back in the cup and hand it to Batatou. She takes it and starts to cry. Clearly, it has been a long time since anyone has shown her such kindness. Certainly not since her husband was murdered. Yâ Moukiétou's eyes are wet and your throat is in knots. In the life you lead these days, you hear a lot of crying around you but, nothing compares to the tears of joy you are witnessing right now. This is a unique moment in time, and you are fully savoring it.

"Wait, let's take souvenir photos," Laurentine Paka cries

out. You did not know she had a camera. She takes her novel out of her bag—it's from the *Adoras* collection and she never goes anywhere without it—and instead of laying it on the ground and dirtying the precious object, hands it to Ossolo then digs back into her bag to take out her cell phone—one of those devices with a built-in camera—which is carefully wrapped in its faux leather case. She is the only one among you to have a phone like that. She takes several photos, then has Moyalo step in as photographer so that she too can appear in one. You ask everyone to take one special photo with Batatou as the star.

Everyone agrees and applauds. You position her in the center of the group, and you stand to the left of her holding one of her children in your arms. Bileko stands to her right carrying the other. After you have scrolled through the photos on the digital device's screen and selected the best ones together, Laurentine Paka erases the rest. She promises you all that her husband will make printouts for each of you. In fact, she calls him right away.

"Since we are organized now, I propose that until our movement is over, we share all of our food." It's Mama Moyalo speaking. "Tomorrow, everyone brings what she can: fruits, meat, fish, anything the stomach can accept, and we will eat together. For those who can't find anything, not to worry; they can bring water to drink for all of us to share."

"Yes!"

"Very good idea."

"I agree one hundred percent."

They echo in agreement. You also think it's a very good idea.

Finally, each of the women goes back to her pile of unsold stones and packs up her things as she usually does before heading home; each with a vague feeling that tomorrow may be different, not just another day.

FIVE

HAVING FINISHED your workday, you are on your way home, walking as quickly as you can in order to arrive before the sun sets. After ten minutes, as you approach the turn onto the path that you usually take as a shortcut, a shadow emerges before you. It seems to be slogging along on all fours, plastered against the hillside it was trying to climb. After a moment, your eyes manage to make out a woman sagging beneath a bundle of firewood. She is so doubled over, her torso practically at a right angle with her legs, that you figure the load she is carrying must be as heavy as a dead donkey. No doubt, it's got to be one of your friends from the quarry. Yes, you immediately recognize her, how could you not? Since you are together nearly every single day, you know all of them and you know each of their stories. Even if now you were all in the same boat, each of you had ended up there through your own path of suffering. And each form of suffering is unique. No one can live or truly understand another's suffering. You know Mâ Bileko's story only too well, and that it is she who is there before you, out of breath as she climbs this slope. If out of all of you one should have never ended up doing this forced labor, it is she. A happy and full marriage of thirty-two years!

Her husband had been a primary school teacher, then a school inspector, which allowed him to travel all over the country. Mâ Bileko had also traveled a lot. Her first trip out of the country was to Paris with her husband, who had been sent as a delegate to a conference on primary education in Francophone countries. She had taken it as an opportunity to travel to Holland where she had bought bundles of Dutch wax, super wax and java wax cloths to bring back. This had allowed her to start her business with the steadfast determination to become as opulent, in every aspect, as the rich Yoruba women of West Africa, the full-figured Mama Benzes, who drove Mercedes Benzes. But it was her trip to China with a delegation of women that had definitively established her success. That trip had opened her eyes. She had understood that she had to turn her back on Europe, old tropism of colonialism, and look to Asia, or else she would merely be continuing the petty trade in pagnes all her life like thousands of other women in the African markets. Taking advantage of a forty-eight-hour layover in Hong Kong, she had bought electronics, CD and DVD players, video games and other gadgets, some useful, others useless. Her big surprise was the cell phones that sold like hot cakes, and not only to the rich. Everybody wanted them, from executives to peons, from taxi drivers to river fishermen. The humble civil servants saved their beer money to be able to afford one. Besides, it had become fashionable, and any young girl felt belittled in front of her peers if her boyfriend did not buy her one.

After a year, she had become a real businesswoman. She had opened several stores and, to keep them stocked, she traveled several times a year in Asia, in the Chunking Mansions of Hong Kong or the trade centers of Guangzhou in mainland China. She never missed the Dubai Trade Festival where the prices of goods were reduced by half. She was making so much money that she had become the breadwinner, her husband's ridiculously low primary schoolteacher salary only supplemental, a kind of pocket change. She had about twenty employees, from store managers to caretakers who looked after her new villa. She drove a Mercedes, and, like any privileged member of society, she had become overweight and, in turn, so had her husband. As a matter of fact, people only called her by the respectful nickname of "Mama Kilo," a way to recognize her opulence literally as well as figuratively. She was respected because she had become rich honestly, through her work and her business smarts, and not by relying on the support of crooked politicians who stole from State coffers with impunity, even though, of course, she had her own network of customs officers and tax inspectors whose palms she greased from time to time, so that they would close their eyes at a lot of things.

Her husband's illness brought out the best in her. She stopped all of her business trips abroad to stay night and day by the bedside of this man for whom her love grew a little more with each passing day. Convinced that she was going to lose him if she did not evacuate him to another country abroad, she started knocking on the doors of Western embassies and, despite the humiliations and long waits in line, she managed to obtain a visa for a health evaluation in one of the best hospitals in the United States, where the Arab princes of the Gulf were treated. Alas, after a month of treatment, the doctors gave her the horrifying news—her husband's cancerous leukemia was incurable, and he would have to be brought back to his country to spend the three or four months he had left to live. Regardless, once back home, she continued to squander enormous sums of money on quacks who claimed to have a miracle cure for the disease that was resistant to Western medicine. But was one not ready for anything, in the face of despair? Despite all of that, the inevitable happened.

When her husband died, she had almost no money left. The enormous expenses she had incurred as she tried to save the life of her companion of so many years, with whom she had raised a girl and two boys, had scraped every last penny of her savings. Her business was on the brink of bankruptcy. In a market as trendy and competitive as electronics, several months of absence was suicide. Competitors selling junk laptops, pirated CDs and DVDs now occupied the void she had left. But that financial and commercial debacle certainly would not have landed her on this riverbank where she was reduced to filling bags of gravel to survive, or on this hill she had to climb every night as she is doing now before you, her back broken under the weight of her brushwood. With her fearlessness and experience, she surely would have bounced back if the family of her late husband had not swooped down on everything she owned like vultures on carcasses.

You are younger than she is, actually the same age as her oldest son. With your swift resolute strides, you have caught up to her.

"You walk so fast!"

"Don't mock me, my child. My rheumatoid arthritis makes it more and more difficult for me to move, but I'm okay."

"Where did you find all this wood?"

"I gathered it here and there. It's not good wood—just dry sticks that burn up very quickly. They don't burn long enough to cook food. A piece of advice, don't use them to prepare cassava leaves. The advantage, however, is that they don't give off too much smoke and they're useful for lighting charcoal."

"You need a gas stove. At your age, firewood is too much of a nuisance."

"I have one, but I don't have any gas. A bottle of butane gas is the price of a bag of gravel." "That's why we absolutely have to sell the bag at fifteen thousand francs. Today, I am in a big hurry, and I won't be able to walk with you. We will meet again tomorrow, Mâ Bileko, and good luck. I hope we have more luck with those entrepreneurs."

"Yes, I hope so too. I already have a full bag and another one three-quarters full. Fifteen thousand francs would be really good. Alright, see you tomorrow. When will you bring your little girl again? Her name's Lyra, right?"

"Yes. She is fine. With everything that's happening, I don't know when I'm going to bring her with me."

"In any case, don't forget to give her a kiss for me."

You wave goodbye and go on ahead of her. You are walking quickly because you are thinking of your children who should be back home from school by now. You are also hurrying because you have to go well out of your way to stop by your Aunt's to pick up Lyra. Before long, you have reached the top of the hill and you turn around to take one last look behind you. From up there, Mâ Bileko's silhouette is tiny, the silhouette of an elderly woman braving the mountain, carrying a load that is wider than her back, her back which long ago had carried, supported and filled children with joy, three children, but which now only transports bundles of wood. But you've got to get on your way. You turn around and keep on walking down the asphalt road, yet not necessarily preventing Mâ Bileko's story of a social fall from grace from coming after you.

•

It had begun at the meeting the two families held in order to take stock of her estate, a few days after her husband was buried, as tradition requires. It is the moment that every woman you know fears, the moment when the mask of hypocrisy that the husband's family members wear—that mask of shared pain and compassion—cracks and makes way for obscene greed. Next to that, all the stresses which tradition has imposed on the grief-stricken widow before her husband is buried look like recess on a playground: staying seated on a mat, barefoot, tousled hair covered with a pagne; not allowed to go anywhere alone, even to the toilet, unless accompanied by two female chaperones, the same two through whom any words either spoken to her by a man or addressed by her to a man must pass. But no, this time it was a feeding frenzy.

The meeting had barely begun when the deceased husband's elder sister opened the hostilities: "Forgive me for speaking before you do, Uncle, and all the other elders who are here, but it hurts so much that I must speak. I'm going to say what I think since we're all family. I was ashamed of the way this woman disrespected my brother's memory during the ceremony after the cemetery. If I had not held my tongue, I would have screamed in front of all the guests. With all the money my brother left her, this woman who has benefited from it all her life found nothing better than to serve cheap drinks to our guests! And was there even something for everyone? Not at all! I saw people fighting over a bottle of beer! What an insult. I nearly died of shame! What does she think she's going to do with this money? Buy new dresses and shiny jewelry for herself now that she has gotten rid of my brother? Oh Petelo, my younger brother, your corpse is still warm, and you have already been forgotten," she concluded, her voice trembling.

Mâ Bileko thought that she was dreaming. She knew that the reception after the burial had been dignified. Cases of good local beer and large jugs of cool palm wine were served to everyone who had accompanied them to the cemetery; and for those who did not drink alcohol, lemonade and fruit juice was offered. Anyway, this sister-in-law never liked her. She was jealous of her from the beginning, pretending to believe that Mâ Bileko had married her brother only for his money because at the time Bileko didn't work. She didn't even have a profession, whereas he was a schoolteacher, thus a public servant, thus rich. Jealous also because, abandoned by her husband after six years of marriage because she had not borne him any children, she had never been able to remarry. But Bileko was not easily fooled. She knew it was all just an act to find a way to take her for all she was worth. That is what always happened when you were both a woman and a widow.

Her husband's uncle, who presided over the gathering, played the wise patriarch rebuking his niece, saying all that was in the past and it was time to focus on the future, especially the children's future. How much money had his nephew left in his account? When were they going to take inventory of the stores? And the suits? The pairs of shoes? Didn't Bileko think that it was time to take all those pagnes and all that jewelry she had and divvy them up among her sisters-in-law and cousins-in-law? As for his own grandson, her husband's uncle's eldest son's child, thus nephew of the deceased, he did not ask for much, the Mercedes would do. And he continued to describe, to count and recount the items he coveted until there was nothing left to add to his inventory.

Now it was the grieving widow's family's turn to respond.

The eldest of Bileko's family spoke and began protesting, though half-heartedly, because he knew the custom and would have behaved similarly if he had been on the husband's side of the family. He asked them gingerly not to take everything, reminding them to think of the children who needed a car to drive them to school, and especially that they leave the house to the widow, again, because of the children. It never occurred to him that the others should not take those possessions because Mâ Bileko also owned them.

What everyone had forgotten was that in spite of her basic education, Mâ Bileko was no longer a backward villager who could be taken to the cleaners, she was an informed woman. They had forgotten that she had been a businesswoman who had traveled around the world, negotiated markets with her European, Arab, and Chinese counterparts. The long-winded speechmaker of the family had barely stopped uttering his cumbersome wordplays and convoluted paraphrases in order to say what had to be said without really saying what had to be said when Bileko sat straight up in her chair. Her face emaciated, her body fatigued from night vigils and mourning deprivation, but her gaze burning with fierce determination, she managed to shout at them in a tone that was unusually disrespectful for a woman in her circumstances. "Where were you all hiding while your kinsman suffered in agony, the same kinsman for whom you now shed crocodile tears? None of you contributed to his medical expenses. Very few of you visited him when he was in the hospital, and now that he's dead you show up and demand that your dear and beloved kinsman be buried in a luxurious coffin and that we offer champagne and Scotch whiskey to all those who attended his funeral. Where were you hiding before he died? Now you want the house, the Mercedes, the pagnes, the jewelry, the television, the stores, the money. But you are forgetting one thing: All of it belongs to me! And I know what is in the best interest of my children, thank you. Didn't you know that your kinsman had a schoolteacher's salary? That I acquired all those assets through my work, my travels, my hardships? I am going to tell you one thing: I shared all of my assets with my husband but, now that he's dead, I am the sole owner of them! You will get nothing, you hear me, nothing! *Nada!*"

If her deceased husband's family was shocked, her own family was even more so and tried to hide their embarrassment. No wife had ever dared to speak to their in-laws in that manner. Undoubtedly, the world was falling apart. Things held no more and soon the hens will rule the roost! The uncle-in-law's shock transformed into anger.

"You have no respect. I wonder how my nephew could have kept such an insolent woman as his wife for so long," he fumed.

"You are a snake! No, a witch," yelled her sister-in-law, "my brother's death was no natural death. She killed him for his wealth. I told you she practices evil. Go search her room. I am certain you'll find talismans!"

Joining action with words, she headed into the house. Like locusts, the other sisters and cousins of the husband rose to follow her despite protests from Ma Beliko's family who shouted uselessly, "Stop, you don't have the right. We will curse you if you touch anything!" They opened and emptied drawers, armoires, and cupboards. They came back with beautiful dresses, wax and super wax pagnes, Bazin fabric and lace pagnes; gold jewelry, rings and necklaces set with brilliant stones. Then, dramatically, a smile of satisfaction on her lips, the sister-in-law came out last and triumphantly placed a large gilt bronze Buddha statue in the middle of the circle the two families had formed. It was the supreme talisman, stronger that anything found in their homeland because it came from the Orient, country of elixirs and magicians that one sees in cassettes of pirated Indian films. A whisper of stupefaction turned into apprehension rose from both sides. Some were afraid to look at the thing, even more so to touch it, and for good reason. Few had seen a statue of Buddha; none of them could imagine that it was sold in the streets of Bangkok or Seoul as commonly as the small wooden statuettes sold in African airports. Her own family was beginning to doubt her and no longer knew how to defend such concrete proof of evil practices.

Mâ Bileko was so enraged she couldn't take it anymore. She got up from her seat, threw off the pagne that covered her head and yelled at everyone, her parents included, to leave her house, her property. That they get the hell out immediately! Or else, she would file a complaint for breaking and entering, theft and intimidation. "One last thing: Petelo, my husband, loved me. We loved each other. I will not be in mourning. Tomorrow, I will braid my hair, I will wear my most beautiful pagne and my most beautiful jewelry. He will look at me from where he is and he will know that I made myself beautiful for him. Anything else, I could care less! Go, get, leave!"

From then on, everything became worse. The husband's side had started yelling that Bileko was the one who should leave the house that was their brothers'—or their nephew's—depending on who was speaking.

"No, the house belonged to the deceased's children," Bileko's family retorted, on the defensive.

"But what children?" the sister-in-law shot back, "With all those trips and those nights she spent in hotels abroad during her so-called supply trips... nothing says that they really are my brother's children."

Those words hurt Bileko deeply and, enraged, she replied that when one was sterile, one could not allow oneself to speak as if one knew how to get pregnant. Besides, it wasn't an accident that the sister-in-law was sterile; it was because she was a witch! Boiling with anger, the latter threw herself at Bileko, but one of Bileko's cousins blocked her and pushed her back forcefully. She fell to the ground. When she got up, she turned her back to Bileko and her parents, bent over, lifted her pagne and showed her bare buttocks, a curse. Total pandemonium erupted in a cacophony of crisscrossing insults, with the cursing sister-in-law's sisters and cousins attempting to break through the barrier of hands and arms that kept them from punching Bileko. Finally, outnumbered and overwhelmed by the turn of events, Mâ Bileko's family retreated in defeat and Bileko was put forcibly into a taxi which brought her to her parent's house.

When she returned the next day along with her aunt and two of her children, she nearly cried. Her personal belongings, at least what was left of them, had been taken out of the house and strewn about all over the veranda. All the locks had been changed. The garage was open, but of course the Mercedes was gone. Enraged, she took a big rock and started banging on the lock of the front door to break it. As if they'd hidden so they could spy on what she was doing, two men appeared. She recognized one of them, one of her husband's nephews, with whom she'd always been generous. They shoved her around, telling her to get the hell out. She started shouting insults at them, which attracted a crowd of onlookers each having their own commentary while the kids tried to defend their mother by kicking them. Finally, Mâ Bileko, her aunt and her kids were thrown out of the house, off the property, into the street, humiliated and abandoned to themselves.

•

She had told you this story one afternoon when, for reasons you no longer remember, you had been the last ones to leave the quarry. You were going back up this same hill, a shortcut that went from the riverbanks to the big paved road. She was not carrying as much weight as today; all she was holding then was her basket of food, now empty. You, on the other hand, in addition to your basket, were carrying Lyra, who was tied securely astride your back. It had been a good day because, after practically a week of absence, the trucks had finally come by and each of you had your twenty thousand francs well concealed somewhere under your clothes. As you walked, you talked and talked about your daily routine of stones and heat, dust and sweat, but also about what you were going to do the next day, because it would be Sunday, your only day of weekly rest. After a while, you had stopped to readjust the pagne wrapper around Lyra, which had loosened a little. Mâ Bileko, who also stopped to wait for you, offered unexpectedly:

"I'll carry her until we get to the road, if you want. It's

been such a long time since I have felt the softness of a child's body against my back."

"Of course!" you'd replied, although you were afraid that Lyra might throw a tantrum and cry because she didn't know this stranger. Quite the opposite though, she smiled when you transferred her onto Bileko's back, as if for her it were a game.

"Oh, little one, let grandma carry you," Bileko said once the child was secure on her back, as you resumed climbing together, slowly. Then you studied her face like you had never done before. Wrinkles traced its entangled folds, but wrinkles mean nothing when the harshness of life ages a person prematurely. At forty, one appears fifty and the shea butter that was applied to the face every evening changed nothing. Still, you had the feeling that she was your mother, your mother who would have left her village, her banana plantations and her cassava fields, to fail on this pebble beach. Passing the child from one back to the other had suddenly created a strong intimacy beyond the natural solidarity that the site had forged among all the women. Your conversation with Bileko became more personal and its meandering led you both to your most painful places.

You disclosed to her that you had never received your diploma because of an unexpected pregnancy and an early marriage. In return, she revealed to you that she had a daughter, a little younger than you, who had been kicked out of school after she was sexually abused by her teacher. Sincerely touched, you had spontaneously asked her daughter's name:

"Zizina," she had answered.

"I would like to meet her," you continued. She had said nothing for a moment, then:

"Sad story. She suffered so much! Thank God, it's fine now. Ever since she read that ad in the newspaper that the UN was recruiting ten women in the country to be part of an all-female police force to go to Liberia, she thinks she's already there. She registered for evening classes, which she pays for herself, thanks to the job that she created with her scooter, mobile supplier of digital refill cards for cell phones and batteries for all sorts of little electronic appliances."

"What type of appliances?" you had asked.

"Calculators, watches, digital cameras, MP3 players. It's going pretty well. Some days we only eat thanks to her." You did not know what she must have read in your gaze since she suddenly stopped and blurted out: "You know, I was very rich once!"

That was how she started telling you her story, a story so deeply etched in her memory that she could recall every last detail. "You cannot understand the pain, Méréana, when I was thrown brutally out of my house, off my land, by those two men and found myself out on the street with my aunt and my two children crying out, frightened: 'Mom, mom, why are they kicking us out of our house?' They were traumatized. And the crowd that was indulging this sight, with wicked pleasure, of the neighborhood's grande dame reduced to a beggar, searching desperately for a taxi to escape the shame!" After uttering those words of shame and humiliation, she fell silent. You did the same as well because you knew that your words, whatever they might have been, would pale in comparison to hers.

You had arrived at the top of the hill, where the path crosses the main road, where your paths diverge. The sun, now large and blood red, no longer warmed, which meant that nightfall was soon approaching. You watched her in silence as she unraveled the pagne from around Lyra and helped you to reposition the child on your back. Lyra had begun to sulk and to resist, not wanting to leave her new grandmother's back at all. The whims of the child made you both laugh and brought back cheerfulness. After all, the day had been good. After having wedged the little girl in place onto your back, and as you were saying goodbye to Mâ Bileko, you couldn't resist asking that nagging question: Why hadn't she sought justice? Because after all, didn't we live in a country of laws as the radio blared every day? She had sighed:

"Don't trust the laws that are on the books. They just write them to please the UN and all those international organizations that give them money and invite them to conferences. The real law— the one that we endure every day—is the one that always gives men the advantage. If you only knew the money that I have spent on lawyers and trials! All of that gobbled up the little money that I had left after my husband's death. All those customs officers and tax collectors that I had bought off, all those so-called friends of my husband to whom I had given discounts on iPods and other electronic gadgets, none of them knew me anymore. That is how I was robbed of everything."

That day, it was with those words that you parted ways and, thinking about what you, too, had endured, you wondered if there were any worse place for a woman on this planet than this continent called Africa.

SIX

THE IMAGE OF Mâ Bileko crushed under her bundle of wood fades little by little and your immediate reality comes into focus: go pick up Lyra, your sister's child, at your aunt's house where she has spent the day, then quickly head home before nightfall to join your other two children who must be home from school by now. Your quarry is three miles away from your home which is not so far after all. You are also lucky because the school is in your neighborhood. It had taken you less than a week to teach the two boys how to get there and back by themselves, the oldest, twelve, holding his nine-year-old younger brother's hand. They must be hungry now.

Perched on your shoulders, the little girl is cooing like a bird, happy to see you again because you are the only mother she has ever really known. As usual, Auntie Turia has already washed and fed her, which is helpful since all that is left for you to do is to put her to bed when you get home. You enjoy asking those silly questions that adults like to ask children her age. Show me your right hand. How many toes do you have on your foot? Do chickens have legs? What did you eat at Granny Turia's? She cannot pronounce the r in her name and says Lila, which by the way, is also a pretty name. Her mother had invented the name Lyra by combining the last two letters of Kaly, her bastard husband's first name—whom she had loved blindly—and the last two letters of her own first name, Tamara. As it often happens with you, as soon as the little girl starts answering your questions, engrossed in the counting of her toes with her childish lisp and pronunciation, your memory of her mother immediately comes to mind and, once again, you start thinking about the bright future you had dreamed she would have. Was it subconsciously to compensate for your own aborted future that you had vicariously invested yourself in the idea of her success?

•

Your mother is a peasant. She cultivates the cassava fields along with a small plantation of banana trees inherited from her mother. She is a practicing Christian of the Swedish Evangelical mission like your father, your village being a Protestant island in a predominantly Catholic region, a Catholicism blended with traditional faiths. He is a pastor—well, people call him pastor because he is the one who directs the spiritual activities of the village, although he has never studied theology and has practically never left his village. With his glasses placed acrobatically on the bridge of his flat nose, he would conduct weddings and funerals, reading the Lord's words out of an old Kongo Bible with red edges. When you saw him running his finger over each line as he read, you did not know if he was really reading or simply repeating what he had learned by heart because you had never heard of him ever going to any school. He is that very type of old-time Protestant, the kind that would never deviate one iota from the morals instilled by the Swedish missionaries who had evangelized your village during your grandfather's time. For him, drinking alcohol is a sin, smoking too, because the smell of tobacco contaminates and poisons the body, the Lord's temple. Admiring the neighbor's wife's swaying buttocks or simply allowing his gaze to linger a little too long on a woman's blouse is equivalent to having committed adultery in your heart and already puts you in the territories controlled by the devil himself. During the dry season and after the bushfires, he used to trade in his Bible and his priesthood for a machete and an axe and accompany his wife in the fields to chop down trees, cutting down groves to clear the area where your mother would make mounds of dirt where she would plant her cassava cuttings, and your sister and you would scatter peanut or corn seeds between them. It was good soil, and the often-plentiful harvest was in no way comparable to the Sahelian lands described to you in geography class.

At that time, your school was located in the neighboring village, four miles away if you took the main road, but you knew some shortcuts, and if you took those paths which go up hills and through valleys, you avoided the road's numerous twists and turns, which snaked around so much it would often run parallel to itself.

Often times the rain would surprise you and you would get home completely soaked; then mama would make you a lemongrass infusion with sugar or honey. Once, it had rained so much that the books and notebooks you were carrying in your cloth school bags were all wet, some pages had come loose while the ink in the notebooks had rubbed off, and the lessons that you had written were nothing more than big blue stains. You were afraid to face your parents because of your carelessness even if it wasn't your fault. In any case, Dad would not be happy because books were expensive. You had no way of hiding the disaster from your father. Worried by the violence of the storm, he was waiting for you underneath the veranda. He spotted the wet objects you were trying to hide behind your backs right away. It was a miracle, not at all what you were afraid of—arguments and punishments—quite the opposite.

"My poor children," he said, "it's my fault, I should have thought about it sooner." Within a week, he bought plastic school bags and a raincoat for each of you. You were not poor thanks to your fields and the banana tree plantation. You were privileged because a lot of students had neither notebooks nor books but only slates; and the teacher had to copy everything you all had to read aloud together onto the blackboard for them. And, since you were not poor, you had everything you needed to succeed, and your parents pushed you constantly to go to school. They had invested immense hope in you and your siblings, but especially in you, the oldest daughter.

The day primary school certificate results were announced, you were in the fields with your mother and it was Tamara who brought you the news, all excited. Your mother dropped her hoe right away, wrapped her arms around you, then gave you a big smile, then hugged you again, and finally started dancing around you and singing. "No more plantation for you," she said, "you have to go to high school. I'm going to ask Turia to host you. You will go live at her house." Your father was smiling when he saw you arriving from the field, a basin full of corncobs on your head. You did not know if he was proud of you or of himself, but in any case, he was happy. When grandmother was still alive, she would always call on the ancestors for everything that was happening to you, good or bad. Father considered the great failure of his life to have not succeeded in converting grandmother, his mother, to Christianity. You often heard them discussing theology and even arguing. He would talk about his one God and the only Son; she, about her numerous gods and ancestors because, she reasoned, "many eyes see better than two." He lived fearing his God and could not yell at him when He abandoned him; her gods feared her wrath because, if one of them had not fulfilled the mission she had assigned to him, she would punish him by ripping a leg or an arm from the statuette that embodied him. You still remember the day that you brought her the first sorrel leaves from your garden in a small wicker basket. It was the first time that you had planted something, your first harvest. As prideful as a five-year-old can be, you handed her the basket triumphantly, and she, the proud grandmother, took you in her arms and told you solemnly, as if it were a secret, that your clan's ancestors had given you the gift of a green thumb. When it was explained to her that your primary school admission certificate was of critical importance for your future, she had assigned to one of her gods the exclusive task of watching over you. Father neither knew nor recognized the ancestors. He addressed his congratulations simultaneously to you, to God the Almighty and to Jesus Christ. "You will be the family's first intellectual," he said, "the first to go to high school and get your diploma, you will earn your university degree and top it all off with a doctorate!"

At twelve years old, the daughter of a self-proclaimed pastor and of a peasant in a remote village, you had never heard of those diplomas. And, when, in front of your whole family you put your brand-new suitcase into the bus that was going to take you to the capital, you understood that a new stage of your life was going to begin the moment the driver turned on the engine, and that rusty-red dirt road that the truck would soon take, that road that zigzagged before you, that disappeared for a moment into the grove then reappeared like a small, narrow strip over there at the top of the mountain then disappeared again, was the path that would lead you to this new life that your parents had wished for you, a life that was different from theirs. The other travelers must have sensed it because, right away, they had squeezed in a little more tightly to give you a seat that was more comfortable. Your mother was waving the headscarf she had removed from her head, your sister her hand, while your father, with grand gestures, was sweeping the air with his holy book. You had not cried.

•

Your roaming thoughts seem to have shortened the way because at the curve in the road you already notice your house, though it seems you had hardly left your aunt's. Your first concern is to make sure that the children have returned from school safe and sound. You fear every day that something will happen to them while you are at the quarry: that is what spurs you to drag them along with you on the days they don't have class.

Yes, they are there, and they welcome you with cries of joy. The oldest comes to take Lyra whom you have taken off your shoulders. The nine-year-old, for his part, has started rummaging through your grocery bag because he knows you always bring them a few little goodies when you return in the evenings. He finds nothing and begins to pout. Obviously, you don't tell him that you're starting to run out of money because you have not sold anything for several days. You console him by explaining that you did not have time to make your usual little stop in the street where the doughnut, grilled peanut and banana vendors sell their goods. Maybe tomorrow. He takes those words as a firm promise, whereas for you they are just those little inconsequential lies every mother tells to console their child.

You enter the house which is already dark. You flip the switch and the lights come on! Who said that miracles do not exist? Your neighborhood has power tonight, and you are happy because the distribution of electricity in the city is like the lottery—one day you have it, the next day you don't. And, when you have it, it sometimes only lasts for a few hours. They call it a "selective power cut." That is why, in addition to your candle reserves, you have your storm lanterns on the ready always stocked with enough oil.

Like every evening, despite their resistance, you make the two boys wash up before having their evening meal to get rid of the grime accumulated throughout the day. While they do that, you put down Lyra who is already dozing off. The oldest finishes his homework quite quickly since today he only has geometry, calculating the area of some simple polygons—a triangle, a square and a rectangle. Then you let them chat with you a little before you send them to sleep on the foam mattress they share and tell them to close the mosquito net. Finally, you can tend to your body.

The water that you have put on to heat is now the right temperature. You remove the bucket from the gas stove and head towards the shower with a wash basin. You use a scented soap to scrub your body, especially your armpits, your pubic hair and the whole area between your thighs and your buttocks. The thick lather absorbs your sweat, the dust and all the grit of the day. Then you rinse off with plenty of water to clear away the soiled suds. You are no longer dirty. Then, squatting over the edge of the basin, you splash the inside of your open thighs several times with warm water. The contact of the warm water with your intimate area arouses a desire in you, a rather strong desire. You close your eyes. Your breathing transforms into an uneven rapid succession of short breaths of air, inhaling and exhaling. You realize that it has been a long time since you have made love, since a man's hard penis has been inside you, more than a year at least, since that fateful night when you had firmly asked that man, who was your husband, to put on a condom if he wanted to make love, that condom he did not slip on which was the reason that today you are a stone breaker raising three children all alone. You had anticipated that being alone—without anyone by your side—would be difficult, but you never imagined it would be so to this extent.

•

Because of Tamara's long illness, you had to stop making your buyer's trips around West Africa a while ago, a business which had been doing very well because, as opposed to the pagne cloth market which was saturated, you were one of the rare ones who specialized in food: smoked shrimp from Lomé or salted fish from Dakar brought in faster returns than super wax pagnes or Bazin fabrics. In fact, you had already started withdrawing from your savings well before you left your husband because you were your sister's sole caretaker. Your parents' contribution was seasonal since it depended on the harvest. All of her friends, even those in her intellectual circle, had deserted her when the word had spread that she was sick with AIDS. When you would run into them by chance, they would shower you with sympathy and compassion, but they no longer hugged you and barely even held out their hands as if you had contracted yaws disease or tuberculosis. And yet, as educated women, they must have known that this terrible illness was not transmitted through a kiss or a handshake. It was not the plague after all! But what to expect from the people of a country that was ashamed to recognize that the disease even existed, and which camouflaged reality by using the term "an invented syndrome to discourage lovers." Nelson Mandela had not been ashamed to share with the world that his son had died of it, and neither were you ashamed about your sister. The only difference—as you always pointed out—is that it was her husband who had infected her.

When you found out that your country had been selected for a low-cost tri-therapy program funded by the Bill and Melinda Gates Foundation, you had rushed to register your sister on the list of applicants. However, after being sent from one office to another, making appointments which each time were pushed back to the following day and unable to find the necessary amount to grease the palms of whoever it concerned, you had never had access to those medications.

Then, when eating had become an ordeal for her because of the pain that knotted her throat, when her skin could no longer bear contact with the sheets because her body was covered with lesions, and when her weight loss had transformed her beautiful face into two big, bright eyes set between a prominent forehead and excessively protruding cheekbones with a thin layer of skin stretching over in an attempt to cover them, you had panicked. And afraid to see her die, you had tried everything: from Indian and Chinese medicines of dubious origins sold clandestinely on the market, to traditional treatments based merely on garlic or wild peppers; from pastors and other Evangelists offering prayers with candles, incense and sacred waters, to the healers who asked you to sacrifice either a rooster, or a sheep to go with the animist amulets they sold you for spiritual protection. What would one not do when there was no longer any hope? She died, in spite of everything. You accompanied her body to the village where your parents wanted to bury her. You took Lyra with you, her only daughter, an orphan at six months old. Thank God, her mother had not transmitted the virus to her during her pregnancy.

After the shock, you had to keep on living, even if only to raise the three children. Fortunately, you were married, you thought. Your husband would help you bounce back. Now that you no longer had your sister, he would be your only support, the pillar you could lean on, surrounded by his love and your children, like your aunt and her husband, like your mother and your father. Cruel disappointment! He had begun by reproaching you for getting too involved in Tamara's illness and neglecting him, then by downright messing around without even waiting for you to come out of mourning the loss of your sister. Or, most likely, he had been playing around for a long time without you realizing it, until that fateful night when the veil fell from your eyes and you had been afraid. Unjustified fear, perhaps, but fear all the same of dying like Tamara. So you had demanded that he use that thin rubber which made the difference between life and death. You did not leave him right away though.

Your aunt had persuaded you to return to your conjugal home that morning when, covered with bruises, you had turned up at her house at daybreak. A woman did not leave her husband for so little. What God had united through the sacraments of marriage could not be undone with a few blows. She was your aunt; she had more authority over you than your own mother, as tradition prescribed. Besides, she was the one who raised you throughout your entire adolescence. She had brought you back to your conjugal home, as if such a home still existed. Anyway, your mother would not have acted otherwise. Your hypocrite husband, with his shifty eyes, showed all the respect that was due to a mother-in-law and swore to all his gods and that he did not understand why you had left the house; he was really embarrassed that a small problem that could be settled between husband and wife was disclosed outside the marital roof. Your aunt agreed with him. It was exactly what she wanted to hear, she who could not conceive of a husband who was not as good as her dear Malaki, a man who had loved and adored her all her life. You were at fault. The man could not be. Satisfied, she left. He had not dared to tell her that the supposedly little problem was that you had refused to have sex with him without a condom.

After that first incident, he played the loyal and respectful husband for a week, then he threatened to look elsewhere if you didn't give in to him. The more you resisted, the more he insisted. He was visibly exhausted by your stubborn refusal—no test, no sex without a condom—until the night he went ballistic. "First and foremost, you belong to me!" he had shouted. He continued, bellowing, that he had paid a dowry to marry you, and that your peasant parents would never be able to pay him back. You immediately shot back that your parents were not poor. As for the dowry, it did not even equal half of the proceeds of the harvest of your mother's banana plantation divided in three. Your answer seemed to have injected an extra shot of adrenaline into his nervous system because he blew up, barking his head off that you did not have a job, that you had no income, that your sister's long illness had ruined you, that without him you would be in the street because you wouldn't know where to go. You sensed that soon he would be out of control and start hitting you. The last time he had caught you by surprise because it was the first time that he had hit you in twelve years of marriage, but it was also true that it was the first time that you had refused him. This time, you would not be caught by surprise. A quick glance around the living room where you were arguing allowed you to immediately spot what could protect you. You moved suddenly to stand beside the table, near the storm lamp. The children, not understanding why you were shouting, were terrified and had gone to hide in their room.

"You think you are holier than the Pope who is against condoms," he yelled, unfairly introducing your parents' Christian faith. You shot back, scathingly, that although you were Christian, you were not Catholic, so the Pope was not your imam. "Shut up, a woman does not have the right to speak to me in that tone!"

"Well, if you want me to shut up, you also have to zip it," you answered him tit for tat. Then, he leapt at you, but you were ready. The storm lamp hit him smack in the face. The glass broke and several shards gashed his face. He was bleeding. Fortunately for him—and for you—the lamp was not lit because the oil that had dripped out of the tank would have caught fire and turned it into a Molotov cocktail.

"I can't see any more, you've blinded me!" He howled like a madman... You could not stay any longer. He could kill you. He could hurt your sister's child. As he writhed around like a chicken with its head cut off, you quickly stuffed some essential clothing and a few toiletries into a bag and asked the frightened crying children to follow you.

You were walking quickly, almost running. You did not know where you were going to spend the night. As you walked, you thought of going to your aunt's, but you abandoned the idea; you did not want to listen to another sermon. One of your best friends since high school, Fatoumata, lived in another part of the city. She would immediately understand your problem and would put you up at least for the night. You hailed a taxi, and you all jumped in. You swore to yourself that you would never set foot in that house again except to collect your belongings—after your aunt and your mother, coming urgently from the village, had failed to make you reconsider your decision. When the AIDS test you'd rushed to get a few weeks later came back negative, you felt like you had literally been reborn.

•

The water against your thighs has lost its heat, and its freshness against your skin brings your thoughts back to the bucket and the basin. You stand up and start drying your most intimate parts before drying the rest of your body. As clean as a whistle, you massage your shoulder blades, biceps, neck and fingers to eliminate the fatigue and stiffness in them and then you rub sandalwood scented almond oil all over your body. Finally, you massage your face with shea butter. You feel more relaxed. You are happy since sometimes you throw yourself into bed still dressed in your work clothes because you are too exhausted to draw water and heat it up to wash and massage your body.

The long day is over and the restful night can finally begin. After a last look in on the two boys to make sure they are sheltered from mosquito bites, you slip under your mosquito net, next to Lyra. It is time to rest your body.

SEVEN

YOUR MIND IS already at the quarry when you wake up. You are only half listening to Radio France Internationale as it gives the African news briefing.

> The President of the Republic of the Congo has spent four hundred thousand dollars on a five day stay at the Waldorf Astoria Hotel in New York. Documents in our possession indicate that he rented a forty-four-room suite to provide accommodation for his family members and the delegation accompanying him. The employees of the hotel were taken aback by the sight of the President's men taking bundles of hundred-dollar notes out of their briefcases to pay the bill which included bottles of Cristal champagne, costing seven hundred fifty dollars each.

> Four Sierra Leonean journalists, who had covered a campaign against female genital mutilation, have been forced to remove their clothes and walk naked in the street by a group in favor of the practice, witnesses said on Monday.
> The journalists were taken on Friday in the town of Kenema in eastern Sierra Leone by members of the Bondo group, a secret traditional organization that practices female genital mutilation, perceived as an initiation rite.
> They undressed the journalists and forced them to walk naked in the town before police and local human rights organizations intervened, according to witnesses questioned by the AFP.

> According to the UN, 94% of women and girls in Sierra Leone between 15 and 49 years old have been circumcised.

For you the only question swirling in your mind was: Will today be different, in other words, will the stone buyers agree to negotiate with you?

The older two off to school, Lyra dropped off at your aunt's, you hurry off. Usually, the sun shines without heat for the first hours of the morning, but today it does not do you any favors because by 8 o'clock it has been beating down as though it was already noon. You thought you would be the first to arrive at the quarry, but once again taciturn Iyissou beat you to it. You would give a cubic meter of your gravel to know what goes on in the head of a woman who saw her child literally ripped from her arms then murdered. You say good morning to her, she smiles back absently and continues to hammer at her stone.

The other women arrive one by one and soon they are all there. They quite naturally gather around you to determine the day's strategy, actually to hear you reconfirm what you'd all already decided two days ago: to sell your bag of stones at the non-negotiable price of fifteen thousand francs by first asking twenty thousand francs, a strategic bargaining price. This circle around you is perhaps also a way for you all to reassure one another.

Each of you returns to her small area and begins her daily routine.

•

Here come the trucks. It's 11am. The wait was not long. The sound of their diesel engines, the gasoline fumes, the dust, the screeching of their tires and brakes, all of it almost makes you jump for joy. You are all relieved. They had told you that they would not come back until you had brought the price back down to ten thousand francs, and yet, here they are. They have come back, proving that they need your stone. But you mustn't show your relief, so you continue to hammer at your stones as though those visitors were completely irrelevant.

Normally, with the arrogance of the wealthy, the buyers would go directly to inspect the bags indulging in the way you would crowd around them like hens in a henhouse scattering around whoever is throwing them grains to peck at. They knew that you were ready to endure all their humiliation so that you could get your hands on those much touted ten thousand francs. They would rant here and there. "Hey you, your bag isn't even full. You think I'm an idiot? Throw a few more pebbles in to fill it up properly if you want me to buy it! What's that? You call that gravel? Go ahead then while you're still here. Just sell me the huge blocks of sandstone you see over there." Kicks to the bag which they knock over to show the seller that her stones weren't broken up into small enough pieces.

In general, the loaders that they brought with them would usually follow only after the bags were purchased. Oddly, today, pretending not to notice the bags of stone, they all get out of their trucks and race toward you: the drivers, the buyers, the loaders. One of them, whom they have chosen as their spokesman or leader, begins haranguing you haughtily. He is wearing black sunglasses to protect himself from the glare of the sun or, more likely, to intimidate you, an American baseball cap on his head, and he walks with a swagger. He threatens you, he tells you that they came back to give you one last chance since there is stone elsewhere, and, if they leave this quarry today without buying anything, they will never return again. End of story.

You all finally deign to raise your heads to look at them.

"We are not refusing to sell,"—it is you who responds because you are responsible for voicing the concerns of the others— "let's get that straight! You've been selling bags for thirty thousand francs that you're buying from us for ten thousand. Since the President of the Republic visited that airfield's construction site and, furious that the work was behind schedule, threatened to put all the entrepreneurs in prison, you took advantage of the situation by raising the price of the bag to fifty thousand francs! Five times the price you pay when you buy it from us. But we also want a piece of the pie. We are asking twenty thousand francs; you'll still make a profit of thirty thousand francs!"

You don't stand when you respond to him, you continue sitting on your seat, a big oval rock with a flat top.

"Twenty thousand francs is our first asking price; we can always negotiate," Laurentine Paka yells over.

A cry of disapproval rises up from the choir of women.

"Quiet," Itela shoots back at her, "let our spokeswoman do the talking. She said twenty thousand francs, so it's twenty thousand francs!"

"She isn't just our spokeswoman, she is also our president," corrects another. "It's twenty thousand francs!"

More haughtily than ever, the man starts talking again, ignoring what you have just said. "When you're illiterate as you all are, you do not speak of things you know nothing about.

You think that your bags are just going to walk over to the airport construction site? And what about the trucks... do you know that in addition to gas you have to change the oil? Grease the axles, charge the battery, put air in the tires, check the brake pads, clean the contact points and other things too technical for you to understand? Do you know that all of that costs money, whereas all you do is sit on your asses hammering, hammering?"

"And yet you come, and you beg us to sell you our stones! You will not get them for any less than twenty thousand francs."

You were a little angry.

"Well spoken, president," the women agree.

"You are ignoring that there's also a very important political stake. Don't you know that the President of the Republic wants the construction to be completed before Independence Day when there will be guests coming from all over the world? Do you want to bring shame to our country? Do you want to bring shame to the President of the Republic?"

"Exactly! If you don't want to bring shame to the President, get out your twenty thousand francs per bag. You will have the stone, the construction site will be finished on time, the President will be happy, and he can party with his guests."

All of a sudden, a piercing cry like the shriek of a half-mad, half-wild creature, rips through the air. Your gazes turn in time to see Iyissou pounce, like a furious beast, and throw herself at one of the truck loaders. The scream came from the depths of her taciturn soul. The truck loader had mistakably placed his foot on one of her bags. Caught by surprise, the man, catapulted far from the bag, bites the dust while Iyissou pounces on him like a panther and starts punching him and letting out brief, hoarse, bizarre cries. Two men, including the one with the black glasses and the American baseball cap, seeing the spectacle, rush over to help their colleague and start punching Iyissou as they try to free him. They should not have done that.

Ya Moukiétou's blood is boiling and grabbing the man with the glasses by the collar, she literally lifts him off the ground and punches him straight in the face with her stonebreaker's fist. His movie-star glasses smash in two and, punch drunk, he collapses. The whole quarry has turned into a battlefield. They throw kicks and punches, but you have your weapons, the stones. Large and small stones that you throw and that hit them in the face, the head, the neck, the forehead, the temples.

Many of them start to bleed. And beware to those who fall, because they immediately have two or three women pouncing on them with their claws of birds of prey, targeting in particular the masculine spot that hurts the most, the testicles. They moan, beg, implore, and some end up crying. Then, they flee. You should see this spectacle of a horde of women in pursuit of a group of panic-stricken, petrified men. A beaten dog always runs away with its tail between its legs, and that is exactly how these men run away. They rush over to their trucks without further ado and take off. Two trucks crash into one other backing up at the same time, while a third misses its turn and almost falls into the ditch before getting back onto the road. Then nothing, the lot is empty.

Joy! Unanticipated joy accompanied by outbursts of laughter. Itela, originally from the village of Makoua, grabs a saucepan and starts tapping on it like a drum. You all begin clapping your hands, dancing, and yodeling. Iyissou enters the circle first. Not only is she dancing and jumping, but she is also talking non-stop, shrieking with laughter as she tells how she caught the man, how she hit, bit, and kicked him. You are all in shock as you listen to this verbal deluge pouring out of this mouth that seldom utters a word in a whole day. Those who know her well explain that the cry that her body released when she hit the man is the same cry that she swallowed the day she was thrust into her taciturn world, when she heard the President of the Republic call her a liar, a storyteller.

That cry that had obstructed her throat came from the long civil war that ravaged the country. As is often the case in such situations, women had paid the heaviest price. Some, like Turia and Batatou, were left widows while others, robbed and raped, had lost everything they owned. Iyissou's story was one of the most tragic. She had managed to get her 18-year-old son out of the country, afraid that he would be forcibly conscripted into one of the rival militias who were fighting one another. He ended up a refugee in an HCR camp in a neighboring country. When one of the militias finally won the war and their leader became President of the Republic, this latter, in a gesture of sincere or strategic generosity, had asked all of the refugees to come back, assuring them that he would personally guarantee their security. While many hesitated, Iyissou took the President for his word and urged her son to come back.

She saw her child disembark among the first refugees. Her strapping young lad was now just a tall emaciated carcass, exhausted by long walks, hunger, diarrhea, and malaria. She had not seen him for two years. That evening, she promised herself that she would give him a nice warm bath and make him eat until he was sated. When he came off the boat landing, she took him in her arms and hugged him tightly, crying tears of joy. But her joy was short-lived because two soldiers from the presidential guard who were selecting passengers approached them. They asked the boy to show his hands. The son of a peasant, he had always helped his mother to clear the thickets with a machete for planting, used an axe to cut tree trunks that would be cut into small wood so they could make charcoal: that inevitably left scars on the palms of his hands, which had become calluses. "This is proof that you handle AK47s," one of the soldiers screamed maliciously, "you are an enemy militiaman." And with that, leaving him no time to explain himself, they threw him into the van that carried him off to his death, and Iyissou never saw him again. She had thrown herself at the soldiers' feet, begged them, tried to explain that he was a refugee who was called home by the President of the Republic. Nothing helped. She had been kicked back brutally by the blows of their boots as the truck with its full load of victims receded into the distance.

Ever since, she had been waiting, hopefully, for a word from the Father of the Nation. Maybe her son was just in prison and still alive. As long as the government spokesperson on the radio kept repeating all day long like a parrot that no child had been rounded up at the city's riverport landing by the presidential guard, she was not worried because, as did many, she had absolute trust in the President. She venerated him by calling him the "Father of the Nation" and she was sure that, as soon as he was made aware of what had happened at the port, he would punish those responsible and bring solace to the miserable parents.

Until the day when the "Father of the Nation" spoke. On the radio. On TV. A press conference given to the international press. He hammered it home that there had never been any massacres at the city's riverport, that all of that nonsense was nothing more than the manipulations of exiled politicians who were making it their business to destabilize the country and take power. He claimed that he was going to appoint a judge who would prove to the eyes of the entire world that the whole story was nothing but a pack of lies. Hearing those words spoken by the "Father of the Nation," for a brief moment Iyissou relived her son being dragged away with dozens of others by the soldiers of the presidential guard. In a state of shock seeing that even the president, her President, could lie to this extent, she had fainted and instead of wailing, instead of releasing her cry of despair, she had swallowed it. She had not spoken since.

And now, here she is in the middle of the dance circle, the circle of joy, chattering, freed by this wretched cry expelled from her body, as Moukiétou and Atareta compete with each other over who can shake their buttocks more vigorously. Moyalo starts a dance from her region, rocking her torso with a swaying motion, and you, not to be outdone, break into a rumba. Oh, how life can be beautiful!

You have to stop your dancing because it is time to eat. Each of you has brought your contribution to the meal as you had agreed yesterday. As there are too many of you to eat together on a single pagne, you spread out two of them to make one large convivial table. You are surprised by the amount of food and especially by the variety. You all eat to your hearts' content as you comment on what happened. The most admirable act, you all agree, was the punch in the nose that Moukiétou gave to the man with the glasses. Spontaneously and unanimously, the group declares that you are no longer merely their spokeswoman, you are President. President because, if you had to make a decision and not everyone were present, you would be authorized to make it, your only restriction being to remain firm and not go below the lowest price of fifteen thousand francs. You thank them for their faith in you and tell them that, now that those people have proof of your fierce determination, they will definitely be back tomorrow with new negotiation tactics because they desperately need your stone. So, you must always remain vigilant.

After finishing your meal, you need to coordinate your strategy for the following day. "Stone is our oil," Batatou yells out, to your great surprise and joy; that is what you have been telling yourself for a long time. Everyone repeats the slogan with cheerful applause.

We do not know by what sleight of hand the beautiful Ossolo manages to produce a bottle of beer. She wants you all to share it, but eleven ounces of a warm drink for fifteen women is impossible. Mama Kody from the Sangha region comes up with the idea: offer it to the ancestors in order to thank them for our victory, instead of palm wine; it will be just as effective, she assures us. The ancestors will understand. Applause. Since no one has a bottle opener, Moukiétou takes the bottle, wedges the cork between her two canines and very skillfully pops it out. The warm beer froths like champagne. She holds out the bottle to Iyissou whom everyone is happy to see so gay; this latter grabs it and, staying inside the large circle that you have formed, offers the drink to the ancestors by pouring it over the ground in a circular motion opposite to the direction of the Earth's rotation, as all of you continue clapping your hands, banging on pots and pans and buckets, ululating and dancing. Grandmother, who had never liked beer, must be having a good laugh looking down on you from where she is now, sitting amongst her peers, the ancestors, of whom she was now a part. You promise yourself that you will offer her the best palm wine that you can find the day when, to celebrate that you have won your struggle, you will all come together again to dance, forming a new sacred circle.

Laurentine Paka, whose presence can never be forgotten for long, is waving her hands about, shouting cheerfully: "Friends, we need to take a photo to remember this moment." The photos she had taken were stunning, particularly the group photo in which you had all placed Batatou and her children in the center. Her husband had had them printed and had distributed them to all of you that same day, before you had left the quarry. You hope that these, the victory photos, will be just as beautiful. You all stop dancing, and you arrange yourselves, in good spirits, in a row like school children. She takes a dozen of them, switching places from time to time so that she can also be in some.

Finally, the show is over. Feeling a release and emotionally drained, you decide unanimously to call it a day, a very short yet full day! Each of you heads over to your own small mound of stones to gather up your things and go home.

●

None of you were expecting the response to be so rapid and sudden. Having dispersed at 11am, the stone buyers came back in full force less than two hours later, at the exact moment when you were all readying to leave the quarry. Only this time, they had not come alone. They came accompanied by an armed commando unit. Although surprised, you yourself were not entirely shocked since the majority of the trucks belonged to real big shots of the regime in power who had a habit of hiding behind anonymous relatives to carry out their often shady business. For them, mobilizing the police in order to defend their private property was completely normal.

It was not an ordinary police force that had turned up, but a militarized police unit, in fact, a real armed militia that had come, apparently to confront dangerous criminals.

A dozen police officers are now jumping out of armored cars with helmets, clubs, guns, and everything. Their leader is wearing a holster with a pistol on his belt. He is parading around with rank insignia but, as you know nothing about military ranks, you decide to give him the title of colonel. He comes toward you, accompanied by three or four of those who had survived the morning battle. One of them is the man with black sunglasses KO'd by Moukiétou, a gauze dressing wrapped around his head like a turban. No need to look, he is very angry. Others are wearing bandages stuck here and there, and you even notice that one is walking with a crutch made from a bamboo trunk. You are scared to death.

Some of the women gather stones, clutching them in their fists, ready to throw them, but you intervene right away, asking them to drop them because this armed gang, the so-called "law enforcement officers," are just looking for the slightest excuse to massacre you with impunity. You muster the courage to walk a few steps toward them, then you stop to let them come towards you. They are the ones who need to approach you because it is your territory. When he sees the others lined up behind you, the leader of the soldiers, the colonel, who until then did not know whom to address, immediately understands that you are the leader and, pointing his finger at you, erupts into anger: "I should lock you all up, you bunch of idiots, for willingly striking and inflicting injury to third parties. Assaulting merchants who want nothing more than to buy your stone. Have you no shame?"

He does not even ask to hear your version of what happened and starts insulting you. For that matter, what is your version of what happened? You are no longer so sure. Wasn't it Iyissou who assaulted that poor man first? No, it was the man with the black sunglasses who wanted to strangle Iyissou; she was only protecting her bag of gravel. But in the end, that is of little importance. The truth is that a bunch of shady businessmen wanted to dishonestly monopolize your livelihood, and you had defended yourselves. But at no time does the leader of these armed soldiers want to know or understand that. You talk to him about selling your bags of stones for twenty thousand francs. He launches into a speech that is completely unrelated to your needs, to your suffering, and to your reality. He talks to you about public interest. He shouts at you that the international airport is a national priority, that it must be finished before the big Independence Day celebration, that guests from all over the world, including the President of the French Republic, are going to be flying in, that your refusal to sell is a sabotage, a deliberate act to tarnish the country's image, the President's reputation abroad, that it certainly will not be laborers like you all who.... Yâ Moukiétou cannot take it any longer and, forgetting that you are the appointed spokeswoman, bursts out: "If the President needs these bags so badly, he can buy them from us for twenty thousand francs! These are our bags; we decide. It's not up to him to tell me what color panties I have to wear tomorrow because they're *my* panties! In the same way, these stones are *our* stones!" Great bursts of laughter from your side which has suddenly perked up with "Bravo, that's it! Well said!" With that, the colonel really gets mad. He yells: "Insult to the Head of State" and orders his men to advance.

Itela asks you what "Insult to the Head of State" means, and you explain to her that that means that you had insulted the President of the Republic. Upon hearing this explanation, Moukiétou gets even angrier and yells over to where the colonel is: "Go tell the insulted President that I would prefer a thousand times more offering him my ass for free to giving him our bags for ten thousand francs!" That was really the last straw!

"Alright, we are seizing these bags. You will come to police headquarters to be paid for them," the colonel orders, "and for ten thousand francs a bag!" And he orders the soldiers and loaders to advance.

"Thieves! Boo, boo, boo… You are not men, boo, boo, boo…" the women start shouting, powerless before these armed forces who are advancing. The moment the colonel hears those insults and those scornful "boo, boo, boos," he yells: "Attack!"

It's a scramble. Boots kicking, rifle butts beating unarmed women. Your stones start flying, but there is no match. You still manage to rough up one of them, and to free their comrade in danger, the men start shooting. Live bullets. You all flee in disarray. You run toward the river, some run toward the giant sandstone blocks to shield themselves from the bullets, and others run toward the high grasses so they can lie flat, hidden from the killers' view. But those who do not manage to run fast enough get caught and are beaten. Finally, after a while, the sounds of human voices and sputtering of gunfire taper off and are replaced by the roaring of the river in the distance, crashing against the rocks as it streams toward the ocean, and by the thuds of the bags of stones, full or half-full, as they are being thrown hastily into the beds of the trucks which start up as soon as all the goods are loaded.

The quarry is not far from the national highway and the gun shots, the shouting and the cries attracted many people who, at first held back by the police presence, are now rushing over since their trucks have now left the scene. Everyone explodes with outrage. One by one, your comrades in combat come out of hiding, some from behind the high grasses, some from behind their giant sandstone blocks. Others, unable to get up, are lying on the ground moaning. You count the wounded: Batatou struck by a bullet in the chest; Iyissou's left arm broken—luckily for her she is not a lefty like you; Laurentine Paka with a gash in her forehead from the blows of the rifle butt... The others are missing: Moukiétou, Moyalo, Ossolo. The soldiers have taken them!

The first thing to do: evacuate the wounded. Batatou's situation is the most worrisome. You must attend to her urgently because she is bleeding profusely. One of the people who has come running to help you generously offers you his car, but the vehicle's small wheels cannot make it all the way down to the quarry, the road being so damaged by the ruts which the fat tires of the trucks have dug out on their trips to get stone. So, you'll have to carry your wounded, climbing up the hill to the passable road in order to reach the vehicle. You have quickly made a stretcher out of two bits of wood and some palm fronds and, with great caution, two men carry her. A second car is available. Iyissou is brought over to it, after her broken arm has been immobilized as is Laurentine Paka whose face is now becoming dangerously swollen around the gash across her forehead.

It's only after the evacuation of the wounded, all to the same hospital, that you realize that Mâ Bileko is beside you, carrying Batatou's two children. You suddenly become aware of your onerous responsibility and at the same time a strong sense of solidarity swells up in your whole being. She offers to look after the two children until their mother is out of the hospital. She doesn't even need to buy a baby bottle because she already has some, she assures you.

"Thank you, Bileko," you say to her, "that's very generous of you. But no way you're taking both. Our solidarity must be shared; I'll take the other baby. I also have a bottle."

That being settled, now the priority is to free your comrades Moukiétou, Moyalo and Ossolo. You decide together that you will all meet at the central police station in an hour, giving you enough time to drop off your personal items at home. You are going to do everything you can to get them out even if it means you will all be locked up. You secure the little one on your back with a *pagne*—by the way what is her name? —and you attack the hill that leads up to the main road, accompanied by your quarry companions and all the men and women who, alerted by the screams and gunfire, witnessed the soldiers' brutality, and came to show their solidarity with you.

EIGHT

AFTER YOU DROP off Batatou's baby at home for your older son to watch, —at almost thirteen years-old, he is big enough for that—you run to your aunt's to pick up Lyra before going to buy powdered milk since you now have another mouth to feed. It is an extra expense for you, but genuine solidarity does not come without sacrifice.

You are at your aunt's just long enough to inform her that your bags of stones have been confiscated by the police and that three of your friends have been arrested, and off you are with Lyra on your back. She does not quite understand the meaning of this cursory update and wants a fuller explanation. You tell her that you are in a rush and that you will call her later to give her all the details.

You stop to buy the powdered milk before going back home. When you took Lyra in after her mother died, she was still on the bottle. Once she was weaned, you do not know why you kept her two bottles in an airtight plastic bin. Perhaps it was destiny that another baby would come into your life. You squeeze the nipples. They are still soft. You throw them along with the two graduated bottles into a pot three quarters full of water to sterilize them. Thanks to the gas stove, it does not take long for the water to boil. You let them boil for another three or four minutes before taking them out to let them cool. Then it all comes back to you naturally: counting the spoonfuls of powdered milk, measuring the amount of water, stirring, shaking the bottle vigorously to make a homogeneous mixture. At first you thought that the baby was going to reject the taste of this industrial milk, which she is not used to having, but not at all. She starts suckling ravenously. Perhaps it's because she is very hungry. A starving stomach does not wait for a gourmet meal. You turn her over onto your knees and tap her back gently. She lets out a burp, no, two. Now that her appetite is sated, she falls asleep almost immediately. When was the last time she had eaten so well? You put her down in the bed which she will have to share with Lyra and tuck her in lovingly. Before you leave, you call the two big kids and give them their final instructions.

•

When you reach the wide asphalt avenue that leads to the prison, there are already nearly fifty people heading there as well. A surprising demonstration of solidarity. Many are men, including Danny, Laurentine Paka's husband. Actually, since any man who lives with a woman sees himself as her "husband," no one really knows if they are legally or traditionally married, if they are engaged or just simply lovers. Laurentine herself makes the situation more confusing because she refers to him as her husband as much as she calls him her boyfriend or her fiancé. But that is of little importance. What matters is that he loves Laurentine, and they are always together. So, to simplify things, you decided to call him by the loose term of "husband." He is outraged and furious about his partner's wound. He seems even angrier than you all are and keeps repeating that that this is no way to treat citizens, especially women. Without anyone asking him to, he starts to direct traffic ahead of you, diverting vehicles, bawling out the drivers who do not comply swiftly enough. Other men are applauding and encouraging you, maybe because you are daring to do what one never does in this country: defy the authorities.

Once you all arrive in front of the police station prison, the prison that is known still today for its torture cells, the crowd spontaneously erupts into punctuated chants of "Free Moyalo!

Free Moukiétou! Free Ossolo!"—three rapid claps—, "Free our comrades!" Your shouting is especially striking because you are sincerely angry, very angry. Not only did they steal your merchandise from you, not only did they beat you, but on top of it they threw some of you in prison. Your collective determination is even greater because, now with this crowd of men and women around you, you no longer feel alone in your struggle.

In this country, dusk is fleeting. Night falls very quickly. You do not know how long this uproar in front of the prison has been going on, but the fact remains that eventually a police colonel comes out. Not the one who beat you up at the quarry with his men, but another whom you do not know. He asks you all to return peacefully to your homes because, according to him, one does not conduct State business at night. And so, just like that, your matter has become State business, no less!

Your coworkers push you forward. As their spokeswoman, you respond, stating firmly that none of you will leave this place without your three friends. Hearing that makes the colonel angry and he shouts back that you are not to dictate to him what he must do, and if within five minutes you have not cleared out, he will have you all beaten with batons. Women, men, the whole crowd starts booing him. He senses that he is no longer in control of the situation and retreats hurriedly, holding his walkie-talkie up to his mouth, probably to inform his command and request instructions. You intensify your cries and chants, which this time are accompanied by whistling and gibes.

After an hour, much to your surprise and delight, you see the city mayor himself arrive, accompanied by... your ex-husband! Why is he here? That's a puzzler. For a moment, his presence unnerves you. Sure, you haven't officially divorced him yet, but you have held the traditional separation ceremony with his family and yours: the circle traced around your body with white chalk and the kaolin marks drawn on your face made you pure again, —and a woman freed from any commitment to this man. But you do not dwell on this fool's presence. Your attention returns to the mayor.

When politicians no longer hide behind law enforcement and put themselves on the front line, it means the situation is serious. In such cases, you have to be on alert because they become such sweet talkers that if you don't watch out, they could sell you your own underwear without you even realizing it. The mayor begins to speak. He is sorry to hear that shots were fired and that there were injuries, but you've got to understand these military men because—as is well-known—it is in their very nature not to get caught up in subtleties. Since your quarries are in his jurisdiction and this is not a criminal case, it is his prerogative to take political decisions. And, to show that he respects you and that he is taking the matter seriously, he makes a point by coming accompanied by Congressman Tito Rangi, who volunteered his services. This latter has very good suggestions for you, and he will not bamboozle you because he is also adviser to the wife of the President of the Republic. "After you've listened to what he has to say," he concludes, "you will return peacefully to your homes because unfortunately—or rather, fortunately—we are a State under the Rule of Law and, in a State under the Rule of Law, there are legal hours to release people. On that basis, your friends will not be released until tomorrow."

The minute he finishes his tirade everyone starts shouting at him. "No, no, no, we will not leave without our friends!"

Instead of keeping quiet, your imbecile ex-husband raises his hand. You know that the moment he catches a glimpse of you, he is going to put on a show. That is how it has always been since you separated. No doubt now, you know why he is there. When he learned that you are the leader of this group of women, or at least their spokeswoman, he immediately got a rush of adrenaline, like a dog in heat. Didn't the mayor say Tito had volunteered his services? Why? Just to taunt you!

After your separation, when you felt that despite his scheming with his friends in the judiciary, you were on the verge of succeeding in making him pay child support so you could feed your two children whom he had completely abandoned, he registered in the President's political party so he could avoid it. And, as a result, he managed to get himself "elected" congressman. He had presented his candidacy in your district but, lackluster in character, he had lost by a large margin in the first round, coming in third after a candidate for the opposition and an independent. But, lo and behold, the independent electoral commission whose members had all been appointed by the President of the Republic not only disqualified the opposition candidate who came first on the grounds that he had disseminated leaflets inciting "tribalism" and "divisiveness," two hours after the end of the official campaign, but they also declared Tito the winner of the second round with three times the votes he got in the first. The ruse was so gross that he kept on adding "democratically elected" to his title as Congressman as if he doubted it himself.

He raises his hand and begins speaking. He seems to be in good health and, you must admit, there is some elegance in the way he is dressed. Whereas everyone else is wearing a boubou or shirtsleeves, he is in a suit. His purple shirt and midnight blue jacket are adorned with a fuchsia tie. A gold chain decorates his wrist. He certainly does not struggle like you do. Try to forget your resentment and listen to him, you tell yourself, maybe he will save the day. Then again, I could be wrong. "Listen, I am here as your congressman because, as I am sure you know, I was democratically elected by you, the people. That means that I am here to represent you to the administration. But I am also an adviser to Madam the First Lady, so I have some authority. Tomorrow, I will convene a meeting during which you will all have the opportunity to declare your grievances, and if we must renegotiate the price of your bags, we will discuss that. Believe me, I am on your side. However, do not let yourselves be manipulated. You may not know it, but the eyes of the entire world are watching us now. Just because your leader or spokesperson speaks well, it does not mean that you need to follow her blindly. Be wary of smooth talkers. You have my word and that of the mayor. That should suffice for you. Return peacefully to your homes now. Your husbands and your children are waiting for you."

And there it was. A good father and a good husband, right? He could not resist making a cutting remark at you. You reply:

"We will wait until tomorrow to discuss a fair price for our bags of gravel. However, we demand that our friends be released immediately, we repeat: immediately. We will not leave without them."

Cheers from your friends and the crowd.

"Who are you to demand anything?" retorts your ex. "Don't be so disrespectful to the authorities. If you keep it up, you'll join the other three in prison."

"Put us all in prison!" the women start shouting.

A man's voice rises, loudly, from the middle of the crowd.

"We know you. We do not trust your promises. How do we know that you are not lying to these women?"

Well, with that, Mr. Tito Rangi, your beloved, goes berserk. He starts yelling. Watch out for flying spit!

"Who are you calling a liar? Me? You call a congressman a liar? An adviser to the President of the Republic's wife? Do you know what we call 'an offense to the authority of the State'? Perhaps you think that your leader here is a paragon of integrity? I have told you that I know her well. She was my wife. She left her home on the spur of the moment. I provide you with this personal information to warn you to be very careful with people who act on the spur of the moment. Listen instead to what your congressman is telling you."

"She left you because you were sleeping around all the time, you womanizer!"

You do not know which woman shouted that. The crowd bursts into laughter. But you are no longer listening. Your blood is boiling inside. You want to wring his neck. Instead of talking about your bags of stones, about your wounded, about your prisoners, no, his main objective is to humiliate you because he has never come to terms with the fact that it was you, his wife, who took the initiative to leave him. It was humiliating for him because, usually, it's the man who boasts about kicking out his wife.

"Careful! You are talking to a congressman, democratically elected by the people, an adviser to the presidency of the Republic. Understand that through your raging temper."

"You were not elected. You were appointed! Cheater..."

More laughter. The crowd's gibes save you because those few moments of diversion allow you to regain control of your temper, which is important. The result is cold lucidity, a cruel desire to do harm. Your arguments do not count anymore now, and you know that this will not be where you will negotiate the price of your bags of gravel. This congressman has only come there to humiliate you publicly; it is he to whom you must reply, as a payback. And if you want to humiliate a man, especially a macho type like him, you question his virility, publicly. So, you stand up straight and you point your finger at him and, in a cunning and ironic tone, you say:

"Tell me, Tito-my-dear-husband-who-knows-me-so-well, since you've been freeloading off of your latest conquest, have you forgotten that you have children? Did you know that real men take pride in raising their children? Is the President's wife aware that her adviser is a disgraceful father? Why don't you take care of that problem before you try dealing with one beyond your abilities?

The crowd goes wild! He was not ready for that blow to the chest or, rather, below the belt. He cannot manage to vomit out words. They are so jammed up in his throat and he starts stuttering. The crowd's boos turn into chants of "Free Moyalo! Free Ossolo! Free Moukiétou"—claps— "Free our friends!"

Completely overwhelmed and disoriented, the mayor and his democratically elected congressman retreat. It is a victory for you because you resisted them, but a very small victory because your friends are still locked up. The only solution is to hold a sit-in in the courtyard of the police station. You alternate singing popular songs with the songs you sing at wakes. You improvise on those songs by creating new refrains that refer to your struggle. Meanwhile, you cannot help but worry: Why haven't the authorities—as is their reflex —already sent their soldiers to beat and disband you with their pistol whipping and billy-clubs? There is something wrong, something off.

Suddenly, the sound of an approaching vehicle intrudes into this amiable atmosphere. A police car. You all panic, and you tell yourselves that this is it. This is the inevitable moment of confrontation with the so-called forces of law and order. You all stand up. The police colonel who oversees the prison—the same guy who threatened you a little while ago with billy clubs—gets out. You all watch in silene, speculating, what might happen to you, as he enters his office.

Suddenly, out of the blue, the two large metal gates of the prison open, and your three friends appear. For a few milliseconds you all stand there, mouths gaping, as if you were hallucinating. Then a thunder of applause. It's one thirty in the morning. You do not believe it. The colonel must have received a call from the presidency because in this country everything comes from the President of the Republic. Moukiétou is the first to come out, wearing a wide smile despite her face bruised from the blows. Ossolo follows, hobbling, though you do not know if her injury is serious. The last to appear, Moyalo, immediately launches into a beautiful speech in Lingala, ignoring her black eye, thanking you all for being there and urging you not to let those thieves take your bags of stones for anything less than fifteen thousand francs.

As spokeswoman, you deliver the final word: There is no stopping now. This is only your first win. The struggle must continue. Tomorrow, you will organize a massive march on this very police station, and you will camp there until they give you back your stolen bags. Your words are welcomed with a thunder of applause.

•

The prisoners had been thrown together into the same cell. Exceptionally, none of them was tortured, but none of them had received medical treatment either. The priority now was to bring them to the hospital and give them something to eat. Everyone cooperated and everything happened quickly and smoothly.

Your cell phone starts ringing. You rummage through your purse to find the phone. You look at the time. It's almost two in the morning. You wonder who could be calling you at this late hour. It's Atareta, the one in charge of monitoring the status of the wounded in the hospital. She sounds desperate. She tells you that, although they arrived at the hospital in the early afternoon, Iyissou's broken arm still hasn't been treated. The hospital doesn't have plaster, or syringes, or cotton, or even alcohol. We have to buy everything ourselves. Where can we find the money? Laurentine Paka is lucky because Danny, her husband, can pay for her prescription. She will give the rest of her alcohol to Iyissou. Batatou is still in intensive care.

You stop the crowd, which is dispersing, and you shout out this information as you ask for contributions. Your quick calculation indicates that you need to collect thirty thousand francs immediately, the price of three bags of gravel. There are plenty of you. If everyone gives two hundred francs, it will work out. You give five hundred. Some hands reach into their pockets and take something out, some unknot their pagnes, and others dig into their purses to make their contributions. Some give coins, others give bills. The final tally is thirty-five thousand francs. It is more than you need. Moukiétou's son asks you not to buy cotton because he has some at home and he also offers three single-use disposable syringes. You call Atareta right away to ask her to stay put and wait for Ossolo's brother who is already on his way to the hospital with Moukiétou's son and the necessary supplies.

There. You are pleased. You did what you needed to do. Still, it is shocking to know that all those women, whom you know only as stone breakers, drenched in sweat under the hot equatorial sun, have other lives, family lives. You learn that Ossolo has an older brother who drives a taxi, that Moukiétou has a twenty-five-year-old child who is a nurse, and that Iyissou—yes, Iyissou—who for so long has been mute and distant from the world around her has an uncle who is a department head at the university.

Now that the tension has subsided, you are suddenly overwhelmed with exhaustion, and you feel hunger pangs. In fact, you have eaten practically nothing all day. All you can think about is eating, taking a shower, then going to bed. Were the children able to sleep without you there? Did your older son tuck in the mosquito net after he put Lyra and Batatou's little one to bed as you had instructed? With this, you are tormented by a sudden anxious thought: What if the baby had woken up and, looking for her mother, had been crying since you left?

One of the protesters tells you that he still has space in his car and would like to drop you off at home. There are already three other women in the car whom he is taking home. Amazing how people who do not even know you could display such kindness and solidarity when the opportunity presented itself. Perhaps the world is not so cruel after all. You thank him. The others move over to make room for you on the seat that is supposed to fit three people, a difficult maneuver since one of the women is, as they say, rather plump. Despite everything, you manage to squeeze in.

You all talk merrily about the day's events as you ride and, hearing the others narrating and exaggerating, the story starts to take on epic dimensions. If you had not been present during the police attack at the quarry, you would have thought, the way they were telling it, that it had been a heroic battle of unarmed, bare-breasted women attacking heavy duty Soviet tanks. Although you secretly find their chatter amusing, you are encouraged by the pride and joy that is beaming on those women's faces, those women who do not even work with you at the quarry and who have probably never broken stone. They are just as worried as you are about the health status of those in the hospital. Finally, the car stops in front of your lot. You get out and the others, relaxed now, rearrange themselves on the seat. Goodbye and see you tomorrow.

You enter the house. To your pleasant surprise, the children are sleeping peacefully, and they even took care to light the storm lamp as a nightlight. You feel extremely proud of them. Batatou's baby is asleep in your bed with Lyra, protected beneath the mosquito net. They followed your instructions.

Before you do anything, you collapse heavily into your armchair overcome with extreme fatigue. You tell yourself that you need to get up and make yourself something to eat, but your body refuses to budge. Then certain images from the day start parading around in your mind. Your ex and his inappropriate, insulting remarks. Why was he so bent on humiliating you in public? Maybe he still loves you despite the ostentatious mask of the scorned chauvinist male he hides behind. Does he realize that he is the reason you sacrificed your life and never achieved the future your parents had dreamed of for you? At twelve years old, when you took your seat in that motorcoach that brought you from your village to the capital—and to high school—you never imagined that the high road before you, which the motorcoach was swallowing up at full speed, would be engulfed in a tunnel from which you would emerge at seventeen, completely ruined.

•

It was the end of year dance, a formal for those who had passed their junior year exams. Must we really be reminded that during those past six years you never repeated a single class from sixth through twelfth grade and that you were always among the top ten in the class and, frequently, the first? That does not mean that you didn't have any fun. You were a fan of your women's basketball team and would always go to support them when they played against other schools. You were sporty yourself. On the track team. Your specialty the two-hundred, four-hundred and eight-hundred-meter sprint events. Of course, despite all those activities, out of loyalty to your family's tradition you never missed Sunday worship at church.

One thing, however, was not among your activities: dancing. You never went to parties quite simply because you were not interested in them. But this time, since you were among the top of your class and this formal dance had been organized for you, you felt obliged to go. Seated on your chair, you watched your girlfriends dancing with the boys, shaking their buttocks, jumping up and down and twirling depending on the kind of dance. Like a princess, you turned down every single invitation. After a while, all the boys had grown tired of your repeated rejections, so nobody else came to ask you. And you remained glued to your chair, like a fool. You would have liked to do the jerk too—the twist, rock out, feel the hip-hop beats, and party like your friends instead of being a wallflower. But the truth was you didn't know how to dance. That's right, at seventeen, you did not know how to dance, and you were in Africa! That's what being the daughter of a self-proclaimed pastor cost you.

But then that boy came over and sat down next to you. You thought you had noticed him once or twice in the schoolyard during the morning break, but you did not really recognize him. He didn't seem so bad, simply dressed though elegant, preppy, unlike the others in their extravagant, if not outrageous getups. You were surprised when he said hello addressing you by name. He told you his name was Tito and that he knew you, because who didn't know the most brilliant girl in the school? You were caught off guard because you were expecting him to whisper something like "You're beautiful" or "the outfit you're wearing is stunning," or even, "You have the most gorgeous eyes in the world!" But no. He spoke of your intelligence, which is rare when a guy talks to a chick. You were flattered and flustered. To hide your feelings, you were modest about it, telling him that getting good grades in class didn't necessarily mean that you were more intelligent than the others and, before he could reply, you changed the subject of the conversation and asked him what class he was in because you had never seen him in any of your classes. He told you that he was a graduating senior and that he was waiting for the results of his college entrance exams which he had taken a few days before. So, he was an adult. The serious type who did math or physics. No, chemistry, lost in his thoughts of atoms and molecules. An adult to respect. You finally mustered the courage to ask him which discipline he had chosen for his exam. Philosophy, he replied. That surprised you because you did not understand how people could still think they could have a career in philosophy when there were so many people who had a Master's in Law or Literature who were unemployed. You said nothing and remained silent so you wouldn't offend him.

As you expected, he threw the question back at you. "Math major," was your response.

His fleeting furrowed brow made it clear to you that he was certainly not expecting a woman to make such a choice and, a little boastful, to show that he also knew math, he came out with the most banal formula:

"a2 +b2 = c2. Pythagorean theorem!" he added triumphantly. "Aside from teaching, you won't be able to do anything with math because all those axioms, theorems and proofs are too abstract," he went on.

"No more than *I think therefore I am*," you replied, beating him at his own game.

"Touché!" he said.

You were charmed by the slapstick way in which he said "touché," bringing his left hand to his chest as he bowed down to you. You smiled. A charming *and* intelligent boy, you thought to yourself. There weren't many of them among those dancers romping around on the dancefloor. You told him that you hadn't chosen math for its lemmas and theorems; it was because you wanted to study administration later, in college, business administration specifically.

"Oh, you mean 'management'," he corrected you.

"Call it what you like, but I want to open my own business," you retorted, "because we can no longer count on the State to hire us."

"True, you can't create businesses with philosophy," he goes on, "but it will teach you to view the world with skepticism."

Skepticism was certainly a philosophical term because you did not know this word. You came clean and told him that that philosophical jargon was too obscure, and that he should express himself more simply with people like you. He smiled—a captivating smile—and explained to you that it meant to doubt everything, to doubt the world. Doubt the world? That did not mean anything. Another philosophical concept as if he were teasing you intentionally. You raised your eyebrows in exaggeration and wrinkled your forehead comically to indicate that you still did not understand anything and threatened, "I'm going to end up asking you the value of the angles of a tetrahedron if you keep speaking in that incomprehensible language".

Again, that smile.

"Enough discussion," he then declared, "don't you want to dance?" Which you were afraid he would ask!

Oh, how you wanted to say yes! But you did not know how to dance. When you forced yourself, you danced like a fool, which was unusual for a young seventeen-year-old girl. You tried to get out of it by telling him you were tired. Could he tell you were embarrassed? Cleverly, he got you out of the bind by telling you that he did not dare ask another girl to dance because he didn't know how to dance himself and, knowing that you were so intelligent and kind, you would be patient and understanding if in his clumsiness he stepped on your feet on the dancefloor. You immediately retorted:

"What makes you think that I know how to dance? Maybe I am worse than you."

"Well then, that's perfect," he persisted without hesitating and, getting up, promptly added: "The more, the merrier. We came here to have fun, not for a dance contest."

You do not recall when he took your hand, at which moment he pulled you off your seat, nor when you got up. You just simply found yourself standing on the dancefloor with his hands around your hips and yours around his waist. And, as if by chance, a slow song was playing.

Crooning music with lyrics like, "my love," "kiss me," "hold me tenderly." A slow dance, during which the DJs kept dimming the lights, you did not know why. During the first three dance steps, you had stepped on his feet three times. On the fourth, he stepped on yours.

"Sorry," he said, "you see, I am also stumbling."

His words calmed you. You relaxed, though you were a little suspicious that he had done that on purpose because, actually, he was a good dancer who knew how to lead his partner. Slowly, surely, without realizing it, your body started swaying naturally to the rhythms of the music. He hugged you a little tighter. You let him. You felt good, had a warm feeling in your belly, and you closed your eyes.

When, with no transition, the music shifted to the beats wrapped up in *coupé-décalé* and the lights were bright again, you stepped away from each other. You were a little annoyed, though you were not too sure why, and you sat back down on your chair without looking at him. He sat down next to you acting as if nothing had happened and told you that you had a good poker face because you were a very good dancer. Although you were seventeen, you had not been around boys much, and a bizarre feeling overwhelmed you. It seemed like your heart was beating faster than normal.

You took a tissue out of your purse and started dabbing sweat that was more imaginary than real so that he could not tell how uneasy you felt. "It sure is hot," he said. Then he asked if you wanted something to drink. Since drinks were free, you said yes because you did not want to be indebted to him in any way. He came back with a blended mango juice. He did not ask you to dance again, and he was right not to because you probably would not have granted him another dance. You no longer remember what you talked about as you sipped your drinks. In the end, he asked you for your address, which you gave him, feeling safe, because you knew you could always just not answer him. On the other hand, you were hesitant about entrusting him with your phone number—your aunt's number—though you ended up giving in.

Obviously, you could not stop thinking about him that night. This had never happened to you with a boy. The next day, though you would not admit it, you hoped he would call. Why else would he have asked you for your number? When, at the end of the day, nothing had come of it, you remembered what your girlfriends who knew boys better than you had told you: That was how boys behaved. They would forget a girl right away just like that, once they had gotten what they wanted. He had gotten what he wanted, a dance with you, so why would he still be thinking about you? Still, you had not gone too far from the phone the whole day. You were on your way to the bathroom when you heard the phone ring. With the time it took you to pull up your underwear and hurry over to the phone, it stopped ringing. You picked up the handset anyway. There was a message on the answering machine.

It could not have been shorter: "Hello Méré? This is Tito. 109.5 degrees. See you." You did not understand. A code to crack? Was he testing your intelligence? You listened to the message again, still just as perplexed. Then you understood. Your accelerated heartrate triggered a wave of emotion that made your chest rise, and you broke into loud and joyous laughter. Luckily, Auntie was not in the vicinity; she would have definitely asked a few questions regarding her niece's mental health.

So, that was it! He had not stopped thinking about you, or at least about what he had said to you when you teased him by telling him that if he did not stop speaking his esoteric philosophical language, you would ask him to find the angle of a tetrahedron! Poor thing must have searched everywhere to find a trigonometry book because the school did not have a library. Or maybe he asked a teacher? This boy is crazy... amazing. Maybe he'll send you flowers!

And with that the phone calls had begun. Was that what it was to be in love, impatiently awaiting his phone call or his name coming into your mind for no reason while you were reading, bathing, or just out for a walk? Then came that unexpected, fateful day. You say unexpected because when you had gotten up that morning, you did not think for a minute that you were going to see him. You were consumed with getting ready to leave the next day for your trip to the village to spend the vacation with your parents. The school year had ended. Your aunt had prepared a long list of what the villagers were most lacking and had given you money to do the shopping. You had done the rounds at the Chinese stores, the West African shops, and the central market downtown, then you had gotten home at around one in the afternoon. You had eaten lunch quickly since there were so many things to pack for your parents, not to mention your own bags. After all, you were leaving for an almost three-month-long vacation. You were trying to fit a big pile of smoked fish into a cardboard box when the telephone rang. It was him.

He began with those ritualistic questions one asked when there was nothing important to say, like how it was going and what you had done during the day. But of course, that did not matter much. The important thing was to talk to each other, to make each other feel like you were still on each other's minds without saying it. The most extraordinary thing was that you had never told each other "I love you." You do not know why he had never uttered them, but, for you, they were not the kind of words the daughter of a protestant minister would let slip out of her mouth very easily. As for kissing, kissing each other open mouth, never! You answered him cheerfully, that you were doing fine, that you had run some errands for your parents and that you were exhausted, and you had to pack everything because you were traveling the next day.

"Why didn't you tell me? I would have helped you run your errands," he protested.

You immediately said that that was not his normal voice, jolly and cheerful, that instead, he sounded serious and gloomy. Was that because you were leaving or because he thought you would have left without telling him if he hadn't called you?

"You sound sad, Tito, what is it? Because I didn't tell you that I was leaving? Actually, I only decided last night."

"No, it's not that. The university entrance exam results were announced, and I am not on the list—I was not admitted. To put it bluntly, I failed."

He choked up. You were speechless. Also shocked because, as far as you were concerned, Tito had the exam, and that was it. Signed and sealed. Never had it even occurred to you that he could fail.

"Are you still there?" he asked after a long silence. "Yes," you said. "I don't understand."

"Neither do I," he went on, barely able to contain his voice, full of desperation. "Come and see me, Méréana. Don't leave me alone. At least come and tell me good-bye before you leave. Really, I feel depressed. I need to see you."

He was pleading, begging. Your heart and your body said yes, you had to go and console him, encourage him.

"Okay, I'll be there in about an hour, but I can't stay long. Tell me where you live."

In fact, you had never been to his place, nor he to yours. Half an hour later you jumped into a taxi and found yourself in his neighborhood, on his street, in front of his property. He may have been waiting for you since you hung up because he was standing in front of the entrance to the property. He let you in. A decent house with electricity. He was renting—a one-bedroom with a living room, a study, a kitchen, and an outdoor shower. Not bad. As soon as you entered the house and he closed the door, without thinking, you had thrown yourself into his open arms. Kisses, caresses. Hard to believe, but those were the first kisses you exchanged since you met that day at the dance. You let yourself go for the first time in your life. Your dress fell, his pants slid down his legs, the hooks of your bra came undone, his shirt flew off, he took off your panties, his underwear and yours slipped down each of your legs then were thrown off with your feet, and you were both on the bed. He penetrated you and you felt a shooting pain which passed. You let out a cry and you gripped him even tighter...

Everything happened so fast. You got up first and noticed there was blood on the sheets and running down your thighs. And you understood. You were no longer a virgin.

"Aaah!" You shriek in anger in your armchair. Why think

about all those memories when there are much more important things awaiting you tomorrow? You lift your cumbersome, heavy self up off the seat and light the gas stove. You place a pot with the beans and salted fish you had prepared the night before over the blue flame. The children left you your portion. After you eat, you have no energy left to wash up. You rarely go to bed without washing off your sweat, dirt, and weariness from the day under a nice hot shower, but it is very late now and, anyway, it will be daylight soon. Since there is no more space in the bed, already occupied by the two little children, you make yourself a makeshift bed for the night by spreading out a mat on the floor and throwing a thick blanket folded in half as a mattress. You spread mosquito repellent cream onto your face, your hands, your arms and all the exposed parts of your body, and you finally lie down.

May you drift off to sleep!

NINE

YOU WAKE UP with a start. Banging on your bedroom window. Everything comes back to you, like a domino effect. The police? No, they would not bang on the window. They would bang on the front door instead with their rifle butts and even try to smash it in if you did not open quickly enough. You hear someone yelling your name. After a moment of confusion, still half asleep, you come out of your brain fog and recognize Auntie Turia's voice, urgent and panicked. You open the door for her immediately. She takes you in her arms and examines you all over as she talks nonstop. "Oh, you're alive, bless the Lord. My neighbor Felly woke me up at five in the morning to tell me that you and the women who work at the quarry attacked a police station last night so you could break some women out of jail, and that, unfortunately, it did not work, and that you my dear Méré were taken to the prison where political prisoners are detained. Abéti, who was listening to us, immediately contradicted the story, reporting instead that you were not thrown in jail, but that you were transported to the hospital because the military who were called to disband your group had broken your leg. That's when Rona came running over to say that she had heard from a woman who knew the sister of another woman who swore she was at the station with you, that not only were you seriously beaten up but also, you were in a coma! My head started spinning. I tried to call you but, when it rains it pours, my phone was dead because we haven't had power since yesterday. I took a taxi in a panic to the hospital. You were not there. I brought just enough money to grease the nurse's palm, or the doctor's, in case they refused to treat you for political reasons because you'd taken on the authorities. They assured me that you were not there. I even thought for a moment that they were hiding the truth from me because you were dead!

"Méré, is what they are saying true? Attacking a police station? What is wrong with you? How can you do that to me my child? Thank God you are not dead, or even hurt apart from that small wound on your forehead..."

You cannot stop her ramblings. Building a dam does not stop the water runoff surging from the mountain after a storm. Instead, you need to let it flow out and wait for it to drain. So, you let her speak until she gets it all out. Her *pagne* tied hastily, her hair a mess because she did not take the time to fix her usual bun, she examines you, touches you, hugs you to make sure it really is you. Finally, she stops.

It's your turn to try to explain. She is glad to hear your version even if, for her, challenging the police and the mayor is doing politics, which, according to her, is against your family's tradition. She attributed her husband's sudden death to politics.

"Why didn't you call me?" She complained.

"It was too late," you reply, "and besides, your phone was dead."

Since you have power, you suggest that she charge her phone right away because a blackout could occur at any time. Like any mother, she still sees you as a little girl, even though you are now thirty-two. So, after she plugs in the device, she looks you over again, thoroughly, to reassure herself that you have not been hurt anywhere. Then she heads into your room to see Lyra, and she is surprised to find two girls instead of one. Laughing, she tells you she did not know that you had had another baby since she last checked. You fill her in on your decision, that Bileko and you are going to take care of Batatou's two children until their mother gets better, or until you find one of her family members who can take the child. She understands the circumstances and offers to stay at your place for the day to take care of the little ones because she is sure that you have got one hectic day ahead of you.

•

All clean now, you are a bit disoriented because today is a new day, a different day, in a word, a day that will be like no other.

While you washed up, your aunt took care of the children and is now preparing their morning porridge. When you get out of the shower, she urges you to have your breakfast before anything else, even before getting dressed. You are truly happy that she's there. She brings you a cup of coffee, the can of sweetened condensed milk, and doughnuts while you sit lazily on your chair listening to the radio, relaxed in the long *pagne* you've tied above your breasts. It's so nice to be coddled once in a while, like a child.

> "An evangelical pastor from a Revival Church and about twenty of his followers chased children through Kinshasa's streets and gutters and beat them brutally accusing them of being 'child witches'. Those kids, mostly between the ages of five and fourteen, are often accused of having caused their parents' illness or poverty. Harassed, beaten, sometimes tortured, they end up running away from home to seek refuge on the streets, if they were not simply thrown out.
>
> When questioned, the pastor stated that his actions were inspired by a revelation from the Holy Spirit who had told him that his six-year-old nephew was responsible for his brother's sudden death, his wife's infertility, and his sister's prolonged celibacy. His nephew, who was denied food for three days, then beaten and threatened that he would be crucified like Jesus with white-hot iron spikes, ended up admitting that he was a witch, that he used a stick and a rooster feather as a plane to travel at night, that he had already 'eaten' three people before his uncle, and that two of his accomplices lived on the streets, where the pastor's hunt had started.
>
> The president of the Gambia, His Excellency, Dr. Alhaji

Yahya Abdul-Aziz Jemus Junkung Jammeh, has gathered
all representatives of his country's diplomatic missions
to share with them his discovery of a potion of medicinal
herbs that can cure AIDS in three days. . . "

"What's that I hear about AIDS?"

You did not think Auntie Turia was listening to the radio
while tending to the gas stove.

Anything that touched on AIDS was a sensitive subject for
both of you since Tamara's death. "Yet another who intends to
cure AIDS with a miracle potion."

"Not the garlic and beets again!"

"You're confusing everything, Auntie, the garlic and beets
is the former South African Minister of Health. This time, it's a
president, the one from The Gambia."

"Those people do not know the harm they are causing.
Anyway, they bring us shame," she concludes, disgusted.

You finish your breakfast and turn off the radio. Now you
can no longer avoid it. You must face the day ahead of you.

All you know is that you will not go to the quarry today,
and the kids will not go to school either. Aside from that, nothing is really planned. You are the spokeswoman—perhaps the
president as Moukiétou suggested—but the president of what?
You do not even know who it is that you are to argue with since
you are no longer face to face with your usual interlocutors—
the drivers and the buyers who accompany them. You will have
to improvise, outline the path as you go. As you dress mechanically, it occurs to you that you must find out how your wounded
friends are. Immediately.

You call Laurentine Paka. Her husband Danny answers.
You ask him how his partner is doing.

"She is doing well, thanks. The gash on her forehead was
well bandaged. She no longer has the shooting pain she was
feeling yesterday, but, uh, wait, here, she's just out of the shower. I'll put her on."

"How are you doing?" you ask her the moment she utters "Hello".

"Better, Méré, but it was horrible when I caught a glimpse of myself in the mirror. No luck for me! The gash is right in the middle of my forehead, and there are several stitches. I have become ugly, Méré, disfigured. I would have much preferred to have my arm broken than wear such a hideous scar on my face. It's worse than Anne-Marie's! Will the scar go away once the wound heals? Do you think I can find a good concealer to cover it up in the meantime?"

Ah, Laurentine, always so coquettish. At a time when you are all facing issues of survival, she is preoccupied with her looks. Luckily, there are women whom neither poverty nor even hunger can keep from wanting to be beautiful. During your breaks at the quarry, she would only talk to you about beauty products, the places you could find American products cheaply, and new skin lotions and creams she had just discovered. She quickly became attached to Anne-Marie Ossolo who knew a lot more than you about what was trendy at the moment and what was already out of style. You suspected that a good part of what she earned from the gravel was eaten up by those makeup products that she used excessively to lighten her skin. You never dared to tell her that those Fashion Fare lotions and powders that she bought at the local market were counterfeit products made in Nigeria, products that contained substances that were toxic and dangerous in the long term. Perhaps now that this struggle had brought you closer, you will have the courage one day to tell her all of that, out of duty. In the beginning, you thought she spent a lot of money too on those romance novels that she always had in her bag, and it was only long after that you realized it was the same book she was reading and rereading and carrying around everywhere with her. You should introduce something new to her, like *So Long a Letter* by Mariama Bâ, which you had read in high school and really liked. But for the time being, you reassure her. You tell her everything will be fine, that you know an effective healing spray. Then you proceed with what is crucial, and what is crucial is to meet all together so you can coordinate your plan. She asks you where the meeting will be. You reply that you do not know yet and that if she has a suggestion, it would be welcome. She promises to call you back as soon as she thinks of something.

The moment you hang up the telephone rings. You press the green button. It's Atareta, the one you designated yesterday to stay with the wounded at the hospital. You forgot about her. She tells you that she has not heard yet from Batatou this morning and that she's off to the hospital right now. You ask her to call you back as soon as she has news and, meanwhile, you'll be trying to find a place for your meeting. She is quiet for a moment then proposes an unexpected but suitable place to meet: the courtyard of the hospital where Batatou is. How stupid of you not to have thought of it! That place offers two advantages: everyone knows it and it's easily accessible. Besides, you would all be near Batatou. It is a way for you to show her your solidarity. What time? The question of time is always a problem in a country where time is always ahead, and people always arrive late. You agree with Atareta to start the meeting at one in the afternoon but, to be sure that there will not be too many latecomers, you decide to announce noon as the meeting time, a good hour earlier. You thank her and ask her to pass on the information.

Again, the phone rings as soon as you hang up. You feel like you're operating a switchboard. This time, it's Ossolo's brother calling from his sister's place. He offers to make his taxi available to you for the day and tells you that he is getting ready to come to your place. Then he passes the phone to his sister. Her leg is doing well. Nothing broken, just some pain in the calf area from being struck with rifle butts, but she can walk without any problem, she says responding to your question about how she spent the night. She asks what you what your plans are for the day since no one will be going to the quarry. You reply that you just spoke with Atareta and that there will be a meeting at the hospital at noon.

"Good idea," she says approvingly, "what did you decide to do?"

You tell her that you don't know yet, but the purpose of the meeting is to find a common strategy to recover your confiscated bags. You ask her to pass along the information to as many women as possible and you tell her that you'll call her back. But, since someone stole her phone, you will have to go through her big brother in order to reach her.

Now, it is time to reach out to your other wounded friends. First Iyissou and her arm. She does not have a phone, but yesterday you found out that she has an uncle who is the head of an administrative department at the university. When you call the number, an electronic voice informs you that your cell phone card no longer has enough credit to place a call. Just your luck! The card costs five thousand francs per unit and, at two hundred fifty francs a minute, that doesn't even give you a half hour of conversation. Letting go of five thousand francs now is not easy and yet you must be able to communicate at all costs with the others.

You have only one solution, even if it makes you uncomfortable: ask Auntie Turia if you can use her cell phone. You return to the living room and tell Auntie Turia that you have no more credit on your telephone card. She looks at you, shaking her head to indicate that she does not understand why you don't just let this matter go. It has already caused so many setbacks. Once again you try to reassure her that you are not involved in politics. You're just fighting for your bags of gravel. She points to the device that is charging: three brief calls, no more, she insists. You thank her warmly. After several attempts through the establishment's switchboard, you finally have Iyissou's uncle on the line.

"Hello, this is Méréana, I work with your niece Iyissou at the river quarry."

"What do you want with me?"

His voice seems hostile, you do not understand why.

"I am the spokesperson for the women stonebreakers. I would like to know how Iyissou is doing..."

He starts yelling before you finish your sentence.

"Who gave you my number? Do not call me again, especially at work! If you are against the government, that's your problem. If you are being manipulated by the opposition, do not get me involved. I am a civil servant, and I do not do politics! And my niece does not live at my house. Anyway, just because I am her uncle, that does not make me responsible for her nonsense. I was disturbed enough by that story about her son being caught as a militiaman, and enough is enough. Never call me again, understood? Never again!"

And click, he hung up. You felt the fear in his voice. You are stunned. What does Iyissou's son's bad luck have to do with your stones? Why is he saying that you are being manipulated by the opposition parties to the government? The President of the Republic, the government, the ministers, the congressmen, the politicians of the party in power and of the opposition are too far, too highly positioned for you people down below. Only your bags of gravel and the daily money they bring are close to you. You start to doubt your actions. Perhaps, without wanting to, you have gone too far? No, your demands are fair.

It occurs to you that Moukiétou's son, who is a nurse, may have news of Iyissou. Before you have time to make the third phone call, your phone rings. You remember, relieved, that even if you cannot make calls, you can still receive them for some time. It must be important information from Ossolo's big brother the taxi driver, or else from Atareta who has news about Batatou. You leap for the phone.

"Hello?" A familiar voice calls out on the other end of the line: "Méré?"

It's Tito, Tito Rangi, your ex! All wound up, he starts insulting you right away, saying that last night you acted like a common whore, humiliating him in public with your big lies.

"You think you had to tell the whole world our family problems and claim that I am incapable of taking care of my sons? And why involve the First Lady in the matter? Not only are you jealous seeing me with chicks who are younger and more beautiful, but your jealousy has turned into hate which is pushing you to do and say whatever nonsense comes into your head."

You are doubly astounded. First that he called, because he hasn't called you once since you separated—it has been over a year. "A man's honor", he used to say everywhere, "she's the one who left, it's up to her to come back." If he had to contact you because of the children, he always went through a third party. Next, by the violence of his words, which made him pitiful and vulgar. You had never known that side of him, even that day when he hit you for the first time. It is true that you had called into question his economic power and, indirectly, his virility— there is no greater insult for a male chauvinist. To think that man had seduced you because he was a philosopher! That had to be in a past life.

"Listen, Tito," you say, trying to speak calmly, "you're the one who started launching personal attacks at me whereas we were there for women's collective advocacy. Anyway, I don't want to argue with you. I have more important things to do today and your rantings..."

"Rantings?" He yells into the handset. "You're the one rambling! 'Women's advocacy'! What rubbish."

"Listen, if you have something to say to me, say it, I don't have time to lose."

"Who do you think you are? Your sister maybe?"

Why is he so vile? You know that bringing your sister into the discussion is a deliberate attempt to hit you where it hurts the most. He knows that the trauma caused by her sudden and premature death is still an open wound in your heart. How can someone be so heartless?

"Tito, if you mention my sister one more time, I will hang up on you..."

"At least she was intelligent and would not have been involved in all the bullshit you are wrapped up in. Fine if you hate me, but I'm going to give you some friendly advice: stop the protests before it's too late."

"That's the mission the people who named you congressman have asked you to accomplish with me, isn't it, me whom the women have elected as their spokesperson?"

It is your turn to be mean. Nothing would exasperate him more than reminding him that he became congressman because of massive fraud during rigged elections. And, just as you expect, he flies off the handle.

"Shut up! I was elected to Congress by the people! If only you were intelligent! But what can you expect from someone who didn't even finish high school and who claims to be leading a bunch of women who are all just as stupid? Go read a little history, and you'll see that the women who have changed things are made of a different moral fiber than you. I'm telling you, Méré, we are not idiots! We know who is manipulating you."

"And who is that?"

"The opposition parties, of course! Right now, there is a meeting of the first ladies of Africa taking place in our capital and the sole purpose of all this unrest orchestrated by the opposition is to embarrass the First Lady of our country, the President's wife and, why not, the President himself. And you all believe that we're just going to let you?"

"And why didn't you say that instead of attacking me in public?"

"I did not attack you. You hate me so much that anything that comes out of my mouth, for you, is a personal attack. All I wanted was simply to warn those poor women about your madness. While the first ladies of Africa give us the honor of gathering in our country, to discuss big problems like the fight against AIDS, malaria prevention, improving the condition of women, you come to annoy people with your little problems about your bags of gravel. You are wrong if you think that we are going to let you disrupt this international meeting."

"We have no intention of disrupting anything, but we will see this through until we recover our bags."

"You're still just as stupid. Your sister..."

"You...!"

You interrupt him. You curse. You who never utter such words, not towards anyone. He remains silent for a few seconds, completely stunned. You take the opportunity to hang up. You know that it is impolite, that an important part of the education your parents imparted to you is to listen to people until the end of whatever diatribe they may come up with, but you really could not take it anymore. And then you didn't want that person blocking your line indefinitely while you are waiting for important calls. Still, you are a bit shaken hearing for the second time this morning that you and your friends are being manipulated by the political parties of the opposition. You were never interested in politics. You only recognize the President of the Republic's face because of the numerous giant portraits of him hanging in public spaces. As for the opposition, you have never met a single member.

On the other hand, Tito has just provided you with an important piece of information which you previously did not have: that the wives of the African presidents are to hold a meeting in your city. To improve the condition of women, did he say? But then why hadn't the First Lady of your country come to see you in your quarry? You look at your hands, the hands of a young thirty-year-old woman with calluses that are becoming increasingly visible from striking the stones, despite the creams you massage them with each evening after you soak them in warm water. Improve your situation? Fight AIDS? Oh, how that First Lady caused you pain just after the death of your sister who had died from the illness. You had listened to her on the radio. It was a meeting to educate the proud combatants of our valiant army for whom rape had become routine. "I ask our soldiers not to rape. Know this: if you rape, you risk becoming infected with the virus as well." Do not rape. Not because rape is an act of violence, a crime punishable by the most severe punishments, but do not rape because women, guilty as always, are likely to infect you, brave soldiers! You felt bad for your sister who went from being a victim to being guilty. No, you could do without those meetings of the leaders' wives.

•

As for Tito, oh that Tito, he does not realize at all the extent to which he ruined your life. He is the reason you are a stone breaker now. The price of a legs up in the air session, just one! The day he had failed his college entrance exam. You had entered his home a virgin. You came out deflowered. But you had never suspected anything then.

The next day, you left for the village, to spend the break at your parents'. Your father organized a group prayer to thank God for your good work at school and especially for passing your junior year—he already saw your diploma in hand and the door to university open—and also, as Aunt Turia constantly praised, for your good behavior in that big city where an adolescent was subjected to all sorts of temptations. Only grandma was missing, she who for her part would have invoked the ancestors, which would have pushed Dad again into launching into one of his diatribes against his mother's "animism, fetishism and paganism".

During the entire vacation with the family you helped your mother as all daughters do, in the village: preparing the fields for the new seeding season which was starting at the end of the dry season, going to the spring to draw drinking water, learning from your mother all the techniques to prepare cassava flour and bread after retting the tubers in the river or in the pond, braiding your friends' and cousins' hair.... Your younger sister, Tamara, your only sister since you were only two daughters in the family, almost never left your side. She was four years younger than you and very much admired her big sister. She constantly bombarded you with questions, some of which were surprisingly naïve and refreshing at the same time. You dodged as best you could those which you could not answer. You also spent a lot of time having her review her lessons, particularly in mathematics. In the midst of all those activities, you did not think about Tito. Perhaps once when you mentioned to Tamara, indifferently, that you knew a philosopher. So, you did not worry when your period was late. You had gotten your first period very early, and it had always been quite irregular.

After the holidays, you came back to the city to your aunt's to start the new school year. It was a pivotal year, the year of the college entrance exam, the year your future would depend on according to your country's educational system. The college entrance exam, a critical test which did not at all take into account your schoolwork throughout the entire year even if it was excellent, but staked all your six years of high school on the results of this one test, which barely lasts two or three days.

You had no problem buying your supplies because, as always after the harvest and crop sales, your parents had put enough money aside to cover all your needs during the school year. Notebooks, pencils, a compass, and books were the things you rushed to buy before school started. No new ruler, no new calculator, nor a new protractor since the ones from last year were still in very good condition. You were thrilled to hold the new books in your hands. That evening, you feverishly flipped through the pages of your math book, admiring all those equations and all those unknown theorems that you were going to learn. Next you opened your chemistry book. You saw two or three formulas written on the left side, then two or three on the right, connected to one another, some with an arrow, some with two arrows placed on top of one another pointing in opposite directions, and sometimes even with a simple arrow that had two heads pointing in opposite directions on either end. You did not understand much yet, but you knew that at the end of the year all this knowledge would be transferred into the large uncultivated space of your brain. There were the most beautiful diagrams also in your physics book, for instance, a beautiful multicolored strip of electromagnetic spectrum going from violet to infrared. You looked at your geography book. You had fun pointing at all the continents, all the unknown places, and pronouncing their foreign names aloud: Reykjavik, Chittagong, Chattanooga, Dunedin, Ushuaia, Kalahari, and especially Ouagadougou which you liked to chant, rolling the delicious syllables around in your mouth. And your history book with its reproductions of photos of our well-known heroes like Patrice Lumumba and other men and women unknown to you.

Oh, how you had anticipated the first day of classes! Your new slacks. Your new pair of shoes. Your old school bag which you had kept for sentimental reasons. Three classes that first day: math, history, biology. Good biology and math professors, but your history teacher had only given you a series of dates for a course titled "Contemporary Africa." 1885: The Berlin Conference under the chairmanship of Chancellor Bismarck. Race to grab colonies. 1914: Senegalese riflemen...To be continued in the next class. Bell.

As you went out, Fatoumata ran to catch up to you. She was your friend. She had never met the Senegalese merchant whose first name evoked the country he came from, an individual who had just enough time to impregnate her mother, then disappeared. Her mother raised her alone by selling firewood and charcoal at the market. She would often help her in the evenings selling her wood and charcoal, while at the same time she studied in the light of the hurricane lamp or by candlelight when oil was lacking, and it wasn't uncommon for her notebooks to bear black smudges from the dust of the charcoal despite all the precautions she took. To prepare for the school year, she sold foufou in the same market as her mom but, despite the latter's help, she did not accumulate enough money to buy everything, and she was still missing two or three books. She asked you if she could photocopy a few pages of your biology book because she did not have the time to copy the cross-sections and diagrams the professor had drawn on the blackboard, as well as the first chapter of the math book because she was worried that she had not noted down certain equations well. You replied that it was not a problem. There was a kiosk on the corner that made photocopies for fifty cents a page. It was when you were leaving the courtyard to go out into the street that you bumped into Tito, Tito whom you had not seen since the day you had let him seduce you.

In fact, when you left his place that day, contradictory

thoughts that were racing through your mind left you utterly confused. On the one hand, your body still felt the pleasure of what had just happened. Never before that moment had you suspected that the intimate encounter of two human bodies could be so intense that you lose your soul and start gasping, grunting, even howling like a wild animal, followed by a feeling of total relaxation a few moments afterwards. It was beautiful and good. But you also felt a sort of unease. Not a feeling of guilt for having committed a sin, but an undefinable malaise for having done something you should not have done. In the end you decided to bury what happened and not do it again.

You were happy to see him again, nothing more. He seemed rather excited and asked you why you had not called him since your return from vacation and why you had not replied to the messages that he left on your answering machine. You answered that you had no particular obligation to him and that there were plenty of other people who did not hear from you. So as not to hurt him, you did not find it necessary to reveal to him that, in fact, you didn't even have his number anymore. Fatoumata, who was a little older than you, immediately understood that it was a private conversation and decided to go make her photocopies while you talked. She took the books and left. As soon as she walked away, Tito repeated what he had said—you did not see the point— arguing that what happened between you created a special bond that connected you. That annoyed you. You retorted coldly that what happened was in the past, a moment of weakness during the euphoria of a successful year's end for you and a moment of consolation for failing his exam. And that was it. Now a new year was beginning, the year of your college entrance exam, and your only objective from now on was to concentrate on your studies. He did not get it, not at all. In a cocky voice, he said that you were kind of his wife because he was your first love and that a woman never forgot her first love. So, you could not just drop him like that. He went as far as to say that you belonged to him. What rubbish! Besides, he had moved, and you had to come see his new place. It was bigger, nicer. That irritated you profoundly.

People always told you that women were emotional, that they clung to their first love and blah, blah, blah. But you realized then that, in reality, it was the men who did not know how to let go. Calmly, you responded that you could not dump him because you were never with him and, with some spite, you added: "You'll be busy with your college entrance exam too, as I imagine you're going to retake it." He did not grasp the irony, but instead came back saying that, yes indeed, the two of you could study better together...

"Enough!" you hollered. "I don't have time to waste, and I have to study. We'll see each other from time to time on the schoolgrounds. Whatever you do, do not call me!" You ditched him there and went to join Fatoumata. For you, Tito was a closed case, a page not only turned but torn out, ripped up, and thrown away.

•

When you still did not get your period, you started to worry. Not knowing what to do, you adopted the Coué method, persuading yourself with each passing day that it would come the next. You felt your breasts swelling. Each morning, you woke up feeling nauseous and then a few pimples started to appear on your face: there was no mistaking it; you were pregnant. You had a hard time believing it. You told yourself that it was unfair. You knew girls who had made love several times without protection and who never got pregnant, whereas you, just once, a single time in a moment of weakness... You thought of your parents. This kind of news would kill them! Your pastor father would die of shame. You thought of Auntie Turia with whom you lived: with her experience, it would not be long before she noticed the changes in your body. You were scared that she would find out about your situation. Besides, you had the impression that this morning, before you went to school, her gaze lingered for a little too long on your breasts; she must be wondering why this sudden breakout of pimples on your face, you who always washed your face so carefully, and perhaps also why the sudden appetite for certain foods.

No, you could not do that to your family. You had to get rid of this pregnancy. How did people go about getting a clandestine abortion? At seventeen years old, panic came quickly. Tito! You had to see Tito, the same Tito you had thrown away like a scumbag a few days earlier in the school courtyard.

•

You looked for him in that same courtyard during the morning between two classes. It goes without saying that your mind was not on the class and your professor noticed it too since she called out to you twice, the first time asking you a question which you could not answer, not because it was difficult, but because you did not follow her explanation at all. The second time she simply stated aloud: "Méré, I find you are very distracted today. What's wrong?" Obviously, you could not say: "I'm thinking about Tito, Madam." You simply blurted out: "Nothing, Madam, everything's fine." During the long break and until the end of classes, you searched for him everywhere unsuccessfully. Where was he hiding?

He told you that he had moved, but you did not know his new address. You did not know any of his friends either and, you could not just shout around that you were looking for this boy. You were beginning to lose hope when you noticed Fatoumata. She wanted to photocopy the third chapter of the biology book.

"Fatoumata my friend, my sister, can you help me?"

"Of course," she replied spontaneously.

You explained to her that you needed to find Tito's address and most importantly, without approaching him; he mustn't suspect anything. Otherwise, there was a good chance he would run away, disappear. We know those boys, always ready to dodge and leave the girl alone in her own shit. Okay, you should not have turned him away, but how could you have known that you'd find yourself in this difficult situation? Too bad, you didn't have a choice anymore. You had to confront him to find a solution, corner him if he tried to run away as you expected.

Fatoumata, so efficient! You got the answer the very next day. Tito had been confined to bed for three days, suffering from a bout of malaria. He was doing better now after taking those new artemisinin-based Chinese therapies, which were more effective than good old chloroquine. He would not attend school for another three or four days because he was anemic and extremely fatigued. Three days? You could not wait so long. The situation was urgent and desperate. You had no other choice. You had to go to him.

You set out for his place after your last class of the day. It was two in the afternoon. You had to take two buses; the second left you on the main avenue, at the corner of the street he lived on. You had to scamper along for another ten minutes, down a sandy alley under the hot tropical sun, trying to decipher the numbers which at times were not marked. Finally, you arrived. A parcel of land surrounded by a limestone wall painted white. Neat and tidy. You entered and noticed the brown door that Fatoumata described to you. You took a deep breath and knocked.

"Come in."

A weak voice. You entered. His mouth opened with surprise. He was sprawled out on an armchair in a small living room, his face emaciated. He looked like an abandoned child. Didn't he have any family? Or a single relative somewhere? An open can of sardines, hot pepper, half a baguette, a bottle of orange soda—that must be his meal. It seemed that he hadn't eaten much. That was the problem with malaria. You practically lose your appetite completely. You took pity on him for a moment, feeling sorry that you did not bring fruits, especially oranges for their vitamin C to help him recover. After his surprise, his face lit up with a big smile and his whole body seemed to have received a burst of energy that made him get up and come toward you with open arms.

"Oh, Méré, how nice of you! You came to visit me? How did you know that I was sick? I am so happy. I knew that you weren't going to abandon me like that. Let me hold you in my arms."

You let him take you in his arms, an embrace that you kept fraternal—no, friendly rather. He signaled with his hand for you to sit down on the sofa as he continued to speak. He was visibly happy. You would think he was cured. You waited for him to calm down then you hit him with the news:

"I'm pregnant!"

Eyes wider than saucers, suspended above a wide gaping mouth, gaze at you. "But... but... what are you saying? Is that true or is it a joke?"

"Do you think that I would go through so much trouble to come all the way to your house just to tell you a joke?"

You responded as calmly as possible preparing yourself psychologically to absorb the shock of what was sure to be denial, the usual "Who says that I'm the father? I cannot believe it!"

You had trouble interpreting his tone of voice and the expression on his face because they revealed neither anger nor panic. It was not what you expected. A little lost and caught off guard, you repeated:

"I'll say it again. I am pregnant."

"Exactly, I don't believe it! You've got to admit, I am virile, anyway! A kid on the first try!"

You sensed a certain pride in his voice, but you did not see where he was going with it. Was he boasting or was he simply being ironic in utter shock and disbelief? When faced with two difficult situations, choose the most difficult one first because its solution will necessarily include that of the easier one.

"So, like all boys you're going to run away? You think it isn't yours? That someone else knocked me up, and I want to put it on you? You think I'm a tramp because I gave in to you the first time. And then when I left your place, I immediately went somewhere else to get laid again, right? Take a good look at me: I was a virgin when you penetrated me, remember?"

The more you talked, the angrier you became and the

more you wanted to use profanity to shock him, so that he didn't take you for some fool who has come whimpering about being deflowered or begging him to have pity on you. You spoke loudly and aggressively to lodge it into his brain that he was just as responsible as you were and that the two of you should confront the situation together. You had seen too many of your high school friends deceived and abandoned, and you would not allow that to happen to you. However, the more you spoke, the more perplexed he seemed, the more he seemed to not understand why you were vomiting out such insanity. He, too, got angry.

"What are you talking about, Méréana? If I wasn't the one who got you fucking pregnant, who was it then? The Holy Spirit? The devil?"

"You... you mean you acknowledge..."

"Are you doubting my virility? Do you also think that I'm sterile? Because I have friends who try to destroy my reputation by telling girls that I had the mumps when I was twelve, whereas it was only an ear infection. I am one hundred percent man, Méré! I hope you don't have any doubts about that."

Talk about a turn of events! Once again, this philosophy student took you by surprise. You had to back up, discretely, to avoid ridicule.

"No, I simply came to inform you of the situation so that we can make a decision together."

"So then, talk to me calmly, Méré. I know you're upset..."

You were relieved. He made the task so simple for you! It was not easy, but you had to reconsider your biases and acknowledge that all boys were not the same. There were some good guys among them. Now that there was no more room for anger, you began pouring out your fears and concerns. You admitted to him that you were afraid. What would your aunt think? What would your father think? For him there was no greater sin than sex before marriage—he liked to use the horrible word "fornication"—and a pregnancy on top of it? What shame! And what about your studies, especially this crucial exam year?

He listened to you silently and attentively. Sincerely moved and empathetic, he replied that he was ready to support any solution you suggested. He especially did not want you to fail your college entrance exam because of him, or that you deceive your parents and that you do not fulfill your dream of opening your own business which you had told him about the first time you met. You came to confront an adversary, an enemy even, and you found before you a friend and an ally. A boy who was generous and decent. You were partners, a boy and a girl, desperately seeking together a solution to a common problem.

The first thing that came to your mind was abortion, naturally. You said that to him. He winced slightly and reiterated that he was ready to accept that as a solution if it was your choice. He urged you, however, to think more about it before taking a definitive decision. You sensed a lack of enthusiasm in his voice. It certainly was not what he preferred, but too bad, it was your body and your decision.

You thought about a clandestine abortion, without your parents knowing. To be safe, the most appropriate place would be a private clinic. At seventeen, they would no doubt require parents' authorization. But that didn't matter much. It was easy to get around that because in this country people can get anything if they have money: false vaccination cards, false birth certificates, false visas, false pay stubs, and even false diplomas. Nothing was impossible. The real problem was finding the money. An abortion in a clinic would cost at least one hundred thousand francs: where would two high schoolers find that kind of money? Even a civil servant would have trouble coming up with it!

Or else, what if we contacted a woman from the neighborhood who... No! You immediately pictured the many girls your age who died or nearly died from attempted abortions in those dodgy offices of clandestine backstreet abortionists; you also imagined the ones who tried to do it themselves following some woman's recipes they had heard here and there: a Nivaquine pill overdose, abrasive vaginal washes made of potassium permanganate, inserting a hodgepodge of crushed wild herbs, supposedly having abortive properties, into the genitals. No. That was not the right path. After all, you did not want to die. You needed to look elsewhere. But there were not that many options: once abortion was excluded, the only other alternative was to keep the child. And accordingly, tell the parents.

As soon as you agreed that you would keep the child, he felt like a man with a mission:

"I am the man. I am going to assume my responsibilities," he cried out immediately, "I'm going to go introduce myself to your parents and tell them that I am the father of the child. Don't you worry, Méré, everything will be fine. I will protect you."

He had slipped from "we" into "I" and you, relieved to no longer be struggling alone, afraid in retrospect of your desperation which could have driven you to suicide if he had refused to assume his responsibility, had willingly let yourself be taken by the hand, to let yourself be led, in other words, to place yourself not next to, but behind him. Otherwise, he would not have thought he owned your body and would not have dared to hit you that fateful day when you demanded he put on a condom, nor would he have allowed himself to humiliate you in public like he did last night.

Suddenly your rage swells, and it takes you out of your ruminations. Who does Tito think he is? Just because temporary circumstances are forcing you to break stone for a living, that does not give him the right to mock you. After all, you went to school, you studied history and math and yes, were it not for that damned premature marriage, you would have passed your college entrance exams. No, even better, you would have been a PhD like your sister. And, why such disdain for those women drooling over every word that comes out of his mouth? So what if those women are illiterate? Does he think you need a doctorate to be an upright woman, a woman of courage? Perhaps he does not know it, but plenty of women with little education have changed the history of their society.

You think of those women from Guinea, the first ones who dared to defy the dictator Sékou Touré by organizing a march on his palace. And, of those Malian women who stood up to another dictator, Moussa Traoré. You think of the mothers of Chile's disappeared under Pinochet's windows, of the women of Argentina who protested their children's abductions. The more you think about it, the more excited you get. And the names of strong women in history come back to you: Kimpa Vita who, in the ancient kingdom of Kongo, led troops against the Portuguese occupation. Rosa Parks who refused to give up her seat on the bus to a white man in a city in the south of the USA. Recalling all those names goes a little to your head and you feel you are close to them. Of course, you do not see yourself heading a procession of women marching on the presidential palace, but what is certain is that neither Tito nor all the African first ladies gathered in a conclave can make you sell your bag of gravel for ten thousand francs.

The telephone ringing suddenly brings you back to the living room and your immediate reality. The thing must have rung several times before you realized it because the ringing stops just as you go to get it. You check if the caller has left a message. Yes, an SMS. "URG, Batatou's condition worrisome. Call back quick." It was Atareta. The message snaps you back into action after the slump you experienced when that bastard Tito came back to haunt your memory. The guy is really antagonizing you. You have to get him out of your head. You cannot let yourself be upset now, at this critical juncture.

You jump out of your chair. You tell your aunt that you're going to join the others, and you thank her for volunteering to babysit. You also ask her to tell Ossolo's brother to follow you to the hospital with his taxi, because, given the urgent situation, you do not have the patience to wait. You exit the house as she pleads with you, like a worried mother, to be careful.

TEN

THE MOMENT YOU step out, a scooter stops in front of your gate. It is Zizina, Mâ Bileko's daughter. She had barely turned off the engine and propped it up on its kickstand before rushing over to you. You immediately grasp her in a warm embrace. You hug her tightly.

Since the day her mother introduced her to you, she has felt a special affection for you and considers you somewhat like an older sister.

"Ah, big sister, I am so relieved. I heard very late at night about what happened to you all and I wanted to be here first thing this morning before starting my usual rounds looking for clients. Is everything fine?"

"That's very kind, Zina. As you can see, all is well, just a few bruises. Moyalo, Ossolo and Moukiétou were detained, but they have been released. Only Batatou is in the hospital."

"Mom told me. I'm not worried anymore. What are you going to do next?"

"Well, I don't really know. Right now, I'm off to the hospital to visit Batatou. After that we'll see."

"In any case, Mom will keep me posted. Good luck, have a good day."

"You too, have a good day. I hope that you sell a lot today... By the way, when is the UN exam?"

"Oh, don't even talk about it, it's in two days. I study very hard every night."

"I know that you will pass. You have nothing to worry about."

"OK, if you say so… Bye, see you later, I've got to get a move on."

She lowers the scooter back onto its wheels, gets on and she's off. Wonderful girl! She was with her mother the day the latter had been humiliated and brutally thrown out of her house and off her land after her father's death. Crying, she and her brother had tried to protect their mother by kicking the men who were dragging her on the ground to throw her out into the street. She was only twelve years old, but that incident had made such an impression on her that she developed a particular empathy for her mother. She lived the difficulties that her mother faced feeding them and paying their school fees quite intensely. That woman, once so rich, had descended into poverty and been reduced, first, to selling goods that she bought on credit from rich West African shop-owners, then finally resolved to break stone on the riverbanks. So, to lighten the burden of this woman who would arrive exhausted at night after a long day of selling her goods at the market, Zizina would prepare the evening meal—the only meal of the day—as soon as she got home from high school in the afternoon. After the meal, she would fry the dough she had kneaded the night before to make beignets, then sell them in front of her property while she studied her lessons by the quivering light of a candle that would sizzle each time an insect burned its wings. Most surprising is that she worked very hard, and she considered those good grades to be some sort of recompense for her mother, proving to her that her sacrifices were not for nothing. Her grades were especially good in geography, a subject that she held dear, until the day the tenured professor, who, it was said, was sick with AIDS, was replaced by another teacher.

It was the new teacher who brought her misfortune. A predator who started playing a game of hide-and-seek with a defenseless adolescent who did not yet know the rules. Each time he returned her homework, the professor would call her into his office on the pretext of congratulating her. At the beginning, it was just flattering words. After some time, furtive caresses accompanied his words and when those caresses became increasingly insistent, Zizina got scared. Her grades started slipping inexplicably when she refused to accept her professor's invitations. Grading a geography assignment, in theory, was not as subjective as evaluating a philosophy paper and yet the teacher found mistakes everywhere. How could you flunk a student just because she wrote *Uyghur* as she had read it in a daily newspaper instead of writing it *Uygur* as the teacher recommended? Even more ridiculous, how could you justify taking off ten points for answering Johannesbourg instead of Johannesburg in response to the question: "What is the capital of Gauteng Province in South Africa?" This was no longer simple harassment. It was his attempt to settle the score.

In those schools where there was no structured psychological support for a young girl in distress, Zizina was lost. She should have told her mother or another adult about it, but who knows what goes through the mind of a teenager. Terrorized on the one hand by the teacher, and on the other not wanting to upset her mother if she ever found out that she wasn't doing well in school anymore: weakened, she was ready to fall into the claws of a predator.

You do not know the details of what happened that afternoon when, coerced and forced, she agreed to go to the teacher's house, except that with his diabolically manipulating promises, threats, and flattery, he managed to abuse the young, frightened girl.

Poor child. After the act of rape committed by her teacher which she did not dare tell her mother about, she was completely traumatized and even her grades which had spectacularly gone up did not manage to pull her out of her exhaustion. She had become silent and withdrawn. Her mother suspected that something was wrong with her daughter, but she could not put her finger on it.

Eventually, she broke down and told her mother everything, and she, rabid with anger, headed to the school to confront the teacher. When the scandal broke, who do you think the school authorities blamed? The young girl, of course, who was called "promiscuous," "a prostitute," and "a bad example for the other girls at school." She was expelled. The teacher denied everything, clearly. Between the words of a teacher and those of a "horny" girl, there is no contest. Thank God he had not gotten her pregnant or given her AIDS.

Just like Auntie Turia, her mother, Bileko, was amazing. She took her by the hand, told her that she felt she was in part responsible for what had happened, and she accompanied her every step of the way on the road to her physical and psychological recovery. And now here she is preparing for a recruitment exam, and if she passes, she will be a UN representative!

You have not gone even a hundred meters before Ossolo's brother shows up in his taxi. He leans over and pushes the door wide open. You get in and sit next to him. He gives you a warm hug, perhaps a little too warm. It makes you realize that you really only know him as Ossolo's brother, and that you should ask him his name since you are embarking on a long collaboration.

"Everyone calls me by my nickname, Armando," he replies to you.

Nice name, sounds Latino, you think. Then, you tell him right away that Batatou is in critical condition, according to Atareta's most recent text to you. You must find out more, urgently. You know there is a kiosk on the corner of the next street where you could make a local cell phone call for only two hundred francs a minute. You need to stop there so you can reach Atareta for more specific information and, also, to know if the other women have already begun to gather in the hospital courtyard.

"No," he insists, as he hands you his own cell phone.

•

It is almost noon when you arrive at the hospital in Armando's taxi. Atareta, who was awaiting your arrival, hurries over to you right away. She is the one you asked to take the wounded to the hospital and help them while you took care of freeing your arrested friends. Of all the wounded, only Batatou is in critical condition. She was hit with two bullets, the first left only a superficial wound, but the second penetrated near a vital organ, which the doctors did not specify, the heart or the lung. In a word, her condition is extremely critical.

What is intriguing to Atareta, she tells you, is that no one from Batatou's family has come despite all the efforts Atareta made to alert them. She must have an uncle, a nephew or an aunt in some city or village. Perhaps you should put out an announcement on the radio during the half hour reserved for death announcements in the afternoon. But your concern now is to see the patient as quickly as possible. Accompanied by Armando who will not leave your side, you follow Atareta to Batatou's hospital room.

To your surprise, the bed she should be in is empty and you do not see her anywhere in the room, even after you've scanned the other beds. You ask Atareta again if she is sure this is the right room. She reassures you again that it is. Worried, and a little panicked, you call out to a male nurse and a female nurse whom you see loafing around down the hallway. This does not seem to please the male nurse who becomes visibly angry. It seems that you should have asked his permission before approaching a patient's bed because he tells you off in no uncertain terms, shouting that you do not just waltz into a hospital room as you please, then adds spitefully that if your patient is not in her bed, it is because someone has already brought her to the morgue. Such inhumanity! You can tell that Armando is losing his temper. You stop him right away by shaking your head and looking him in the eye. This is certainly not the time to make a scene. The female nurse senses your distress.

Looking at you, Armando, and Atareta, she understands right away that you are not looking for trouble. You are respectable people and undoubtedly it was your anguish that led you to overstep the hospital rules. She places her hand on her irritated colleague's arm and, sympathizing with you, explains that your patient's condition has worsened and that she has been transferred to the intensive care unit. The three of you thank her warmly while her colleague standing next to her shamefaced seems embarrassed about his rude behavior.

You rush to the ICU and when you reach the unit, the duty nurse asks if you are the victim's family. You explain to her that you are her comrades in struggle. Only her husband or another family member can see her, she insists. You explain in vain that Batatou does not have family, that you are the ones who have her two children and everything else, but the nurse remains completely inflexible. For the time being, there is nothing you can do except go to the meeting and inform the others.

As Armando follows you, Atareta leads you to the place where the women from the quarry are assembled. She leads you to the hospital's famous mango tree, a tree with a thick, robust trunk, whose thick foliage casts a vast shadow offering better protection from the sun than a parasol. Because of the cool air circulating under its canopy, it has become the place where people prefer to cool their heels while waiting for visiting hours rather than go and sit in the stifling unairconditioned waiting room. Today, your friends from the quarry have taken the courtyard by storm, sitting on the ground, on the grass, on small stools, and on makeshift chairs. You are quite surprised to see that they are on time. This unusual punctuality is a testament to the strength of their commitment. They are all there: Moyalo, Ossolo, Moukiétou, who were detained last night. Laurentine Paka who, despite the stitches on her forehead, managed to conceal them with makeup. Iyissou with her arm in a cast. Bileko with Batatou's child on her back. Bilala your beloved sorceress... also present are your fellow travelers: Laurentine's always-present "husband," Moukiétou's son, and so many others whom you do not even know.

When she sees you arrive, Moukiétou gets up from the stool she was sitting on to give her seat to you. You refuse, indicating to her that she is your elder and that you cannot take her seat and let her sit on the ground. Everyone starts teasing you, one shouting that you are the leader, another that you are their president, and yet another that you are the boss, but all of them clearly indicating that your new role takes precedence over the etiquette of honoring and respecting your elders. You finally give in and sit on the stool as they applaud. You may think that with all this cheerfulness they have forgotten the gravity of the situation, but when the racket stops and all their eyes turn to you the moment you sit down, you know that this is not at all the case.

You have never led a meeting in your life. You are not like your sister, Tamara, who led dozens of them, first as the leader of the student movement when she was at university, and later as an organizer of several meetings, some of which were international. But that does not matter. You feel at ease because this is not a union meeting. It is a discussion among colleagues to take stock of what has happened over the past few days since you decided to sell your merchandise for a little more money. Does your confidence come from the fact that you know that your cause is just and that it is reassuring to know that there are still just causes in this world?

You begin, first, with the bad news concerning Batatou, and you have Atareta confirm what you say because she has been following the situation since the day before. After several questions and exchanges, you all decide that whatever decisions you take from now on, the first thing is that all of you will assemble in front of the ICU after the meeting and demand that at least some of you be allowed to visit Batatou. The names proposed to go see the patient are: you, obviously, Bileko, because she accepted to care for one of the patient's children, and Atareta, because she is in charge of keeping up with the situation.

Now it is time to take on your real problem. You begin by reviewing the facts and you end by saying:

"The first thing to do is to recover our stolen merchandise. The problem is that we do not know where those people have brought our stones."

"They must have already brought them to the airport construction site," one voice yells out.

"What to do?", you ask.

There is no immediate response, but they start talking amongst themselves. You look around you. Since you are all gathered outside under the mango tree in the vast hospital courtyard, you have not gone unnoticed, and because everything is a spectacle in this country, your animated discussion has attracted quite a few onlookers. They begin talking amongst themselves as well because they also want to know what is going on. Their noise is distracting to the women. Irritated by these intruders, Moukiétou raises her hand.

"I see people here who are not from the quarry. I'm referring particularly to the men. Many of them are security officers who have come to listen in on what we are saying so they can report it to the police."

"There are women spies as well," says Anne-Marie Ossolo. "They can be more dangerous than men."

You try to speak but, since no one can hear you well, they have you stand on a chair. From this new height, you can better assess the size of the crowd. Nearly a hundred people, which is surprising given that this is an impromptu meeting for such a little-known cause. Unlike Moukiétou, you welcome the presence of the undercover State agents, who are there indeed. You are delighted that they are there so that they can see for themselves that you are demanding nothing other than to sell your merchandise at the best price, and the reports they will write for their superiors will only bolster your position.

"Everyone can watch, even the spies because I know they are here. They can fill out their reports however they want. All I ask is for them to be honest, to tell the truth. However, only the women from the quarry are allowed to speak and make proposals."

"I am speaking to all the informers, men and women," Moyalo shouts, "go tell your bosses to give us back our bags."

Her words are met with resounding applause.

"And tell them that they are thieves, too!" Moukiétou adds, sparking laughter and cheers.

You are happy with Moukiétou's and Moyalo's interventions, and especially with the reaction their words have provoked because it shows that these women are concerned and worked up enough to confront the authorities.

"What are we going to do to get our bags back? Does anyone have a proposal?"

Women whisper to each other, but no suggestion comes. Then, Iyissou from whom you have not heard much until then, says:

"We have chosen you as our spokesperson... "Our president," another specifies.

"Yes, our leader," Iyissou goes on. "That means we trust you. Suggest something and we will follow you."

"Yeah, suggest something to us," other voices chime in.

You are caught off guard. You thought that an idea would come out of your discussion, and yet they are asking you to come up with one yourself. You do not know what to say. You did not prepare a speech to read. You stammer for a moment, then an idea suddenly comes to mind: a march on the police station. Perhaps as a consequence of those thoughts you had mulled over after Tito's unnerving call, the words now come to you clearly and easily, not from your head, but from your heart.

"Dear sisters and comrades, we are women trying to earn our living by breaking and selling stone. Among us are women who went to school and women who do not know how to read. There are young women and older women. There are married women, single women, widows, and divorcées. We do not expect the State to pay our salary. No, we are working women and all we want is for our merchandise to be bought at a fair price." The crowd's applause gives you even more confidence. You want to speak to all the women who are there with you, whether they are from the quarry or not, but also to the men and women spies who are present. You continue by providing the background from the past two days for those who are not aware of it yet. You talk about the new airport, about the upsurge in the price of stone, about your refusal to sell, and about the violent repression. And you continue: "Unity is strength. It is because there were dozens of us outside the prison that they released our friends Moukiétou, Moyalo, and Ossolo. I am telling you, my sisters, that that is the way we will get back the bags they stole from us. Those men who stole our gravel think that because we are women, we are going to keep quiet as usual. When they beat us at home, we say nothing. When they throw us out of our homes and take everything we own when our husbands die, we say nothing. When they pay us less than they are paid, we say nothing. When they rape us and we file charges against them and they tell us that we asked for it, we still say nothing. And now they think they can seize our rocks by force, and once again, we will say nothing. No! This time they are wrong! We have had enough! Enough!"

Still standing on your chair, you continue your harangue. You did not know that words could have this intoxicating power. The more you speak, the more exhilarated you become, you feel outside of yourself, you are no longer you. You are no longer Méréana. You are one of history's Pasionarias! You are that Black American woman whose name you no longer remember, but the leitmotif of a famous speech she gave at a women's convention comes spontaneously to mind: "Ain't I a woman?"

"Is our only lot as women to suffer?" you cry out from the depths of your heart. "No, no, no! We will go camp out in front of the police station with our mats and our children, and we will not leave until they have given us our bags back or until they have bought them from us!"

"For twenty thousand francs," yells one woman.

"Yes, for twenty thousand francs or for the new price we are going to negotiate, but, either way not for ten thousand francs like before. Whether rain or shine, we will stay outside that police station with our mats and our children."

"And our husbands too," yells another woman, "they have

to be of some use!" Laughter and applause. From the crowd of onlookers, a voice yells out:

"I know that we do not have a say here, but those of us women who suffer at the market, we are going to join you, we are going to march and camp with you. We will bring our children and our husbands too, since as the sister said, they have to be of some use."

You yourself are stunned by the turn of events. When they had you get up onto that chair a few moments ago, you had no idea what you were going to say, let alone do, and now here you are heading up a legion of women volunteering to go and take the police station by storm. Were you being a bit hasty?

Amidst the applause and enthusiastic cries, Moukiétou, firebrand as usual, yells out: "Let's go there now. What are we waiting for?"

The police station is not very far from the hospital, about half a mile. You can be there in a half hour if you leave now. It seems to be unanimous. Now you can get down from your improvised podium.

As you are turning around to grasp the back of the chair to back down like you get down from a ladder, you notice a hand waving above the crowd. Your gaze moves down the arm to make out its owner and see Bilala's face. You cannot believe it. If it were another woman, Moyalo for instance, or Ossolo or Moukiétou, who were used to talking and giving their opinion even when it was not asked, you would not have paid any attention. The final word had been spoken and there was nothing more to add. But Bilala who never spoke up at meetings and even when pressed to do so always replied that she agreed with the decision taken or to be taken, if that same Bilala raises her hand to voice her opinion, there is good reason to be concerned.

Initially, before you knew her story, you thought that her shyness came from the fact that she came from the village—a "country bumpkin", people said—and had never been to school. You quickly realized that that explanation did not hold water and that courage, intelligence, and a sense of responsibility were not dependent upon scholastic and formal education. Bileko, Moukiétou, Atareta, and all those other women with whom you rubbed shoulders at the quarry daily were proof of that. On the other hand, you suspected that she, Bilala, had been profoundly scarred by the way she had left her village, at night, hunted like a wild animal, hiding in the forest, walking more than twelve miles before she dared to come out onto the main road to borrow a vehicle that would take her to get lost in the big city, the capital. Anyway, she was very lucky to come out of that alive. She was the mother of six children. Her troubles had begun when her three youngest children died over the span of four years, two of malaria and one of sickle cell anemia. Her husband's family held her responsible for the death of her children, calling her a witch, and it was not long before they threw her out of his home. The hardest for her was when her own children ran away from her, afraid that she would "eat" them next. She still had tears in her eyes when she told you that story. And what always happens in the village, when someone is accused of sorcery, happened: a gang of youths led by one of her own children set her house on fire one night while she was sleeping, thinking she would burn alive. Luckily for her, she was already at the edge of the forest when the arsonists noticed that she had managed to escape through the small window at the back of the house. They were all waiting for her at the front door where they expected she would try to escape the inferno, and if she did, they would be there, ready to stone her to death. They pursued her like a pack of dogs after their prey, but she knew the forest better than those young boys. She's sure she walked three days before she emerged onto the main road, far, very far from her village. Despite everything, she was able to safeguard all her money because, being the clever, experienced peasant she was, she always tied coins and bills into the folds and knots of the *pagne* she wore. After such a story, who would not try to be discreet, or invisible even? But there she was, raising her hand.

You get back up onto your chair, wave your arms around and shout:

"Wait, wait, do not leave yet... it's important... Wait."

Intrigued, everyone falls silent.

"Bilala wants to say something. I believe it's important."

When a chaotic crowd of a hundred people suddenly falls silent, the silence can be intimidating. Bilala lowers her hand as if she already regretted standing out. You gesture with your hand and make eye contact to encourage her.

"Go ahead, Bilala, speak!"

"We must not march. The soldiers will kill us. They always shoot when there is a protest. They even shoot when the people protesting are sitting down. My uncle was killed when he protested with other retirees in front of the National Pension Fund because he had not received his pension for over sixteen months. I do not want them to kill Méréana. We need her. We must not march."

You are stunned. So stunned that for several seconds you do not know what to reply. Then, stammering:

"But... but... Bilala... it is for everyone to decide... you should have spoken up before... now it is too late..."

"You were speaking so well I did not dare interrupt you. My fear of you getting killed grew stronger. I had to raise my hand. We must not march."

When one does not know what to say, one must keep quiet. But you cannot keep quiet because you are the spokesperson—no, the president—and you are leading this meeting. So, when one does not know what to say and one cannot stay quiet either, one must make others speak and listen to them. So, you address the crowd.

"You have heard Bilala. She does not want us to march."

"If she is afraid to march, she does not have to march," cries out Moukiétou. "Sitting on our behinds and staring at our breasts will not bring our bags of gravel back to us."

"It's true," puts forward another whose voice you cannot identify in the crowd. "She does not have to speak when..."

The rest of her words are drowned out in the brouhaha of the crowd because now everyone is talking all at once. You are afraid that the meeting could descend into chaos because of your weakness, because of your lack of authority. A leader must be decisive. To be decisive means executing what has been decided, despite the momentary doubt that came over you when you were getting ready to step down from your chair after your passionate speech. You raise your arms and shout:

"Democracy is the voice of the majority. Everyone here, except Bilala, agrees that we must march on the police station to recover our bags. There is no further discussion. Let's not lose any more time."

Again, you move to get down from your chair when Iyissou's booming voice—you recognize it is hers—holds you back once more:

"I think Bilala is right. Remember, they have killed college and high school students. My uncle, who works in the Dean's office at the university, told me that the security forces pursued those poor students on campus and shot at them."

"Iyissou, if we had not protested yesterday in front of the police station, you would still be in jail."

"The reason they did not shoot last night is because they were caught off guard," a voice intervenes supporting Iyissou's argument. "Today, with all of their spies here, they know what we are going to do and, believe me, they will be ready and waiting for us."

The commotion is at its height. Everyone begins talking all at once again. You do not know what to do anymore and you are angry at yourself for being weak and letting Bilala reopen a closed debate. At the same time, however, you are happy about her intervention because you yourself had the fleeting impression that you were jumping the gun by advocating this march without having examined all the intricacies of such a decision beforehand. Oh, being a leader is not easy!

More and more women now are taking the side of those who are opposed to the march. You feel you are beginning to lose your confidence a little. Carried away by the rhetoric of your speech, and no doubt also, even if you do not want to admit it, by your desire to prove blow by blow to Tito that you are not at all intimidated by his threats—quite the contrary—you had forgotten the reality of your country, a reality that you know better than anyone since, alongside your sister, you were practically on the frontlines of the student protest to which Iyissou just alluded, which indeed resulted in the death of ten youths. How could you have forgotten that here, citizens who protest are not merely dispersed by riot police with batons, teargas, and water-cannons? Here, the army is deployed, and they shoot live bullets and unfailingly leave dead bodies in their wake. Only once, to your knowledge, was the army's intervention milder: they did not shoot their guns. They only used the butts of their rifles to disperse the old retirees' sit-in to demand their pensions. There were only broken ribs, fractured arms and legs and two men in their seventies in a coma, one of whom was Bilala's uncle. All the other protests were subject to blind repression. Seven dead among the workers at the mining company who were demanding severance pay after the Chinese-operated uranium mine closed. Nine dead among the crowd that shouted: "Hypocrite, murderer" at the Head of State who had come to lay flowers on the grave of his political opponent. As for the students, it was even more tragic since the evening before their protest, your sister tried, in vain, to dissuade the organizers from marching.

That was before she was married and was still living with you and Tito. Four of them showed up, three boys and a girl, to talk with her. You invited them to sit in the living room and you called Tamara who was reading in her bedroom. After you offered them something to drink, you retired to the porch alone to rest. Tito had not gotten home yet.

After a while, they were talking so loudly that you could hear without intending to. First, you recognized Tamara's voice, immediately countered by a male voice:

"I disagree. It's irresponsible."

"But that's the only way the government will hear us and listen to us. When it sees hundreds of students in the street…"

"Thousands if we manage to mobilize the high schools and middle schools," added another male voice.

"Yes, when the government sees thousands of youths in the street, it will give in. The Minister will agree to meet with us and consider our demands."

"You watch too much TV"—Tamara's voice— "You have seen the people protesting against the authorities in Paris, London and Ottawa, and maybe even Johannesburg. You have seen police armed only with batons and shields to protect themselves from stones being thrown. You have seen photographers and journalists reporting on the most minor blunders and you have heard about investigations of police brutality. Quit dreaming! Aren't you aware that in our country they shoot at the crowd? With live bullets? Are you trying to get shot?"

"We will put the school kids in the front. They won't shoot at twelve-year-old kids, will they?"

This time, it was the young woman who spoke.

"I am shocked, Ida. I did not think you were so cynical. At this point, why don't we put women in front as well? They won't shoot at their daughters and wives, right? Oh, my God, you do live in this country, don't you?"

"You are too timorous, Tamara. So, for you, we must do nothing. No scholarships, no books at the library, no computers, no laboratory materials—no problem—we must not protest. We must do nothing!"

"You are twisting my words! At most, you don't trust me. I did not say we should not protest against our miserable study conditions. I just said we need to do it more intelligently. With a sit-in at the university, on campus, for example, instead of throwing hundreds of children in the streets."

"And just what will keep them from sending the army into campus buildings?"

"Okay then, let's hold a peaceful strike. Let's ask all students to stay home," Tamara counters. "I am a law student," said the one who seemed to be the leader of the delegation, "and I can tell you that our Constitution gives us the right to protest, to march..."

"Our Constitution is a piece of paper that the president can change at any time, or just ignore and you know it..."

"Listen, Tamara, we are going in circles. The majority of students at the Student Union Office have decided to organize a march for tomorrow on the Ministry of National Education. You are in the minority. You have to accept the decision and show solidarity with the movement."

"I cannot support a suicidal decision."

"So, you are not coming tomorrow?"

"No!"

"Deserter! You might as well resign from our student office," says a voice which Tamara had identified as Ida's.

"It's too important a decision to leave up to the five of us. We must call a general assembly to present our views," Tamara insisted.

"We don't have time for that. If the students elected us, it's because they trust us to make decisions for them. That is what democracy is. If you do not come tomorrow, we will release you from office and have someone else elected to your position."

"But you are going to be slaughtered!"

They did not leave on good terms. Only the girl whom she called Ida hugged Tamara good-bye as they usually did. Tamara had watched them leave and then, her voice sad and resigned, said to you:

"They are playing with fire. They are going to get themselves killed."

In fact, the next day, the security forces aimed and fired. The official death toll was ten, including, unfortunately, poor Ida.

As you stand on your chair before all those women speaking at the same time, you feel like Tamara is there among you. Her voice fills your mind as if you are possessed by her. "Aren't you aware that in our country they shoot at the crowd?...

We must protest more intelligently." Those words are swirling about in your head. You feel as though you would be betraying your sister if you supported this march. Bilala is right. True, she is in the minority, but she is right. As Tamara's example showed, in a democracy being in the minority does not necessarily mean that you are wrong. You have now completely changed your mind. You no longer want to hold a massive, noisy protest on the streets, in front of the police station. But how to retract your words after that Pasionaria-style speech you gave, perched on a chair before those fifteen women whose bags of gravel had been infamously stolen? Those fifteen women, lost among the multitude of onlookers, who were merely demanding what was rightfully theirs. No, you cannot. Yes, you must! People can, people must change their minds when they realize they are wrong. Thank God, Tito is not here to see the pickle you've gotten yourself into. He was right about one thing: Tamara would have known how to get out of this mess. You must speak, you must...

Laurentine Paka's raised hand above the crowd is like a lifeline. Give her the floor, and while she speaks you will have enough time to think a little more about how you are going to get out of this mess. You start flailing your arms and, after several attempts, you manage to impose silence.

"I have a suggestion to make, but I am not sure if it's a good one," she says.

Everyone turns towards her. When a woman is loved by her husband, it is obvious right away, and Laurentine is. Her partner, seated next to her, is holding her hand. You sense, however, that she is annoyed, but you don't see why. You do not want her to feel ridiculed, and you encourage her to express her opinion, insisting on the fact that all ideas are good, even those that seem the most unexpected, all the while praying—secretly—that she does not suggest something like going to meet the President of the Republic himself. Your words give her courage and she goes on:

"Congressman Tito Rangi must know where our bags are. He could perhaps..."

You must have cringed hearing Tito's name because Laurentine immediately stopped speaking, leaving her sentence hanging in midair. You were expecting anything but that. You lose it for a moment, and you want to scream that under no circumstances do you want that individual involved in your business! You had subconsciously made the rash decision to march on the police station so you could lord it over him, show him that he is not so important, and that you would not be intimidated by him, a decision which you were entangled in now. But you have got to keep your cool because hundreds of eyes are upon you. Whatever you do, do not give the impression that his name upsets you. Instead, show that you can rise above your own resentment so you can judge the situation with complete neutrality, as you should as the people's representative. As you try to pull yourself together, Moukiétou, once again, saves the day.

"Oh no, not after everything that bastard said last night. Yes, last night! How shameful that a state official would launch into such a low and personal attack. We will never forgive him for that. It is true, you were not there last night, Laurentine, otherwise you would not have uttered his name in the presence of all these women."

Moukiétou seized Tito as an emotional outlet for her usual misandry, but hers is not the last word because next Bileko takes the floor:

"We can use that bastard to achieve our goals."

"We do not want any scheming. Our fight must be clean," says Atareta.

"If you think you can make it in this country without getting your hands dirty, you are deluding yourself," Bileko continues. "Believe me, I know about that."

"The trees that grow the most beautiful fruit have roots submerged in dung. If the congressman can help us find our bags, and that is the point, what's the harm?" Moyalo adds in her impeccable Lingala.

"Congressman or not, root fatteners or not, the reality is

that he despises women," Moukiétou cries out. "Didn't you hear what he said last night to Méré? He thinks he is indispensable, like all men. When I get home tired at night and need to relax my body, I have my woman friend who lives in the house I rent massage me. Her hands are softer, more inviting, gentler than any man, rich or not, congressman or not. So, as for that man, when I was in the depths of my cell, I thought of him, and I wanted to kick his butt."

You are losing control of the meeting now that each of the women is speaking as she pleases, interrupting each other. From the march and how to recover your goods, the discussion has turned to Tito. Is that man going to haunt you your entire life? You glance over at Danny, Laurentine's husband, who is listening silently. You think to yourself, here we go, he must be ruminating about his own stereotypes, thinking that all women are good for is getting into catfights and, on top of that, over a man! Really, this is all your fault. You let your personal problems become an obstacle to solving your collective problem. You must find a solution.

"Stop talking all at once. I am leading this meeting. Who cares about Tito? What we want is to find a way to recover our goods. I suggested earlier that we march en masse all the way to the police station and that we hold a sit-in until our demands are met, but others remarked that that was dangerous because the security forces would shoot at us. Just because I made the first proposal does not mean I must not listen to others' arguments, especially if they are well-grounded. Yes, it's true, in this country the security forces do not use batons. They shoot. We had a taste of that at the quarry yesterday. The result of that is that one of our sisters, Batatou, is in a coma. It is truly a miracle that they did not attack us again when we went to demand that our imprisoned comrades be released.

"They were not expecting it," someone shouts.

"Yes, but today, they will not be caught off guard. The informers are among us. Let's plan the march for another time and let's try to come up with an intelligent strategy that is less dangerous but just as effective."

Without realizing it, you spoke as Tamara would have and you can feel her smiling at you from wherever she is.

"Laurentine has just suggested one," Bileko says.

You dig your heels in again. Anything besides involving Tito.

"Laurentine's idea is not bad," you say. "Except, it is better to deal with God directly than with his saints. Tito is nothing. He talks a lot, but he has no power. We must speak directly with the commissioner who took our sisters prisoner yesterday. Let's appoint a small delegation to meet him."

Everyone thinks that is a good compromise. Even Moukiétou, a fierce supporter of mass demonstration, acquiesces.

"I nominate Méréana to lead the delegation," shouts Bilala, who was the one who sparked this change of strategy.

"No need to nominate her," another voice declares, "she is already our president."

"Silence, silence," you interrupt firmly. "Let's not make a mess of things. Let's proceed step by step. First, let's remain clear: everyone can speak, but only the women directly involved, in other words the women from the quarry, have the right to make decisions. Next, since we cannot all go to meet the commissioner, we will need to establish the size of our delegation, then we will need to select those who will be members. And, since it is late in the day, we can only begin our work tomorrow."

Then things happen more smoothly. You quickly agree on a six-person delegation and, obviously, you are selected to lead them. After the other five members are selected, hearty applause adjourns the meeting. You notice Danny spontaneously kiss his beloved Laurentine, and his gesture moves you deeply, you do not know why. Laurentine smiles and brushes her hand over where he had kissed her, perhaps to smoothen her makeup smudged by the touch of his lips.

Now it is time to visit Batatou.

ELEVEN

AS ATARETA LEADS the delegation towards the building where the intensive care unit is located, you yourself are surprised by what is happening. You had never imagined that breaking stones by the riverside would bring you to head a women's liberation movement. You look around at the women selected to go with you to the meeting with the commissioner: Moukiétou, chosen for her outspokenness; Bileko, for her cosmopolitan experience—had she not brilliantly negotiated with business-men from Hong-Kong, Dubai, and Singapore? Bilala, perhaps because she had been the first to suggest the idea of a march; and, finally, Iyissou, whose arm in a sling will bear witness to the repressive brutality against you. Of all of them, you are the only one who is out of place. None of them went to school, or if they did go, they did not go beyond elementary school. None of them chose to break stones. Each landed here via different paths, their situations having left them no choice, no alternative. They will probably do this work their whole lives, until their poor bodies give out. You can see it clearly: beyond her brash humor, Moyalo is sometimes crippled by rheumatism. Moukiétou has already crushed her finger with her hammer twice and, if Bileko is not blind in one eye now, it's only because her right eye miraculously survived when a rock splinter embedded itself into her eyelid. And this work hardly covers their food, health, or clothing costs. In other words, it is barely enough for them to survive.

For you it is different. You are there for a specific reason: to make a hundred twenty thousand francs. You have a specific but urgent need for the money and no one you know either wants to or can lend you that amount. A friend of yours told you about the quarry, which you had never heard of, and said that if you worked for six weeks, you could produce enough bags of gravel to make that amount. You gave yourself seven weeks, no more. Once you have the hundred twenty thousand in your nest egg, you can register for that information technology school that offers a three-month IT technician training program with internship placement at companies. You are educated. Your future is not grim like these women's. Of course, there are hundreds of high school graduates in this country who are unemployed and even dozens with university degrees who, even if they're not crushing stones, are just small vendors with stalls in the city markets, but that does not shake your confidence. More importantly, once your demands are met—the price increase for your bags of stones, you will be able to get out of that forced labor camp even faster. You must therefore do your best to make this movement a success. Tamara would have expected nothing less of you.

You have all arrived in front of the building. Clearly alerted by all the commotion in the hospital courtyard, a man in a jacket and tie flanked by another in a white coat are standing at the entrance. He explains that he is the Hospital Director and that he is aware of your concerns and understands your grief. Because authorization to visit patients is not an administrative decision but a medical one, he has brought the head of the intensive care unit to discuss this matter directly with you. You are all pleasantly surprised by this man's courtesy and good will. Since the beginning of your movement, this is the first time that a man with a modicum of power has treated you with so much kindness. The effect of this is a bit unsettling because whereas you had set out for a confrontation, you instead find yourselves before a man full of compassion and good will. The doctor addresses you and explains that, strictly for medical reasons, only two people can visit Batatou's bedside. You quickly decide on the two: you, of course, and Atareta, the liaison officer, if you can call this the role you assigned her.

Batatou is lying down on a thin mattress laid atop a metal bed frame, with an oxygen mask over her mouth, two tubes in her nose, her body covered with a sheet. You can barely see her chest raising to the rhythm of her breathing. She cannot smell anything, see anything, or hear anything. She is in a coma. A clunky air conditioner is making more noise than cooling the air, leaving beads of sweat across her forehead. You want to tell her that you are all thinking of her, that you are all praying for her, and that her two children are safe. You concentrate so intensely on these ideas as if by some miracle, telepathic waves could pierce through the fog of her coma and enter her consciousness.

Atareta begins sniffling. Seeing that, the doctor gently but firmly moves you away from the patient's bed and has you exit the room. He does not try to hide the truth from you. Batatou's condition is serious. The worst can happen at any moment. You wipe away the tears streaming down your cheeks, which you cannot hold back.

The Hospital Director, ever so courteous, informs you without mincing his words that Batatou's hospital bill is already three hundred thousand francs, and he would like to know who is going to pay it. And that is not all. You urgently need to buy antibiotics that cost seventeen thousand francs per box. None of you can pay such a sum, even if you all pooled all of your savings together. But you cannot reply "No one" to his question. Upon hearing such a response, who is to say he would not disconnect the tubes that are sustaining your poor Batatou? In a firm voice you reply: "Our organization," as if you had an organization. This seems to alleviate his concerns.

The two of you find the rest of the delegation anticipating your return to the waiting room. Your friends get up from the metal benches they are sitting on and rush over to you, their eyes burning with so many questions. You gesture with your hand for everyone to sit down and you let Atareta report on what happened. Before she even finishes speaking, some are already crying. You step in to instill a bit of hope.

Then you all leave the waiting room and go outside. You look at your watch and see that it is already five o'clock. You have a strange feeling that on the one hand the day has been very long, and on the other that the hours passed very quickly. Everything is swirling around now in your head. You cannot even think anymore, as if your brain cells have been fried. In this state, it is not a good idea to demand more from yourself. It is better to let yourself rest. So, you turn to your colleagues and declare that it is too late to continue the discussion here since there are other urgent matters to attend to. For one, the children who have been left alone all day. You are thinking not only of Lyra but also of Batatou's daughter whom you have taken in. You are also thinking of Auntie Turia who surely needs to go home. The others are probably also thinking about the tasks they have neglected. Everyone agrees and you set a meeting time to meet in front of the ICU the following day so you can first check in on Batatou, and then to plan before your important meeting with the commissioner.

You say your goodbyes and each of you goes on to tackle your own individual end-of-day tasks. You head towards the large exit gate which lets you out onto the main avenue so you can take a bus home. The hospital courtyard is empty and sad—hard to imagine that a few hours earlier there were dozens of women bustling around, discussing their future underneath the big mango tree that you see over there, behind the building.

You have only one desire, to leave this courtyard, tinged with a sinister hue by the twilight sun, as soon as possible. The best way is to take a taxi even if it is much more expensive, rather than waiting for a bus. As luck would have it, a taxi is there, parked right in front of the gate. You head toward it to negotiate the price of the fare, but the driver must be monitoring the exit gate because, before you even get close to the car, he opens the door, jumps out of his seat, and starts coming towards you, with a smile on his face showing off all his teeth. It is Armando, Anne-Marie's big brother.

Surprised to see him there when everyone has already

been gone for a long time, you cannot think of anything else to say besides uttering his name in disbelief:

"Armando?"

"Well, yes, you see, I'm still here. I was waiting for you so I can drop you off at home. After a long grueling day like today, it's too tiring to wait for public transportation, then fight for a seat in a jam-packed bus."

"That's nice, thanks. Where is your sister?"

"I don't know. She must have rushed home to wait for that man she cannot manage to ditch despite all the troubles he causes her. You should talk to her. Maybe she'll listen to you."

"Anne-Marie is very beautiful."

"Yeah, a beauty that almost killed her. That's what you call the devil's beauty."

"Don't speak ill of your sister. I like her a lot."

"I'm not speaking ill of her. I love her very much, too. I just want her to listen to me and forget about that guy that she cannot forget. And he's married."

"All brothers say bad things about their sister's boy-friends."

He goes around the car and opens the door on the passenger side. You are surprised by this sudden act of gallantry. At any rate it is not common here. He gets into the driver's seat and, instead of starting the engine, he hands you a bottle of cold orange soda as if it had just come out of the fridge.

"You must be thirsty."

Yes, you are thirsty, and you are very happy with the offer. You take it and thank him. However, a little alarm goes off in your feminine alarm system, that innate system which, so far, has allowed generations of women to survive men's advances. You smell something. Pay attention, proceed with caution! When a man from whom you have asked nothing suddenly showers you with thoughtfulness and kindness, you have to be on your guard. But your thoughts do not go very far since he begins talking, excitedly. He hands you a flyer which he takes out of the glove box of his car:

"We have support. We have support," he repeats.

You have no idea what he is talking about. He hands you the paper. The headline in red letters jumps out at you: WE SUPPORT WOMEN'S RIGHTS. Shocked, you settle into the seat of the taxi, and you start reading as the car takes off:

Once again, the autocratic and anti-democratic power has struck. This time it is poor innocent women, our mothers and sisters, who have been brutally beaten and tortured at their workplace and in the authorities' jails, while all they wanted was to negotiate the selling price of the product of their work, until then bought at a vile price by greedy contractors, the majority of whom are related to the men in power. If we needed any more proof that this country was in full drift toward fascism, this is it. We need change. It is time to drive these unscrupulous men out of power. They are embezzling State money with impunity as they crush the people in misery, like these women fighting for their daily bread.

Opposition parties, consolidated in the United Opposition Rally for Change (UORFC), will meet tomorrow morning to decide what action to take to support the demands of these women. The victory of these women workers will be one more step towards evicting these corrupt politicians from power and from their clique.

You read it again. You either do not understand or, rather, now you understand why Tito accused you of being manipulated by the opposition parties and why Iyissou's uncle got such a scare when you called him. And yet, none of you has contacted any politicians from the opposition nor any politician at all.

You are thirty-two years old now, and since you were born, it is still the same president who reigns over this country despite the incessant crying and screaming of the parties that claim to be the opposition. Oh, yeah sure, by an unforeseen accident of history, they did manage to make him relinquish power for about five years, but he took advantage of their incompetence, their divisions, and their appetite for power so that he quickly turned the situation in his favor. He took back his job by force and then, in order to avoid repeating the kind of historical confusion that had made him lose his seat, he rewrote the Constitution to grant himself a single term of ten years and, now that his term has come to an end, he is preparing to change it to omit this limitation. And the opposition is there, arguing endlessly, making and breaking alliances, and distributing leaflets; whereas, while they are barking like dogs, the President's procession continues quietly on its way, crushing even the slightest resistance along its path. So, you figure, given the uselessness of their actions for over thirty years, an association with those people would bring you a run of bad luck more than anything else. Anyway, your fight has nothing to do with theirs. You are not looking for a regime change or to unseat the President. All you want is to sell your bags of gravel for a better price. In a word, you are not "playing politics," as Auntie Turia would say.

"Ossolo, I do not understand why these opposition people wrote these leaflets."

"Ossolo... Ossolo... My name is Armando."

"Sorry, Armando, it's the fatigue."

"They want to support you."

"We are not playing politics."

"You are saying that too, Méréana? What does that mean: 'not playing politics'? Anyway, if you don't take care of politics, politics will take care of you."

"We do not want those opposition people. They're going to muddle our message, which is simple and clear: to sell our bags of stones for fifteen thousand francs."

"I thought it was twenty thousand."

"Um... yes, twenty thousand francs. But I think I can tell you: Twenty thousand francs is a negotiation price. Our objective is to go from ten to fifteen thousand francs. It is certainly not unreasonable to ask them for five thousand more francs! You don't shoot people for five thousand francs!"

Emotionally drained, you lean back into your seat and close your eyes, wanting nothing more than to listen to the purring of the engine hiccupping from time to time when the car hits a pothole. Armando must have realized how tired you are because he no longer utters a peep. Thinking that it will help you relax, he takes out a CD from its case and slides it into the player on the dashboard. What do you hear? Parafifi, not just a song, but a very old song from the 1950's, a lover's lament by the Congolese singer Kabasele, addressed to his ladylove, whose name was Félicité:

> *Félicité*
> *Young woman of extraordinary beauty*
> *Today you have sown sorrow around here I beg you, grant a glance*
> *At Paraïso, the man sitting next to you*
> *Who is giving himself to you, body and soul Félicité*
> *When I think of the two of us*
> *My blood begins to boil*
> *A single glance from you*
> *And I lose all control*
> *Your teeth are like diamonds*
> *Your eyes drive me crazy...*

You sense that it was no coincidence he chose this old-time hit from back when neither of you was even born yet. Obviously, it was intended for you. Oh, men! Does he take you for an ignoramus or what? And he thinks he's being smooth! Yeah, more like clodhopping!

"Can you turn on the radio, please?" you ask him, before the transfixed lover can start his second verse.

"You know, Méréana, when the circumstances are right, sometimes I like to listen to these old songs which are classics now."

You saw it coming. He is expecting you to ask him: "And which circumstances are those that are right in this moment?" so that he can launch into his predictable spiel. You do not take the bait.

"I would really like to listen to the latest news, please."

Reacting to your stern tone of voice, he grudgingly does as you ask, no longer knowing how to make his move, which he had undoubtedly meticulously prepared.

"In Zimbabwe, militants of the ruling party ZANU-PF have initiated a forced collection from national companies in order to fund an extravagant celebration of President Robert Mugabe's eighty-fifth birthday. The party's menu features two thousand bottles of Moët and Chandon or Bollinger 1961 champagne, five thousand bottles of Johnnie Walker and Chivas, eight thousand lobsters, two hundred pounds of jumbo shrimp, four thousand portions of black caviar, three thousand ducks, sixteen thousand eggs, three thousand chocolate and vanilla tarts, and eight thousand boxes of Ferrero Rocher chocolates. Eighty cows, seventy goats and twelve pigs will be slaughtered for the banquet.

The businessmen are each required to contribute between forty-five and fifty thousand American dollars to the 21st February Movement, the youth organization named in honor of the president's birthday.

Zimbabwe is officially the world's worst economy. Last week the Central Bank took away twelve zeros from the national currency to fight hyperinflation estimated to be at two hundred thirty-one million percent. The rate of homelessness in the country is at ninety-four percent, and the current cholera outbreak has already resulted in four thousand deaths of the eighty thousand people infected.

Sports: the soccer team..."

"Stop in front of this kiosk please, I'm going to buy a phone card."

He stops the car. You get out and buy one. The sacrifice

of the five thousand francs is imperative because being able to communicate with the others now is essential. Since the kiosk is not far from home, you tell Armando that you are going to continue by foot. A little walk will relax you. He objects and gets out of the car. When he finally understands that you will not change your mind, he offers you his services for the next day. You do not say no, nor do you say yes. You simply promise to call him, and you thank him. He tells you goodbye hugging you warmly, perhaps squeezing you a little too tightly against his chest.

TWELVE

YOU ARE IN for a big surprise when you enter your property: Fatoumata! You do not believe your eyes. Fatoumata, your high school friend whose home offered you and your crying children refuge that evening when you fled your husband's house in a panic. She no longer lives in the same city as you. Now she lives in the port city, the country's economic capital. You cannot remember when you last saw her. When Tamara died, she took a week off without pay to stay with you and help you overcome the shock of losing the person who was not only your little sister, but also your child. It meant so much to you.

You run towards each other with open arms. Hugs. You look at her. Fatoumata, the girl who used to photocopy your books because she did not have money to buy them, the girl who sold charcoal at the market with her mother and roasted peanuts in the evening on the street corner in the flickering glow of a candle so that she could buy notebooks and secondhand clothes. Now this girl is better off than you. It is a cliché to say that faith and perseverance in work pay off, but Fatoumata is living proof. An entry level accountant, at first, at a local branch of a petroleum company whose logo is a large shell, she climbed all the way up the ladder and is now sales director.

"What a surprise, Fatou! How long have you been in town?"

"I arrived last night for a meeting with the Minister of Oil and Mining. But before all that, tell me, is it true what I heard this morning when I arrived at the Ministry, that you are leading a group of rebellious women?"

"Rebellious women?"

"Yes. People are saying that you collectively threw stones at the President of the Republic's procession and that you were even arrested. What is that all about?"

"And you believed it?"

"Of course not. That's why the moment the meeting ended I rushed over to see you and find out more."

"Listen, I break stones on the riverbanks. I need money."

She does not believe her ears. She is shocked. She definitely must be thinking that her high school friend has sunken very low.

"Oh, Méré, come on. You know that I am here. I can always lend you money."

"I know, but I didn't even think to ask you."

"What do you mean, you didn't think to ask me? Now, forget all of that. How much do you need to get by?"

"It's not about the money anymore, Fatou. That is not what is motivating me anymore. It's all those women!"

"At least tell me what's going on."

You both sit down, and you tell her everything. She listens to you in silence, nodding her head from time to time. Then she says:

"You remind me of Tamara. The same passion. Is that in your blood or what?"

You laugh and you tell her that she knew Tamara as well as you did and that there is no comparison between the two of you. You chat more about everything and nothing as you share a glass of local beer. Finally, you walk her to her car.

"Thanks, Fatou. That's so nice of you. Let me look at you again. How long has it been since we've seen each other? A year, maybe a year and a half?"

"No, you're thinking of that time I came to stay with you

after Tam's death. We saw each other well after that. Don't you remember? When I came to see you in a panic... I came and went back the same day."

"Of course! How could I forget that? Speaking of that, you are glowing! Seems like things are still going very well, as they say."

"Oh yes, couldn't be better. I can't believe what I went through to get to where I am now. I am happy, Méré. Once again, thanks to you."

"And your husband, how is he?"

"I have never seen a man pamper a child so much. You won't believe this but the boy looks more and more like him. Anyway, we're happy, and that is what's important."

She gets into the car.

"I'll say it again, Méré: don't hesitate to contact me if you need money."

"Okay, I'll think about it. Thanks again."

After one last wave, she takes off. Another cliché of which Fatoumata is again living proof is looming in your mind: money doesn't buy happiness. If she is happy at home now, it is not because of her money.

When she got married, she was the kind of woman that every man dreamed of having—beautiful, educated, faithful, and she was earning a more than comfortable salary as an accountant at a large oil company, especially when compared to that of her husband, who was the head nurse in a medical office. But, after three years of a childless marriage, pressure began to mount on the husband's side of the family to kick her out of the house or at least for him to take a second wife who could give him children. He would continuously twist a knife in the wound during every argument, throwing in her face the fact that she was barren. Besides, not only did he start coming home later and later, and did not even pretend to hide where he was coming home from, but he also started outright sleeping elsewhere. And everyone knew that he had a "second office", meaning a mistress. If she complained, he would reply cruelly:

"Give me a child before you start nagging me!" Deprived of her husband's support, humiliated and denigrated by her in-laws, and mocked by the women in her life, the beautiful and plump Fatoumata started to suffer from stomach pains, lose weight, and wither away. She became anorexic and was on the verge of depression.

Everything came crashing down one evening, during a reception the oil company held in honor of an executive from Benin, a colleague who, at the end of his contract, was to return to his country. At the end of the evening, Fatoumata, realizing that he had to fly out early the next day and had forgotten to sign an important accounting document, called to tell him that she was going to drop by. He took her into the living room and, after signing the document, offered to have one last drink since they would never see each other again. Banal at first, the conversation became more and more intimate. Drunken with words of tenderness and affection that she had not heard for so long—and perhaps a little intoxicated by the champagne bubbles—she had given herself, wholly.

Four weeks later, when her period did not come, she took a test and knew she was pregnant.

On the one hand, unable to live with the joy of discovering she was fertile; and, on the other hand, living in the fear that someone would find out that she had cheated on or betrayed her husband, she sank into a deep depression. One night, she thought of you. High school memories, maybe, when you put her in charge of finding Tito when you discovered you were knocked up. In desperation, she called you that night and, without explaining anything, told you that she absolutely had to see you and that she would catch an emergency flight the next day. A round trip day flight.

At the airport, if you had not known that it was Fatoumata, you would not have recognized her. She was not that beautiful, cheerful woman, always smiling, whose chubbiness was so endearing. She was a sickly woman, like a tuberculosis patient, with an emaciated face.

She told you all the details of her ordeal and revealed to you the situation she was in. Then you started discussing all the possible options.

The simplest solution was to tell her husband that she was pregnant and to say nothing else. This lying by omission implicitly meant that he was the father and so the ostracism of which she was victim would cease. In the end, he would be happy to have a child. You had to choose between finding happiness at home and living a lie. The truth is that sometimes a lie can save a marriage more than total frankness. That was the solution you had finally embraced.

As she was about to leave for the airport, a perverse thought came to your mind. A lie or not, that guy should not get away so easily after all the physical and moral abuse he had put your friend through.

"What if you humiliate him this time?" you heard yourself suggest innocently to Fatoumata. "What do you mean?" She asked, intrigued.

"Listen, if that guy, just passing through, got you pregnant the first time, that means you're fertile! That you are not sterile! Fatou, you know our men: if during all this time your husband has not had children outside the matrimonial home, if he has not gotten his mistress pregnant, it is not out of love for you, it is simply because he is incapable of..."

Before you had finished your sentence you saw her mouth fall open and her eyes slowly widen. Her eyeballs were glowing curiously. For her it was a moment of almost divine revelation. You were not surprised that she had not thought of this before. For generations, women had so deeply internalized the discourses of domination and guilt that men had assigned them that, for most of them, it went without saying that a man was never the one who was infertile. It was always the woman. If there is an imperfection somewhere, always look for the woman first. You continued your sermon.

"You have two choices before you, Fatoumata. Either you

can live with your secret and save your marriage, forgetting all the humiliation you have suffered, or you can reveal the truth and take your revenge by exposing that man as sterile and incapable of impregnating a woman. Though still happy he can get it up! Whichever you choose, stick with it."

"You are incredible, Méré! I had never thought of that. But you're right! I have suffered too much. I want to tell the truth and make him shut his mouth. Too bad if I look like a fickle woman, I am ready to live with that."

She was silent for a moment, then looked at you:

"To think of all the times I thought about committing suicide. I would have killed myself like an idiot, and for a guy with degenerate sperm!"

"Wait, Fatou. There is a third option that's even more satisfying. Do not reveal anything in public. Tell the truth only to him. Talk to him. Tell him that for some time you have been wondering about which one of you was sterile. He will reply, as one might expect, that of course it can only be you. Then you'll calmly retort that it cannot be you since you have found a man, a real one, who has impregnated you. Leave him with the dilemma to either publicly disavow you, thereby revealing that he is unable to impregnate a woman, and thus to become the town's laughingstock, or to keep quiet and protect his manhood. You can bet your bottom dollar that he will choose the second option. And besides, I bet he will be begging you to keep the secret."

She smiled enigmatically as she left. You never found out what was said between her and her husband or what kind of pact they made with each other, but the fact remains that after several months, Fatoumata was radiant once again. She was back to that joyful woman you had always known whereas the poor man lived in constant fear that someone would find out that he was not the real father of his son.

•

It is past six in the evening when you leave Fatoumata and get back to your property. You hope you have not taken too much advantage of Auntie Turia's availability. As soon as you enter, you hear her voice calling to you from the porch where she is sitting:

"Thank God, you're back. I hope that you did not do anything stupid."

"Don't worry, Auntie, everything went well. Tomorrow, we will meet the police commissioner to recover our bags of gravel."

"Did you schedule a meeting?"

"Not exactly. We intend to demand one."

"How so?" Auntie Turia asks, a bit skeptical.

You outline the plan very concisely, omitting anything that might cause her to worry.

"If you get this meeting, ask only for your bags. Do not play politics. Politics is not good."

You realize that Auntie Turia is trotting out exactly what you said to Armando, and you realize right away that it means nothing. Apart from love and making love, what is not political? Demanding better schools, better health care, a neighborhood soccer field, a decent salary, everything is. The difference lies in the fact that some make a living from it while, for others like you and the other women, it's a one-off, like demanding an appropriate selling price for your bags of gravel. But you cannot say that to your aunt.

"Okay, Auntie, I will not play politics. Thank you so much for watching the children."

"I fed them all, and the two boys are doing their homework, I think. I had a lot of trouble with Batatou's little one. She kept crying for her mother. In the end, she accepted me. I washed her, and she eventually drank her bottle and fell asleep. Tomorrow, you need to give her a light corn porridge. She is big enough for that and it will also keep her from getting diarrhea because it's likely she will not digest that artificial milk well."

"And Lyra?"

"Oh, that little one loves her Maw-Maw. She played big sister and then she conked out too.

She wanted to tuck the baby into bed."

She leaves the porch and follows you into the house. The two boys have finished their homework and are playing a game whose rules seem quite complicated to you. The older one yells out: "Hi, Mom!" giving you a big wave, whereas the younger one gets up to come and kiss you. He forgets to ask for the do-nuts you had promised him last night. You go peek into the bedroom. Lyra is sleeping next to Batatou's daughter. It's as if they have always lived together, two little angels, one of whose mothers is in a coma at the hospital. Everything is fine.

Without your having to ask, Auntie Turia offers to come back again tomorrow to watch the two girls while the boys are at school. You thank her profusely and you accompany her to your front gate:

"Don't hesitate to call me for anything. My cell is charged now. Take a hot bath—I have already heated the water in the big tinplate bucket—eat, and try to sleep. Alright, see you to-morrow."

She puts her arms around you, and you kiss each other warmly on both cheeks. You watch her as she walks away, disappearing into the night. Your mother's big sister, a widow, who knew how to survive the brutal death of her husband, who now leads a quiet, balanced life, living off her sewing shop. If only you could say as much for yourself!

You send the two boys to bed because tomorrow they have to go to school. They sulk a little and then get to it. You test the water that Auntie Turia prepared for you. It really is hot. Although you are starving, you decide to wash up before you eat. Take off the clothes you have worn all day and put on a *pagne*. Grab a towel and some soap. Pick up the storm lantern and take the bucket from atop the gas stove and, finally, head to the outdoor shower. You are suddenly overwhelmed, though, with extreme fatigue. So, you decide to rest, even if it's only for five minutes, before you do anything else. You collapse onto the chair, which is used to cushioning your carcass, routinely exhausted from your days of hard labor. But tonight, it is not only your body that is exhausted. Your brain is too.

You sit down and, with your back firmly pressed against the back of the chair, you take a deep breath and release the air slowly from your lungs, hoping that this long yoga-style exhale will carry a little of your fatigue away with it. You kick off your shoes and the fresh air caresses your toes which were confined for so long. You close your eyes to rest them as well. Everything is calm around you. You do not hear the children's breathing, not even the two boys who are actually right next to you, hidden behind the screen. Auntie Turia really took good care of them. You are lucky to have her. More than your mother, she is the one who raised you, guided you in life from the tender age of twelve until you were seventeen, when an unexpected pregnancy thrust you into a premature marriage. But even with that ordeal, again she was the one who came to your rescue. It was her unexpected but remarkable behavior during that drama that kept you from making the foolish mistake of a teenager, who saved your life and who helped you to get yourself back on track toward a future which seemed completely destroyed to you. That all happened very quickly, by the way, in a single afternoon.

You had locked yourself in your room. From your window, you could see Tito who, as promised, came to announce the news to your aunt. He was accompanied by an elder of his family, an uncle perhaps. You did not have the courage to go out to introduce this boy whom she did not know and who just suddenly appeared on her doorstep. You were ashamed of what you had done, ashamed of having disappointed your aunt after all she had done for you, all the advice she had given you.

Ashamed that people might judge her, believing that your idiotic behavior was because she had been a bad mother. So, a sense of guilt added to your shame.

You had no idea how Tito introduced himself, nor how his

relative presented the issue but after about ten minutes, maybe less, after she led them into the living room, Auntie's loud voice, hesitant between anger and disbelief, called to you. You felt a rush of hot air and your armpits began to sweat. But there was no way for you to avoid it. You had to go. You wondered if that was how prisoners on death row advanced towards the execution post: with their heads down and heavy hearts. You entered the room and just stood there, near Tito. Auntie looked at you both, but remained silent for a few seconds, seconds that seemed like hours to you. Perhaps to calm down.

"Méré, do you know this boy?"

"Yes, Auntie."

"Who is he to you?"

"He's... he's a high school classmate."

"Is that all?"

Then, you no longer knew how to respond. How do you tell a mother that that was not all, that you had gone to his house, that he had undressed you and then you had let him screw you, and gotten you pregnant?

"Is it true that you are pregnant?"

"Yes, Auntie."

There, it was done. You've said it. Even if it was in a low, almost inaudible voice.

"My God, my God, what is happening to me? I suspected something, but I would never have thought this! I trusted you so much! You realize that... Please go wait outside," she said bluntly to Tito and his relative.

The two went out immediately. Hopefully they would not run away and leave you alone. As soon as the door closed after them, everything that Auntie held in her chest exploded.

"Méréana, how could how could you do this to me? You, whom I have always held up as a role model. You who have always been among the top of the class, an exemplary young girl who never comes home at ungodly hours. How did you manage to get pregnant in the streets? And your parents. Did you think about your parents? About your father the pastor? You are going to kill him! He is going to have a heart attack when he hears what you have done! My God, what is happening to me? And my little sister, your mother, what will she think of me? That I did not give you good advice? That I did not love you? Shame, shame, shame on me, shame on you, on your parents, on your family… Oh, I trusted you, Méréana! How could you have done this to us?"

Each of her words hit you, hurt you, wounded your heart, and yet, you knew that they were justified and that your words would have been just as harsh if a girl you were raising under your roof had done the same. Suddenly, you felt alone in the world, abandoned by everyone, orphaned. You could not take it anymore. The dam burst and you started to cry. At seventeen, it's easy to bawl. You did not even cry with dignity, in silence. Instead, heaving sobs interspersed with hiccups accompanied your tears.

But then, through your fog of tears, you saw a figure moving toward you and her open arms wrapped you in a firm and warm embrace. Your head snuggled up against the hollow of her breasts, you surrendered completely and allowed your body to absorb the maternal love and kindness emanating from all the pores of her being. You were no longer an orphan. You were safe in your Auntie's arms. You knew that she loved you and that she would help you through this. So, you began to cry with greater intensity, this time with tears of deliverance, tears that, while freeing you, were also releasing those words that came from the bottom of your heart and which escaped between two sobs:

"Please forgive me, Auntie Turia, forgive me for having disappointed you. I love you, Auntie, help me, I beg you, help me."

She continued to hold you in her arms, caressing your back, arms, and face without a word. It was only when, exhausted and emptied of your tears, when you finally stopped crying, that she began to speak, her voice full of tenderness.

"My dear girl, forgive me if my words have hurt you. I was in shock. I share the responsibility for what happened to you. After all, you are only a child. I should have told you about the real things in life, explained to you the changes that your body was going to undergo when you came to me distraught about your first period, the bloodflow you knew nothing about. I should have told you about the feelings and desires that would accompany the growth of your breasts and the bulge of your buttocks. I should have warned you about boys who would flatter you every time they would gaze at your breasts, the curve of your back and the movement of your hips when you walk. I should have warned you that, like predators lying in wait, they would play hide-and-seek with you until you gave in to them. But I did not do any of that. I respected the foolish taboo that one should not talk about sex with one's daughter. I spent my time preaching to you about abstract virtues like Love, Fidelity, Abstinence and all the rest while you did not even know what a simple teenage crush was."

She fell silent for a moment, then, with a small self-deprecating laugh, continued:

"I even talked to you about sin! But what is a sin for a fifteen-year-old girl? An adult invention for sure. Oh my God! If I only knew! Well, the damage is done. We are in this mess together. You can count on your auntie. I will get you through this. I will get us through this."

She squeezed you against her with one last embrace then walked over to the door and brought in Tito and his uncle—yes, it was his uncle. She had you sit down on the couch next to her and seated the uncle and nephew opposite you.

"Well, now that the harm is done, what do you propose?" she said, addressing Tito.

As tradition requires, the elder would have the first word. And the uncle wanted to speak, but Auntie interrupted him somewhat abruptly.

"Let him speak. He is responsible for the pregnancy, not

you. What do you intend to do now, young man? Help her abort?"

Tito looked at you. That was the option you had considered then but gone back on for lack of money. But, if Auntie now supported you in this option as her question seemed to indicate, you would choose it without hesitation. That is what Tito must have been thinking as he looked at you, arching his eyebrows questioningly.

"We thought about it and..."

"Well, think no more," Auntie interrupted outraged. "Abortion is out of the question, you hear me, Méré?"

"Right, Auntie, we scrapped the idea."

"Good! Anything but that," Auntie went on.

"We decided to keep the child. I am the father. I'll take full responsibility," said Tito, trying to sound firm and self-assured.

"With what means? You're a student with no job."

"As Tito's uncle, I will commit to provide everything that will be needed for the birth," the uncle finally dared to say. "Baby clothes, diapers, a cradle, and even a stroller, if necessary," he added for good measure.

"Yeah, right. Buy baby clothes and disappear. I know how boys deceive girls in this country."

"Oh, no," Tito said, indignant. "I am not one of those hooligans who gets a girl pregnant and then vanishes into thin air. The proof is that I came before you, not alone but with my uncle to show that I am involving my family. I came to assume my responsibility. I will take care of Méré and my child."

Those words seemed to calm Auntie. She had jostled them a little in order to have clear answers and gauge Tito. She looked at him for a moment, then began to address all three of us moving from one to the other without transition.

"Your nephew seems serious to me, and I am happy that Méré did not fall for a no-good. Of course, I would have liked for this not to happen but it did, and I must assume my role. Méré, you are my daughter. I will support you. I will help you, and I will take care of the child. The problem is Méré's parents. How are they going to take this? Méré is their oldest daughter. They have invested a lot in her. I will have the difficult task of going to the village to bring them the news and make them understand that it was an accident that could happen to any girl this age. For now, let's keep this a secret between the four of us until I speak with her parents about it."

She kept her promise. The next day, she left for the village. She explained to you that she had to go there alone, without you. Things would be easier that way. She stayed there for three days, three days during which you lived in restless agony barely able to eat anything. How would your father, so pious, take what he would consider defilement of the body, the Lord's temple? And your mother, so proud of you, the village's first girl to go to high school?

What Auntie Turia told you upon her return was a bomb: marriage! You had thought of everything except about getting married. You were speechless. She hadn't given you any details about her meeting or about her discussions with her sister and your father nor how they had taken the news. She simply explained that marriage was the best option for everyone. Never had you thought you would get married so early. Quite the opposite, because, at that time, all you thought about was your future. Your high school diploma, firstly. Then, a bachelor's in applied mathematics and an MBA. Finally, opening your own modern company capable of manufacturing high-tech trademarked products adapted for tropical climates. Wouldn't this premature marriage shatter that dream? Not necessarily, Auntie reassured you. All in all, it was better than being a single mother with no financial means. You could not count on your aunt's generosity forever. Whereas with a husband...

So, you accepted it. Your parents came to the city, and you had a traditional marriage in Auntie Turia's compound. Everything went well. You parents did not complicate things at all. They were happy with a symbolic dowry. The official wedding ceremony was held immediately and your father, Bible in hand, had even proudly escorted you to the Protestant church for the nuptial blessing. The only one missing was your late grandmother along with her ancestral procession and the statues symbolizing their powers. But Auntie Turia was, once again, at the center of everything. She chose your wedding dress, supervised every aspect of the ceremony, led the procession to the house of your husband, a delighted Tito Rangi, as if he had been waiting for you all his life. She helped the two of you begin your life as a young couple and, most importantly, as young parents when your first child was born.

Oh, how Auntie had been right! Gradually, you learned to appreciate Tito. Initially, it was not true love like every teenager imagined, kissing under a starry sky, but your love for each other increased gradually, deepening at its own pace. You had established trust and complicity between you, which became stronger when your child was born. Tito was so kind, so available, always ready to satisfy your every desire. And Auntie was happy to see the two of you, happy to have contributed to her niece's happiness. She had become more important to you than your own mother. She was the one to whom you would run anytime you had a problem you could not solve. And she is still there for you now, always so generous, always so ready to help...

Enough about the past. You need to wash up, eat, and sleep because tomorrow will be as rough as today. Not your usual routine fighting stone. No. Tomorrow your fight is with the men who shamelessly want to exploit you. You get up and go over to get the bucket. You must have been daydreaming for a long time because the water is not very hot anymore. You reignite the gas and leave the bucket to warm up while you get ready for the shower.

The shower does you some good. Now you are only thinking of one thing: collapsing onto the folded mat and thick blanket which is your bed since you gave up your actual bed to Lyra and Batatou's child. And that is exactly what you do after devouring—God, were you hungry! —the dish your aunt prepared. You lie down naked beneath your pagne. After a while, you bring your knees to your chest to caress them, then stretch out, sighing languidly. You think about your body, how it has not been touched in over a year... You let your hand linger over your breasts, still firm despite two pregnancies, place it flat on your stomach and start massaging for a moment, then move it downward to play with your pubic fuzz. You are moist between your legs and have butterflies in your stomach. You continue touching yourself. Now you are completely relaxed. Lying on your side curled up into a ball, you place a pillow between your thighs. You pull your knees up a little more.

This fetal position allows you to better place the pillow between your legs. You squeeze your thighs and let your imagination make love to your body as you slowly drift off into a deep sleep.

THIRTEEN

IN THIS COUNTRY, seeing a police car stopped in front of your house at five in the morning is never good. Nor at five thirty, because it is five thirty when a white van, whose siren seems to be regulating the sound frequencies and rhythms of its flashing lights stops suddenly in front of your compound.

When you hear the brakes screech to a halt and the sudden silence of the siren, you know that the raid is targeting your house. You jump up from your makeshift mattress, rush to the living room, lift the net curtain a couple of inches, and look out the window. Three men rush out of the van like jack-in-the-boxes. One is wearing a pair of black glasses and brandishing an AK-47. They give two rifle butts and four kicks to your entrance gate, a sheet of corrugated metal nailed to a wooden frame held together by two leather straps functioning as hinges. It comes crashing down, and the three men walk right into your courtyard.

The first to your front door is the officer with the Kalashnikov. He is definitely the commando leader because he is the one to shout after they beat down your door with their rifle butts: "Open up and come out with your hands up! And make it quick, or else I'll shoot!"

The man is out of control. You must open the door quickly before he follows through with his threats. As you are heading towards the door, you realize that you are naked underneath your *pagne*. You panic. You run to your room and very quickly throw on some underpants. Then you grab whatever is in arm's reach. Your work clothes: an old pair of jeans worn to shreds from kneeling on the gravel and a t-shirt, faded from all your sweat and multiple washes. You barely get the t-shirt over your breasts when the plywood door is smashed to pieces. Two of the three men are already in the living room when you get back, overturning chairs and knocking over the table. Their leader, the gunman, has the rifle pointed at you, apparently to cover his men. Your two boys wake up with a start, terrified. They hug each other tightly, standing up against the wall, while in their room the two little girls, who had also been woken up by the all the ruckus, start to cry. And you, helpless, and not understanding anything, stand there frozen like an idiot, mesmerized by the barrel of the gun which is staring you in the face.

"Are you Méréana Rangi?"

"W… W… Why?" you finally manage to stammer. "What is going on?"

"Are you, Méréana? … Answer…"

"Yes, yes, that's… that's me… but what is going on… What did I do?"

"Let's go! We're taking you in. Outside!"

A quick mental flashback: the women's spokesperson perched on a chair, lambasting law enforcement, calling for disobedience so you can retrieve your bags of gravel. You understand everything now. In this country, people can disappear without a trace. The entire world must know that you have been picked up, otherwise you are a goner. You need to be shrewd. You ask if you can go get your shoes in the bedroom. "No dilly-dallying!" shouts the leader with the AK-47.

Your aunt's number is programmed on autodial. Press one right button and it will ring on the other end. Quick, Auntie, pick up! She picks up.

"Auntie, the police have come to arrest me. Come quickly. The children are alone." You hang up immediately. No more than ten seconds. Armando. You dial his number:

"Armando, warn the other women. The police have come

to arrest me."

Six seconds. You are finally pretending to look for your shoes when you see one of the men sticking his head in through the bedroom door frame, to make sure you are not trying to escape. You have just enough time to slide your feet into your sandals, those cheap plastic sandals that Chinese merchants sell at the markets.

You come out of the bedroom and, suddenly, decide to resist. Why would you let yourself be dragged like a docile sheep being brought to be sacrificed? You tell them that you refuse to leave, that in a country under the rule of law, citizens are not arrested without an arrest warrant and certainly not at five in the morning. You should not have said that! It is too much for them. One of them pulls you toward him and toward the door. You push him away. He shoves you and sends you flying out of the house. You try to regain your balance with several small hurried steps to no avail and fall on your behind. Angry, you instinctively try to kick the officer leaning over you, trying to pick you up. Although you do not manage to reach him with your kick, he gives you a hard slap which slashes your bottom lip. Blood stains your t-shirt.

"Handcuffs," shouts the leader.

Despite your awareness of how useless your movements are, you keep kicking. It takes two of them to pull your arms behind you and put on the handcuffs. They drag you into the street by force. Your two boys snap out of their drowsiness and follow you into the street screaming and crying for their mom. A crowd of onlookers has already gathered in front of your compound, drawn by the sirens and the men in uniform. The police throw you into their white van. Again, the sirens, the flashing lights and they shoot off at top speed.

●

You are particularly afraid because you do not know where they are taking you. Central headquarters would have been reassuring, or even the prison, though you know that people are tortured in those places too. But at least those are official places where they are careful now that no one dies there, ever since that scandal three months ago when about twenty people died from suffocation. There were thirty of them piled up in a cell which should not have even held fifteen. No, what you fear most is them bringing you elsewhere, to one of those unmarked places which do not even figure on the maps of human rights groups, and there were plenty of those places. You study your abductors. Hard to say whether they are army, police, or military police, their outfits being a hybrid mix of the three uniforms. Anyway, nothing surprises you anymore in this country where the different militias, incorporated into law enforcement after the accords that put an end to the civil war which ravaged the country for so long, often dress imaginatively.

Your worry, however, is replaced with bewilderment when you realize that the cop car is heading neither to the prison nor to an unknown location. Instead, the vehicle's route is familiar to you: the sandy road leading up to the main paved avenue, the roundabout, a right turn, going up the avenue that goes to the stadium, passing the boulevard where the big military parades happen, a left turn... Your brain records each of these topographical details through the small, barred window which allows a little light to filter into the inside of the truck. Your confusion only grows when the vehicle, after taking a series of turns at top speed like the police cars do in American movies, finally stops: you end up in the courtyard of the Ministry of Women and Disabled Persons. That's a puzzler!

•

Two rows of seats facing each other form a hallway in a building which is not much to look at: this is where the agents who kidnapped you leave you after they take off your handcuffs. They smoke and talk outside, leaving you alone, knowing that you cannot escape. You understand that this is the waiting room. You hesitate for a moment then choose the seat you think is the most comfortable, among the wine-colored faux-leather armchairs whose shabby appearance is accentuated by their headrests and seats, clearly worn by the numerous necks and bottoms to whom they have offered a haven of rest while their owners waited anxiously for the minister to deign to receive them even for a minute. If as the sign indicates it really is the Ministry of Women and Disabled Persons, it must not be of the highest priority for the government when you compare it with the Ministry of Oil and Mining where your steps led you several times when building your case asking for a triple therapy treatment for your sick sister, a case which remains open, by the way. But why have they brought you here?

Now that you are seated alone in this hallway which resembles a tunnel, your mind starts racing. Why they came looking for you is a no-brainer. You are the spokesperson for the women and your demands must be starting to seriously tick off the law enforcement officials. But why bring you to the Ministry of Women and Disabled Persons instead of to the Ministry that deals with issues of police and public order, the Ministry of the Interior?

The only plausible explanation is that the Minister wants to receive you and talk. After all, isn't she in charge of women's issues? But you dismiss that idea because who are you anyway but some unknown woman among thousands of others who are toiling away in this country, with no degree, separated from your husband, a single mother, a stone breaker, so why would a State Minister waste her precious time receiving you? And then, as far as you know, demanding a better price for merchandise is not an issue that is particular to women. And, besides, for a meeting with a high-level state authority, you do not go drag someone out of their bed in the wee hours of the morning. You finally make up your mind: they have brought you here to give you an earful, to order you to put a stop to your movement immediately. Who better to bawl out a woman than another woman? But you will not let yourself be intimidated. You will defend your cause. After all, what does the Minister know—she does not even do her own daily groceries—about women's daily struggles?

The wait is becoming long. You think of the children.

Auntie Turia must certainly already be at the house. And what about Armando? What was he able to do? You tap on your jeans pocket and notice that in your haste and panic, you did not have the reflex to slip your phone in there.

The Ministry's civil servants start arriving one at a time. Most of them ignore you, but some, surprised to see you there, acknowledge and greet you with a nod of the head. However, none dares speak to you. After a minute, the cop leading the mission comes and sits next to you. He does not have his black glasses or his Kalashnikov. Nor does he say anything to you. You wait. Finally, a secretary comes out and tells him that the Minister is ready to receive him with his package. He gestures for you to get up and the two of you follow the lady, him behind, you in front. The secretary opens the door, lets you in, then disappears.

In all your life, you have never entered a Minister's office, much less met a real live Minister. With your cheap plastic flip-flops, your dirty jeans frayed in places, your blood-stained t-shirt, yellowed from absorbing your sweat and the quarry's ochre dust, with your swollen lip and disheveled hair, feeling intimidated in spite of yourself and not knowing what to do, you stop midway between the door and the Minister's office.

Never would you have imagined that a Minister could be so dumbfounded! Her mouth wide-open, her eyes spellbound, she is looking at you as if the ceiling had fallen on her head or as if an extraterrestrial had landed in her office.

"But... but... what... what is going on?" she asks.

Finally, she looks past you and at the police officer.

"Boss, this is the person you asked us to bring in first thing this morning..."

"But... but... you beat her up? What is wrong with you? Did I tell you to brutalize her?"

"Resisting arrest, boss! She kicked us and even tried to bite us."

"Well, I would have done the same if I had been treated

like that! Once a henchman, always a henchman. You make me ashamed. That is not how we treat citizens... I am shocked, Madam, and I am truly sorry about this. What they did to you is unacceptable. You cannot stay in that state. Go home and take the time to wash up and get dressed. I will be in my office all morning. I will give instructions for how to get in when you come back. Sorry once again, Madam, and my apologies."

She turns toward the police officer:

"Bring her back home immediately. Treat her with dignity and respect. Understood? Otherwise, you will be dealing with me."

"Yes, boss."

He gives the military salute. You do not say anything, because you do not know what to say before a Minister who is angry and apologizing. A Minister who apologizes is unheard of in your country! You simply bow as a sign of respect. When you start moving to follow the agent, she upbraids him once more, her anger still obvious:

"Bring her back in my car, understood? With the motorcade."

"Yes, boss."

He practically stands at military attention when he opens the door for you.

FOURTEEN

A COP ON a motorcycle, ear-piercing siren blaring, followed by a Minister's car. In the car, you, Méréána, sit in the back, while your former jailer-turned-guardian-angel sits up front beside the driver. You look around as you pass through the city and watch in disbelief as your car goes through red lights without stopping and vehicles get out of the way or pull off the road, as traffic officers windmill their arms directing them to move aside. You are totally confused. For a minute you even think that somewhere in your brain your neurons have short-circuited: a few hours earlier you were beaten, handcuffed, and thrown into a paddy wagon. A few hours later, here you are sitting comfortably on the back leather seat of a ministerial car accompanied by a bodyguard and a cop on a motorcycle. You do not know where you are anymore. You have completely lost your sense of time.

Obviously, a Minister's car accompanied by a motorcycle cop does not go unnoticed in a poor neighborhood. A crowd of onlookers has already gathered before the vehicle even stops. Those people are definitely wondering what a State authority is doing here, showing up at this place which has never been at the center of its concern except during electoral campaigns when it sends its agents to distribute money or t-shirts and *pagnes* with the faces of its candidates and of the big Chief stamped on them. The bodyguard is back to his old self. Sporting his black glasses, he opens his door the very second the driver puts on the brakes and a second after that, his hands are already on your door handle as the vehicle comes to a full stop. Between the moment he clicks on the handle to open the door for you and when you get out of the vehicle, during that small fraction of a minute, complete silence falls as if all the people there were holding their breath, waiting to see the illustrious figure who was about to appear. And who do they see get out of the car? A woman hideously dressed, in cheap plastic sandals, hair disheveled like an old widow, with a swollen lip, Méréana! But who cares? Their eyes do not register that. They are all entranced by the symbols of power, the car, the motorcycle, the bodyguard. When they recognize you, their neighbor, they break into hearty, spontaneous applause. You catch bits of chatter here and there: "Méré's been appointed minister…", "Finally, we have a minister in the neighborhood too…", "She knows my two unemployed children well…", "I haven't received my pension for three months, Méré will take care of it…" and so on. Auntie Turia, no doubt alarmed by all the hubbub, shows up too. Surprised, she stands frozen, her eyes darting back and forth between the car and the motorcycle on one side, you on the other, her head bouncing back and forth like a ping-pong ball. You raise your hand and wave. The gesture is met with another round of applause. You walk over to Auntie Turia, put your arm around her waist and the two of you disappear into your courtyard.

Your children come running to greet you. They are all fine. As expected, Auntie Turia has taken very good care of them. To her question: "Am I crazy or what? You leave me a desperate message saying that you've been kidnapped, and then you show up at home in an official car, carefree, like a princess. What is going on?" You joke, saying: "Haven't you heard? I've been appointed Oil Minister." She shakes her head as if she has definitively made up her mind about you. It is clear now: her niece has lost her marbles.

You become serious again and tell her what happened to you. She in turn tells you how panicked she was, how she rushed over to your place to find Armando already there with his taxi. The poor guy this very minute must be sweeping every prison and police station trying to find you. Hearing that, you call him right away on his cell. He is very happy and tells you that he will arrive shortly. What a nice guy, that Armando! You can finally get ready.

•

What does one wear to go meet a Minister, especially when you have not bought any clothes in at least a year? You wonder if you even still know how a distinguished woman must dress, since all you wear every day is your stonebreaker's outfit, a pair of jeans and a t-shirt, the same outfit you threw on this morning when they came and nabbed you. You rummage through your closet. You start with the *pagnes*. You take one out that isn't too faded, tie it around your waist, put on the blouse, tie the head wrap, look at yourself in the mirror. No, you don't like that one, you don't feel good in it. You take it off and throw it hastily onto the bed. You take out another, then another. You have the feeling they are all out of style. Then you remember the two big *boubous* you brought back from a trip to West Africa a long time ago. The first is a dark blue *bazin*, the neckline embroidered with golden lace. It has been at least a year since you last wore it. It looks good on you, but the dark blue color darkens your skin tone a little too much. Maybe the other one, a rich *bazin* in white fabric would illuminate your face better and emphasize your breasts. You unfold it and put it on. Unfortunately, you have lost a lot of weight. You're swimming in it. You throw it on top of the other clothes strewn across the bed. What to do? You rummage again and you take out a dark brown linen ensemble that you have not seen for ages. You choose a beige caraco to go with it, which you button carefully, then you slip on the skirt and pull it up to your waist. When you zip it up, it fits perfectly on your hips. Then you put on the matching jacket over the caraco. You open your jewelry box and spill its contents onto the bed. The one-hundred-franc coin you keep there, a coin that's practically become a fetish, rolls onto the floor. You pick out some silver earrings. You put everything back into the box, including the coin. You try to put on some lipstick to cover up your injured bottom lip a little. Definitely not high heels, black loafers. You turn around and look at yourself several times in the mirror: you look like a professional and competent woman. The clothes sometimes do make the woman.

When you step into the living room, the reaction is unanimous: you are gorgeous! Everyone "oohs" and "aahs" in admiration. You are surprised to see so many people in your small living room. Auntie Turia has pushed the folding screen and the mattress it was hiding against the wall to make more room. The news of your arrest has traveled far and wide, so several women from the quarry, your comrades in struggle, are there, as are Armando and Laurentine Paka's husband. In fact, Laurentine, with her cell phone camera in hand is the first to shout: "Look how beautiful you are, Méré!", and the others follow with their comments. Laurentine and Anne-Marie even demand that you take a photo with them.

Since there is really not enough space in the living room, you have everyone go out into the courtyard so you can brief them quickly. You explain to them that you were invited by the Minister who oversees women's issues but instead of sending a formal invitation, you were dragged out of bed at five in the morning and beaten. The Minister lost her temper and ordered her agents to drive you back home in her official car so you could wash up and get dressed properly. That said, as for why you were invited in the first place, you give up, although you have an idea. What is it? Refusing to sell your gravel.

You propose gathering together after your meeting with the Minister at the same place as yesterday, under the big mango tree in the general hospital courtyard. Several people object to the choice of place because of the presence of interlopers. We have to keep to ourselves. Finally, you decide to meet here, at your house. Auntie Turia certainly will not be happy, since she is obsessed with the idea that you are "playing politics".

Everyone accompanies you to the car. Armando is devouring you with his eyes, you can feel it. So, you pay attention to the way you are walking, which makes you lose your natural gait and realize the way you swing your hips. You realize that you are not entirely indifferent to his presence in spite of what you claim. Thank God you didn't wear the heels.

The driver is already behind the wheel and the moment the bodyguard sees you arrive, he rushes to open the door for you and then stands there straight as a pole. The complete reverse of the way he threw you into the paddy wagon! As a rather childish revenge, you intentionally make him stew in his own juices as you take your time getting to the car, stopping to say a word to Laurentine who is taking a selfie next to the vehicle, asking Auntie Turia a question that takes her a while to answer, asking Armando to do whatever it takes to contact the other women from the quarry… Finally, you reach the car. The guard steps aside. You get in, sit down in the back on the right side, settle in comfortably, and cross your legs. He shuts the door and hurries to get into his seat in the front, next to the driver. The motorcycle revs its big engine, activates its siren and you're off.

Not for long. You have not gone more than ten yards when the front right wheel suddenly hits a pothole. You are thrown forward and, if you had not had the reflex to grab the back of the bodyguard's seat, your skull would have shattered against the ceiling of the vehicle. The engine stalls from the impact.

"Come on, pay attention, for fuck's sake, the guard lashes out at the driver, then turns his head toward you as if he realized how vulgar his language was and says: "Oh, sorry, madam. You know how these neighborhood roads are…"

"You don't have to tell me, I live here," you retort, settled back into your seat looking as serious and dignified as the Queen of England.

The driver is frantic. He has restarted the engine and managed to get the car out of the hole by slamming on the gas only to promptly end up stuck in the sand. Despite the driver's frenzied acceleration, the car will not budge. Its wheels are just spinning. At least it is not the rainy season. You would be in a real quagmire. Still with your haughty grande dame attitude, you call out to the bodyguard:

"For Christ's sake, do something!"

He gets out of the car and starts to push. Deep down, you are really enjoying yourself as you watch this man who dared to handcuff you early this morning pushing, panting and sweating. Is this what revenge is? The car still does not budge. Suddenly, a swarm of kids, thrilled by the spectacle, swoop down onto the car, laughing, screaming, and chirping like birds. They start pushing it.

Their combined arm strength causes the car to finally get out of the sand-filled crater.

"One hundred francs, one hundred francs," the children scream, demanding their reward.

Your guardian angel pretends not to hear them and dives into the car, which peels out before he even shuts his door. The kids pursue you for a minute then give up as you leave them in the dust. You take pleasure in making one last quip at your torturer turned guardian angel:

"Your bosses don't need to make roads in our neighborhoods since they all drive 4x4 SUVs."

You have reached the main avenue. Once again, all the vehicles pull over so you can pass. So, this is what power is! You close your eyes and inhale the smell of the leather seats. You savor the coolness of the air conditioning. No stones to break, no dust, no scorching sun, no sweat... Now you understand why in a poor and above all else corrupt country like yours, people not only hold onto power but are ready to kill to keep it. You understand the three-thousand-dollar suites at hotels, the seven hundred fifty-dollar bottles of champagne, the mistresses...

Life has its bag of tricks: not in your wildest dreams would you have ever imagined that one day, setting out to demand a better selling price for your bags of gravel you would end up all dolled up in the back seat of a ministerial luxury car with a bodyguard and escort. Oh, if only Tamara could see you now!

Finally, the ministry courtyard. Your Cerberus does not bring you through the waiting room. Instead, he takes you through a hidden door that leads directly to the secretary's office. The latter is not surprised to see you. Quite the contrary! She receives you as if she has been waiting for you. She stands up at once and tells you respectfully that she is going to see if the Minister is alone and ready to receive you. She comes back immediately and, with the same consideration, takes you to her boss's office.

FIFTEEN

SEATED AT HER desk, the Minister welcomes you with a wide smile and points to the sofa. You sit down.

"One second, I'll be right with you. I am almost done signing some urgent papers."

When that soldier brought you into this same office early this morning, you were still shaken and startled and had not really looked at the Minister. All you registered was her anger which now seemed to be quelled. Now that you are seated on this sofa, although tense and still a bit intimidated, you have the time to observe her as she signs her important documents.

She is older than you, you would say late forties. Or fifty? Short, straightened hair with bangs, lots of makeup, her lips glistening in red, she is wearing a tailored V-neck fuchsia blouse, low-cut enough to show her up-lifted bust. You find her earrings very chic, white gold with inlaid diamonds, although they are a little gaudy, the kind of jewelry people buy duty-free at airports or on planes. She must have quite a few miles on her Frequent Flyer card. And you thought you were so chic and stylish in your classic brown ensemble!

"There," she says.

You flinch and immediately lower your eyes, not to be caught out by your gaze revealing you were watching her.

"Marguerite?" she shouts.

The secretary hurries in, as if she were waiting to be called.

"I signed the urgent letters. The others can wait. I will sign them as soon as I've finished with Madam Méréana."

"Yes, Madam." She takes the file and exits.

You stand up. The Minister stands up, walks around her desk and waits as you, still intimidated, walk toward her.

She takes off her glasses, tries at first to put them in the right pocket of her blouse but ends up hanging them in the notch of her V-neck. You notice right away that she is wearing leather pants. They do not make her look tawdry, which is not easy especially when a woman is not very thin. You finally have the chance to see her from head to toe. With her sleek hair that makes you imagine that she spent quite a bit of time and dropped lots of cash at the hair salon, her makeup, her designer pants and blouse, her leather open-toe heels, she is the archetype of those middle-aged African women, with very Europeanized beauty, who are often heads of ministerial departments or representatives of their country in international organizations. She extends a jeweled hand to you. You take it in yours and shake her hand respectfully. You cannot tell whether the glimmering jewel on the ring is a diamond.

"Let's sit down."

"Let's sit down," she said, not "sit down": worldly woman. She knows how to welcome people and put them at ease. You sit down on the upholstered chair across from her and she settles into her ministerial armchair.

"You are better than you were this morning," she says with a wide smile. "You're gorgeous, I love your ensemble."

"Thank you."

"Coincidentally, brown and orange are my favorite colors. I didn't say it, but all my friends are outraged every time they visit me because I had my entire kitchen painted orange."

This trivial ice breaker relaxes you a little. You smile but say nothing. She studies you for a moment then goes on:

"Once again, I am truly sorry about the way my agents treated you. I did not ask them to arrest you. I am the Minister of women's issues and, if anyone is supposed to be aware of a woman's daily problems, it is me. When I found out that some women were beaten by the riverside, I naturally wanted to know more about it. My agents indicated that you were the person to see. I asked my cabinet to contact you right away to arrange a meeting. And they kidnap you! No matter how much we explain to them that democracy is also respecting citizens, they still do not understand. Dear me, it is hopeless! I insisted on having you escorted back home in my car to set an example, to teach them a lesson. Anyway, let's forget all that, and thank you for coming."

You are pleasantly surprised by her words. "Thank you for coming," she said? The idea that one could turn down such an invitation from the Minister, much less to be treated with such respect in the formality of her office had never occurred to you. Just to hear her saying the words "thank you" makes you sympathetic towards her or, rather, inclines you to trust her.

"Thank you, Madam, I... I do not know what to say. I admit that I did not think I would be received and treated with so much respect by a Minister, especially after the beating my friends and I endured the day before yesterday, and after the way your agents dragged me out of bed by force this morning. Thank you very much, I am sincerely humbled by your words."

"Don't thank me," she says with an affable smile. "Respect for the citizen should be the norm. I heard that one of you was in a coma."

"Yes, Madam Batatou, the mother of two surviving children of triplets."

You watch her. She closes her eyes for a fraction of a second like a boxer who has taken a punch that hurt him but does not want to exteriorize the pain, then she asks:

"Tell me exactly what happened."

Encouraged by her words, you explain. The more you talk, the more confident you feel. She is a minister, she is in the government, and she takes care of women: if someone could do something for you, if someone could change the situation, she could. Isn't that what a minister is for? You finish your briefing with a description of the clash with the police and conclude with an appeal:

"Is wanting to sell our bags of gravel for twenty thousand francs instead of ten thousand a threat to the Republic and the government? We have already suffered too much, Madam, and on that we will never compromise!"

She is silent for a moment following that last sentence which you uttered so passionately. You wonder if you have come on too strong. Careful Méré, do not antagonize her after all her gestures of goodwill toward you.

"First," she says, "you need to calm down. You do not need to accuse the government for its blunders, and blunders exist everywhere, even in the countries that are examples of democracy like France or the United States of America. Obviously, that does not mean people cannot do anything about them and I have not been indifferent to the situation. I lost my temper when I found out that not only did they beat you, but that they also shot live bullets at you. Shooting at women who are merely demanding a better price for their merchandise is unacceptable, at least for me. My role is to help you, but above all else I want to be clear about the story. Can you honestly tell me that there is really nothing else behind this demand?"

"Of course, Madam. What do you mean, nothing else behind this demand?"

"I just want to be sure that no one is behind this, that this is not political manipulation."

The question disappoints you a little coming from her because she is showing that her mind works just like all those men and women who have an ounce of authority, for whom any spontaneous demand cannot exist. On the other hand, it is a legitimate question given her position.

"You can be sure," you reply firmly.

She opens a file and takes out the UROFC leaflet you had read in Armando's taxi. You are so shocked you start to panic.

"So, you are telling me you have never seen this."

Her tone has changed. Her tone is curt, and any trace of affability has disappeared from her face. So, this was all a façade?

"Well, yes, Madam, I have even read it. They are doing what they want, and it has nothing to do with us."

"Yeah, you want me to believe that a group of illiterate women, a bunch of little drudges living hand-to-mouth took the initiative to plan a protest march in front of a police station and no one is behind it pulling the strings?"

"I am surprised to hear you say that, Madam, how can you say that you promote women's rights if you have such contemptuous ideas about them?"

"It is not contempt. I know my people better than you do."

That irks you deeply and you lash out at her, losing control:

"You sound like the White people who used to say: 'I know my niggers'. We are not your negresses, Madam."

The words had barely come out of your mouth and you regret them already. You must not forget that that woman is the minister after all. You become afraid.

"What are you saying? Do you think that I don't know that you are the leader?"

"I am not leading anything, Madam," you say trying to sound respectful.

"Well, what on earth made you force those poor unarmed women to attack the security forces? That was so stupid!"

You do not know what has come over you, but in an act of childish pride, undoubtedly piqued by the word "stupid", you say: "We were not unarmed. We had our stones!"

"And what did that get you, besides a poor woman in a coma?"

You say nothing. You are starting to get the feeling that maybe you have not explained yourself well, maybe your words made her believe that you were the ones who first assaulted those soldiers and their commander.

"Didn't you threaten to march on the police station and, who knows what else, maybe after that on the presidential palace itself? Are you trying to tell me that my sources are lying? And do you know where I get that information?"

"We are women demanding a better price for our bags of gravel."

"Women who throw stones... women who stone the security forces."

"They shot at us with assault rifles, Madam."

"Because you cast the first stone. And you are their leader, right?"

"I am only their spokeswoman."

"It's manipulation! Why did you choose this specific moment to make your demands?"

"Because the circumstances warranted it..."

"That's right! Exploiting the meeting of the first ladies of Africa to wreak havoc!"

"That is not true! We did not even know that there was a meeting of first ladies of Africa. All we are demanding are our twenty thousand francs... "

"You do not throw women out on the streets for twenty thousand francs! Do not take me for an idiot! You will not sabotage this conference for twenty thousand francs! And take me down with you!"

She is silent for a moment and takes a good look at you. Since you are maintaining a respectful silence, she resumes more calmly, conciliatory even.

"Television cameras from the entire world are watching our country right now. This meeting is very important because it is celebrating the tenth anniversary of the meetings of the wives of African Heads of State. What could be more ridiculous than seeing women being violently repressed, displayed on screens across the world while these ladies are meeting? If such a case were to occur, who would be the first to be criticized? Me! And my ministry. They will say I am incompetent. I only ask you one thing: Put an end to your movement immediately. You could pick it back up after the meeting when the eyes of the world are no longer on us. And you have my word. I will then support you to the end, one hundred and fifty percent. This is important to me and to the ministry. It is practically a matter of national interest!"

So that was it! All that kindness was not for your beautiful stone breakers' eyes, but for her ministry, for her to ingratiate herself with the President and his wife. In response to her suggestion to resume your demands when the cameras of the entire world are turned away from your country, you want to say: "So that you can repress us even more violently behind closed doors," but you resist your impulse and reply reasonably.

"Twenty thousand francs is perhaps nothing to you but for many of us it can mean the difference between life and death, Madam."

You feel your tone of voice is just right, calm, collected and respectful. It has an effect on her because she gives you that affable grand dame smile again…

"Madam Méréana, let's be serious. Tell me exactly what it will take for you to stop clamoring."

You like the question because it is direct, straight to the point. A simple and direct question requires a simple and clear response, especially one that is operative. Her response to your response will allow you to determine whether, behind her lip service, she is truly capable of making decisions. You need to be as clear as possible. And convincing.

"First thing: Make them give back our bags of gravel which were stolen by the police."

"Let's say confiscated, because the police do not steal."

"For us, it is theft, Madam. They have no right to steal the fruits of our labor, of our sweat. That we will never accept!"

"Noted. I will discuss it with the Minister of the Interior, and he will listen to me now that he knows I have the backing of the President's wife."

"And what if they cannot locate our bags?"

"I will do everything in my power to compensate you."

"At our new price: twenty thousand francs, not a cent less."

"I will do my best."

"Second: Those who attacked us yesterday must be punished. Do we not have laws in this country? Or does the law not apply to us because we are women? One of our friends is in a coma. Who is going to take care of her orphans if she does not come out of it? Her hospital bill is already three hundred thousand francs. Where will we find the money?"

"I will advocate on your behalf for the State to take care of those costs, but I'm telling you now, it will not be easy."

"Why not? Politicians and their relatives are evacuated abroad for health reasons for less than that, sometimes for a cold, without even seeing the expense!"

"Whoa, hold on. Let's not exaggerate."

"I am not exaggerating anything. Do you really know the extent of our suffering, Madam?"

Her friendly façade cracks once again and is replaced with a stern look and a pontificating voice.

"Your suffering? You may not know it, but I was appointed Minister of Women because I specialize in their suffering. And I did not sleep my way to the position in case you were ever inclined to believe that. I have attended more than twenty national and international conferences on women's problems, and I know all the statistics. Do you want me to tell you about it? About male domination over women? About domestic violence, dowry disputes, forced marriage? About widow inheritance? About rape and resorting to rape as a weapon of war? About genital mutilation? About witchcraft, AIDS, malaria? About gender vulnerability which can only be fought by enhancing women's capacity and empowerment? And with all that, you want to suggest that I do not know about women's suffering? Do you know that when my ministerial term is over, I will look for international funding to create an NGO dedicated to improving women's access to economic resources?"

She stops to catch her breath. Does she think you are impressed by this discourse which is nothing more than the official politically correct human rights discourse international institutions promote, with their formatted vocabulary and loose consensus? Does she not know that you are Tamara's sister? Tamara who, when she came back from one of those conferences or meetings, would often describe this type of woman to you, the type that international institutions recruit as experts, be they ministers, directors of various projects or of NGOs, consultants and other types, who are worldly, flawless in communication and public relations, who fly from international conference to international conference, all expenses paid, but who in reality often know nothing about life on the ground. Out of everything she has just told you, there was not one concrete example regarding your daily experiences.

What does she know about how hard your work is, how much labor is necessary to shatter a large rock under the heat of a wood fire or of burning tires, the dangers involved in turning the large blocks from the shattered rock into rubble, the time needed to produce a bag of gravel, the price you women pay with your bodies, not to mention the numerous accidents? You say nothing. Your silence makes her believe that you are blown away, impressed by her performance and that you no longer doubt her expertise and competence. Assured that she has reestablished the natural order of things, she becomes more conciliatory and her affable smile from the beginning of your conversation returns.

"I'm going to tell you what I have already done to show you that I take this problem very seriously. When my agents informed me that several of you were incarcerated at the prison, I immediately picked up the phone and called the Minister of the Interior. As expected, he almost sent me packing. He spoke to me about "troublemakers", and "reestablishing order, especially now", as if the Republic's defense depended entirely on him. He is one among many who thinks that the Ministry of Women and Disabled Persons is nothing but a foil to attract the international community's good graces in order to receive development aid. But no, my ministry does not take a back seat and now more than ever is the time to show it.

"As Vice-President of the meeting's organizing commit-tee, I have direct access to the President's wife. Immediately af-ter I was rebuffed by the Minister of the Interior, I was able to reach her on the phone. I played the fear card. I painted a dra-matic picture of the situation, arguing that if the prisoners were not released immediately, thousands of women would rush to the palace where the meeting was happening. I let her imagine the consequences.

"Every cloud has a silver lining, in the sense that in most of our countries in Africa, the President's wife has a certain authority over the members of government. Horrified by the idea of seeing a deluge of angry women broadcast on interna-tional television while the aim of the meeting she was presiding over was specifically to show off what she does to improve the lot of those very women, she took her cellphone and called the Minister right away. I don't know what they said to one another but less than half an hour after that phone call, your colleagues were released."

"Oh, the mystery is solved. We were all surprised at how easy it had been to get our friends released and particularly with no violence to us, the demonstrators."

That is how she manipulated the wife of the Head of State to free you, by turning you into horsewomen of the Apocalypse. A real powerful woman. Despite yourself, you cannot help but admire her, to tip your hat to her.

"That is my job. You can count on me for the rest. So, here's the agreement. I will work on getting your bags back and helping you cover your friend's hospital expenses, and you will help me by immediately stopping your demonstrations. It's a win-win situation."

"And also allow us to sell the rest of our bags for twenty thousand francs. Those we are not able to get back will be reim-bursed to us at the same price. That is not much to ask."

"You know, in any negotiation there is always a compromise. You do not always get what you want."

"We are not at that point yet, Madam."

"I know, I know. But you understand that I cannot just let women suffer and do nothing, so I am going to do my best. After all, it is for them, for you, that I am bending over backwards to this extent. Leave a list of the names of all the women who work at the quarry with you and your telephone number with my secretary. I may even contact you again before the end of the morning because I want to resolve this problem as soon as possible."

"I don't know how to thank you, Madam, for being kind enough to receive me and for hearing our version of the facts. Once again, I was very touched by the way you welcomed me, and I trust you."

She gets up and you do the same. When you clasp the hand she is extending to you, she studies your face as if she were trying to decode something that is beyond her control.

"I have to admit, when I read your file, I did not expect to speak with someone like you. You are educated, intelligent... How did you end up at a quarry breaking stone?"

"It's a long story but, you know, 'gender vulnerability' and 'women's lack of access to economic resources'..."

She is not sure how to take your answer.

"I see," she says. "I hope that we will have the opportunity to talk about it another time."

She hasn't seen anything. You also do not see when you will have the opportunity to tell her about your descent into this stone nightmare. You bow your head slightly and exit.

SIXTEEN

YOU LEAVE THE Minister's air-conditioned office and find yourself, a little disoriented, in the humidity of the street. Despite your having spent close to an hour in her office, you are not sure what to think of her, divided between antipathy and admiration. Everything is spinning in your head. You need to sit down for a moment to assess what you got out of your meeting with her and to give your mind a little time to digest all the information you were just bombarded with.

There is too much noise and bustle around you: you have to squeeze through all the passersby crossing your path, avoid the bicycles which all but ignore the rules of the road and come at you head-on on the sidewalk, the beeping putt-putting cars emitting noxious black smoke. You look at your watch. It is almost one o'clock. Knowing that it is past noon suddenly makes you hungry. You have not eaten anything since the morning and your metabolism is definitely in a hypoglycemic state because you feel a strange weakness come over you. Yes, you need to sit down and eat something and think. A nice glass of fruit juice will re-energize you.

You head to the first café you find, a nice enough place despite its pompous name, "Café des Anges." It is a bakery with an area reserved for customers to eat and drink. You sit down. It has been a long time since you set foot in a downtown tearoom and offered yourself the small pleasure of such simple things like a chocolate éclair, a butter croissant, an apple tart, or a little madeleine.

You pick up the menu, a rectangular card folded in half, placed upright on the table. Glancing quickly at it, you notice that the least expensive drink costs five hundred francs. In the neighborhood where you live, five hundred francs is a lot of money. With that much, you could order a mushroom or ham omelet, a cup of coffee with a side of buttered bread, and still have money left over. What do they do to be able to live here and afford such prices? You have two thousand francs on you. A Coke costs five hundred francs. An orange soda costs six hundred fifty. You are not in the mood for a Coke, but you feel you have to have one in order to save a hundred fifty francs, which is what a bus ticket back to your neighborhood costs.

You see the waitress arrive the very second you set the card down. A young girl who looks tired despite the smile displayed on her face. She probably started working very early this morning, a little like you, when you go to the quarry.

"Hello, madam, have you decided?"

Her voice is respectful, not the mechanical and indifferent voice of overextended café waiters working long hours. She looks at you. You can sense her admiration, her admiring your gorgeous brown ensemble which makes you look so sophisticated. She definitely sees you as the model professional woman she would have liked to be, instead of wandering from table to table at the beck and call of customers with often questionable behavior. You feel somewhat vain. You do not want to disappoint this young girl and give her the impression you are counting out your change as if you were tight-fisted.

"Orangina," you answer right away.

You barely have the time to take out your cell phone before she is back with the bottle. She shakes it well and serves you.

"That's six hundred fifty, madam."

You had forgotten that here you have to pay as soon as you are served. You hand her a thousand-franc bill. She rummages through her apron and hands you your change. Being generous, you tell her to keep it. "Oh, thank you, madam," she replies, pleasantly surprised, because here it is not customary to leave a tip. She leaves. You do not know why, but you are happy, and you take your first sip.

Now, call. Get in touch with the others. Share your news. You do not know why Armando's name comes to mind first. You justify it by telling yourself that it is because he has a taxi and could be a contact person. You have his number on speed dial so all you have to do is select it and press the green button.

"Méré, where are you?" a rushed voice says. "How did it go?"

"I finished with the Minister. I had a very interesting and encouraging discussion with her. I think we have a good chance of getting our bags of stone back and at the price we set. We have to meet immediately. I'm heading home right away."

"How are you getting home?"

"I'll jump onto the first bus."

"No, stay there, I'll come and get you. Where are you right now?"

"At Café des Anges".

"Oh, oh! That's why your voice sounds like an angel." You pretend not to hear the remark and you carry on:

"You don't have to come and get me, you know, I can take the bus."

"No, wait for me. I have a customer with me and I'm dropping him off downtown exactly in the area where you are. I'll be there in fifteen minutes. Stay there."

"Okay, if you insist. That will give me time to finish my drink."

"What are you drinking?"

"Never mind, take care of your customer. See you in a bit, thanks."

As soon as you take your first sip your thoughts return to the Minister. Your antipathy towards her is clear now. She is a woman of power who does not hesitate to manipulate people to get what she wants. In her power struggle with the Minister of the Interior, didn't she manipulate the President's wife by depicting us as a horde of furies ready to sweep down onto the presidential palace? And again, she had no reason to bawl out the person she sent on a mission in front of you, the military officer who dragged you out of bed at five in the morning. One does not humiliate one's subordinate like that for others to see. If she did it, it was deliberate, to make sure you would see that she was the one who wielded power, and you needed to know that. You see what she is up to now. She plans to exploit your protest movement to consolidate her career as Minister. Fake smile, fake compassion, how could anyone like such a person?

But no sooner have you reached that conclusion when your antipathy for her is replaced by admiration. In reality, she is a career woman, and you like career women. Wasn't your sister Tamara one? It is good that women like that exist so they can resist men, men like the Minister of the Interior who plays the macho man. After all, would it really matter if by exploiting the situation to save her job, it ended up achieving your demands? That would make her an objective ally more than anything else. Is she an opportunist? Why wouldn't a woman in politics be as opportunist as any average male politician? In the end, you like her. In fact, you have it wrong: the real criterion to gauge a politician is her effectiveness in solving problems, not her likeability or how nice she is. This minister, for the little you know about her...

Your phone rings and interrupts your ruminations. Auntie Turia? Or perhaps Atareta wanting to share news of Batatou? You look at the screen before putting it to your ear. You do not recognize the number.

"Hello, yes?" you say.

"Madam Méréana Rangi?"

"Yes?"

"This is the Minister's secretary. I'm the one who received you a while ago. It is urgent. The Minister wants to see you immediately. She is waiting for you in her office."

"But I just left!"

"I know, but it really is urgent. Where are you now?"

"Nearby, at the Café des Anges."

"Good, I will tell the Minister that you will be here in about ten minutes."

"What is this about?"

"I cannot tell you. All I know is that she wants to see you right away. You are top priority."

"Well, it must be awfully important. Alright, I'll be right there."

What now? Even if you have no reason to worry because, after all, the Ministry of Women is not the Ministry of the Interior where, as is well known, people summoned there sometimes disappear without a trace, it is still useful to inform your family members and friends when you receive such a pressing, unexpected invitation. Your phone indicates that you have less than six minutes left on your calling card. You must be careful and keep at least two for emergencies. You call Auntie Turia and give her the information, leaving her no time to ask useless questions that would use up the few remaining minutes. Armando. You dial his number, let it ring twice and hang up before he picks up. When he sees your number, he will definitely call you back. It's what you call "beeping". And you're right because he calls you back that very minute. You explain to him that you have been called back urgently to the ministry and you don't know why. He asks you to wait for him so he can go with you. You can't. So, he suggests following you to the ministry. You tell him that is not necessary and that he should continue cruising for customers instead. He refuses to listen and says he will wait for you at the entrance.

You get up to leave. On your left you notice the fresh, delicious pastries displayed on the shelves. You immediately think of your children when you see the madeleines. You feel a little guilty that you indulged yourself at the café without them. Except for the doughnuts, often too fatty from being deep-fried in palm oil, that you sometimes bring them in the evening, it has been a long time since you have brought them a real cake.

Sometimes you wonder if you are a good mother. There have been times you sent them flying when, getting back home exhausted from the quarry and needing some peace and quiet, the mere sound of their voices irritated you. Worse still, there were times you wondered whether it wouldn't be better to offload them on their father, so you could have some free time and breathe a little. Why should he live a cushy life with that bimbo for whom he bought a luxury car while you slave away like a forced laborer? After all, you did not make those children by yourself! Luckily, you collect yourself fairly quickly from those moments of lassitude.

Yes, you must admit, it is not easy to be a single mother.

You buy three madeleines with the money you have left, one for each child. After carefully wrapping them in parchment paper, you pack them in your purse. Indeed, it has truly been a while since your poor kids have gotten a special treat from their mother.

•

The secretary greets you with a big smile when you appear at her door, as if by showing up you just saved her job. She gets up and goes right away to tell the Minister that you have arrived. In less than a minute, a woman leaves the Minister's office. Her meeting was probably cut short or postponed because you are the priority, of course. She is elegant and dignified, wearing a greyish-brown blouse and a light violet *pagne*. The regal bearing of her neck is accentuated by her headwrap wound in a spiral. She looks at you and smiles questioningly, most definitely wondering what makes you someone more important than her.

The Minister stands to greet you. You can feel a sense of urgency, as if having you sit would have wasted precious minutes.

"I did not think I would call you back so quickly. Just after you left, I received a phone call from the President's wife. I do not know what the Minister of the Interior reported to her, but she was very upset with you. 'I want you to bring that girl to me, the one who is leading protests while I am about to receive distinguished guests. I want to see her before the end of the day,' she ordered."

"I am not leading protests," you object.

"You will have to explain that there."

"Am I really going to meet Madam President?" you ask in disbelief.

"Yes, and try to be polite. And respectful."

"I am always respectful, Madam."

"More than respectful, reverent! Don't forget that she is the wife of the Head of State. Go now, don't waste any time."

As soon as the secretary sees you leave, the lady whose meeting you interrupted gets up and asks her if she can go in now. The secretary tells her to wait a little until she is finished with you. Meanwhile, three other women have come to swell the ranks of those requesting an audience with the Minister.

Ironically, it is the same van that took you away this morning which will be taking you to the President's residence, with the same driver. This time no flashing lights, no sirens, no bodyguards. Since he is not aware that the Minister sent you home to change clothes in her official car with her own driver at the wheel, you can sense that he is confused and understands nothing, probably asking himself if he is living in a world that has lost all meaning: this morning he was driving a girl who was handcuffed, manhandled like a criminal, dressed in old clothes, and now she is this chic lady he is chauffeuring to the President of the Republic's residence. As a government driver, he has seen all kinds of things, so that nothing shocks him anymore.

When you exited the Minister's office, you could not find Armando's taxi even though he promised you he would be there. Perhaps he did not have time to get here yet, considering how brief the second meeting with the Minister was.

First rule of survival in this country: always inform someone of where you are going. You again hesitate between calling your close family, Auntie Turia, or Armando. With Auntie, you run the risk of her keeping the information to herself, or at least of her not getting the word out enough.

You end up settling on calling neither and decide instead to beep Laurentine Paka. You tell her that at this very moment, you are headed to the private residence of the President of the Republic where the First Lady has summoned you, and that she must let everyone know. She remains silent for several seconds as if her brain is incapable of processing the information just transmitted to her, then reacts: "Thank goodness you are well dressed! She will see that just because we crush stone, it does not mean we are incapable of getting decked out." Good old Laurentine!

You probably have only three or four more minutes left on your phone credit. You should save them so you can call the others after your meeting. You flip your cell phone shut, put it away and settle down for the ride to the private residence of the President of the Republic.

SEVENTEEN

IT IS EASIER to get into heaven than into the private apartments of the President of the Republic and the First Lady.

The first roadblock is at the tall gate that opens into the courtyard of the complex. The two soldiers guarding the roadblock ask where you are going and if you have a mission order or a summons. The driver explains. A call made to you-don't-know-who confirms that they are indeed waiting for you, just you, not the driver; he is asked to turn around. You therefore have to cover the last few meters on foot. As you watch the guards, you have a vivid recollection of the day Iyissou's son was arrested. He was coming back from a refugee camp when he was beaten, loaded into a truck and taken to an undisclosed destination. What if these soldiers had been part of the sinister commando that raided the landing docks of the city's river port that day?

You move toward the second roadblock, which is more sophisticated with a security booth, armed soldiers, and two tanks with their guns pointed toward the avenue that leads to the high wall surrounding the buildings and the entrance gate. You notice the video cameras that are no doubt recording your every movement.

A woman soldier frisks you, pats you down to make sure you are not hiding a bomb in your panties. She confiscates your cell phone, your bag of madeleines too, then waves you through. Apparently, you are no longer a danger to the Republic. Finally, you enter the premises of the President and First Lady's private residence.

First, the space. Coming as you do from a densely populated neighborhood where one's living space is a mere few square meters and where a small room, sometimes the same bed, is shared by several people, it is hard to fathom how one person could have so much space for himself. You admire the mown green lawn, the sprinkler spraying, its arms swiveling with each spurt of hydraulic pressure. Palm trees including the traveler's tree, with its fan-shaped leaves. Two magnificent peacocks are strutting about on the lawn, one spreading its beautiful tail spotted with specks of bluish sheen. A little further on, you can see deckchairs under umbrellas. And the pool, of course.

While you are staring in amazement at this verdant paradise, a guard calls out to you and signals to follow him to the waiting room. You pass by a garage where you count one Aston Martin, two Japanese SUVs and an empty spot. A Rolls-Royce perhaps? You let your imagination run wild for a split second: you have never seen a Rolls. Maybe, like the Minister of Women did, the First Lady will have you driven back in hers or in one of the luxury SUVs?

The guard escorts you into the sitting room and asks you to take a seat and wait your turn. You look around. My God! You wonder if you can lay your buttocks on one of those luxurious leather armchairs or, modestly, make do with one of the benches. While you are at it, you opt for the luxury armchair, after all, your buttocks are worth just as much as the country's First Lady's, right? The seat feels soft, you place your arms on the armrests and you settle comfortably into the chair. It's really much better than that armchair at the Ministry of Women and Disabled Persons, with its springs that poked through the back of the chair and kept you from nestling in. But you are not the only one in the room. Three other well-dressed women are waiting too, two squeezed on the sofa, the other, younger and alone, is sitting stiffly on one of the benches. They all outright ignore you, perhaps they take you for a rival who is here to beg for help from the woman the national radio calls the "Mother of the Nation." They continue to ostensibly watch the television or, rather, the televisions because there are five—two with giant screens—each tuned to a different channel. On the French-language channel, people are playing *Questions for a Champion*. One of the English channels is showing *American Idol*, the other, CNN, an American 24-hour news channel, is streaming more advertisements than news, and then there is the Arabic channel, Al-Jazeera. Just after showing some traditional dances, the last TV, tuned to a local channel, is re-airing the speech the Head of State gave last night.

Comfortably seated in your cushy chair, you look up at the ceiling. Although you are no expert in architecture, you are sure that those delicately molded geometric structures must have cost a fortune; you wonder if the faux rustic columns standing in the four corners of the room are made of real marble. At the end of the room, there is a bar and several bottles of wine and liquor lined up behind the counter. The space must also be used for receptions, you think. Maybe champagne, instead of water, would flow if you turn on the faucet you notice over there, behind the bar, since it seems to be the drink of choice in these circles. Your head begins to spin. Never before have you seen such luxury, never would you have imagined that in this country all you had to do was go through a gate to find yourself on the other side of the mirror, in a world where poverty and misery do not exist and where one does not have to break stone in order to survive. A world where one probably does not even die because how can death reach you when you live in the middle of such insolent luxury?

After waiting several minutes, you are called ahead of the women who were there before you into an office or rather a living room, and finally there you are, face to face with Madam First Lady. You've only seen her through televised news programs when she makes donations to Childhood-Solidarity, her organization which she describes as non-governmental, even though everyone knows it receives three quarters of its funding from State money. Plump, she is wearing, unlike the Minister, African attire which plays to her advantage, a three-piece ensemble, the pagne and the head wrap made from the same fabric. It makes her look dignified as a leader's wife should look, and at the same time gives her a reassuring maternal look. A little toward the back is a woman with a notebook, probably her secretary. No doubt about it, you are impressed. Without getting up, she says:

"You are Méréana Rangi?"

"Yes, Madam."

"Hello."

"Hello."

"Sit down."

You sit down, stiff, petrified almost. It is still difficult for you to realize that you are sitting there, face to face with the country's First Lady, in her residence. And yet, although the minister warned you that the President's wife was very upset with you, the few sentences she has spoken up to this point did not ring of anger.

"You are young. You could be my daughter, you know. You look nothing like the fury you've been described as. So, you're really rallying women against me?"

She hits you with those words suddenly, without warning. You are intimidated, you do not know how to react, or even what to say.

"Uh… uh…"

"Uh what? You know, I know everything."

"I think there's some misunderstanding, Madam First Lady. We're not rallying anyone against you, we're just women asking for a better price for our bags of stones."

"It seems you threw stones at the police. Is that reasonable?"

"We were under attack by gunfire."

"One of you is in a coma?"

"Yes, Madam."

"It's sad, all of that. So you see where it leads when one does not follow the appropriate channels to make protests? You've heard of the NGO Childhood-Solidarity, haven't you?"

"Yes, Madam."

"And do you know who runs it?"

"Yes. You do."

"So then, why didn't you come to see me to discuss your issues? Don't you know that that NGO also deals with women's issues?"

"Because... because... demanding a better price for one's merchandise is not a woman's issue."

"What bizarre reasoning. Are you a woman or not?"

"Yes, but not in this case."

She looks at you oddly.

"Excuse me? Sometimes you're a woman, sometimes you're not?"

"Uh... no... I'm talking about women's demands."

You are definitely doing a poor job of explaining yourself because she clearly does not understand and interrupts you, tactfully, not suggesting that something is out of whack in your brain.

"Listen," she goes on, "there's going to be a big women's celebration in our country. It will not just be a First Lady's event because as Mother of the Nation, I want all the women in our country to participate. There is no issue you could have that I cannot resolve."

"Our bags of stones... "

"I know. You want to sell them for twenty thousand francs, you want someone to return to you the bags that were confiscated by the police because you refused to obey and attacked the policemen. I know all of that. All of that will be taken care of; but, as that may take some time, I'm going to ask you one thing: cease your protests immediately and any demonstrations while the matter is being resolved. I do not want any unrest or any perception of unrest hanging over the country while my guests are here. I know you are a reasonable young woman, and that you would not want this conference or this country to fall apart. Nor would you want the President to be shamed in front of the rest of the world."

"It will be difficult for us to stop our protests because... "

"Listen, my child—I can call you my child because I am as old as your mother—you are their spokesperson. I've been told how well you speak, how at a meeting in the hospital courtyard you kept those women from marching on the police station. That's what I appreciate about you, the intelligent way you have of seeing a situation in front of you and the courage to change opinions about it. That's why, in spite of my very busy schedule at the moment, I took the time to meet with you and, better yet, I had you in before all those women you saw in the waiting room and who have been waiting for hours to be seen. That can only prove to you the high regard I have for you. I know those women will listen to you if you tell them to stop your protests while I address your matter. I give you my word that I will do that. Tito Rangi is a deputy now, and that's thanks to me. Better yet, he is an advisor to the President thanks to my intervention."

The mention of Tito's name irritates you.

"Tito has nothing to do with this."

"It's to make you understand that what I did for him, I can also do for you. You think I don't know anything about you? Your sister for example. We never met, but I respected her because she was a woman who honored our nation. Be responsible like she was. Ask the women to stop their protests. If they do, I will personally see to it that the matter is settled—I've already made it my business anyway. How do you think your comrades got released so easily after committing aggravated assault against the police?"

She stops speaking and looks at you, which means she is waiting for an answer.

"Because of your intervention."

"Exactly! I'll say it again, this meeting with the First Ladies, this big celebration of our country, is too important to me."

She stops again and looks at you. You say nothing, not because you don't know what to say, but because you are trying to figure out how to formulate a way you can articulate to the First Lady, the Mother of the Nation, your outright refusal to betray your friends by renouncing what has already cost you so dearly. Remind her that one of you is in a coma? Seeing that you are not taking the bait in spite of all the compliments she has showered you with, she says sharply:

"I know that you need a hundred twenty thousand francs."

With that, you panic a little. How did she know that? What else does she know about you?

She persists:

"A hundred twenty thousand francs is no problem. I am very sensitive to women's suffering and it's that sensitivity that can at times pass for maternalism. Helping women get by, gain their independence from men, helping them take their destinies into their own hands, it's what I live for. Otherwise, what would be the use of being the First Lady? And of being a mother? You may not know it, but I am also a mother."

"I fight poverty by going into the battleground, into villages where I distribute palm oil to women, medicine, powdered milk for their babies, mills to grind foufou and tables and benches for schools. Once I even took responsibility for the hospital bill of a woman who had given birth to quintuplets! Better yet, I insisted to my husband that the number of women in the next Parliament must double. We will thus move from fifteen percent of women today to thirty percent, a major step toward complete equality in a very near future. And then there's my program to fight HIV/AIDS. Heeding the advice of the Churches, I've just added abstinence and social reintegration of prostitutes because the fewer of those there are, the fewer people with AIDS and the fewer people at risk of contracting AIDS there will be. Know that this fight I am leading against AIDS and for development is cited as an example throughout the whole world. The choice of our country to host this important meeting is not by chance, but rather a consecration, a recognition of the work that I do. Do you see how important it is now? I am going to take care of your personal problem right away. For the rest of your demands, they will be dealt with immediately following the conference. I give you my word."

She turns to the woman you believe to be her secretary, who takes a thick manila envelope out of a drawer and hands it to Madam. The latter places it down conspicuously on her desk.

"In this envelope, there is well more than you need to get by. For your studies, for your future. It's yours."

You are absolutely stunned! You have heard about corruption, you know it is rampant in the country, but you have never confronted it. Up to this moment, there was absolutely no doubt in your mind that you were incorruptible but right there in front of you is that envelope. All you have to do is extend your hand, take it, put it in your purse, no questions asked, and all your problems will be solved. By tomorrow, you'll be able to pay the fees for your computer courses and in six months you can maybe open your own school, your own business, and just like that, realize the broken dream of your youth. And you will no longer deny your children the simple pleasures one is entitled to at that age. In any case, in life, one must know how to seize an opportunity and often that opportunity, unlike the mailman, rarely rings twice at your door. And after all, she stole that money from the State's coffers, right? That means it belongs to you a little as well. So, why not reap the benefits of it?...

With her experience in corrupting people, the lady has become adept at reading facial movements and can immediately detect who can be bought off right then and there and who will hesitate and need a little push to get over their wavering reluctance. She must consider you in the second category since, after observing you for a moment, she continues in a soft voice, intending to sound reassuring:

"What happens in this office stays in this office. No one will ever know anything. Here, take it."

For the first time since you have been in there, she stands up. Standing in front of you in her gorgeous outfit, her presence is even more intimidating. You look up at her. She walks toward you, the envelope in her hand. She holds it out to you. You look at the object, a fat manila envelope. It is sealed. You do not move an inch. She watches you for a moment then taps on your shoulder three or four times and says in a motherly tone: "Go ahead, take it, it's nothing, it's just to help you." You contemplate the object again for a few seconds then suddenly you grab it and shove it in your purse. The transaction is complete. You get up. Then, the great compassionate lady, modestly triumphant, wraps an arm around your shoulders and says with a knowing smile:

"Don't make it more of an issue than is necessary, my child. And don't worry, you are not the first person to be reasonable and choose where your priorities lie. In about two hours, a television crew will be advised about your meeting where you will release a press statement announcing that you have decided to cease your protests until the end of the First Ladies of Africa meeting. It will not be a betrayal. In fact, to the contrary, the President of the Republic will consider your decision a patriotic gesture toward the nation. Good luck. I'm counting on you."

She turns away from you and returns to her armchair. Her problem solved, she has already forgotten you. Her secretary escorts you out. If she were a man, you would consider her a "henchman" of the First Lady of the Republic. Can we also say "henchwoman"? Your mind does not register anything on your path out of the presidential residence. Only when the humid warmth suddenly assaults you do you realize that you have already exited the air-conditioned buildings. At the security booth, you are handed your cell phone but not your bag of madeleines. You ask for them. Threatening, the guard replies that all you left was your cell phone, nothing else. My God, soldiers who swipe madeleines? You do not insist. You take the phone and you put it in your bag on top of that manila envelope worth its weight in thirty pieces of silver.

EIGHTEEN

AN ARMED GUARD leads you out of the security perimeter of the presidential compound and leaves. You are now in the street, alone, on foot. You wonder what kind of fantasy went through your mind when, while marveling at the luxury cars neatly parked in their lot like thoroughbreds waiting in their starting gates, you dreamt for a few moments that you would be driven home in one of them.

You walk briskly. You grow irritated: the heat, the uncomfortable feeling of sweat under your armpits, the ensemble you thought was so classy, now stifling with its too tight caraco and too snug skirt. Thank God, you did not put on high heels. And your purse seems so heavy now with the envelope in it. Why did you accept the money? At any rate, you had no particular inclination whether to accept the money or not when you grabbed the envelope and stuffed it in your bag. Your gesture was automatic, a matter of course, a foregone conclusion. Why? You do not know. Or maybe subconsciously, up against her domineering presence, you got scared that she would be insulted by your refusal, and crush you on the spot, if you insulted her by refusing it. Or else, like a card player, you thought to play a clever hand, and attempt to outsmart her? But actually, you took that envelope spontaneously... like a fool! A sudden rage surges in you at that thought. You are furious at yourself for being slow-witted. The comebacks you should have made to that woman suddenly jostle in your head, clear and plain as day.

She says that she knows your suffering because she distributes gifts in villages, but since when, Madam, is charity a way to fight poverty in a country? Let's leave the one-off actions, the donations, the emergency aid to the humanitarian organizations, the ones who know how to do it, and whatever one may say, save lives... and then leave. When you run a country, fighting poverty is not a media-driven campaign of sprinkling donations upon villages and then leaving like relief NGOs do. People's real lives, women's in particular, begin after the television cameras put the covers back on their camera lenses, after the prefects who greeted you have concluded their hollow, laudatory speeches, after the welcoming pomp and spectacle has ended and after you, complacent, leave the village. Then you will find out, Madam, that your visit changed nothing. Malaria, non-potable water, the inability to access medical care and the lack of benches or books in schools are still there, as is the misery of their impoverished human lives, worth less than one US dollar a day.

But wait! She said that she knew your sister. Yeah sure! All you have to do is type her name into www.google.com and there are pages about her, or, if you don't want to google her, all you have to do is look at Wikipedia. And she had the audacity to say that she held her in high esteem! But your sister would have yelled to her face that a merely formal gender parity between men and women at the National Assembly could not make up for an equality that does not exist within society, a society where women are still beaten, disowned at their husbands' discretion, expropriated of all their assets when they become widows! Parity must begin from below. Electing women must start at the local level because a woman on a village or district committee, a woman in a key position on a town council or in a company, has more real power than a woman suddenly named deputy at the National Parliament!

AIDS? Still blaming prostitutes? Appalling.

You should have reminded her of her own advice to the

military when she advised them to stop raping... because of the risk of them being infected by women carrying the virus. How contemptuous. You lose it. Luckily, we do not practice female genital mutilation in our country, otherwise that woman would have fought against it by advocating: "Gentlemen, please, we must fight against female genital mutilation because a circumcised woman will give you less pleasure in bed!"

Actually, you are cursing yourself more than you are that woman. You are boiling inside because you are suddenly ashamed that you were so intimidated that you did not dare defend your friends properly. No, your sister Tamara would not have been as slow-witted as you. In fact, all those comebacks you just thought of are in the passionate letters full of discoveries, of wonder and thoughts she kept sending you from New Zealand, that island at the edge of the world where her work with militant Māoris impacted her as a student. You had carefully filed those letters with her other belongings you decided to keep after her death. For a long time, you kept them in the room she stayed in while she was still living with you and Tito, that period when you were not only her big sister, but a mother too. You did your best to raise her so that she did not make the same mistakes you did, so that she would become what your parents wanted you to be, but which you never became.

As soon as you received news from the village that she had passed her primary school certificate exams, which would allow her to go to high school, you immediately told your parents that you wanted her to live with you and Tito, before Auntie Turia could make the same request. Tito was wonderful, and you will always be grateful for all that he did for Tamara despite the hatred he has had for you ever since that night when you slammed the door in his face. He thought of Tamara as his little sister as much as you did. He bent over backwards to remodel the small outdoor room, a half garage and half storage room attached to the house, into a nice interior bedroom, opening a door through the wall and converting the exterior door into a window. Even before he had his job as Director of Learning and

Teaching Technologies at the Ministry, he always managed to get all the books Tamara needed, which allowed you to save a little bit of your cashier's salary. He helped her with her philosophy courses and later, when you bought her a Mac laptop, he guided her through the first steps of mastering the appropriate software. You supported her in math, of course, especially in statistics. But she became independent very quickly because she was learning more and more things that the two of you had not learned in your day, barely four or five years earlier.

From the start, what really mattered to you was to make sure that that young girl's future— she was only thirteen at the time—would not be forever compromised by an unwanted pregnancy. You were navigating between two roles, that of a mother and a big sister. In the beginning, you told yourself that you would monitor the growth of her breasts, the development of her hips, that you would make sure she never came home too late and that you always knew the friends she was going out with, until she turned sixteen. Then you would take her by the hand, sit her down and explain all the obstacles ahead. But things went much more quickly than you planned, and everything changed dramatically one afternoon when she came home from school.

She stopped for a moment in the doorway to adjust the bag she was wearing slung over her shoulder when, in a fraction of a second, your eyes caught a glimpse of things they had never noticed until then: slightly swollen lips in the middle of a relaxed and radiant face, a bust that was noticeably curvaceous for her age, hips swaying in a nonchalant, feminine way, subtly suggesting that the girl had crossed the threshold of puberty, and that perhaps she had even tasted the forbidden fruit. You panicked! She had just turned fifteen! What were you thinking? Didn't you know that children of that generation grow up so quickly that you can easily be fooled? Mama—or maybe it was Grandma—often told you: "You should give a child advice before she goes to the dance, not after she's back." Was Tamara already back from the dance party?

True, one mustn't procrastinate when facing pressing

issues, but one needs not rush things either. Questioning her right there, at the door, after her cheerful "Hi Méré" would be a mistake, the behavior of a panicked big sister. Instead, you have to act like a mother, Méréana, so, cool it.

So, you went through your usual routine. You made dinner and ate together after Tito came home from work, you told each other the little twists and turns of your day, Tito fixed the cupboard panel which had come off its hinges, Tamara washed the dishes, you had the child brush her teeth and go to her room to go to bed. Then the fateful moment arrived.

You went to her door and knocked. She asked you to come in. You entered and you sat down on the edge of her bed.

You had thought: If I start beating around the bush, I will not be able to say what there is to say. So, you tackled the subject head on, if not abruptly. Auntie Turia or Mama would have handled it differently, but they were her mothers whereas you may think, you were only a big sister:

"Have you already slept with a boy, Tamara?"

Dumbfounded, her mouth and her eyes opened simultaneously. After a few seconds, she shook her head as if she misheard the question.

"Excuse me?"

"You heard me. I am not going to repeat the question."

"Méré! How can you…"

"No, don't take it the wrong way, Tam, I trust you."

"So why the question? Do you suspect something?"

"I would just like to give you some advice before it happens… and even if it has already happened."

"You know I would never do such a thing. What would you think of me? And Mom, especially after what happened to you?"

"Exactly, I would not want what happened to me to happen to you. I got very lucky because I had a woman like Auntie Turia by my side."

"Don't say that. Tito is a generous soul and you have always been a role model for me, and I respect you a lot."

"I got lucky, that's all. Just imagine the consequences of my recklessness that day if Tito had had a disease. Don't be mistaken about the meaning of what I want to tell you: virginity is not important in itself; it is made to be lost anyway. What is important is how you lose it and with whom. Today, the pill is not enough for a young girl because it's no longer just about avoiding pregnancy. There are all those sexually transmitted diseases, the old and the new ones, the worst being HIV. So, little sis, whatever happens, be careful and stand firm about the condom."

"Thanks, I will always keep that advice in mind. Right now, I don't have a boyfriend and I'm not thinking about that."

"I wasn't thinking about it either when it happened. There is what we want and what happens. We must be equipped in advance to face those unexpected life events."

She did not answer, and you kept quiet. It seemed to you that her brain was processing the information you just gave her.

"That's what I had on my mind and what I had to say to you, Tamara."

Then you got up to leave her room. In a spontaneous gesture, she jumped off the bed where she was sitting and hugged you.

"Thanks, Big Sister."

Those words, "Big Sister," so full of affection, penetrated deep into your heart and you hugged her back more tightly. Never had the two of you felt so close, like best friends. At last, you gave her a little kiss on the cheek and closed the door on your way out.

You never spoke about it again and, up to the time she triumphantly passed her high school diploma and received that rare scholarship for the University of Otago in the city of Dunedin in New Zealand, you never found out whether your little sister had lost her virginity while she was still under your roof, even when that boy she would later marry after she got back from abroad, was already assiduously courting her. Anyway, you did not want to know, and you did not try to find out. Only once did she allude to this conversation in one of the letters she regularly sent you from abroad.

A persistent car horn snaps you out of your thoughts, oscillating between anger and tender memories. What got into that driver to stir up the whole neighborhood with the piercing sound of his horn? He couldn't do more if he wanted to get the clowns of the presidential guard to come out. You look... and it is Armando that you see, flailing his big arms to signal to you to come over to him and his parked taxi. Seeing him suddenly brings you back to reality. My God, you forgot survival rule number one, to always indicate where you are. You had turned off your cell phone when you entered the presidential residence and, for sure, Auntie Turia and the others must have been panicking, not being able to reach you or leave you a text message. You walk toward Armando who runs toward you with open arms. You spontaneously start running too and fall into his arms. He hugs you tightly and you hug him back. You are happy to have this physical contact, this comforting warmth after two intellectually exhausting duels with two powerful women. The feeling of his hand on your back does you good... But wait, what has come over you, Méré, letting yourself go like this? Didn't your experience with Tito teach you anything? Do not let yourself be fooled by a man's kindness. Also, what is he going to think? That the poor fool has fallen for his charm? You have to get a hold of yourself, Méré, before he gets cocky. You push him away suddenly as if you were bipolar. He is a little surprised but says nothing and picks right back up with business as usual, as if nothing happened.

"You had us scared to death! Why didn't you give us any sign that you were alive? Your cell goes automatically to voicemail on the first ring. When Laurentine first told me that you were called to see the President's wife, I did not believe it. I insisted that you were at the Ministry. I went there looking for you, I went all the way to the secretary's office and told her I was your brother, that you asked me to come pick you up. She replied that you left her office a good hour earlier and refused to tell her where you were going. All I could do was follow you to the presidential palace, as Laurentine told me. I practically got myself killed for you because at one point my car was stopped by soldiers who ordered me to turn around immediately or else... They told me that I had crossed the security perimeter of the residence of the Head of State. So, I came to wait here just in case. Why didn't you call me, Méré? Don't you know that people can also disappear in the residence of the Head of State?"

He spouts this all out as you walk. Once you reach the taxi, he opens your door and closes it behind you after you sit down, then goes to get behind the wheel.

"We shouldn't hang around here," he says and takes off at full throttle. He navigates the first turn poorly, apologizes, then asks: "So, how did it go?"

"It was horrible!"

"What do you mean, horrible? Didn't you explain to her that... "

"Let me reassure the others first."

You unlock your phone. You call Auntie Turia. She screams, happy to hear your voice. You remind her that you do not have much credit left and that you have to cut your conversation short so you can speak with the others. "But everyone is here," she says. You ask her to put Laurentine Paka on, to whom you say that you are on your way home, in Armando's taxi.

"You can use my telephone if you have other calls to make. I still have lots of credit," he suggests.

"No thanks, not at the moment."

"So, what do you mean it was horrible?"

"I can tell you one thing, Armando: I no longer need to work at the quarry. I am rich!" The car swerves and climbs up onto the sidewalk as Armando looks at you, dumbfounded.

"Careful, watch the road!"

He slows down, then pulls back onto the road and stops.

"I don't understand, Méré. You... You... " He leaves the sentence hanging in the air.

"Yes."

You open your bag, take out the thick envelope and throw it onto his lap. He looks at it, floored, not daring to touch it as if he feared it contained a bomb that would detonate if he picked it up.

"Elsewhere, corruption is hidden. It takes place under the table. In our country, it is not hidden. It happens right out in the open. Go on, we're going to share the envelope, fifty-fifty, just the two of us. We will be rich."

"But... but... Not you, Méré!"

"Why not? I need money too. Don't you?"

"But... but... you think it's good to... your friends... How much is in there?"

"I don't know. Count it!"

He finally dares to touch the envelope. He picks it up and hands it back: "But you haven't opened it yet. It is still sealed."

"That's a good thing. I've changed my mind. Don't open it."

He says no more. You look at him, amused. Then you suddenly burst into a fit of uncontrollable laughter, a resounding laughter accompanied by endless hiccupping which shakes your whole body. Tears stream down your face. Armando looks at you, stunned, thinking you have definitely lost it. After a long while, you stop laughing. You suddenly feel good, your chest light, your head clear, your mind relaxed.

"Let's hurry, let's join the others. They must be waiting for us impatiently." "And... and the envelope?"

"Keep it, I trust you."

NINETEEN

SHOUTS OF JOY burst forth when Armando's taxi stops in front of your lot. They are all there, all your friends from the quarry. They come running, jostling each other around the car, open the door, and applaud. Did they think they would never see you again once you penetrated the lair of the presidential palace?

They follow you into the courtyard which has been converted into a meeting hall with two dozen chairs arranged in a big circle, and in the middle, a single armchair takes center stage. Glancing at it quickly, you can tell it is not the good old warped, used armchair you collapse onto every night to rest your body and replay in your mind all the day's frustrations. It is Auntie Turia's beautiful armchair with the padded backrest and wide seat. Why and how did this chair end up here? You have neither the time to think about that nor to utter a word before you are assailed with questions and pushed over to the celebrated armchair. Among all the racket, you still manage to hear Auntie Turia's voice, shouting: "She must be hungry. Let her eat first!" It is true. You are hungry and thirsty, but even so, you cannot ask these impatient women to let your having something to eat take priority. After all, the day has been just as long for them. "I am not hungry," you lie lightheartedly, "just a little thirsty."

You pretend to ignore the armchair to which you are being led and you sit on a chair. Everyone starts shouting: "The armchair, sit in the armchair." You object. You do not want any privilege, you are all equal here and, you add, if anyone should sit in it, it should be the oldest of you all, in this case, Mâ Bileko. The latter, who is holding Batatou's child on her lap, reacts immediately, with authority:

"No, no, you are the one who must sit in this chair! We know that we are all equal here, but it is not about us nor about you. It's about the others. If we want our interlocutors to respect our spokeswoman, they have to know that we respect her too. That is why we want you in a dignified seat. Why would our presidents hold onto their "armchair" if it were not the symbol par excellence of their power?"

All the women applaud. What can you say? Nothing? What can you do besides acquiesce? You get up from the chair and walk over to the armchair and, so as not to be too formal, you gesture playfully as they cheer and laugh. And you take your place. Except for Armando, Laurentine's friend, Danny, and Auntie Turia who are watching from the porch, no one outside those of you who work at the quarry is present. You understand that your friends do not want the chaotic hospital scene to happen again and had decided to exclude all interlopers. Sort of a meeting behind closed doors but under open skies.

You begin your report. You fly quickly through the morning procession and your meeting with the Minister. Concerning the latter, seeing the suspicion on their faces, you insist upon the fact that it is exactly because of her no qualms and realistic political attitude that you can count on her. Then comes the most difficult part, your meeting with the wife of the Head of State. You are totally honest.

"I was intimidated, of course, but I still think I made myself clear, that we will never cease making our demands. Unfortunately, she did not want to hear that. Just like the Minister, she thinks we are illiterate, uneducated women and therefore we cannot think for ourselves, or that we are being manipulated by men from the opposition. She also thinks that if she just pays me off, I will ask you to put a stop to everything and you will all just follow me blindly... "

Before you finish your sentence, indignation and anger have set in. Who does she think she is, that woman… when was the last time she bought her own groceries… we'll have to invite her to break stone with us for a day… what, are you kidding? You think the poor thing will last even a half hour… at least, she does not think that it's the ones wearing the pants that are hiding behind our *pagnes*… rather, she is the one hiding behind the first ladies of Africa so she can rob us… I say it's not the police station we should be marching on, it's the airport so we can welcome each of the first ladies as she gets off her plane… All their voices and words are coming at you at once. You wave your hand several times shouting: "Wait, I haven't finished…" They finally quiet down, and you can go on.

"She paid me off to torpedo our movement. I do not know how much she gave me but given how thick the envelope is, it is a lot of money. I turned it over to Armando.

All heads turn to Armando. The poor guy was not expecting it and as dozens of eyes suddenly point at him, he seems confused for a moment, like an antelope caught in the cross-beams of hunters' flashlights.

"I locked it in the glove compartment. I'll go get it."

He comes back with the envelope, confident now and happy to play a lead role next to you. He asks everyone to notice that it is not open, showing the wide adhesive tape that sealed it.

"Open it in front of everyone," you tell him.

He pulls on the adhesive tape without much success, it is glued so well. He takes a small jackknife out of his pocket and makes a small slit in the envelope. He slides the sharp blade of the knife into it and opens the thick papaya-yellow cover with a sharp noise like tearing paper. Finally, he empties the contents onto the small stool sitting beside the armchair.

You all follow every one of his movements in absolute silence. He starts counting aloud. Six small packets, each containing ten ten-thousand-franc bills, five with ten five-thousand-franc bills, ten with ten thousand-franc bills, and the rest, ten packets of ten five-hundred-franc bills each. All in all, one million CFA francs! Brand-new bills as if they are hot off the press. None of you has ever seen so much money in a pile like that, except maybe Mâ Bileko back when she was a big retail trader on the Asian and African markets. You look and see that Iyissou is wide-eyed, Moyalo is speechless—she has lost her verve and her Lingala—Moukiétou' fists are clenched... you do not know why, but you are relieved. Yes, you do know why! So, breaking the silence you say:

"Thank God, Armando was waiting for me when I came out of the President's palace. I do not know what I would have done or what would have happened to me if I carried that envelope around with me any longer. I don't even want to think about it."

"They are capable of sending someone to steal it from you and then spread the rumor that you hid the stash from us," Anne-Marie Ossolo yells out.

"All that money scares me," Bilala says. "We mustn't touch it."

"We have to give it back," Iyissou goes further.

"It is not her money," says Moukiétou, "it's the money her husband has stolen from the people. It is our money."

"Let's just take the amount we need to reimburse our stolen bags and give back the rest," Moyalo says.

"But if we pay ourselves with stolen money, we too are thieves," Iyissou insists.

"I am telling you she will be furious if we refuse this money," you add as supplemental information. "She was so sure that we would take it that she has already rushed television and radio crews to record my statement saying that we are putting an end to our demands."

"Let's share this money equally, in public, for everyone to see, and let's say where it came from. That way she'll understand what we do with corruption money. And stealing from a thief is not stealing. We are just paying them back in their own coin."

"For me, it's simple," says Laurentine, who hadn't said anything until now. "Since that woman is going to come down hard on us if we refuse her gift, we might as well take it and continue our demands anyway."

You were all going in circles. Auntie Turia, who has been watching you from the porch, raises her hand and asks to speak. You eagerly give her the floor.

"I know this is not my business, but I wanted to say this: you either accept this money and uphold your end of the deal, which means immediately ceasing your demands for a higher selling price for your bags of gravel, or you return the money to the sender, and you continue making your demands. That's what is morally correct. There is no in-between. Otherwise, it is playing politics."

"One million, that's a lot of money for us, Auntie."

You do not know why you said that. She looks at you a little astonished but says nothing. Mâ Bileko takes the floor.

"Listen, if we refuse the money, we not only run the risk of persecution, one way or another, but we also risk losing the quarry. Don't kid yourselves. They will always find a good reason to keep us from going there or to simply close it. If we accept this money, not only will we be no better than the people who beat us up and stole our bags, but we will make it even more difficult for any women who are exploited to make future demands. Do not forget that the small market traders are watching us, and they admire us. After all our suffering, with poor Batatou in a coma for having demanded a higher selling price for her bag, I do not see how we can just let everything go and continue selling our bags of stone for ten thousand francs. It is not a question of morals. It is about our dignity."

You all applaud spontaneously, Moukiétou being the most enthusiastic among you. All right, it's decided: you will not accept this money. You will not allow yourselves to be bribed. That said, what to do with the money and how to give it back? Armando cannot simply jump into his taxi, park in front of the palace gate, hand the envelope to the guard and say: "Here, I came to return Madam's envelope." It's not so simple.

After a moment of silence, Auntie Turia raises her hand again. "Go ahead, Auntie."

"I listened closely to what Mâ Bileko had to say. I spoke before about morals. She spoke of dignity. She has just said something very important, which could reconcile the two—dignity and morality: she spoke of Batatou. Batatou is in a coma. She has sacrificed her life for this fight. She is single with twins, with no support and obviously cannot pay her hospital bills. Why don't you give her the money?"

"I applaud you, Turia," says Mâ Bileko right away, "that's what we must do! I hadn't thought of that."

Yes, that's it, a nice way of responding to the arrogance of all those who think that you are insignificant because you have neither money nor power. You are unanimous, no sooner said than done: take the money and allocate it in full for Batatou's care, and make it known publicly, on the radio and on television, without hiding where it came from. Obviously, it goes without saying that you will continue pushing your demands. Satisfied and relieved, you adjourn the meeting and ask everyone, before going home, to wait until you announce the decision you have all taken to the TV crew which will soon be here. At that very moment, your cell phone rings.

You frantically rummage through your purse to take out the phone you threw in earlier. It could be an important call. It could be the Minister wanting to know what came out of your conversation with the First Lady. Or maybe it's the First Lady, herself! You press the button to answer the call.

"Hello, yes?"

"Méré?"

You nearly drop the phone. Rangi! Tito Rangi. He is seriously starting to piss you off. Will he ever stop harassing you?

"Don't hang up. I have something important to tell you."

Everyone is looking at you. You have to stay cool. "Speak," you say, trying to sound calm.

You get up from the armchair and walk out of earshot. You do not want to make a scene if his words, yet again, drive you up the wall.

"The President's wife called to tell me she is very pleased with you. You did well to accept everything she proposed to you, including the envelope. I am the one who told her about your problems, and you see how she has reacted. She is a remarkable woman, ever generous. You don't think anyone would make someone suffer for some hundred twenty thousand francs! Despite what you believe, I don't hate you. Besides, you are the one who left me. I know you sometimes regret your rash decision, and if you want to come back home… "

"Oh, so the money was to get me back? I thought the President's wife bought me off so I would betray the others and stop our demands."

"No, no, that's not what I said. The money is not to buy you off. It's not a bribe. It's just compensation for using your influence to avoid embarrassing our country in front of its distinguished guests. All work deserves pay."

"Oh really? I thought that was what we were asking for, decent pay for our work."

"It's not the same thing! You women are in the streets, throwing stones… we do not negotiate with people who violate the law. I hope you've understood. We are counting on you."

"Yeah, you can count on me."

"One more thing. The President's wife does not want the statement to be given by one of those illiterates who carry no political weight. She wants you to give it since everyone knows who you are now."

"No problem, Tito. I will write it and read it myself. I wouldn't want you to lose the congressional position her husband appointed you to… "

"Don't start with me. Our conversation has been civilized up to now. I have been elected by the people, and you know it. When we finish this call, I will inform the leader's wife that you have accepted all her conditions. And you'll see, you will not regret it. Ah, another thing: it would be great if you could throw in some praise for the First Lady in your declaration."

"Sure, and if you want, I'll even add it was thanks to you that I agreed to read the statement myself."

"You don't have to, but anyway I love it when you're reasonable like that. The journalists are already on their way, they should be there soon."

"You really know everything, don't you? Even the one hundred twenty thousand francs I needed."

"Everything you are interested in, concerns me."

"And everything you're concerned with interests me."

"What is that supposed to mean?'

"It means what it means. Okay, I have things to do, bye."

You hang up before he can reply. You are happy and annoyed at the same time. Happy because you kept your cool. You were able to hold back your anger. Annoyed because you know now that he was the bastard who concocted the story about you for the leader's wife. And wait! In his magnanimity, the man says he is willing to welcome you if you come back home! He does not even realize that he is the one who keeps chasing after you, harassing you while you just find him more and more revolting. Oh yeah, he'll get his statement.

You return to the others. You tell them that you have just been informed that the television crew will arrive shortly to record your statement. So now you have to agree on what to say and who is going to speak.

You easily agree on the terms of the statement. The only debate is about whether to announce on radio and TV that you are demanding the fifteen thousand francs, which is your ultimate price, or, as a bargaining tactic, maintain the price you set when you were negotiating with the buyers, which would allow you to appear to concede by letting go of five thousand francs at the end. You settle on the second proposal. However, complications arise regarding which one of you should make the public statement. Everyone unanimously nominates you, but you refuse. You do not want to. You explain to them that since you were the one who went to see the Minister and the President of the Republic's wife, your fight must not come down to just one person. You need a new face for those who will be watching on TV. As you say that, out of the corner of your eye, you see Laurentine Paka take out her mirror and start to put makeup on. But she is not who you are thinking of. You're thinking about the "peasant" among you, the most "illiterate" one, the one who only speaks your national language, Kikongo, the one who does not know a word of French, the language that is used to record official statements: you think of your beloved "witch," Bilala. Is there a better way to snub your nose at Tito and his boss than presenting Bilala as the symbol of your determination? You share your idea with them. You plead. You argue that since the Minister treated you like little illiterate drudges, incapable of making any decisions on your own, you need to put her face-to-face with one of those illiterate women to prove the contrary. The argument is well-received, and some even add to it. Bilala is surprised to be asked to take on the role, hesitates, then finally accepts. Now, you are ready.

As you expected, it is not just one journalist who shows up with his cameraman carrying a hand-held on his shoulder, there are several of them. Madam has done well. Of course, there are two official journalists, one from the national TV station and one from the national radio station, but there are also local correspondents from the BBC, RFI, Voice of America and Radio South Africa. You are astounded beyond words. Had your small, insignificant movement, started by fifteen women breaking stone at a small quarry by the riverside and demanding a little more money for the product of their work, become such an important event to the point of attracting the international media?

Since it is the first time these journalists are meeting you all, they do not know whom to address. So, on their own accord they split into two groups, one heading toward you, the other toward Laurentine, as would be expected since among all the women present, you are the only two wearing Western clothes. That is enough for them to decide who the leaders of the movement are. In fact, many more are heading over to Laurentine than to you, no doubt because she is better dressed and perhaps more beautiful. Between your brown ensemble, no doubt elegant but a bit tight and stern, and what Laurentine is wearing, there is no contest: an artfully washed-out denim skirt which ends just above the knee, matched with a pale yellow sleeveless blouse, to which is pinned a broach with fake gems sparkling as if they were real, accentuating the tragic beauty that the stitches give her face. You never found out what led Laurentine to this quarry. Her care-free attitude, her display of vanity, her love for sentimental novels and the constant presence of her friend by her side, all that seems out of place. But behind her apparent transparency, is she hiding something dramatic that no one suspects? The cameras click, flashes burst. Laurentine has her fifteen minutes of glory.

"We come to record the statement regarding the ending of your demands," the journalist from the official TV channel says to her.

Those around you also hear the question, causing them to leave you and all rush over to Laurentine, believing they have found the accredited spokesperson. But she, with a wide sweeping motion of her arm, extends her hand toward you and tells them somewhat grandly:

"Méré is our leader and our spokesperson. She is the one you must talk to, and we are all behind her."

Like a gaggle of geese, they all come back toward you. And you gesture toward Bilala:

"Bilala is going to make our statement. She is ready, and she is waiting for you."

In fact, as you had all urged her to do, she is sitting in the armchair you were occupying earlier. You asked her to remain seated when she makes your statement, seated like a chief who is respected, who is owed respect. After two or three days of protesting, you have all also learned that, even with a just cause, a good performance is crucial if you want to be taken seriously. The TV journalist looks Bilala up and down, then turns to you.

"We prefer you," he says.

"It is not for you to choose who our spokesperson is," you retort. "The authorities who sent us insisted that it be you."

"Since you're the one who dealt with the Head of State's wife courtesy requires that you be the one to respond." adds the guy from the radio.

"I told you, Bilala will make the statement."

He seems uncomfortable with that and whistles discretely in your ear: "Not in that outfit!"

It is true that Bilala's *pagne*, long out of style, washed, wrung out, dried, and rewashed a thousand and one times, is certainly not high-quality. And the headscarf she is wearing is transparent in places, where all the successive washing and rinsing have worn the thread much too thin. On her feet, she is wearing those plastic flip-flops the Chinese flood our markets with. You do not know how to say it but in her modesty and, shall we say, poverty, her entire being gives off a certain authenticity that is difficult to define, which makes her look even more dignified, sitting like a queen in that throne-like armchair standing proudly among the other chairs. You turn toward the journalist and say to him, out loud to embarrass him:

"You mean you do not want her to make our statement because she is wearing a *pagne*? Are you ashamed of our culture and of the way our mothers dress?"

"We don't care what you think," Moukiétou shouts. "If you do not want to take our statement, the foreign radio stations are here."

"What! You don't like her scarf?" adds Anne-Marie. "Just wait and see."

Everyone is frozen, staring at her. She is holding a three-foot-long *pagne* in her hands. Where did she pull that out of? She lets it unfurl and flaps it in the wind with a snap. She takes

Bilala's headscarf off and hands it to Mâ Asselam who is closest to her. With rapid agile movements, her two hands and fingers expertly transform the *pagne* into a head covering that sits atop Bilala's head like a tiara, finishing it all off with two intertwined double knots. Nice work! A real magician that Anne-Marie! You all erupt in spontaneous applause as Bilala says with a wide smile: "Oh, thank you, thank you!" That small touch has transformed how she holds her head and makes her dignified look stand out even more, somewhat veiled by her poverty.

"So, you still don't want her?" says Moukiétou, still angry. "You want her to put on a long evening gown?"

"No... no... it's not that," the journalist stammers, confused, "it's just... the statement is very important... She will be seen by our foreign guests... I was told the First Lady, in particular, is waiting..."

"So, what are you waiting for? Go ahead!"

You are the one who interrupts him. He has no choice. He either accepts or loses his job. In any case, you do not need him. The foreign press is there and that is enough for you because their credibility holds more weight than those servile TV and radio stations. He gives in and tells his cameraman and sound engineer to start rolling. The BBC, RFI, and Radio South Africa already have their mikes on.

"Mama Bilala, you have decided to suspend your protests at the request of the wife of the Head of State who cares very deeply about women's issues in our country. Please make your statement live on the air."

"Thank you," Bilala says with a little smile. "I am ready."

Very slowly and clearly, with the distinct accent of the local forest people, she begins speaking in Kikongo.

"My name is Bilala."

"Stop!" the journalist says. "We want a statement in French. Our foreign guests also need to understand."

You are furious. He can go to hell. Here, we speak in the

language of our country.

"Go on, Bilala, don't worry about him!" you say, with the rest of the women's approval.

"My name is Bilala. I am speaking here on behalf of all the women who break stones by the riverside. This is what is happening. The traders who were selling bags of gravel for thirty thousand francs and buying them from us for ten thousand are now selling them for fifty thousand. They are making a forty-thousand-franc profit! We want to sell our bags for fifteen... twenty thousand francs. But the traders have a problem with that. We do not know why. In response to our protests, they sent the armed police to our work site on the riverbank. For no reason, the armed police beat us, injured us, and threw us in prison. One of us is in a coma now.

This morning, the Minister of Women received us and promised to help. We thank her from the bottom of our hearts. After the Minister, Mama President summoned our spokesperson. At the end of their discussion, she gave her some money and ordered her to cease our protests immediately. We all met, and here is what we have decided.

"Mama President, we accept this money"—she holds up the fat envelope and shakes it in front of the camera—, "thank you very much. But this money will all be saved to pay our friend Batatou's medical expenses, and for her children. Batatou is in a coma, her life hanging by a thread. Meanwhile, we will absolutely maintain our two demands because we are not asking for charity. We will continue to protest until, one, our stolen bags have been returned to us and, two, our bags of gravel from now on are purchased for twenty thousand francs. If we do not get our stolen bags back by this evening, tomorrow we will hold a protest march on the police station. That is all we have to say."

You all applaud loudly, and your bravos and ululations are amplified by the crowd of onlookers who came running when they saw the media and press in front of your lot. Bilala did a fantastic job, especially when you know she was not reading a speech—and oh, waving that fat envelope in front of the cameras was a master stroke! You are all so proud of her. She has just shattered the myth of the illiterate woman who is unable to express her demands independently. The national TV and radio journalists, on the other hand, are looking quite gloomy. They had come to record a surrender, and instead they got a declaration of war. What fate does their supervising Minister have in store for them? You, however, are all pleased. Your point of view has been heard, and the foreign radio stations will further amplify your message since all of them broadcast to your city on FM radio.

What else to do now except wait? At any rate, you are sure that the police, who have your bags, and the Minister or the Head of State's wife will react very swiftly because the first of the invited First Ladies is supposed to land tomorrow. You got that information obligingly from the ineffable Tito Rangi.

•

The day seems to be well advanced when the journalists finally leave, followed by the onlookers who assembled in front of your lot. But actually, it is not that late. Only a little after 4PM, which means there are still two hours of daylight left. Now that all those people are gone, you begin to assess the situation and take a few important decisions as a group. First, that you will hold onto the fat envelope and Bileko will manage it. Next, that Atareta will be in charge of several important missions: go to the hospital to inquire about Batatou's condition, then to the pharmacy to buy the most urgent medications and, finally, pay a visit to the television network to leave a photo of Batatou with a press release to broadcast because despite the two you already issued on the radio, not a single member of her family has yet to show up. The photo will be more effective. Don't they say a picture is worth a thousand words? Mâ Bileko takes eighty thousand francs out of the fat envelope and hands them to Atareta who goes right away to look for a taxi. Finally, by mutual agreement, you all decide to meet the next day at 11AM in the courtyard of the hospital where Batatou is fighting for her life.

You start folding the chairs to arrange them in a corner of your lot. You ask where the chairs came from and learn that they were rented for one hundred francs each. "It's not that expensive," Laurentine Paka asserts when you raise your eyebrows finding out the price, "not even the price of half a bag of stone." Anyway, they were not obliged to rent those chairs, because you could have sat on benches, on mats, or even on those bricks that are piled up in a corner of the compound. But no, despite all the difficulties at present, they preferred to make the sacrifice and chip in to pull together the two thousand francs needed to rent those twenty chairs to make the meeting appear more formal—more respectable. For sure, for those still in doubt, the message could not be any clearer: these women must be taken seriously!

The task completed; everyone starts to disperse to go home. Despite his persistence, Armando understands that you have no desire to keep him around and that it is time for him to make up for the part of the day he has lost. He generously takes his sister Anne-Marie, Bilala, Moukiétou and Iyissou in his taxi and before taking off, he manages to find a way to kiss you good-bye and offer his services once again, if need be.

Your courtyard is empty now. Only Mâ Bileko is still hanging around, talking with Auntie Turia. She is waiting for her daughter who is supposed to come pick her up so they can go home together. The two women, like two grandmothers who are old friends, have laid Batatou's two children down, side by side, on a mat covered with a mosquito net. Mâ Bileko is sitting in Auntie's beautiful armchair which has just been brought back to the porch. You tease her saying she looks quite good in that seat. She is sitting there with the natural posture of a CEO. "You're the one, Méré, dressed as a beautiful modern young professional woman, giving off the impression that you are—it's difficult to explain—a natural leader. I am really very happy that we chose you to represent us." Feigning modesty, you wave at her and go back inside the house. It is time to make yourself comfortable.

TWENTY

YOU ARE FINALLY out of your ensemble, feeling cozy in your pagne and sandals. By the time you come back from your room, Bileko has already left. You are sorry you did not have a chance to say good-bye and sit down on the armchair she was on, that armchair which turned out to be so unexpectedly important. Now that the meeting is over and everyone has left, it is nothing more than an ordinary piece of furniture among others, and you take the opportunity to tease Auntie about it one more time.

"I see this armchair has finally left the exhibition hall and can now face reality: contact with buttocks..."

"Sure, make fun of me. Luckily, I had this gorgeous piece of furniture!"

"But how did it end up here?"

"Bileko!"

"Bileko? How so?"

Amused, she tells you the story. After all the chairs had been set up, Bileko asked that you be seated on a chair that was distinct from the others, preferably an armchair, which, according to her, would raise your stature with the people who are following your struggle. Then, Auntie Turia showed them the old armchair in your living room. When Bileko set eyes on that old moth-eaten piece of furniture with its brown faux leather backrest resembling a scalp infected by ringworm, she lost it: "Don't you know that a chair is an attribute of power? We need a suitable chair that conveys the integrity of our movement! We will be the laughingstock of everyone if we have our spokesperson sit on this old thing." She went on, explaining that when she was a bigwig businesswoman negotiating deals in Asia, she always made sure to show off her most beautiful finery because that commanded respect. Applauding her colleague, Laurentine chimed in: "She's right. They must respect us."

It was after that passionate defense that Auntie suggested her armchair, "which is still brand-new," she added.

And it is true, the piece of furniture is new! As many grandmothers do, she always keeps a transparent plastic slipcover on it. You often tease her saying that an armchair is made for massaging buttocks not to be stared at beneath a plastic cover. And that is how that armchair ended up here, standing brazenly among those white polystyrene chairs.

"Mâ Bileko is a remarkable woman," you say. "I am so happy you two get along so well."

"Not only did Batatou's babies bring us closer, but our ages too. We chatted like two old ladies who have heard and seen it all in this world. Nothing can surprise us anymore."

"You two are not that old. You're fifty-eight, and she can't be over sixty. At your ages, you are not as old as Methuselah. You're just young grandmothers."

"At any rate, we hit it off right away, and we have become friends. I asked her to come and visit my sewing studio when your protests let up and you can get a little rest. We would have still been yapping if her daughter hadn't arrived to pick her up."

"Zizina was here? She is truly extraordinary, that girl. Did she come on her moped?"

"Do you know her well?"

"Yes, very well. She thinks of me as her big sister, and she has shared a lot about her life with me. Sometimes she reminds me of Tamara."

"She just took some exams to be recruited into a women-only police force that the UN intends to form to send to Liberia or DRC, I can't remember which."

"Liberia. So, that was today? She told me about it, but I had forgotten the date. I wish her lots of luck, not only for her, but also for Bileko. Hard to imagine that the same woman who is now so destitute that she has to break stones to live and gather dead wood in the bush to cook her food, once raked in millions in her life, then lost everything for the simple sin of suddenly being a widow."

"You don't say!"

"Yes, well, at least she had children!"

At those words, a brief tic contracts Auntie's face, betraying the effort she made to hide the impact of such a treacherous blow to the heart. "My God, why did you say that? You ought to think before you speak. You ought to get a flogging for that blunder!"

"Right, 'at least she had children', she repeats your words, trying to sound neutral, but you notice a certain bitterness all the same.

"No, Auntie, that's not what I meant. You know that. I meant that, to strip her of everything she owned, her in-laws did not have the convenient excuse, incontestable in their eyes, that she did not give her husband children."

"I understood perfectly well what you meant, Méré. You are completely right to think that this is no reason. Would you like to know why my dear husband Malaki's family did not succeed at throwing me out, even though I did not give him any children? And believe me, they tried."

"Uh, because he left a will. A legal document leaving you all his assets."

"Are you kidding? What value does a will have in this country, especially when it comes to inheritance? Tradition is stronger than any legal text you can draw up."

"So then why didn't the family evict you from your husband's home?"

"For fear of fetishes! That's right, not for fear of justice or out of compassion, for fear of fetishes! Knowing, as everyone does, that if he did not resolve the situation while he was still alive, his wife would find herself out on the streets the moment he closed his eyes, my husband concocted an unbelievable trick. Since all of them—uncles, aunts, nephews, sisters—whom he suspected would go after our assets believed in the power of fetishes and were afraid of sorcerers as is often the case here, he decided to outdo all juju practitioners.

He very cleverly spread the rumor that he was well-versed in the occult practices of the Orient, in particular those from India, and that he was therefore under the protection of spirits that were unknown in our latitudes, spirits more powerful than all of West Africa's marabouts' talismans combined. Also, those talismans from the Orient would even stand up to the spells cast by the pygmies of our equatorial forests. He came up with the idea on two missions he made to India as a high-ranking officer in our army. At any rate, to corroborate this rumor, he hung up a huge picture of the third reincarnation of the Hindu god Vishnu in the living room, in which the god was represented with the head of a wild boar and four arms whose hands each held a symbolic object—a wheel, a sword, a conch shell and a mace. It is terrifying when you see it for the first time and I admit, even I took some time to get used to it. It was nothing like our statuettes, our ancestors' nkisi kondi, bristling with nails, a small symbolic mirror in the center of its abdomen, and feline claws and cowrie shells driven into the rest of its body. In case Vishnu's presence was not enough to get the message across, he had placed a massive, potbellied Buddha conspicuously in the center of the living room coffee table. Even better, he explained, while the power of our local fetishes died along with the death of their owner or the person they were protecting, theirs, the ones from India, had the inverse function. They were dormant, hibernating, and did no harm to anyone as long as their owner was alive. But the moment their owner breathed out his last lungful of air, they would automatically start bustling about to protect everything and everyone that he asked to be protected after his death.

"And, believe me, Méré, it worked! Nobody dared come and tell me to get out of the house except one of his nephews who wanted to seem bold. I must admit that coincidence helped me too. One fine day, said nephew landed up on my property at the crack of dawn, got me out of bed with his screaming and banging on the main door of the house. 'Enough! This has gone on long enough!' he was shrieking, screaming that all those stories about fetishes were nothing but nonsense. He was giving me forty-eight hours to clear out of his uncle's house. And besides, he would repeat, he was being charitable to me, otherwise it was chop-chop! What did it matter to him that I swallowed up a good part of my salary for the purchase end renovation of that house?

"The moment he stepped off the property, one of the pieces of paper he was holding and had waved around in my face flew out of his hand. He wanted to catch it, took one step into the road... and wham, got mown down by a car that was speeding past: he was killed instantly. Of course, as was to be expected, it did not take long for the rumor to spread that his death was attributed to Vishnu, enthroned in my living room in his third avatar, who dealt him a blow to the head with his mace. That the blow had cracked his skull and suddenly, like a disoriented beast, his coordination impaired like a decapitated chicken, he had thrown himself underneath the wheels of the car. That was the fate that awaited those who dared to evict Malaki's widow: their punishment was worse than AIDS. They would go mad, be condemned to wander the city in rags, and end up squashed by a car. How could anyone still doubt the power of the spirits who were protecting me after that impudent nephew's brutal and unexpected death? After the accident, all those people finally left me alone. They were greedy, for sure, but not rash."

"What a story, Auntie!"

"Well, yes. That is why I, a childless widow, still live in your uncle's house. OK, that's enough. It's getting dark, I'd better see to the children before I go. And you too, take care of yourself now. You haven't eaten anything since this morning."

With that, she gets up and calls them in. Lyra comes running first, as usual. With such a loving grandmother, wouldn't you do the same?

Usually in the evenings, after you give the children a bath and help them with their homework when they have it, you eat with them. Then, once you've sent them off to bed, you rest for a moment to let your body and your mind wander so you can release the stress of the day. When you can, you finish with a hot shower, which helps you drift off into the land of dreams. But today was no ordinary day and your usual routine does not fit in. You cannot eat decently or think before you cleanse yourself of the day's dirt and sweat. The fatigue too, from trekking around from the Ministry to the Presidential Palace, from the attempted bribery to which you were subjected, to your public demonstration of defiance. You have to wash up first. So, you start with a hot shower.

Two buckets full of water. You scrub your body with a loofah soaked in soap suds then use an entire bucket of water to rinse off. You come out feeling light and clean. You can feel your pores breathe. You were in there for quite a while because you see that Auntie has already bathed and fed the children and is getting ready to leave. You thank her and walk her to the outside gate. You cannot walk her any further wearing only a pagne over your naked body, a towel on your head and flip-flops.

"You don't want me to spend the night? There will be at least one witness if they come looking for you again like they did this morning."

"Don't worry, Auntie! Now that the whole world is aware—didn't you listen to the international radio stations? —, they will not dare take me away. In any case, my cell battery is charged, and I still have credit. If anything happens, you'll be the first one I'll call."

"Be careful anyway, my dear. See you tomorrow. Go now, put the children to bed."

She hugs you, then turns and goes. You do not turn around right away to go back inside. You stay for a moment and watch her shrink into a dot that slowly and silently disappears beneath the light of the moon. When you finally turn around to head back to the house, Auntie's silhouette fading away into the shadows remains in your mind like a dark spot lingers on your retina after being exposed to a bright light. You feel guilty and sad about mistakenly bringing up a painful part of her past which she had managed to bury—not having children. From the words that you uttered, 'well, at least she had children', it was the 'at least' which gave her the impression that you approved of what had happened to her, it was the 'at least' that, like a treacherous arrow, pierced the armor beneath which she had managed to contain her suffering.

Oh, if you could only give yourself a whipping! You would have known nothing of that buried suffering if she herself hadn't confided in you during one of those intimate moments where you both had let your guards down. Her own sister, your mother, you are sure, never as much suspected that pain, much less your sister, Tamara. She told you during a conversation: "You know, Méré, I did not give birth to a child, so I do not know the joy and pain of motherhood. Which hurt for a long time because Malaki and I wanted so much to have one. But now that he is gone, I don't regret anything anymore since I have you and your sister. I don't think I could have loved a child from my womb any more than the two of you." Oh, Auntie Turia! Our mother's big sister, your elder mother!

TWENTY-ONE

THE TELEPHONE ringing wakes you like an alarm bell. You look at the time. To your surprise, it is already six-thirty. You get up, sit on the edge of the bed, and pick up the phone, hesitating to press the button that will establish communication. You let it ring two or three more times so you can enjoy those few fractions of a second to reboot your brain, get your still foggy mind working again, because you have not slept well. You did not sleep well because, the moment you began drifting gently off to sleep, lulled by the soft pitter patter of the light rain that had started to fall, doubts about the way you reacted to the First Lady's offer began swirling around in your head. Not so much about the fact that you refused to obey her orders, as the way you dramatized your refusal on a giant technicolor screen. As much as you are looking for excuses, as much as you tell yourself this is all Tito's fault, that it would have been completely different had he not called you right at that moment with that arrogant, somewhat contemptuous tone he now displays towards you, or that, actually, all the theatrics were not directed at the President's wife but at Tito, it changes nothing.

You cannot easily discard your responsibility. You are the one who is accountable for this reckless act, and the consequences could be grave. Tamara would never have made such a mistake, letting her personal feelings and resentment prevail over the general interest. How can you make up for that? All those thoughts suddenly interrupted by the telephone ringing became jumbled in your head, keeping you in a state of fitful half-sleep throughout the night. What if it is the President's office calling? Or the Minister of the Interior?... You give in and press the green button.

"Hello?"

"Hello, Méré? It's me, Atareta."

"Atareta?" "Yes."

It is not the police. You are relieved, but only for a fraction of a second because you understand right away. Batatou! This must be about Batatou!

"Sorry for calling you at this hour when the roosters have barely begun to crow. I just saw Batatou. Her condition is serious... critical. You need to come. There are decisions to be taken. I cannot do it alone."

"Oh my God! I'll be right there. Are you at the hospital?"

"Yes. I might go out for a bit to inquire about some formalities, but I will not be far. Just call me."

"OK. I'll do my best to get there as soon as possible."

You hang up. Batatou! Obsessed with your fixation on Tito, she had slipped out of your mind. She is the one who has paid the heaviest price in your struggle. Without what happened to her, you might not have had the determination to continue, the courage to defy authority, even if that courage was on the brink of recklessness. Get dressed and jump in a taxi so you can get to the hospital as soon as possible. But wait, it's not that simple. You cannot leave the children, including the baby, alone, just like that. You look at the two littlest, Lyra and Batatou's daughter, sleeping peacefully on the bed you left to them. What else can you do other than ask for Auntie Turia's help once again?

When she picks up, you reassure her right away that everything is fine. "No, Auntie, nothing happened to me... yes, yes, the night was fine... the children too... It's about Batatou... no, no, she did not die, but Atareta just called to tell me that her condition is critical... yes, I need to go right away to be with her at the hospital... that's right... oh, thank you, Auntie... I'll wash up and get dressed and wait for you to get here.

I'll make you tea if you want... okay, you prefer coffee... al-right see you, thanks again."

You hang up.

Hurriedly, you wash up and get dressed: quickly but securely tie an orange pagne around your waist, over your underpants, and over your bra, put on a blouse with three-quarter-length sleeves.

It's what you call "Popo style", a fashion inspired by Beninese women. Not exactly formal wear, but practical for a day that is sure to be hectic. You automatically turn on the radio, then put the water on for tea and coffee. Unable to just stand still because you are anxious, you pace between the gas stove and the wide-open window, keeping an eye out for Auntie Turia to arrive.

> "Some young schoolgirls have been disfigured by acid for daring to go to school. Those responsible are men, believed to be Taliban. The situation turned violent very quickly. Out of nowhere, motorcycles appeared in a cloud of dust. After forcing high school girls to remove their veils, the men sprayed acid on their faces using a water gun. The most seriously injured is Atefa, her face melted and her right eyelid nothing more than a pile of flesh stuck to her eye socket. Her nose was eaten away by the acid down to the bone. Her sister, Shamsia Neema, despite her face being completely burned, stated loud and clear defiant toward their aggressors: 'Even if they do it a hundred times, even if they have to kill me, I will keep going to school.'

Your mind is already at the hospital, with Batatou. As soon as Auntie arrives, you will rush to find a taxi. But where can you find a taxi at this hour, in this neighborhood? Quite naturally, you think of Armando and his taxi. The guy is starting to be indispensable to you. You know he is just waiting for an opportunity to help you out, but you just do not want to give him one. However, the day could be long, and you may need to make several trips. A car is absolutely essential. So, after weighing the pros and cons, you decide to call Armando. Doesn't necessity often trump reason?

"Armando?"

"Yes... Oh"—he recognizes your voice—, "what a nice surprise and how nice to be woken up in the morning by such a beautiful voice!"

You pretend you did not hear that.

"It's Méré."

"I know! Your voice..."

"Sorry to bother you..."

"You never bother me..."

"Batatou's condition has deteriorated significantly. I just received a call from Atareta. I need to get to the hospital urgently and maybe also make some other stops."

"Oh my! I'll just brush my teeth and throw on some pants, and I'll be right over. Does my sister know?"

"Not yet. I will update everyone once I see Batatou and can assess her situation accurately."

"Oh my God"—he has completely dropped his playful tone, which touches you—, "this woman must not die! We must do everything in our power to save her. You were right to call me. I'll be right there."

To your great surprise, Auntie Turia arrives in Armando's taxi. He spotted her when she was about 150 feet from your house and insisted she get in the car. Such an angel, that Armando! You extend your hand. He understands that this is no time for hugs and shakes it. The coffee and tea are ready. You serve Armando; Auntie helps herself. He takes the coffee gladly and drinks it rather quickly as Auntie Turia bombards you with questions about Batatou. Questions you cannot answer at this point. Finally, after you agree with her about how she is going to spend the day with the children, Armando and you jump into the taxi and head to the hospital.

TWENTY-TWO

YOU DO NOT need to look for Atareta. She is standing in front of the hospital's main gate. She is crying! Your heart sinks in your chest. If Atareta is crying, it means the worst has happened. As soon as she sees you, she hurries over and throws herself into your arms. You hug her tightly and, between two hiccups, she manages to let out: "She died." Tears begin to fall silently down your cheeks as well. Although moved too, Armando tries to encourage you. "We have to pull ourselves together," he says over and over again, "there are many arrangements to be made."

You walk silently up the stairs to the floor of the intensive care unit where Batatou was. Her body is still in the corridor of the room where she took her last breath, covered only with the blood-stained pagne she was wearing the day she was wounded. You are outraged. Not a single sign of respect, not even a clean, white sheet to cover the body of a deceased person. Our grandparents' time, when people still respected the dead, has certainly passed. You mention that to the nurse who greets you. With absolutely no empathy, cynical even, he replies that if the hospital asks each patient to bring their own bandages, needles, medicine and rubbing alcohol to be treated, you cannot expect the hospital to put a white sheet over a body for free.

He opens her medical record.

"The family has to identify the body before it is transferred to the morgue," he says. "Are you her family?"

Did Batatou have any family? You issued a radio statement intended for her family, but no one came forward. If she does not have any family, they are going to refuse to give the body to you and a few days later they will bury her anonymously, perhaps even in a mass grave. Who knows? You don't hesitate for a second.

"Yes," you answer. "Her cousin."

"I'm her uncle," Armando says, following your lead.

"I'm…" Atareta starts to say. The nurse interrupts her.

"Two are enough. Your IDs."

You hand him yours and Armando hands him his driver's license. He writes down the information he needs.

"Go to the appropriate office to get the death certificate. Don't forget, the body will not be released to you for burial until you pay the hospital fees and the morgue expenses. Alright, you can bring your cousin to the morgue now," he concludes as he hands you a slip of paper.

An orderly pushes the stretcher as you follow in silence. You can tell that for him this is routine. He is showing as much emotion as if he were transporting a sack of cement to deliver to the depot. He does not go far. When you reach the end of the hall, he stops in front of the stairs.

"The elevator is broken. You'll need to bring down the deceased. That's not part of my job."

You are so shocked by his words you just freeze with your mouth half-open. Atareta, on the other hand, expresses her outrage, shouting: "And how do you expect us to bring the body down with no elevator?"

"Carry it on your back like all the others do… It's not my fault the elevator isn't working. If it is broken down, it is broken down!"

Armando does not seem to be disturbed at all. In a calm voice, he asks the orderly: "You can help us, right?"

"Uh… yes… I know some people who will help you for a fair price. They are specialized in that sort of work. I can go get them. They're not far. They're waiting at the elevator in the lobby."

"Go get them."

The man immediately bounds down the stairwell, skipping four steps at a time.

"This is scandalous! A hospital without a working elevator!" Atareta says, still boiling with rage.

"First, you need to start by asking if there is running water, if there are toilets…"

"I know, Armando, I know. But still, we are in a university hospital!"

"Monsieur Armando finds this all normal," you say sarcastically, finding nothing else to say.

"Armando is a taxi driver, Madam Méréana," he says, suddenly irritated. You don't know why. "If you only knew all he has seen in this country! If you only knew how many times he has transported the dead and the dying in his taxi because there was no ambulance! If you only knew how many babies he has seen die from malaria convulsions from not receiving an emergency injection because the hospital did not have a single syringe! Can you two imagine the parents' despair when after having spent a fortune on taxis driving around looking for an all-night pharmacy where they could find vials of Quinimax solution, they watch powerlessly as their child convulses to death because they were unable to find a syringe to inject her with the life-saving solution?… Armando could go on like that for a long time, Madam! Luckily, thank God, there are people who know how to capitalize on such situations. No running water in the hospital? There are people who run up and down the stairs to sell you water jugs. No bathrooms? There are people who visit rooms, offering to empty bedpans or dispose of soiled bandages. No elevator? There are people who go up and down the halls, offering to transport the bodies of patients who had the bad taste of dying upstairs. That is how patients get water, excrement is removed, corpses are carried to the morgue, and everything works out. So why complain about it? And, if people find nothing wrong with it, why go out of the way to change things since what is daily routine elsewhere is a miracle here?

It's a miracle when we turn on the faucet and water gushes out. It's a miracle when we flip on the light switch and electricity flows. It's a miracle when you're at the hospital and you are offered a pill of aspirin for free. That is the reality of our country! Armando is beyond indignation, Madam, and he is not upset with that poor boy because he too is merely profiting from the system. You can be sure that he is in collusion with those corpse bearers, and he will get his commission on what we are going to pay them: isn't he the one who procured the merchandise for them? While we wait, I'm going to find something more decent to cover Batatou with. I'll see you downstairs."

Then, he in turn goes down the stairs, step by step, slowly. Atareta and you look at one another, dumbfounded by his unexpected dramatic exit. Since you have known him, he has never spoken to you in that tone. Was he offended by the way you addressed him? Was it the sarcasm in your voice or the "Monsieur Armando" that he could not digest? Or was he just putting two stuck-up bitches who thought he was clueless in their right place? And yet, there was no anger in his voice. Much to the contrary, it was composed and conveyed true emotion. Yes, that was it. Atareta wept at the site of Batatou abandoned in the corridor. You shed silent yet abundant tears. Armando, either not able to or not wanting to also cry in front of these two women sniveling and moaning, was filled with indignation and had exploded with the stories of a taxi driver, an old veteran who has seen it all, experienced it all. However, behind his blunt words, is a man full of compassion. You are further moved by the fact that, unlike Atareta and you, he did not know Batatou. You suddenly feel respect for this man whom, since the day you met him, you had never really taken seriously. A man whom you had deliberately limited to the cliché of taxi drivers as being chatty and superficial.

Two men, accompanied by the orderly, finally appear: "They're going to bring the body down," the orderly tells you.

"But how?", Atareta protests, "They don't have a stretcher."

"They don't need one. It's a spiral staircase and maneuvering a stretcher is difficult. The body can slip and fall, and that would not be decent or nice. But don't worry, it's not the first time they're bringing a body down. These are professionals who know what they're doing."

While he is talking, the famous professionals arrange the *pagne* covering Batatou, tying it around her corpse. Then, one grabs her feet, the other her head, and they start going down. Her body is not stiff yet, which means that they do not have too much trouble bending or slightly contorting her to negotiate the stairwell's spiral geometry. The two of you follow them while the orderly takes up the rear. The descent seems endless and the spectacle unbearable, seeing the body jolting around between the hands of those two like a vulgar bundle of cheap cargo. You finally reach the ground floor, and they set the body down on a stretcher that was already there. You do not thank them. You simply ask coldly:

"How much?"

"Two thousand francs," one of them replies, stone faced.

That very moment, Armando arrives with a white sheet. Seeing you rummaging in your bag, he wants to know how much the porters asked for. When he hears the amount, he is incensed and turns to them.

"Two thousand francs? You're kidding! It's two hundred francs per floor when you bring up a patient. You think I don't know that? Don't tell me it's more difficult going down than going up."

"It's two hundred francs for a living patient. A corpse is more expensive…"

This discussion is becoming obnoxious. Arguing like junk dealers about your colleague's corpse which is still warm is more than painful. It's indecent.

"Forget it, Armando, I have the money… Here, here's your two thousand francs…"

"Take it and get out of here," Armando says, still furious.

Atareta unfolds the white sheet and covers the body carefully. When she is done, the orderly who had kept quiet during all that time grabs the stretcher and heads toward the morgue.

The three of you follow him.

The morgue is not far. The orderly asks Armando to go with him into the cold room to see the cabinet where the body will be placed. Luckily, Armando is there. You do not have the heart to see that depressing room again, where your sister's body stayed, a room full of corpses, some of which were lying on the floor because they were not brought in by relatives or simply because they were homeless and died on the sidewalk. Too many horrible memories. You feel immensely grateful to him and, despite your reluctance, his presence is comforting.

After a moment, he comes back with a receipt and hands it to you: C76A. That is the number of the cabinet where your friend now rests. Tears start streaming down your cheeks again.

TWENTY-THREE

BATATOU IS DEAD. Killed. The image of her stiff body being tossed around in the stairwell keeps playing in your mind as you leave the morgue and head toward the hospital exit. How could life be so cruel as to take Batatou, a woman who never challenged her condition as an exploited person and who would never have joined your protest had she not been compelled to do so by your decision? Perhaps she only accepted to go along because of all those questioning looks darted at her when for once, she took the floor in public? In fact, as much as you know, for example, important details of Bileko's or Moukiétou's lives, you know very little about Batatou's, except for the fact that she gave birth to triplets and that one of them, as well as her husband, had died.

What intrigues you most is that not a single relative has yet to come forward despite the two radio announcements and a televised bulletin with her photo that you broadcast last night. Apart from a young Rwandan woman, a refugee who told you that she was alone in the world, with no father or mother, no brothers or sisters, no uncles, or cousins because they were killed during the genocide, you do not know a single individual in Africa who doesn't have a single relative, no matter how distant. That is why you need to be absolutely certain that Batatou has no family at all before you bury her.

The news of a person's death generally spreads very quickly, and you are sure that the women from the quarry will start showing up at the hospital well before eleven o'clock, the scheduled meeting time. Her death has turned a simple demand for some bags of gravel into a tragedy. Who will be held responsible? What happens next? Will there be a criminal investigation? Things are really beginning to spiral out of control.

The very moment you step through the hospital's main gate, your cell phone rings.

"Is this the number the TV gave regarding a certain Batatou?" a voice asks as soon as you utter "Hello".

"Yes... Do you know her? Are you a relative?"

You turn on your speakerphone and gesture for Atareta and Armando to come listen.

"No... I am not family... I saw the photo on TV, and she is the spitting image of one of my neighbors. At first, I hesitated because the resemblance could be purely coincidental, but the details, that she was a stone breaker, that she had triplets but only two are left, relieved any doubts, all the more because it's been two or three days since she's been home. Also, I know she doesn't know anyone in this city. Taking all of that into account, I thought it had to be her, even if two or three details didn't match."

"Yes, she may very well be your neighbor." "You said her name is Batatou?"

"Yes, at least that's what she went by... "

"Batatou... Batatou... " she says aloud, as if searching her memory. No, I don't know her by that name. But... "

"Hold on a second. I'm going to ask my colleague here next to me if she knows her by another name."

"I can't talk much longer. I'm in a kiosk. It costs a hundred-fifty francs a minute and I only have three hundred francs."

"Give me your number quickly and I'll call you right back."

You repeat the numbers she dictates to you while Atareta

writes them down on her palm with a black Bic pen, lacking any paper at hand. She hangs up.

"Do you know if Batatou had another name?"

"No," Atareta answers.

"She told us that Batatou was a nickname she'd given herself because she'd had triplets. *Tatou* means "three" in her language. Nobody thought to find out her real name. I'm going to call that woman back and ask her to come to the hospital to see the body and confirm it's her neighbor.

"You can use my cell," Armando offers, "I put ten thousand francs worth of credits on it this morning before I stopped by your place."

How could you refuse? You take the device as he hands it to you. You thank him.

The call does not go through on the first try. Which does not surprise you with such an unreliable telephone network. On the second try, you get: "Due to high call volumes, your call cannot go through. Please try your call again later." Bad luck. Finally, the third time works.

"Hello? Is this the kiosk?... Is the lady who just spoke to me there?"

"What lady? This is a public kiosk, Madam, and there are a lot of ladies making calls here.

What's her name?"

"Uh... she didn't give me her name... Say Batatou, call Batatou, she'll recognize the name... Please, it's urgent."

For a moment, there was silence, then you hear: "Batatou... is there a Batatou here?" Silence again, then:

"Hello? Yes, I'm the one who talked to you... I was saying that the photo and the information that was given matches with what I know about my neighbor, but not the name or the fact that she had a husband who'd been killed. She was never married."

"Listen, would you be kind enough to come to the hospital to see if it is her?"

"I live very far, and I don't have any money for a taxi."

"Take a taxi. We'll pay the driver when you get here."

"No, really, I can't. I'm preparing cassava that I need to sell tomorrow. It's already boiling on the stove, and I can't turn it off. Why don't you come here to see where she lived? That could help you."

"That's a good idea. Describe to us exactly where you live, and we'll be there right away. Thank you so much, it's really kind of you to leave your cassava on the stove to come to the kiosk to talk to us, and to have spent your money."

"Don't mention it. She considered me her only real friend, almost like a sister."

"I'm going to let you speak with someone who knows the city well."

You hand the phone to Armando who goes over the directions several times. The three of you decide that Atareta will stay at the hospital and wait for the others.

•

One cannot say that the neighborhood where Batatou lived is a model for urban planning. You had to turn around several times after going down several streets that turned into narrow alleys covered in garbage or cut off by insurmountable ditches. The rain that fell the night before makes driving treacherous because it is impossible to know whether the layer of stagnant water covering parts of the road is hiding deep potholes. Armando's greatest fear is breaking the vehicle's driveshaft each time the tires fall abruptly into those concealed holes. After a while, by dint of getting bogged down in the deep ruts dug by the vehicles that drove through them before you, you decide to give up and continue by foot. Armando masterfully manages to raise the vehicle onto a shoulder which has miraculously appeared on the side of the road.

Right away, you are assaulted by the smell. A rotten smell wafting through the air from the garbage dump on the roadside. You instinctively take out your handkerchief and hold it over your nose like a gas mask, but to no avail. The smell seeps through the fabric, goes straight to your throat and invades your lungs. You feel as if you are suffocating. Armando and you leapfrog the garbage which the rain washed onto the road: plastic bags, biomedical waste, household rubbish and, you are sure, human waste because when you don't have toilets, you defecate in nature. Four children, barefoot and with bare hands, are rummaging around in the heaps of trash. A little further, another sitting all alone on the heap of garbage is eating a piece of bread. You keep walking. The first houses are just on the edge of the dump, and you wonder how their inhabitants can live with such a stench. About fifty yards further, with the smell strongly reduced, the air becomes more breathable.

From afar, you see a woman waving her arms like a windmill as she comes toward you yelling: "It's here, come this way." She is quick to catch up with you. "I'm Adama," she introduces herself. She explains to you that when she saw you arrive, she immediately figured you were the ones she was waiting for. She asks you to follow her. In the street, a dozen kids are kicking a ball around. Just as you get up to them, the goalkeeper, guarding a goal marked with two bamboo sticks, lunges and misses the ball which ends its trajectory in the muddy water-filled open sewer. While the other team congratulates one another yelling: "Goal... goal...," he retrieves the ball, puts it back in play, then, pinching his nose with his fingers, blows it loudly, gets rid of his mucus with a flick, and wipes his hands on his t-shirt. Further down the road, two even younger boys and a girl are having fun digging small ditches and, using their hands as shovels, amass mud to build embankments. You finally arrive in front of Adama's compound.

She invites you in. In a corner of the courtyard, resting on three large stones, a water bucket filled with cassava wrapped in wild leaves is boiling. The cover is a large jute bag. A young girl with a pagne tied above her breasts is drawing water from a well nearby. When she sees you, she puts down the bucket she is holding and comes to greet you.

"Get out some chairs for our guests," Adama says to her, and, turning toward you: "This is my daughter. She's getting ready to go celebrate a friend's birthday, but before that, she is going to another friend's to get her hair braided."

The girl comes back with two plastic chairs, just like the ones you rented for your protest. Adama sits down on a round wicker chair.

"Do you want something to drink?" she offers.

"No, thank you. That's very kind, but we don't have time. We're really in a hurry. The other women are waiting for us at the hospital."

"Where are the children?"

"They're with us."

"Well, as I told you, the photo looks like my neighbor, but her name is not Batatou. Her name is Vutela."

"Vutela!... Do you know any family members?"

"She had an aunt. At least that's how she always referred to her. Unfortunately, she died about four years ago. She didn't have anyone else, and I am her only friend. But are we talking about the same person? Aside from going to the hospital to identify her, what proof do you need to be sure that Vutela and Batatou are one and the same person?"

"I don't know," you say. "Maybe we'll find something after we visit her house."

"Let's go find out."

The three of you stand up. Before leaving for your presumed Batatou's house. Adama first goes over to the hearth, moves the embers around under the bucket, adds some wood and, using a pot lid as a bellow, fans the fire, turning the smoke into glowing flames. Then she asks her daughter to watch the fire and not to leave until she is back.

Batatou aka Vutela's abode is seven houses down on the same street. A small rectangular shack made of baked bricks. Weeds are already starting to invade the lot. Adama knows where her friend hides her key. She retrieves it and opens the door. A musty smell festers in the house which has been closed for several days now. She opens the big window to let some air and light in. The house has two rooms. A shabby living room, with a cushionless armchair and two chairs beside a small table on which a pot and two plates sit piled on top of each other. Two fat, ash-grey cockroaches, surprised by the light, scurry across the table, then disappear. At the back, the kitchen utensils are arranged on a shelf. Adama lifts the pot cover. A rotten smell escapes, and she immediately closes it. It must be the meal Batatou had prepared to eat in the evening, after she got back home from the quarry. Now it is crawling with maggots.

Next, Adama enters the second room, the bedroom. You feel as though you are violating the owner's privacy by going in, but you must. You wait for Adama to open the window of the dark room before you enter.

No need to look. Yes, Vutela is Batatou. The proof is right there, on a small table next to the bed: one of the photos Laurentine Paka took with her cell phone the day you decided to raise the price of your stones. You remember that photo very well. Batatou is standing all smiles, flanked on each side by Bileko and you, holding her two children in your arms, surrounded by all the others, Moyalo, Moukiétou, Ossolo, Atareta, Iyissou, Bilala, and the rest, except Laurentine who took the photo.

"That's you!" Adama exclaims pointing you out in the photo.

You return to the living room. Adama sits down in the armchair, her eyes fixed on the photo. You sit down on the chairs.

"She never showed this to me," she says.

"Maybe she didn't have time to. We took these photos only two days ago." "Did she tell you she was married?"

"Not to me directly. When I arrived at the quarry, she was already there and everyone called her Batatou, and they told me that her husband was killed during the looting. She never denied it."

"Vutela never married. Worse, she had a morbid fear of pregnancy. She told me several times she would rather die than be pregnant. Besides, she panicked when she felt a man was a bit too interested in her. A real phobia."

You do not understand anything anymore. Who would have guessed that a person as modest and unassuming as she was could have such deep secrets?

"You were her friend. Tell us about her. I represent the women from the quarry, and you can trust us just as she trusted us. We had become her only family. Right now, one of her children is with me and the other with one of us. Tell us about her."

She stays silent as if she were having an internal debate with herself, her eyes still fixed on the photo. Finally, she raises her head and looks at you, then shifts her gaze to Armando. Their eyes meet and he, not sure how to gauge her look, suggests stepping out and leaving the two of you alone. She tells him he may stay, but Armando decides to step out anyway. It's just the two of you now, two women trying to decode the life of a third woman.

"Perhaps it's better he left. Since you are her friend, I can reveal the secret that binds us. I don't think I'm betraying her. We became very close because those despicable soldiers did it to us together."

You're in shock. Mute, stunned. You pull yourself together and dare say the word she could not utter.

"Did it... did it... You mean they r... raped you? She never told us."

"Why would she tell you? Some things are better left unsaid if you want to lead your life without being judged by people who cannot understand."

"What happened? How did it happen?"

"It's not an easy thing to talk about... The murderous madness of the victorious soldiers was unleashed on our neighborhood when we were coming home from the market. The attack was so sudden and unexpected that there was total panic. We bolted, abandoning our goods. The two of us ran together, she and I, but no matter our speed, the gunshots were getting closer. And we were out of breath anyway. In the blink of an eye, we spotted a dilapidated house in a lot lost in tall grass, with part of its front wall crumbled, while the part still standing held a doorless wooden frame. There was no roof. It was what we needed for refuge because no one would dream of looting the ruins of a house. We hurried not inside but behind the back wall in case they decided to look inside the shack anyway. We found a man there who had had the same idea and, trembling with fear, he placed his pointer finger over his lips, instructing us not to make a sound.

"I think the soldiers saw us enter the compound, because barely had we settled behind the wall, and they were already coming in. With great fanfare, they looked inside the house as we thought they would and when they didn't find anyone, they went around it.

"And there we were, three frightened beings. And they, four armed roughnecks. The man who was with us immediately threw himself on his knees, pleading with them for his life: they did not even listen to him, and with a bullet to the head he toppled over backward. They threw themselves on us, shouting the most vulgar words. When the first one started to unzip his fly, Vutela went crazy. She started yelling: 'Kill me, I'd rather you kill me.' Two came at me. Two at Vutela. Then a fifth soldier came dragging a woman who was resisting as much as she could. I don't know what that soldier had smoked, but he seemed completely nuts. He threw the woman down and, wrestling her to the ground despite her kicks, forced his penis into her mouth. Her mouth full of him, the woman started grunting. Then, suddenly, the soldier leapt several yards, howling wildly, blood spurting out from his penis, lacerated by several bites. The soldier who did it to me first and then passed the baton to his counterpart, jumped furiously onto the poor woman, shoved the barrel of his Kalashnikov into her mouth and fired. And for good measure, he shoved the barrel into the vagina of the woman whose head was already in smithereens, then shot again. The horror. We were close enough to be splattered with sperm, blood, and bits of human flesh. When they finally left, dragging their buddy who was still pissing blood, Vutela fainted, bleeding from her vagina.

"I suffered much more for her than for myself because she was a virgin when those soldiers assaulted her. No man had even touched her before that. Isn't it dreadful that her first experience with a man had to be that?"

"Yes, it's dreadful. A woman's worst nightmare."

"Worse, she who had always sworn that she didn't want to have any children found herself pregnant a few weeks later…"

"You mean the triplets…"

"Yes, those children are the product of that rape."

"And yet, she loved them so!"

"Yes, she loved them. It was not easy for her, especially in the beginning. For a long time, her feelings were torn between repulsion and love for them. Repulsion and perhaps even hate, not only because of the physical suffering she endured during the delivery. She especially hated them because those children, *her* children, reminded her of her rapists and their bestial breathing over her, and that they were the result of what those men planted inside her. But the moment she felt it, her hatred was disarmed by the innocence of those children who did not ask to be born, and who, in their own way, were victims too. Paradoxically, that same physical suffering which drove her to hate them reminded her that they were in reality her own flesh and blood. A strong feeling of affection for them would overcome her then, and she would hold them in her arms to protect them from the suffering of the world. Is that what maternal love is?"

"I understand. It is not easy to put yourself in the shoes of a mother of a child conceived from a rape. You were very lucky you did not get pregnant."

"Yes, but I lost my husband. When he found out that I was raped, he threw me out of his house without any regard for me, saying I was a… defiled woman! He never understood my suffering."

"Did you have children?"

"Yes, a daughter, the one you met a little earlier."

There was nothing more to say. The two of you keep quiet—she, perhaps replaying the images of the horror like a movie in her mind, and you, respecting her silence. Finally, she comes out of her recollections and asks:

"What are you going to do now?"

"Now that we're sure that Batatou is Vutela, if no relative comes forward, we are going to make arrangements for her burial. Let's not touch anything, we'll deal with all that later. Let's leave now, let's close up the house."

She closes the two windows, and you exit the house. She closes the door and while she goes behind the house to put the key back where it is kept, Armando asks you:

"So?"

"It's a sad story. I'll tell you later."

To get back to the taxi, you have to return to Adama's house. The three of you walk in silence. You cannot stop thinking about Batatou because everything you just found out about her intrigues you: her phobia of men, and especially her terror of becoming pregnant in a country where not having children is still shameful, a stigma. How many women have been disowned for being barren?

"What are you going to do about the children?"

Adama's voice interrupts your thoughts.

"We don't know yet. We'll see after the burial. I still don't understand why she was so afraid to have children."

"Not afraid of having children. Afraid of being pregnant, of giving birth. She was worried sick throughout the whole pregnancy."

"Why didn't she abort?"

"You think it's easy to get an abortion?"

No, it is not easy. You think about your own situation, about what happened when you were seventeen. Luckily you had a woman like Auntie Turia by your side to help you.

"You're right," you acquiesce, "it's not easy. I know."

"She took some time before she trusted me enough to tell me her story, and I have never told anyone. Now that she is dead and you are taking care of her children, I can tell you with a clear conscience.

"First, I must say that we got very lucky because three weeks after those bandits attacked us, a Doctors Without Borders team arrived. I don't know what would have happened to us without those doctors. Dead, probably. They gave us antibiotics and repaired Vutela's vagina which was in terrible shape. They're the ones who discovered she was pregnant. The more her belly grew, the more anguished Vutela became, and the more she had nightmares. When she was six months pregnant, her belly was huge, but we didn't know she was carrying triplets. Then one night in her eighth month she woke up with terrible abdominal pains. I stayed with her the whole night, trying to calm her as much as I could with potions and massages as we waited for daybreak so I could bring her to the hospital. She was burning up with fever. With a wet towel, I tried to cool down her body. I thought: that's it, she's going to die, as she became delirious and started crying out incoherently 'I don't want to... don't die... don't leave me, mother... you are not alone... yes, I'm here, my dear sister... the flies...'

"At dawn, I ran to find a taxi. I did not go to the market that day. I asked my daughter to go and sell my cassava for me. It was a sudden malaria attack which could have killed her. Very dangerous for a pregnant woman, the nurses told us. They kept us there all morning. They put her on an IV drip, of course not before first making sure I had enough money to pay for it. When the drip was finished, they let her rest for another hour and released her midafternoon with some pills that Vutela was to take for a week.

"I came back to see her at night and brought her some rice porridge. After I got her up on her feet and poured the porridge into a deep bowl, I sat down beside her and asked if she felt strong enough to eat by herself or if she needed me to help her. She started to cry. I didn't know what to say or do. I just sat there in silence and let her tears flow. When she'd gotten it all out, still sniffling now and then, she said to me:

'I don't know how to thank you, Adama. What you've done for me, my own family wouldn't have done.'

'Of course, Vutela,' I protested, 'anyone would have done what I have. Tell me if you have a relative in this city. I'll do anything to find them. Or else, tell me where your village is. I can send a messenger there.'

'I don't know anything about my family anymore. My parents, if they are still alive, must think I've been dead all this time.'

'Dead?'

'Yes. I fled my village when I was thirteen. Because of what my older sister went through. She was fourteen when my father married her to a forty-year-old man. Oh, how she cried and cried the day of her wedding! She was so miserable! At fifteen, she was pregnant. Her belly was so big, it seemed like she had turned into some sort of round ball. And then came delivery time. It was horrible. I hope to never see such a scene again in my lifetime. Mama always told me that the sun must not rise or set twice on a woman giving birth. Sadly, that was not my sister's case, who suffered hell for three days. They were screaming for her to push, push and she tried to push, howling.

When, exhausted, she couldn't anymore, they told her that she was lazy because she was not pushing enough. In fact, the baby's head was too big and was stuck in the birth canal. She was sweating, yelling, and she fainted several times. They placed wet towels on her forehead and gave her little slaps to bring her to. I was too young to understand that the reason for all this suffering was that my sister's body was not developed enough to carry a baby. It was only on the fourth day of her ordeal that a midwife arrived. They had sent someone the night before to the health center to get her. To get there, first they had to borrow a pirogue and then walk an hour to the place. By the time the midwife arrived, the fetus had already died, and she had to take it out with forceps. My sister survived, but I'm telling you, I preferred that she died rather than live through what she experienced.

"I don't really know what happened during those three days when she was in labor and excruciating pain, but a hole must have opened up somewhere in her body, where the pee and poop come out, because she could no longer hold it in."

"Oh my god," you exclaim, interrupting Adama's story. "An obstetric fistula."

"Is that what it's called?" she asks.

"Yes. In fact, it's an abnormal orifice between the bladder and the vagina or between the vagina and the rectum, when blood circulation to the vaginal tissue has been blocked for a long time."

"Anyway," Adama goes on, "what she told me after was difficult to hear..." Pausing sometimes to sniffle with little hiccups, she continued her story: 'She stunk of urine and feces. Nobody could stand being around her anymore. Her criminal husband disowned her immediately, saying she was no longer a woman. He even claimed that what happened to my sister was a punishment from the gods or the ancestors for I don't know what taboo she defied. We couldn't bring her to the health center because nobody wanted her in their pirogue. The poor girl! She spent her days in a wood cabin on the outskirts of the village, alone, abandoned, with a swarm of flies around her. I was the only one who spent time with her, brought her food and water. It was not easy. Sometimes the smell would make me vomit, but she was my sister. Even Mama didn't stay with her as much as I did because she too believed that her daughter must have broken a taboo, otherwise what happened to her wouldn't have happened. Three weeks later, she came down with a sudden fever, and within forty-eight hours she was dead, alone in her cabin. I'm the one who found her body in the morning. I found her lying there, on the ground, covered with hundreds of flies buzzing all around. It was awful, the way they got into and blocked her nostrils just like they did her mouth, which had stayed open in death. She was my sister, my big sister. I used to play with her. I felt so alone!... That is when I became terrified of getting pregnant and giving birth. Even today, at twenty-six, I'm scared shitless and my heart pounds like crazy whenever a man gets near me.'"

"Now I understand," you say.

Adama nods her head and replies:

"Wait, that's not all. There's more. Let me finish telling what she confided in me that night."

"Sorry, go ahead."

"She continued: 'Barely three months after my sister died, one early afternoon, I saw people gathering at our place, including the fisherman who was the richest man in our village. Rich because, while everyone else had thatched or palm roofs, his roof was made of corrugated sheet metal. The women were sitting on one side and the men on the other. They were speaking in proverbs that I did not understand and from time to time, they would share kola nuts and palm wine. I was thirteen and Mama made me sit next to her on a mat.

'And then my father called me and told me to come over next to him. I got up and stood before him. He asked me to serve some palm wine to the fisherman who had put his sunglasses back on, another sign of wealth. When I handed him the glass, my father said: "My daughter, this is your husband!" Surprised and afraid, I let the glass fall and ran off crying. Angry, my father yelled after me. A man chased me and with his long strides, quickly caught me. My father started scolding me. The fisherman, however, spoke kindly to me, telling me that I had nothing to worry about, that I would eat well at his house, that he would buy me nice clothes and even a watch and some shoes like a city woman, and so on. I wasn't listening. I just sat there next to Mama with my head down. Finally, they left. I was happy. I thought it was over.

'Usually, I would wash up by myself at night before going to bed, but that night, Mama made me wash up earlier and, to make sure I was nice and clean, she scrubbed my body with a luffa. She told me to get dressed because we were going to go out, and my aunt's arrival only deepened the mystery. It was only when I saw the fisherman's sister arrive that I understood.

'All those women dragged me to his house despite my kicking and screaming. I only stopped protesting when my father told me to shut up in his authoritarian voice because we were taught since we were very little that we must always obey our father, and later our husband. Mama carried my things. The women had a long discussion with the fisherman who promised them he would treat me like his own daughter who was the same age as me and that he would not rush things and would give me time to get used to his house, etc. Then all those people abandoned me there, closing the door behind them. I was trapped. I couldn't escape because it was night outside and, at thirteen, not only are you afraid of nocturnal animals but also of devils, witches, and ghosts who—we were told—walked the night with the owls.

'The fisherman told me to follow him into his bedroom. Afraid, I obeyed. He showed me the bed—a big bed—and said smiling: "This is your bed." That is when I got a good look at him for the first time. An old man, fifty years-old, even older than my beloved sister's husband, a bald spot atop his head and white hair on the side. His hideous smile exposed his gums and several missing teeth. "Don't be afraid, I'll be back," and he disappeared. I sat on a corner of the bed, all hunched up. I did not know what was going to happen to me.

'He came back. Wearing only his underwear and a loose-knit shirt. He asked me to lie down. I refused and turned my face toward the wall, so I didn't have to look at him anymore. "Look at me!" he howled. When I turned around, he had on neither underwear nor undershirt, exposing his broad torso speckled with grey hair, his paunchy stomach and horror of horrors, the bit of stiff flesh between his legs which was moving up and down with jerky movements like a snake head. I immediately imagined the beast who impregnated my sister, and I screamed. That did not stop him. Since he was stronger than me, he picked me up and threw me onto the bed. But what I lacked in strength, I made up for in flexibility and agility, so I bounced off the mattress. As he attempted to grab me, I kicked him below the belly which must have hurt because he bent over himself screaming. I got out of the room, pulled the door open and was outside, in the night. I was no longer myself, no longer afraid of the wild animals or demons and ghosts that inhabit the moonless nights. I couldn't go to my parents'; they would bring me back to that guy's place the following day and apologize. I remembered the cabin where my sister had been quarantined. It had a strong door. That's where I spent the night. I didn't sleep a wink because I could hear the footsteps of panthers who had smelled my scent and were prowling around the house, and I was listening to the owls, the sorcerers' birds, ruffling their wings before taking flight, I felt the breath of the ancestors and ghosts who were leaving their world to haunt the earth at night... no, I didn't sleep a wink.

'I left my refuge at the crack of dawn, afraid of being surprised by the people from the village. I wanted to run away, far away. I knew there was a fishing village two hours walking from ours. No one knew my family there. I arrived exhausted, but I was afraid to enter the village. I sat under a tree and, my body giving up, I dozed off.

'When I woke up, a woman, older than my mother, was standing by the foot of the tree. In fact, I woke up to her shaking me gently. She asked me who I was. I did not dare give her my name. I gave my sister's, Vutela. Yes, I have been Vutela since that day. My sister's name had become mine. I had become my sister. I told her I didn't have any family, that my parents had drowned on their way home from a wedding ceremony held in a village far from our home, when their pirogue was charged by a hippopotamus and flipped over. I was lucky, or unlucky, to survive the wreck. The name of my village? I did not know because I was too little when all that had happened. Since then, I lied again and again, living here and there, wherever people are willing to welcome me.

'I think she believed me and was moved by my little tale. She gave me something to eat and told me that a young girl should not wander around like that, alone, that many awful things could happen to her. She asked me to come with her to her village, a little further up the river, because she was here only to buy fish.

'I stayed with her for almost a year. Even my parents had not shown me so much affection. She had a younger sister who also loved me very much. She took me with her when she decided to leave the village to try her luck in the city. She died four years ago. She left me this plot and this house.'

"That's Vutela's story as she told it to me that night, while eating the boiled meat I had brought for her. A week later, she still had pain, but that time it was labor pain. The malaria attack had caused a premature birth. We were lucky once again because the Doctors Without Borders team had not left the country yet and one of their mobile teams had returned to the area. Thank God. Vutela's vagina was so damaged, she could not give birth naturally. Her triplets were delivered by caesarian."

Now Adama is silent. You also do not say anything for a moment, still shocked by all she has revealed.

"Tell me," she resumes, "when will the burial be? I want to be there. That way she will see me from where she is now and will know I have not abandoned her. I'll keep your group photo with me."

You realize that you arrived at her compound a while ago and that you ended up having the conversation standing in front of the entrance gate. You thank her once again and offer to reimburse her for the telephone charges she incurred. She refuses outright. Then you ask if she has cassava to sell. She does. You buy six, two for you, two for Auntie Turia, and two for Armando. It comes to more than what she paid for her telephone call.

TWENTY-FOUR

CRIES AND LAMENTS. Howling. Songs and tears. A crowd has already gathered in front of the hospital's main gate by the time you arrive with Armando. The news really did travel fast. Before the car even stops, the women rush over to you, eager for an update. Atareta, whom you left to greet them, is visibly overwhelmed by all these people, many of whom are not from the quarry. In any case, apart from confirming Batatou's death, she did not have anything else to tell them. Seeing your colleagues from the quarry crying, singing, and moaning makes your throat tighten and your eyes well up with tears. But you must not cry. You must not let yourself be overcome with emotion. They expect more from you, that you talk to them, comfort them. Even if that changes nothing about the reality of the situation, that Batatou is dead.

When you get out of the taxi, the first thing you notice is Mâ Bileko's hand flailing about. You understand that she has something to tell you. She comes over and whispers in your ear that it would be better not to have the meeting here at the hospital. You discuss briefly with her, come to an agreement, and ask her to inform the crowd. She raises her arm and waves her hand up and down like a wing flapping, to ask for silence. The voices lower enough for her to be heard.

"The hospital courtyard is not an appropriate place to discuss the tragedy that has befallen us. Anyway, there are still many details that are missing. For that reason, we, the women of the quarry, are going to meet this afternoon at Méréana's to discuss and make the necessary decisions. Decisions concerning Batatou's funeral and how we will proceed with our protests. As for the rest of you, we thank you for your sympathy. We will release a statement on the radio during the obituary announcements to specify when and where the wake will be held and what we intend to do. Thank you very much."

The crowd finds the proposal reasonable and starts to disperse in awkward silence, as if, after the public outcry and tears that welcomed you, each of those women resigned herself to the fact that their friend was dead, and they would each have to live with their personal, individual pain. You notice that Laurentine and her partner are heading toward the bus stop, whereas most of the other women are walking. Armando, once again, insists on bringing you in his taxi, but since there are four seats, you ask Bileko, Anne-Marie and Iyissou who are nearby to go with you. You do not want to be alone with him. Your body and your mind are too tired.

•

You arrive ahead of the others, followed by Laurentine and her beau. Auntie Turia, aware of Batatou's death, is surprised to see you back so soon. You hand her the cassava that you bought from Adama and let Mâ Bileko explain the situation while you go see the children. Bilala, Iyissou and Laurentine start setting up the chairs right away. Little by little, those who walked start coming in. In her managerial role, Bileko orders drinks—bottled soda and water. You will need it because it is hot and you all are thirsty, especially those who walked from the hospital. Finally, everyone sits down, and you start the meeting.

Your friends are more relaxed than they were this morning, now that the reality about their colleague's death has sunken in and their emotions have settled a little, even if their anger is still smoldering. You are the only one who knows Batatou's sad story and that her real fake name is Vutela. No one knew her real name, not even Adama. You decide not to talk about it though since she hid it while she was alive. In any case, your emotional attachment was to the name Batatou, not Vutela.

After some discussion, you quickly agree that burying Batatou the next day would give the impression that you are ridding yourselves of your friend in haste. So, you must delay the burial by at least a day so you can plan a decent funeral.

"A decent funeral?" probes Bilala, the one who was your voice when you announced your decision to the world, that the money you so graciously received from the President of the Republic's wife would be entirely reserved for Batatou. "Not only decent, dignified!"

"Not only dignified, majestic," Iyissou adds, "we have the money."

"Yes," Moukiétou says, "those people need to know that we know how to bury our dead." Yes, you think, without saying so, that would be a real slap in the face to Tito and his corrupt gang.

"She must be buried in the downtown cemetery where all the important politicians are buried," says Laurentine Paka, for once sitting without her guardian angel. "In fact, all the prominent financial and political figures are buried in that cemetery. It's expensive," she goes on, turning to Bileko, "but we have enough money, right?"

"Yes," the other confirms, "we haven't even spent half of the one million yet." Everyone applauds both Bileko's proposal and her effective management.

You all discuss the details of how to implement your decisions. You divvy up the tasks rather swiftly. First, among those who are to take care of the chairs, the sound system, the coffee and sugar, the lanterns, everything you need to make sure the vigil will last throughout the night; then among those who are to take care of all the administrative paperwork, including the death certificate and the purchase of the grave. Mâ Bileko is at the center of it all, ensuring stewardship of Madam the First Lady's embezzled money.

•

Normally, the peak time at wakes is around ten at night since that is the time those who have come early because they do not plan to spend the whole night overlap with those who come late because they plan to stay till morning. But tonight, the court-yard is already full at eight. There are so many people, they are spilling out into the street. Spending the night at a wake is no walk in the park because the nights are chilly and the mosqui-tos unbearable. The women coming for the whole night arrive all bundled up with a mat and a blanket under their arms.

For your part, the organization is near-perfect. Strings of electric lanterns light up the courtyard—let's pray there isn't one of those unplanned power cuts you're so used to. You have added benches to the chairs to accommodate all this crowd. A CD-cassette player with a built-in amp and speakers is ready to take over for the mourners, once they take a break after several songs. You have enough plastic mugs and cups to distribute the coffee you're keeping hot thanks to some wood fires you have burning underneath two big pots each placed on three large stones set up in equilateral triangles. In anticipation, you also set up a team of volunteers ready to intervene in case of any trouble since at these organized vigils to honor the memory of the deceased, serious incidents often occur. Children or neph-ews, for example, beat to death and sometimes even burn alive elderly family members, because they have the misfortune of having white hair since that, for them, is the sign that those people are sorcerers, therefore responsible for the death. Gone are the days when Africa respected her elders and their white hair was considered a sign of wisdom. But that is not what wor-ries you tonight. What concerns you tonight is that the music, the lights, the coffee, will attract those young hoodlums who will take advantage of it all to make it a dating venue with their boyfriends and girlfriends. Which too often leads to jealous showdowns and altercations that inevitably result in bloody brawls. You want nothing of the sort. You really want Batatou's wake to be calm and dignified.

So, you take the mike. You thank everyone, especially those who are not directly connected to your quarry but who have come to support you in solidarity. Then you announce the decisions you have made. You are interrupted by a round of applause when you announce that Batatou will be laid to rest downtown. Atareta takes over to give other details and to answer questions.

When Atareta finishes speaking, the singing resumes. Anyone who knows how to sing or play an instrument starts singing, playing, or simply clapping their hands. But they are not sad songs. Some have a rather gay rhythm. You are not a good musician, not a good singer, but it doesn't keep you from trying to keep the beat with the maracas Atareta handed to you.

Nights of vigil can be long, especially when, after the singers are tired, you start playing songs on cassettes or CDs no one is really listening to. That is when those who decided not to stay the whole night go and the others regroup according to affinities to chat, confide in one another or to revel in cheerful stories. It is also the time when the young people either start flirting or fighting. But all of that only lasts a few hours before people start to really settle in for the night. The music stops. The women who brought their mats spread them out to lie down, bundled up in their *pagnes* and blankets. The men focus on getting as comfortable as possible on their chairs. At around two o'clock in the morning, all you can hear is snoring interrupted by crushing mosquito slaps. You, wearing jeans and thick socks to protect you from getting bitten, settle comfortably into your armchair, ready to conquer the night as it progresses toward the first light of dawn.

TWENTY-FIVE

Méré, do you know how to say "a flower" in Māori?

"He puti puti!"
Isn't that beautiful? :-)
Tam.

●

"Big sister, big sister."

A voice, as if in voice-over, interrupts your dream. A charming dream that sunk you back into one of those text messages Tamara used to send you often on a whim. Tamara was like that. She did everything passionately, sometimes on impulse, sometimes with thoughtfulness and care. A text just to let you know how to say "a flower" in Māori. Now that you think about it, you should have asked her how to say "star" in that language.

The voice insists. Your sleepy brain wakes up with a jolt, finally recognizing the voice.

"Sorry to have woken you up, big sister." It is Zizina, Mâ Bileko's daughter.

"No, I wasn't really sleeping… just lost in a daydream."

"Must have been a nice dream. You had a big smile on your face."

"I was dreaming about my little sister, Tamara. You now, you look a lot like her, Zizina."

"Thanks. A shame I didn't get to meet her, I really would have loved to."

She rummages through her purse and takes out a small packet with a dozen prepaid phone cards. She hands you a five thousand franc one.

"This is my contribution to Batatou's funeral. I know you have a lot of calls to make today. I asked my mom to give it to you, but she insisted I deliver it personally."

"Thank you, that's really kind of you. We'll make good use of it."

"Good, I'll go now. I'm going to go wash up quickly then I'll meet you at the cemetery. And, on my way, I'll try to sell a little."

"Your mom told me your small mobile business selling phone cards and electronic accessories for cell phones is going pretty well."

"Yes, since I'm the first to do this kind of door-to-door sales on a moped, I don't have much competition yet. But I'm sure a lot of people will start copying me. It may not seem so, but it's a risky business. I could get hit by a car or assaulted in some remote neighborhood. That's why I'm happy to sell down-town, especially at the stoplights. The problem with downtown is that you have to constantly play hide-and-seek with the po-lice, and most of them are shady."

"I'll walk you out."

She had brought her moped inside the compound and locked it, afraid it would get stolen.

You exit the compound.

It is five-thirty in the morning. The sky is barely starting to brighten, the stars that watched over you through the night have already disappeared. Once in the street, she props the bike on its metal kickstand, allowing the back wheel to turn freely, gets on and pedals in place full speed, playing with the throttle.

The engine turns on.

"See you later…"

"See you… By the way, how did the exam go?" Her eyes light up and she grins from ear to ear.

"Mama didn't tell you? I was accepted, among the top five!"

"Bravo!" You give her a warm hug. "I'm really happy for you."

"Thanks, and for Mama too. She gave me so much! I will never be able to repay her."

"Don't worry about that, that's what moms are for. They're sending you to Liberia, right? I hope it won't be too dangerous."

"I don't think so. It's not a combat unit, it's a paramilitary police unit to patrol the streets of Monrovia, the capital, catch bandits and help form a national police force. In a country coming out of a war and where there is such a strong rape culture, a robust all-female unit can make a difference."

"An all-women unit? That's amazing! I don't know of any precedent."

"We are the first African unit of its kind. The very first was made up of a contingent of Indian women. They are in Liberia now. We are going to replace them. You'll see, big sister, we are going to frighten those men," she adds with a smile.

"I hope not," you say, also smiling. "You mustn't frighten men. They'll consider it revenge. Revenge is never a healthy solution because it reeks of vindictiveness. It should be respect instead. We need to teach men to respect women. When do you leave?"

"In a week, but not directly to Liberia. We'll spend three weeks training first in Accra, in Ghana."

"That's an English-speaking country."[1]

"*Pretty good, thank you!*" She bursts out laughing. "Ok, I've got to go. See you this afternoon."

---

1. In English in the original text.

She turns the gas handle and takes off. You watch as she drives away. A success story. Who would have believed it knowing, as you do, that after her father's death she hit rock bottom? And now the girl is going to be a UN representative, an ambassador for peace. Who wouldn't be proud of her? She is he *puti puti*, that one.

You go back inside the compound. Apart from two or three women lagging behind, rolling up their mats and blankets to go, the compound is almost empty now. Wakes always end early in the morning so people can get to work on time. The courtyard is littered with plastic bags, paper cups, and cigarette butts. You'll have to sweep up before people come back tonight after the burial, for the final vigil to bid Batatou farewell. Apart from that, everything is in order. Now, it is time for you to go lie down for an hour or two before you tackle the day ahead, which is already proving to be a busy one.

TWENTY-SIX

FROM WHEREVER He keeps an eye on the mortals who come knocking at the door of His paradise, God must have been impressed by the way you accompanied Batatou to her final resting place. It could not have been a more dignified burial for that poor woman with no family, who had been so mistreated and humiliated in life.

Since the downtown cemetery is not far from the morgue, you all decided to walk. Escorted by two motorcyclists in formal dress, a brass band led the procession in a sonic halo of trumpets, trombones, drums, and cymbals glistening beneath the sun. The hearse followed, at a walking pace, with a large portrait of Batatou on top. Since Batatou did not have any close relatives, Mâ Bileko and you took their place in Armando's taxi, directly behind the hearse. Behind the taxi, behind the women from the quarry who distinguished themselves from the rest with their white t-shirts stamped with Batatou's effigy, was the immense crowd of men and women who came to pay their last respects to your fellow stone breaker. That is how you arrived at the cemetery, to the rhythm of the hearse's sirens, the crowd singing tunes introduced by the brass band and the brass band, in turn, picking up tunes launched by the crowd. Weighed down with floral wreaths, the casket was taken out of the hearse and carried to the grave on the shoulders of the women from the quarry. An evangelical pastor whom you did not know, probably from one of those revival Churches teeming in the country, gave a long, impassioned sermon about salt, sulfur, fire and other cosmic cataclysms, to vilify all the tyrants of this world who cause poor people like Batatou to suffer. He promised them that the wrath of Jehovah would befall them within the second coming of Christ. Then, after praising the happiness awaiting Batatou in the other world, he asked several times, though he made no effort to answer: "Where, O Death, is thy victory? O Death, where is thy sting?" Three women from the quarry spoke after the pastor ended his sermon and closed his Bible. The last one, choking on her tears and emotions, was unable to finish her speech. At long last, the floor was yours.

Feeling the mixed emotions of rage and pain, you said that you would have preferred that Batatou have a happy life on this earth rather than in the afterlife; that the corrupt dictators who mistreat their population should be judged here and now like common criminals by the International Court of Justice, not wait for Judgement Day. You strongly reaffirmed that you would fight to the end to see that the demands which led to your friend's death are met and, lastly, you swore on behalf of all of you to take care of her twins. 'Where, O Death, is thy victory?' asked the pastor. His victory was that he took a very dear friend away from us," you finally concluded, then threw the first clod of earth onto the coffin being lowered into the grave.

•

The courtyard will soon be full again for the final vigil. You find it's a good thing that, after the sadness and the tears at the cemetery, people can get together once more to celebrate the life of the deceased with song and drink, dancing and laughter. While you wait, you want to spend a little time with the children whom you have not seen all day long.

While you were at the burial, Auntie Turia prepared a large bucket of water for you and, even before you had time to sit down and rest your legs after the long ceremony at the cemetery, she suggested that you take a shower right away. Usually, you use hot water to wash at night, but today you use cold to refresh your body burning from the sweltering heat. When you get out of the shower, you feel cool and fresh. So hungry you could eat a horse, you devour the food she prepared for you, and she watches you eat for a while. Satisfied, she decides to go home to check if everything is fine there, promising to come back a little later in the evening, so she too can pay her last respects to Batatou.

You are sitting on the porch on Auntie Turia's now famous armchair; Batatou's daughter is on your lap. She must be starting to think that you are her mother since she attempts something that resembles a smile when you tap softly on her cheeks. Lyra, playing the big sister, trots toward you with a bottle in her hand wanting to put it in the little one's mouth as she has no doubt seen Auntie Turia do. You explain to her that Baby has already eaten and isn't hungry. She is not happy to hear that and begins to pout. The two boys are happy to see their mom too and try to tell you about their day at school despite Lyra constantly interrupting them. At that very moment, surrounded by all your children, you feel as if you are bathed in the plenitude of a self-sufficient world at peace with itself. The universe could disappear, and you would not even notice.

After a moment, they leave you and start playing amongst themselves. Batatou's baby has also fallen asleep. You get up quietly and place her gently on a mat. You look at your watch. You still have at least two hours before the first people start to arrive for the vigil. You pick up your radio, turn it on, and sit back down on your armchair with the backrest fully reclined. You close your eyes to relax and listen to the music.

"The Chinese are increasingly exploiting the forests of central Africa to respond to their colossal needs for tropical wood, without the slightest regard for regulations and often with the complicity of local authorities. 'At the rate the Chinese are cutting the wood here, we fear that four years from now certain rare species of the Chaillu forest massif will become extinct,' warns a farmer from the village of Ngoua-2 in the south-west region of Congo-Brazzaville. Graver still is that they are also razing young plants without reforesting afterward.

People are also noticing an influx of Malaysian companies who, like the Chinese, are invoking South-South or Afro-Asiatic cooperation to justify the predatory attitude of several among them. Those companies have acquired logging rights for four to five million hectares of natural forests in the Congo basin (Cameroon, Gabon, Congo, Equatorial Guinea, Central African Republic), implementing extensive exploitation methods which have resulted in full-scale natural disasters on the island of Java, on the Solomon Islands and in Papua New Guinea.

A young thirteen-year-old girl, Aisha Ibrahima Duhulow, has been stoned to death before a crowd of several hundred spectators in a stadium of the port city Kismayo in Somalia. She was raped by three men while on her way to visit her grandmother. Along with her father, the young girl tried to file a complaint with the al-Shabaab militia, faithful to the Islamist leader Hassan Turki who controls the city, but the militia opted instead to accuse her of adultery.

Before several hundred onlookers, the young girl was buried up to her neck, then about fifty men started throwing stones at her head. The stones used for the lapidation were neither large enough to cause instantaneous death, nor small enough to be harmless. Aisha Ibrahima Duhulow was dug up three times, pronounced still alive by nurses, then put back into the ground to be finished off. The young girl screamed and cried endlessly: 'Don't kill me, don't kill me.'

The guards opened fire on her parents and some witnesses who were trying to save her, leaving one child dead. The Islamists offered their apologies for the child's death but showed no regret for the stoning of Aisha Ibrahim Duhulow.

We would remind you that stoning, which is not at all mentioned in the Koran, is consider anti-Islamic by numerous respected Muslim scholars. . . "

Your blood curdles in your veins. You cannot listen anymore. Killing a thirteen-year-old girl with stones! Twice punished, once by being raped and a second time by being stoned. The only reason? She was born a woman! Help, men have gone mad. God, those men who are throwing stones are claiming to do it in your name: if you do not stop them, if you let this heinous crime go unpunished, then you too have gone mad, just like them. Seized with weariness, you feel weighed down by all those beings whose lives are stolen every day, simply because they are not born the right sex. Poor Aisha Ibrahima Duhulow being among them. You turn off the radio and cry.

The telephone.

You jump. Somehow you manage to snap out of your dismal thoughts and pull the phone out of your pocket. You do not recognize the number on the screen.

"Méréana Rangi?"

A woman's voice which seems familiar but you cannot manage to identify it. "It's me, the Minister who received you two days ago."

"Oh, of course! What a surprise!"

Surprised, you are. Normally, a Minister would never call directly. They always go through their secretary. This woman really does things her way.

"I have very good news for you and your colleagues, Madam Rangi. We just came out of an extraordinary meeting of the steering committee for the summit of African First Ladies, presided over, as you know, by the wife of the President of the Republic herself. My point of view prevailed, and it was decided that all your demands will be met."

"Ex... excuse me?... You're saying..."

"... that everything you asked for has been granted. From now on, you can sell your bags of gravel for twenty thousand francs. Regarding the bags you lost, it would have been too complicated and, above all, would have demanded too much time to verify who has how many bags. I made a proposal to pay each of you the equivalent of what five bags at twenty thousand francs each would cost, and it was accepted. I think it's a good compromise."

"That really is good news, Madam. I look forward to sharing it with my friends. But what guarantees us this decision will not be reversed?"

"Me, obviously! I am not the type to reverse her decisions. And the President of the Republic's wife, of course, magnanimous and generous as she is, despite the fact that you refused the proposal she made to you and took her willingness to help you as attempted bribery."

"And the Minister of the Interior? We do not trust him. He's the one who gave the order to shoot at us."

"Don't worry. The minutes were signed by the President's wife in her capacity as Chair of the summit and countersigned by me, as well as by the Minister of the Interior, who was present at the meeting. It is irrevocable. I forgot to tell you, but he will certainly be contacting you to confirm what I just told you. So, expect a call from him or from his office. I was anxious however to be the first to tell you because you know how much I am invested in this case and how much I have fought to see it through to a successful conclusion."

For a few moments, you are silent. Taking that as a sign you are reluctant to believe her, she proceeds:

"The stakes for this tenth summit of the African First Ladies are very high for the image of our country and its leader. It is absolutely imperative that nothing, especially a protest by women throwing stones, disrupts the opening ceremony which will be tomorrow evening, with a show and a gala dinner. So, everything needs to move very quickly. You will have your money in the morning before the official opening of the summit."

"I thank you from the bottom of my heart, Madam. You said you would help us, and you kept your word."

"I only did my work and the work entrusted to me by the President of the Republic."

"I'll share the good news with the others as soon as they all get here. They will be really pleased. Thank you again."

"I heard your friend's burial was quite spectacular."

"We did what we could. Though we would have preferred her to be here tonight to celebrate this victory with us."

"I understand. You will have what is owed to you tomorrow in the morning before the official opening of the summit."

"Thank you, Madam."

She stops talking, but you sense an ellipsis and that she has something else to say to you.

You are silent too for fear she will change her mind. "I'll tell you something, Madam Rangi."

"Yes."

"You are a tenacious woman. You have commanded my admiration and I hold you in high esteem."

"Thank you, Madam," you say, surprised and confused at the same time.

"Thanks to your protests, you have revived the importance of the Ministry of Women and Disabled Persons. I admit, you have a great deal of courage."

"Is it courage when you do not have a choice and are obliged to do what must be done if you want to survive?"

"Yes, because you could also just be intimidated and give up."

"Thank you," you reply, since you do not know what else to say.

"You're welcome."

You think that is the end of the conversation and that she is going to hang up, but no. She goes on.

"You know, all the conferences I've attended, all the statistics I boast about did not make me aware of the reality of women's suffering as much as the few minutes I spent talking with you... Since you left my office, there is one thing that keeps bothering me. How is it that a young woman of your disposition, who expresses herself so well, ends up being a stone breaker?"

"I believe I already told you, Madam."

"Not really. Would you be interested in coming to work with me at the Ministry? Someone like you would be very useful to have in my cabinet."

What did she say? You? Go from stone breaker to cabinet member? Is this some sort of joke? Another form of bribery in disguise, or does this powerful woman truly think you could be useful to her? When you do not know what to respond to a question but have to respond anyway, you have to evade.

"I don't know, Madam, your offer is so unexpected. I'll think about it. For the time being, I'll attend to our demands."

"I understand. When all this is over, call me back, I mean it. Good-bye and good luck."

"Good-bye, Madam, and thanks."

She finally hangs up. You sit quietly for a moment in your armchair, still confused by her final words. But suddenly it all comes to you—the full meaning of the information the Minister passed on to you. Elated, you leap out of your chair and do a few dance steps, then you jump up in the air and roar like a lion. In bewilderment, the children watch you, wondering whether their mother has suddenly lost her marbles.

TWENTY-SEVEN

TONIGHT IS THE final vigil. It is nine o'clock and the courtyard is already full. The mood is gay. Even the songs which seemed so sad last night have cast off the cloak of death and become "Should auld acquaintance be forgot," as if you were accompanying a friend who is leaving on a long trip. The drinks help too, especially the palm wine and the awful local beer of which some have already gulped down two or three bottles. Anyway, at least in death, Batatou has received the love and consideration she was denied throughout her life, even if that does not make up for it. But as humans, you and your colleagues have done all that needs to show to the eyes of the world that one life is worth no less than another.

Long before the meeting with your colleagues from the quarry, the news of your victory was already known to all. Now that you are all gathered at the back of the compound, away from the crowd and the noise of the vigil, you report to them exactly what the Minister told you. An unconditional victory. In fact, you got more than what you had hoped for: you thought you would sell your bags of gravel for fifteen thousand francs rather than ten thousand, and you ended up selling them for twenty thousand francs, which is double! None of you has more than three bags confiscated by the police—personally you only had two—but here you are being paid for five at full price. And you're fine with that since, it's only fair, you have to be compensated for the two days of work you lost.

When you finish your report, they all respond with energetic and warm applause. You are proud of your victory, not so much for getting what you wanted, but for the way you got it. Indeed, this was not one of those epic struggles to change the world which your sister Tamara was fond of. No, this was nothing but a selfish small-scale struggle to get more money for your bags of gravel. But even if it was no storming of the Bastille, you put your lives on the line: you were beaten, imprisoned, injured by bullets, and you lost one life. That counts.

You look at Iyissou, you look at Moyalo and Moukiétou, you look at Anne-Marie Ossolo and Laurentine Paka, you look at Bilala… all those women will have a minimum of one hundred thousand francs in their hands tomorrow! In the harsh trade of breaking stone, they never dreamed of seeing so much money all at once. From now on, they will know that in this world no battle is lost in advance, there are some fights that can be won. Their lives are going to change, so is yours.

It is during that joyous moment that you see Zizina arrive, her face beaming. Her mother, Bileko, is sitting next to you. You turn to her:

"Look, it's Zizina. She must have something urgent to tell you."

"To tell us," she replies with a mysterious grin, the meaning of which you don't grasp.

The young woman walks toward you, places her hand affectionately on your shoulder and greets the group excitedly. You all in turn greet her warmly.

"Mama gave me the news about your victory. I'm so happy about what is happening to you."

"Thanks so much, Zina," you say. "Your mother told us you also worked at the quarry at one time."

"Only for a week. I couldn't hold out. I don't have your strength."

"You were right to leave," says Laurentine Paka, "that's no job for a beautiful and intelligent young woman like you."

She laughs.

"I come to see you because I too have some good news to share. All of you know that I passed the UN exam to be part of a police force in Liberia. Well, the trip scheduled for next week was suddenly pushed forward. Just before I went to the cemetery, I received an urgent letter informing me that a UN chartered plane is arriving tomorrow, and I have to board in the afternoon for Accra."

She is interrupted by the women's applause.

"So, I come to say good-bye to you, to my mother's friends, because I think of you as my mothers and big sisters."

"You are our child, the child of us all," Moukiétou says. "We are so happy for you. Have a good trip and may God bless you."

You are all standing around her, each of you in your own way wishing her good luck and a safe journey. After all your demonstrations of affection, she decides to go. You escort her out of the compound to where she parked her moped, locked up to a post. She puts the engine in gear, climbs onto the seat, starts the motor and windmilling her right arm to bid you all, takes off. You follow her with your eyes until the moped's red taillight disappears into the night.

"We should give her a farewell gift. She is our daughter."

It is Bilala who has just spoken. You look at her. Very moved, she wipes a tear. Bilala, accused of being a witch by her own children who would have burned her alive had she not had the presence of mind to jump out of a window in order to escape.

Everyone accepts her idea. You put Anne-Marie in charge of choosing and buying the gift, first thing tomorrow morning. All you have to do now is join the rest of the vigil. You keep your cell phone handy in case the Minister of the Interior's office tries to contact you.

TWENTY-EIGHT

YOU REALIZE SOMETHING out of the ordinary is going on when you notice all the commotion by the entrance to the compound. By the time you get up to inquire about it, they have already entered: two individuals followed by a third, who is armed, probably a bodyguard. You immediately panic when you recognize the first: Tito Rangi in person! How dare he come here and defy you on your territory? Calm down, Méré, stay cool, composed. Rattled by Tito's sudden appearance, you pay no attention to the person accompanying him, or rather, whom he is accompanying, the Minister of the Interior—in the flesh. Who wouldn't recognize the Minister of police, law and order, the man who crushes protests, imprisons students and political opponents, sends the police to pick you up no matter what time it is in the morning or night? Why is he coming in person? To intimidate you? Or else, now that your business is settled, he is coming to express his good will, thus sending a strong signal indicating that the dispute is over and that the Republic, at last reconciled with its children, is rushing one of its senior officials over to attend the wake of an ordinary citizen whose rights have been recognized at long last? All those thoughts are swirling around in your head.

You walk over to greet them. Should you shake Tito's hand when he holds it out to you?

Sure, why not? No, why would you do that? And why not

a kiss on each cheek? Since your separation almost over a year ago, you had never met face-to face. He had made it a point not to speak to you directly—and even that doesn't happen often—but to pass through an intermediary to enquire about anything involving the children. A pathetic loser. Pathetic and vain, babbling like the failed philosopher he is. It has been a while since you observed him so closely. With his Versace suit, his Weston shoes, and his burgeoning paunch, he is the very caricature of a parvenu who is suddenly rich because of politics. Seriously, dear girl, what could you have seen in this guy? Were you just naïve, or what? To think that not only did you live with him for over ten years, but you sacrificed your career so he could advance his! Ignore him.

"Hi, Méré. Surprised to see us?"

Reeking of satisfaction, he is the first to open his big mouth, with the goofy grin of a crook who has just pulled off an underhanded coup. Don't be surprised, Méré, it's always the underlings who speak before their master. Forget him. Put him in his place.

"What makes you think that, Tito? Didn't you know? We've been waiting for the Minister to arrive for quite some time."

Without giving him the chance to reply, you turn to the Minister:

"We have been awaiting your arrival, Mister Minister," you say confidently, "please follow me, let's find a place where we can talk calmly."

"Very well," he says, "but I would like to address the whole group."

"All the stone breakers from the quarry," Tito cannot help himself from adding.

"Really," you say ingenuously, "the Minister doesn't know that all of us are stone breakers?"

"Yes, yes, I am aware of everything," the latter says hurriedly, as Tito, from the look on his face, seems ready to eat you alive.

"That's not a problem, Mister Minister, we are all here. Please take a seat while I gather them all together."

You lead the three men to the porch; you have them sit down, offering as protocol requires, the Minister Auntie Turia's beautiful armchair.

•

Facing the Minister, Tito sitting next to him with a Samsonite briefcase on his knees, you are fifteen women stone breakers who decided one morning not to be ripped off anymore and to stand up to demand a fair price for your merchandise. To make it clear that the sixteenth, Batatou, is among you and with you, you left one chair conspicuously empty in the middle of the first row, opposite the Minister's chair. He cannot not understand. Sitting comfortably in his chair, legs crossed, he raises his eyes toward Tito who, after counting each of you with his eyes, says to him:

"I think we can start, Mister Minister, they are all here."

"Good," the latter begins. "I know that you are already aware of the decision the government has taken in your regard. However, until you are told officially, it is only a rumor. I am here to give you official confirmation. I wanted to come personally rather than send one of my officials, to show how important it is to us to resolve this issue. No one knows this dossier better than Deputy Rangi, adviser to the President of the Republic, temporarily assigned to the office of Madam the First Lady, not to the Minister of Women and Disabled Persons whom you went to see. Not only has he participated in all the meetings, but he is the one who recorded the minutes, including those of our last meeting, which is the one that interests us here. He is going to tell you about the decisions that were taken. Then I will answer any questions you may have. Tito?"

"Thank you, Mister Minister. As the Minister said, the President of the Republic, through Madame the First Lady, President of the tenth Summit of African First Ladies, in his magnanimity, has responded positively to your requests. From now on, you are authorized to sell your bags of gravel at the minimum price of twenty thousand francs. You will be compensated for your lost bags, on the basis of five bags for each of you at the rate of twenty thousand francs. That is one hundred thousand francs for each of you, which is a nice chunk of money. I know that very few of you have ever had so much cash at your disposal. The money is ready, and the checks have been made out according to the list of names your spokesperson submitted to the Ministry of Women and Disabled Persons."

Tito opens the briefcase he has on his knees and takes out a stack of checks. He reads each name aloud. Paying close attention, you notice there is one in Batatou's name. When he is done, he hands them to you. You count them again and hand them to Mâ Bileko to keep safe and sound.

"The Public Treasury will open a special window. We ask that each of you cash your check in the morning so we can officially close this case before the opening ceremony of the summit in the afternoon. It is very important. That's it, I've told you everything and, as the Minister said, you may direct any questions you have to him."

"I would have preferred that you paid us in cash. I've never set foot in a bank, and I have no ID card," Iyissou says.

The Minister replies calmly, with a reassuring smile:

"Don't worry, I'll take care of that. Show up tomorrow at the window with someone who has an ID. With one of your friends, for example. We could also give power of attorney to your spokesperson so she can cash the check in your name."

There are no other questions. Everything is fine, too fine actually. All you have to do now is wait for the Minister to leave so you can celebrate and dream about your future plans. But he does not get up. He uncrosses his legs and, resting his forearms on the armrests, leans forward and begins speaking. Your seventh sense goes on high alert.

"Now that the government has met all your demands, I have a small favor to ask of you in return. It is not me who is asking, but the wife of the head of State who, as you know, is presiding over the tenth anniversary of the summit of the wives of heads of State from the entire African continent and guests coming from all corners of the world. It is a very important meeting for our country's standing in the world."

He pauses while your brain is racing a hundred miles an hour, in vain, to get a head start on guessing where the Minister is going with this.

"As our adviser to the President, Deputy Rangi, stated so well, it is thanks to that woman's greatness of mind that you got what you got. And she does not want to stop there, she wants you to be honored by the international press. So, she is asking you to take part in the opening ceremony of the summit tomorrow afternoon. A bus will be provided for your transportation. Like all honored guests, a special place will be reserved for you in the front row with a big sign reading "Women of the River Quarry" or any other name your group chooses. When Madam the First Lady of our country enters with her distinguished guests, you will rise with the entire room, and you will applaud spontaneously and warmly. The national television network has already received an order to take several close-ups of you. You will be stars. The whole world will see that in our country women's issues are taken into consideration and treated seriously. The Head of State's wife will be pleased and proud of you, the President of the Republic will be pleased and proud of you, the entire country will be pleased and proud of you. Look, we are not asking much from you. Simply that you stand up and applaud the President's wife."

He is done. He settles back into his armchair and waits for your reactions. No, rather, your reaction since, taking you for the group's leader even though you are only their spokesperson, you are the one he looked at as he uttered that last phrase. His words are so steeped in hypocrisy that you understand what the catch is right away. By dint of giving orders and everyone obeying him in this country, he believes the entire world is made up of nothing but half-wits. You are all silent, thinking about what to say so as not to offend the Minister of law and order. Bileko looks at you as if to say: "Let me reply to him." You signal for her to go ahead.

"We are very grateful for what the leader's wife did for us. First, she gave us an envelope with one million francs, which we used to bury our friend killed by the police for want of medical care, and then, as you say, it is thanks to her that we got what we got. Tell her on our behalf that what she has done up to now is more than enough for us and, once again, that we are more than grateful. She need not be concerned with us anymore. We do not need any other accolades."

Turning toward the other women, she calls out:

"Isn't that right, friends, that we do not need any other accolades?"

"No, we don't need any others," they answer in unison, as do you.

"Besides, tomorrow we won't have time," Bilala says. "We need to all be at the airport to present a gift to our daughter who is going abroad."

You all agree. You find the reason Bilala gave to be brilliant, the sudden idea of all of you going to the airport to give Zizina her gift.

"Don't you give a damn about anything? The President's wife extends an invitation to you, and you refuse?"

Tito. He can never keep his mouth shut.

"Our daughter is more important than your Madam President," Moukiétou retorts.

"Don't be so ungrateful after all she has done for you," Tito insists. Then, under the pretext of checking the time on his wristwatch, he theatrically pulls his fist out of his jacket sleeve so you see that the watch is a Rolex.

You look closely at this character. He doesn't even have the decency to dress appropriately for a wake. Instead, his outfit reflects the color palette that dandies refer to as "summer colors", even if that season is unknown at your latitude. But, despite his fitted orange jacket with two decorative pocket flaps and buttons on the bottom of the sleeves, his striped, mauve microfiber tie with orange dots, falling mid-waist and flapping over a white shirt, his fitted pale blue pants with no belt, his crocodile shoes, despite or because of all that, the poor guy still gives the impression of being a parvenu. On top of that, he is not even good-looking. And to think that in another life, when you believed you loved this guy, he called himself a philosopher and taught you the word "skepticism"! Now he's a parrot who doesn't even pay attention to what comes out of his mouth. A real loser, that guy. You can no longer keep quiet.

"That was not a gift your Madam President gave. Do you think we do not understand the game you are playing? You want to buy our allegiance because you are supposedly charitable? First, she wanted to buy us with one million and since that didn't work, she wants to have us another way. No, we are not for sale, Sir. You cannot take back what we got because you did not give it to us."

Unlike your demeanor at the Ministry and at the presidential palace, you speak unafraid, perhaps because you feel safe here, on your territory, strengthened by the solidarity of all these women around you.

"You've forgot that one of us died for those bags of gravel," Moyalo says. "We are not going to your party tomorrow. We will all be at the airport."

"Even if it weren't for the airport, we would not go to the ceremony," Moukiétou takes it a step further, you can feel her adrenaline rising. "We are not prostitutes."

"You will come to the ceremony tomorrow, for God's sake! I will block the access to the airport and if I need to, I'll keep that plane from landing or taking off," the man fumes. "I am the Minister of the Interior!"

He was certainly not expecting this rebuff, especially not coming from women he thought were weak and defenseless.

"You're going to keep a UN chartered airplane from landing or taking off for no reason?"

He is surprised by this piece of information because, although he was aware that a UN airplane would be landing tomorrow in this country, which is his fiefdom, he did not know that one of the passengers on that plane would be the daughter of one of the women from the quarry. Not knowing what to say, he gets up from his armchair, threatening "That's not going to happen, you'll see," turns his back and leaves. Tito trots along behind him with his briefcase, like an obedient poodle. He finds the time to stop for a moment though, and looking at you in a way that would kill you if looks could kill, explodes: "To find a person dumber than you, you'd have to fly to the moon!"

"You'd have to fly even further to find anyone more pathetic than you, to Saturn!" you bark back.

TWENTY-NINE

ONCE THE DELEGATION has gone, you stay for a while longer to discuss how the meeting with the Minister went. You find Bilala's idea brilliant—all of you going to the airport to bid farewell to Zizina. You also all agree to be at the Public Treasury as soon as the windows open so you can withdraw your money before noon at the latest. That will give each of you enough time to go back home, put your money away, eat, change, and meet at the airport with time enough to spend at least an hour with Zizina before she boards. That settled, each of you returns to her place at the vigil.

Auntie Turia, who was back as she promised, watched your meeting with the Minister and Tito from a distance. You go sit next to her and she asks you to tell her what happened. You give her your report, not leaving out the part about how much of an idiot your ex was is. She acts as if you did not mention him at all, which annoys you a little, because you would like her to support you unequivocally in your resentment. Unlike you, she simply cut him out of her life. "Even speaking ill of a man who has abandoned his children is giving him more respect than he deserves," she told you one day when you had launched once again into one of your diatribes against Tito. "Ignore him and move on with your life." Right, but he does not ignore you!

"A visit from a minister. You really are something!" she concludes after listening to you.

You see that she is tired. After all, she spent her whole day here, taking care of the house and the children. There is no need for her to spend another sleepless night on an uncomfortable mat with mosquitos, after last night. She has already paid more than her respects to Batatou. You keep on insisting until she finally agrees to go home and sleep. You help her with her blanket, and you exit the compound together. You decide to walk some of the way with her, which will give you a respite from the wake's mood you've been immersed in since you came back from the cemetery. Armando is standing out front talking with someone and sees you arrive. He breaks off his conversation and hurries over to you.

"Auntie Turia, going home so soon?"

He calls her Auntie too like you do, you notice.

"Yes, Armando. Méré doesn't want me to stay. She thinks I'm too old to spend two nights in a row at a wake," Auntie Turia says smiling, to tease you.

"I completely agree with Méré. Not because you are old, but because she will need you again tomorrow. So, you need to rest."

"I can see you are all plotting against me."

Armando likes that comment. He laughs.

"Better yet, Auntie, we're not going to let you walk, I'll bring you in my taxi."

"No, no need to do that, you know I don't live very far."

"It's an order, no discussion," he says with a big smile. "Follow me."

Amused, you watch the two of them getting along like two little kids playing. With measured steps, Armando is already four or five yards ahead of you. All you have to do is follow him.

Auntie is sitting in the back and you are in front with Armando. You drive slowly, the headlights piercing through the dark night.

"Good news, Auntie. I have a CD of old songs. I'm going

to play one for you and I am sure it will bring back some memories. You might have danced to this tune when you were a young girl."

"What song is it?"

"I'm not going to say. I'll let you come up with the title."

"You only like the oldies, don't you?" you point out to him.

"No, I have some new popular ones too. But I listen to the old stuff because they're classics of our popular music. They have an old-fashioned charm that I like."

As soon as she hears the first guitar notes, Auntie Turia says: "It's *Marie Louise* by Wendo Sor Kolosoy, the founding father of Congolese rumba. She starts singing the Lingala lyrics along with Wendo:

> *Marie Louise Kombo na yo mama!*
>
> *Marie Louise, what a name!*
>
> *How can you not marry a woman with such a name? Why are the in-laws refusing to let us get married When we love each other?*
>
> *They secretly insult me They secretly speak ill of me*
>
> *Because of you Marie Louise*
>
> *Let them know that I am their son-in-law And that I, Wendo, love Marie Louise.*

When the song is over, she says to Armando:

"You see, you're wrong. I didn't dance to that tune because it is not a song from my day, it's from my parents' generation. It is the seminal song of Congolese rumba. You chose the right version, the original from 1948. Back then people used to say you mustn't sing *Marie Louise* around midnight because evil spirits listening to it would not be able to resist getting out on the dance floor disguised as beautiful women and handsome men. Woe to those who fall under their spell! Wendo made another version ten years later, in 1958, turning the beautiful rumba into a cha-cha. He shouldn't have because it stinks. I don't like it."

You are impressed. Because of Armando, you are finding out that that woman had a youth, just like you did. That she danced, dated, had boyfriends who tried to kiss her one night on a street corner... Good old Auntie! You cherish this moment of nostalgia triggered by an old-fashioned tune that made a person of the previous generation come alive. A wave of emotion wells up in you, and spills over to fill the car, transforming it into a cocoon of tenderness.

When you arrive in front of her lot, Auntie Turia gets out and thanks Armando. You get out too to accompany her inside. You wait for her to open her door and turn on the light and then kiss her good-bye, till tomorrow. She hugs you and says:

"Armando is a really good guy, don't you think?"

"Um... yes... he's... he's nice," you stammer in reply. "Try to sleep a little anyway. See you tomorrow."

You go out and find Armando waiting in his taxi.

He manages to make a U-turn in the narrow street. You are sitting next to him in silence. He is not talking either. The undefinable atmosphere of happiness triggered by Auntie Turia seems to still be floating in the car which, because of the dark night surrounding you, gives the impression of a safe haven created especially for its two passengers, Armando and you. You close your eyes.

"Méré, I see a café across the street. Let's stop for a minute and have a drink. I'm thirsty."

"There are drinks at the wake."

"It's not the same. Besides, it's going to be a long night, no sense rushing."

You hesitate, then say to yourself: Why not? You also want to have a drink. Plus, after all he has done for you today, refusing would be too mean. You settle into a table at the back of the room. In these cafés and bars, the music is often too loud. That is not the case here. It is rather soft, like background noise, which is already a good start. You order a fruit juice. He gets a coffee. You do not even pretend to offer to pay for your drink when he takes his wallet out because you know he will refuse.

"Auntie Turia is truly an extraordinary woman," he says.

"Well, she is my aunt, what do you expect!"

"Do you know you resemble her?"

"It must be hereditary."

"Tell me something, was your sister Tamara like you? I'm sorry I never got to meet her."

"She was more beautiful and smarter than me. You have no idea how much I miss her."

"You are also very beautiful, Méré."

"Yeah, yeah, go on, say it, I am the most beautiful woman in the world, etc. Come off it, Armando, that doesn't work with me."

"Listen, I don't know all the women in the world, so I cannot say that you are the most beautiful of all. That would be a lie. But one thing is sure, of all those I do know, you are the most beautiful."

Touché. If you were lighter-skinned, he would have seen you blushing. To cover up your embarrassment, you change the subject.

"Tomorrow is going to be a big day for us. We are finally going to reap the fruits of our struggle."

"You are a mystery to me, Méré. You are not like my sister Anne-Marie. You are intelligent, educated… how did you end up at this quarry breaking stone?"

"It is a very long story, and I am not going to bother you with it. Perhaps another time."

"No, Méré, I insist. Who's to say we're going to have another opportunity like this? I am asking because it is important to me."

You are touched by the sincerity in his voice.

"Well, if you insist! No mystery at all... Fine, listen, if you want to know... I did not pass my college entrance exams. Not because I was incapable, but because I had an unplanned pregnancy and married young. You're surprised, right? I bet you did not know that! I am not the ideal woman you think I am. I had to drop out of school before the end of the school year. Got married in a hurry to a philosopher and stayed with him for twelve years.

"A philosopher?" he asks, surprised. "You mean Tito? Tito is a philosopher?"

"Yes, a philosopher who actually taught me a lot."

"For example?"

"Skepticism."

"What is that? You know, I did not study for long, much less philosophy."

"It means doubting everything."

"Doubting everything! What is that supposed to mean? And what use was it to you?"

"No use," you say with a smile, "except when I doubted where he had been one night when he came home late stinking of beer. I'll spare you the details. After our wedding and the birth of our first child, we decided that he, as is expected, must at all costs continue his studies, at least pass the college entrance exams which he failed the previous year, and I would take mine later. Men are always given priority, right? While he was going to school, we had to live. Luckily, I had Auntie Turia to babysit the little guy. First, I found a job as a cashier, then as head cashier at a store that sold computers and electronics. I was the main breadwinner of the family for almost five years, while he only worked small part-time jobs. In the meantime, our second unplanned surprise was born, which put an end to my wishful thinking about going back to school. In the end, I never did.

"All that effort and sacrifice ended up paying off though. Tito finished his Master's in Information and Communications Technology for Education and immediately found a good job at the Ministry of National Education as director of the institute in charge of introducing those new technologies in teaching. The job title was more impressive than the salary, but it was not bad for someone starting out like he was. We could finally live comfortably.

"That is when I decided to take a little breather, and I took a month off to travel. I went to West Africa, which is where I got the idea to start a business selling shrimp and smoked fish instead of pagnes. I visited Ouagadougou, that city whose bizarre and mysterious name has always fascinated me, since the first time I discovered it, on the edge of the Sahel, on a map in my high school geography book. I also went to South Africa, Mandela's country.

"And then my sister got sick. I had to take care of her. Because of my repeated absences, the store where I was working ended up firing me, and at the same time my marriage started falling apart. Here too, I'll spare you the details. We separated a little after my sister passed away. As they say, when it rains it pours. A few months later, I found myself completely broke, carrying three children around, one of whom was my sister's, while my ex-husband, who had gotten into politics, and was bolstered by several successive judgements of the courts in his favor, stubbornly refused to pay any child support."

"Oh, I see. And that's why you went to break stone."

"No, not straightaway. Often you need a big shock in life to wake you up. I went from one menial job to another, with just enough money to live day-to-day. You know, you settle into the routines of menial jobs very quickly."

"I know what you mean. I experienced that before I got my own car."

"One evening, I was relaxing on the porch. I was especially exhausted because I got up very early, at four thirty in the morning, to go to the bus station and wait for the greengrocers' trucks bringing fresh fruits and vegetables from the villages in the countryside. The women line up so aggressively, you have to be among the first to even hope to buy what you want. But it is worth it because a crate of vegetables can earn double what you bought it for, and you can make triple what you paid for a bunch of bananas if you sell them retail in threes. What is interesting is that you always manage to sell most of your merchandise within the day.

"But that day it had rained all the night before, one of those violent storms that are so frequent during the rainy season. Only one vehicle came. Here and there, a bridge had been carried away by the violence of the waters or the embankments on the side of the road were so waterlogged they slid down into the roadway, blocking any passage; and in one place, the road had collapsed due to erosion, and elsewhere, the road had become such a pool of mud that even vehicles with a dog clutch got bogged down. Beyond all hope, we waited until the middle of the afternoon, then we had to accept the fact that no trucks would be coming that day. So, to buy what we would eat that evening, I had to draw on the money I was going to buy the fruits and vegetables with. My budget was tight. Once I got home, I made the calculations. I had just enough money left to buy two crates of vegetables and one bunch of bananas the next day. Which meant that I did not even have enough to pay for bus fare and I had to walk to get to the main bus station. Which also meant that, next morning, I had to get up even earlier, at four A.M.

"Then I noticed a woman, accompanied by a child, standing in front of my property. Intrigued, I asked her to come in. She walked up to the gate, holding her somewhat shy-looking child's hand.

'Your son popped my child's balloon,' she lashed out with no introduction, 'you need to give me a new one.'

"I did not know what she was talking about, so I called my younger son over. Yes, it was true. One of those children's lightweight rubber balloons, the kind you fill with air and let float at the end of a long string. He told me it burst when he was inflating it. No big deal, really. Frankly, I don't understand what people are thinking, making such a big fuss out of so little? Couldn't she wait till the next day?

'And how much does the balloon cost?'

'One hundred francs.'

'A hundred francs? You come and disturb me at night for a hundred francs?'

"I was not happy at all. One hundred francs! A ridiculous amount, a measly coin. I was determined to humiliate her for that pitiful hundred-franc coin she came to nag me about: instead of handing it to her, I would throw it at her so she would have to bend down to pick it up off the ground, in the mud, if she didn't manage to catch it in the air. And I would make sure she didn't catch it.

"But the very second I was about to stand up, I remembered I didn't have one hundred francs to give her. A measly one-hundred-franc coin! How shameful! What to do? I remained frozen in my armchair, searching my mind for a way to get myself out of the situation, which led her to repeat:

'All I'm asking for is one hundred francs to buy a new balloon for my son. I did not come looking for a fight.'

"Again, what to do? The gears in my brain were spinning a hundred miles-an-hour to come up with a solution. No matter what, I could not admit to her that I did not have the one hundred francs, after the scornful tone and haughty attitude I had greeted her with. And so, I came up with something clever. I turned to my son:

'What color was the balloon?' 'Green,' he replied.

'Well, I'm not giving you the hundred francs. Who's to say you're going to buy a balloon with it and not use it to go get a bottle of beer instead? I'll reimburse you in kind. Tomorrow I will bring over a green balloon for your son.'

'Don't treat me like I came over here begging for money. I have never come to you before.

'Give me my hundred francs and I will go. I have other things to do, and I need to get up early tomorrow morning.'

"In the end, she understood that I was not going to change my mind and she left with her child.

"Her final words, 'I need to get up early tomorrow morning,' still ringing in my ears, immediately brought down my anger. I did not need to be mad at her. We were both in the same boat, two destitute mothers, working our fingers to the bone so we could put food on the table for our children and survive. Did I know why she had to get up early the next day? To go clean houses in town? Or perhaps to do the same commute I did, by foot, because just like me she did not have those one hundred francs to take a bus? I felt ashamed for having humiliated that woman, a mother who was merely trying in her way to show her child that she loved him and that she was doing what she could to protect him from the adversities of the world. I confess that tears began to stream down my cheeks.

"Glued to my armchair, unable to move, I kept thinking and thinking about that hundred-francs coin. I did not even have one hundred francs, can you imagine? No, Méréana, I said to myself, you cannot go on like this. Going from one odd job to the next will end up killing you—and what if you wake up ill one morning? You let yourself go too far. Wake up, snap out of it, do something, move! You have a brain, so use it like a mason or a carpenter uses his hands! My thoughts were spinning out of control.

"When I was working in that shop that sold computers, I noticed there was an enormous demand for computer technicians. If I could master important word processing, image processing and management software, I would be guaranteed a job. I could do that. I was a brilliant student in high school, and I was preparing my college entrance exams with a specialization in mathematics. There was a private school which was just starting a custom-made training session, exactly what I was looking for. A three-month program of coursework with business internships for a total cost of... two hundred thousand francs. Where in hell was I going to find that kind of money when I did not even have a hundred francs?"

"The stone quarry...," Armando says.

"Not at that point. I wanted to borrow the money. Auntie

Turia made eighty thousand francs available to me. For the rest, I would ask friends, banks, and set up a tontine where I would be the first on the list to collect the money. But none of my efforts were successful. I did not know it would be so difficult to come up with one hundred twenty thousand francs in a country overflowing with oil, whose president can afford to pay two hundred thousand francs for a bottle of champagne abroad. My time was limited. I needed that money in the next two months, before registration closed.

"That is when I heard about this rock quarry by the riverside. I immediately made the calculation and, at ten thousand francs per bag of gravel, all I would need was to produce twelve to make the amount I wanted, and that could be done in six weeks. That is what I finally ended up doing and that is why I am sitting here in this café with you today."

"My God, what a story! I admire you even more than I did before. When does registration close?"

"In exactly two weeks. That is why our protests must succeed."

"How many more bags do you need to sell or fill to reach the amount you need?"

"I've already sold eight bags. I need to sell four more. Actually, I only have to fill two more, barely a week's worth of work, since I have two full ones among those the police stole. But now that each bag is earning me twenty thousand, I already have the amount I need. I don't even need to go back to the quarry anymore, but I will go anyway to finish filling those two bags, otherwise I will feel like I did not finish the job I started."

You fall silent, feeling that you may have talked too much, and you listen to the music playing in the background. He stares at you for a long time then reaches his arm across the table and places his hand on yours. You quiver imperceptibly. How warm, affectionate, comforting his palm feels covering your hand! You would like him to leave it there, forever… But, you pull your hand away abruptly.

"I think it's time to join the vigil," you say. "The others will wonder what happened to us." You stand up. He gets up too and follows you to the car.

Without a word, he slides a CD into the player and Rochereau's voice pours out, with the lyrics of one of his most beautiful songs, dedicated to a woman:

Kitoko e tondi yo na nzoto, Maze
Na mona moto nini na ko mekana na yo te

Maze
Your body is pure beauty
No one compares to you
Your face is like no other
So radiant and elegant!
When you walk past, heads turn
You drive all the men crazy…

You listen. Is the choice of this current hit song innocent on his part? Of course not. Does he think you are as beautiful as Maze, the woman in the song? Why are you asking yourself such useless questions? Just let yourself be rocked to the sound of Rochereau's entrancing voice. Enjoy this feeling of floating inside a bubble of love.

From afar, you can see the lights of the wake and, at times, hear voices and songs carried by the wind. There are so many people keeping vigil that they are overflowing into the street, so you cannot park in front of the compound. You find a spot much further away. He stops the car and, just as you are opening the door to get out, he says:

"Méré, did you ever pay back those one hundred francs to that woman for her son's balloon?"

The question surprises you as much as it makes you feel bad. In a sad yet sincere voice, you reply:

"Alas, I never did, Armando. The next day, coin in hand, I searched the entire neighborhood for her, for this woman whose name I did not even know. I never found her. When I got back home, I placed the coin in my jewelry box. It is still there, and I see it each time I open the box. And each time I look at it, it reminds me that I will always have a debt toward someone, somewhere."

"You are so compassionate, Méré, and so generous!"

You are touched by his remark and, impulsively, you lean toward him to give him a light kiss on his cheek. But as luck would have it, he turns around at the same time to look at you and your kiss ends up planted on his lips. You do not have time to pull yourself together before yours open under the firm pressure of his tongue. And yet, this was not supposed to happen, Méré. Too bad for you!

THIRTY

DESPITE THE ALL-NIGHT vigil, you wake up feeling light in mind and body. None of the worries that usually overwhelm you when you wake up are weighing on you this morning. Even the radio which you immediately turn on is giving only good news: the election of the first Black president of the United States of America; convincing results of a malaria vaccine; the opening at the Hague of the trial of a warlord from Eastern Congo whose troops raped and assaulted thousands of women and children; a French magistrate declares admissible the complaint made by a number of NGOs against the presidents of the Congo, Gabon and Equatorial Guinea about assets and ill-acquired property in France... All that is missing is the news of your victory. You feel like you are truly in a state of levitation, like planet Earth on that poster Tamara gave you, one half of a blue globe flecked with white clouds, floating merrily beyond the lunar horizon.

You thought you would be the first in line at the door of the Public Treasury, but Moukiétou, Iyissou and Laurentine Paka are already there when you show up. Laurentine Paka is alone, without her boyfriend who almost never leaves her side. A little afterward, you see Armando arrive to drop off his sister. When she sees Anne-Marie, Laurentine rushes toward the car. Those two women have a particular connection, perhaps because each of them is beautiful and elegant in her own way, and they like to talk a lot about fashion and beauty products. You head over to join them.

Armando is happy to see you and you, for your part, are not displeased to see him again.

"Good morning, Méré, the wake did not tire you out too much?" "A day like today is worth the weariness," you reply to him.

"Armando has volunteered to come back and pick the three of us up as soon as we withdraw our money," says Laurentine, delighted.

You feign indifference.

"That's not necessary, I can walk or take the bus."

"Don't be ridiculous. Women loaded with cash in a jam-packed bus? The pickpockets would have a ball," Armando answers back.

"I'll have Moukiétou go with me," you say. "Who would dare come near us when they see the muscles in her arm?"

That sparks laughter.

"Don't listen to Méré," Laurentine interrupts. I'll call you as soon as we're done." "OK, ladies. Later."

He gets into his taxi, gives three short honks, and takes off.

It is eight o'clock on the dot when the big bank's doors open. A public establishment that opens on time? Unheard of in this country. Which means that the President of the Republic and the relevant ministers gave strict orders to those officials. You are all inside with a bustling crowd when you hear an announcement: "The women from the quarry by the riverside, please report here... the women from the quarry by the riverside..." You do as they say. You are all there: Ossolo, Bilala, Iyissou, Bileko, Moyalo, Moukiétou, Asselam, Itela... An agent leads you into a waiting room which is even more luxurious than the one at the Ministry of Women and Disabled Persons and asks you to wait a few minutes.

He is not gone long; in fact, he comes back almost immediately with a man in a jacket and tie, wearing glasses, his hair cut so short he looks bald and so grossly overweight that he walked with a stilted gait. As if his disability were not enough, a smugness bordering on contempt emanates from his voice when he addresses you.

"Good morning, ladies. I am the Manager of this establishment. I do not usually receive clients myself, but I wanted to make an exception for you despite my very busy schedule. I hope you appreciate it. To make things easy for you, I ask you to sign your checks and bring them to the teller here. Then, ID in hand, you will go to a special window I have opened for you. That's it. Have a nice day."

He turns to leave. Get out of here, lard ass, all we want is to withdraw what is owed to us, you think secretly. Apparently, your opinion is not shared with Mâ Bileko, who calls out to him just as he is getting ready to leave the room.

"Mister Manager, please. We do not intend to go line up at any ordinary window. We want to be paid here."

The man turns around. He cannot believe his ears.

"Who do you think you are? I am the Manager here and I organize my services as I see fit. You will go to the special window which has been opened for you if you want to be paid. I have customers who come to withdraw over a million here and they wait in line. And don't bother me again, I do not have time to waste. I give the orders here and..."

"Méré," Mâ Bileko interrupts him turning toward you, "the Minister of the Interior gave you his direct line when he came to mourn with us yesterday evening. You wrote it down. Can you call him?"

"Of course," you say readily, like an actress taking her cue although nothing had allowed you to anticipate what she just said, "I have it in my contacts."

You grab your bag, open it and plunge your hand in. But, before you even take your phone out to make the call, the man swallows two or three times, as if he suddenly realized that he had knotted his tie a little too tightly.

"You did not let me finish... I was saying that I'm the one who gives orders around here and... and that... there is no problem if you want to be paid here. I will take care of everything. I am going to give instructions for you to be paid right here."

A forced smile and he is off, his ego deflated by at least a cubic meter. You all look at Mâ Bileko. "What does it matter where we get paid as long as we are paid?" your stares seem to ask.

"It's is a matter of dignity, my friends," she replies to your mute interrogation. "We are not only fighting for a better price for our bags, but for people to respect us as well."

She has regained her reflexes as a prosperous merchant who negotiated with the most important businessmen and women of this world before winding up, like you, at this stone quarry by the riverside.

•

When you exit the bank, you are pleased. Each of you measures her victory by these crisp brand-new ten-thousand francs banknotes. It blows your mind to see so many new bills: do those people make them every morning? You watch Bilala, your "peasant woman", as she takes her bills out, counts them again in disbelief, then puts them back into their envelope. What goes on in a person's mind who sees her dream almost fully realized?

After a brief discussion, you decide on the time you should all meet at the airport to say good-bye to Zizina, then each of you goes her way.

THIRTY-ONE

AS PROMISED, Laurentine calls Armando, but he is on the other side of the city with a customer on board and cannot meet you until at least half an hour from now. You decide to go to a cafe so that you will not have to wait for him in front of the bank. It just so happens that Café des Anges is not far, and that is where you go.

The young waitress who served you the last time you were here is again on duty. She recognizes you and greets you with a big smile. She probably has not forgotten the generous tip you left her last time. She seats you in the best spot in the room and takes your orders.

"Champagne," Anne-Marie Ossolo jokes, "we have just robbed the Public Treasury."

"We do not serve champagne," the waitress answers, not getting the joke. Why would she?

"No, it's a joke," you reassure her.

You order an Orangina again, Laurentine and Anne-Marie each order a can of imported beer. You all start drinking and chatting as you wait for Armando's call. Laurentine, chatty and excited, starts talking about her plans. She wants to open a beauty salon where a woman can find everything she needs to make herself beautiful, hair straightening and make-up products, skin-lightening lotions, hair extensions, wigs and on and on, even teas to help with weight loss.

"I will only sell authentic, tested products, which I will import from Chicago and New York, from Paris and London, maybe from South Africa; not those tainted products coming from Nigeria or the former Zaire, real poisons for your skin. I won't sell any Chinese products either!"

You listen, amused. As she takes a mirror out of her pocket to look at herself, you turn to Anne-Marie:

"And you?"

"Now that I have the money, I can get my revenge!" You do not understand.

"Your revenge?"

"When the bags I still need to fill are sold for twenty thousand francs each, I will have more than two hundred thousand francs. Tonight, I'll pay my back rent, settle half of what I owe to that West African, then I'll go buy myself the latest Super Wax, and go provoke, scoff at, and trap that stupid bitch. She'll see. She is the reason I'm in this mess. She destroyed my beauty. Do you think I'm going to let her off just like that? Oh, if you only knew how much I have been waiting for this money!"

Surprised by the violence of her words, you are completely in the dark because you have no idea what she is talking about. Apparently, Laurentine knows, since she says:

"That's for sure. She deserves to be taught a lesson after what she did to you. Tell Méré. You can trust her. She is not the type to betray a friend."

"Betray?" you ask.

"Go ahead, tell her, Laurentine. I get so enraged just thinking about it! My blood literally boils."

"Anne-Marie is, or rather was, Bokola's mistress."

"Bokola? You mean Gustave Bokola, the extremely wealthy businessman?" you ask, astonished. "The one who owns three bakeries, two gas stations and I don't know what else? Some even say he traffics in diamonds."

"He is also a politician, a senator," Anne-Marie adds.

"One Sunday night...," Laurentine goes on.

"No, it was a Saturday night," Anne-Marie corrects her.

"It doesn't matter," Laurentine continues.

"One Saturday night, she didn't have anything to do..."

"It's not that I didn't have anything to do, I was having issues..."

"Same thing. She was having issues because her boyfriend, the one before Bokola, had just broken up with her..."

"No, I'm the one who broke up with him."

"Listen, Anne-Marie, tell it yourself, since you keep interrupting me all the time."

"It's because I want Méré to really understand the context."

"Why did you want to break up with him? Because he wasn't cute?" you ask, teasing her.

"Oh, no, he wasn't bad at all. Charming, the kind of man women fall for at first glance, but he was miserly. Hard to find anyone stingier! It was always a struggle to get the rent money out of him. He didn't even give me enough to buy a bar of soap. What is the use in having a boyfriend if he doesn't dress you, feed you, doesn't pay your rent, in other words, if he doesn't take care of you? The 'banging' was good," she says smiling," but that is not enough. You also need cash."

"Banging"?

"Well, yeah, 'banging'. When two bodies collide in bed, you know."

"Oh, I see," you say with a smile.

"A good boyfriend must offer three things: the 'bang-bang', the bling-bling, and the bucks", Laurentine informs you, seeming to know what she is talking about.

"So, I ditched him," Anne-Marie picks back up. "He's such a poser, I'm sure he has already found some other idiot to support him. After the breakup, not only was I feeling lonely, but I also really had issues. I was broke, the end of the month was coming, I needed to pay the rent by myself, I couldn't count on anyone, and I especially did not want to ask Armando to help me. Because of all that swirling around in my head, alone in my room, on a Saturday night no less, I was at the end of my rope. After a while, I jumped up, took one look at myself in the mirror and said to myself: 'Anne-Marie, you are young, you are beautiful, you need to enjoy life. Staying cloistered in here isn't going to solve your problems.' I needed to get some air, go out, and dance to snap out of my depression.

"I got all dolled up in a little blouse and a short skirt, full make-up, and went to Jenny's, a dance club where I knew the manager who often let me in for free. I had just enough money for a local beer, but that wasn't a problem since I know how to make a drink last when I need to.

"I had barely settled in with my drink when this guy comes over and starts smooth-talking me. Being born and raised in this big city, I know all the guys' tricks and I can tell a smooth talker who is only trying to screw you and then disappears— the ones we call 'players'—apart from the serious person you can have a conversation with. This guy was among the former. They really are unbelievable, those men. For them, just because a woman is alone in a bar, calmly sipping her drink in her little corner, she is looking for a guy. I strongly rebuffed him and bluntly sent him packing. After him, two other clowns came to try their luck and I turned them away in the same manner. I had enough, I just came to take my mind off things because I was bored at home, not to be picked up by some boor. I suddenly felt bad and all I wanted now was to finish my drink as fast as possible and go to bed.

"That is when I saw a waiter come toward me, with a bottle of beer and a glass on his tray, a Danish beer, I think, the most expensive in the house. 'From an admirer,' he said to me as he turned to show me a table diagonal from mine. A man was sitting there, alone. With a wide smile, he waved his hand as if to confirm that, yes, it was from him. The waiter said to me: 'You can change it if you prefer to drink something else.' – 'A margarita,' I immediately said because I needed something a little stronger than the beer I was drinking. When the server came back with the drink, he told me the gentleman who had graciously offered the drink would be delighted if I would share his table, but in no way should I feel obliged. I hesitated, then thought to myself: Why not, there's nothing wrong with accepting an invitation, especially from such a considerate man. The rest of the evening went really well. He was a perfect gentleman, as opposed to those ladies' men whose intentions are clear before they even approach you."

"So, it was Gustave Bokola," you say.

"He himself! At the end of the evening, he suggested dropping me home since it was too late to find a taxi. I lived alone at the time, so there was no problem. He took me in his big, air-conditioned car with fat tires and tinted windows. I'll admit I was impressed. It was the first time I got into one of those vehicles I used to admire from afar when I would see one in the city, sometimes with women in them who were not as good-looking as me. When we arrived in front of my house, he asked if he could see me again. You all know that a woman must never say yes right away, she must make herself be desired. So I told him I wasn't sure if I wanted to see him again. 'Oh, but I would really love to, Anne-Marie. Listen, here's my private number, it's my cell, you have nothing to fear. Call me when you want to.' Oh, his cell phone, very practical, I thought right away, telling myself he must be married."

"And was he married?" you ask.

"Married, with five or six children, I think, but that's not my problem. I didn't ask him to come over to me and start flirting. 'I don't have a cell to call you,' I replied to discourage him. But my reply had the opposite effect. 'You don't have a cell? No problem. Another reason to call me. You will have one tomorrow, from me.'

"I always wanted to have a cell phone, all my friends had one. Why should I refuse the offer, especially when I didn't even ask for it? And, even if he offered to pay my rent, why should I refuse? It's not because you've been helped once by a man while you were going through hard times that you are a prostitute. I've never been a whore, I am not one now and I'll never be one. I called him the next day from a payphone. He asked me to meet him in a fancy hotel downtown. He had kept his word; he had a cellphone for me. That is how I met Gustave. We were together for two years, no problems. He was part of my life, and I became attached to him."

"So, you were his 'second office'?" you conclude.

"Yeah, if that's what you want to call it, but"—she smiles—"who knows if in his eyes I did not become the primary, given the time he spent at my place?"

"The 'bang-bang', the bling-bling, and the bucks" Laurentine chimes in.

"As for the 'bang-bang', not so great. But the bling-bling and the bucks, I really had it all. I moved into a gorgeous apartment, and he took care of everything. Need the latest pagne? Here you go. Jewelry? Here you go. Anything I wanted, and it was immediately in my hands. All I was missing was a car, but it wouldn't have been long before I got one if his wife hadn't ruined everything. Armando looked unfavorably on all this and often gave me hell but, you know, big brothers usually don't understand anything. After all, it was my life, and I was happy."

"Have you seen his wife?" Laurentine asks you. "Skinny as a rail. No, worse. A needle! Not even a booty to bounce on the mattress. Can you imagine her in bed? Her poor husband must think he is making love to a skeleton. I understand why the guy was in love with Anne-Marie. You should have taken pity on that woman, Anne-Marie, and sent her vitamins or hormones to fatten her up a bit."

"I don't know if that bitch was premeditating it, but everything came crashing down one afternoon. Are you still interested, Méré?"

"Of course."

"I'll let Laurentine tell the rest."

"This is the part of Anne-Marie's story I like the most," she picks up. "I would have loved to have been there! That afternoon, she was invited to a celebration of the end of a period of mourning."

"I asked Gustave to come with me. He refused, giving me

reasons I simply could not believe. It was only afterward that I understood why."

"You know, Méré, it is at this party where we cast off our mourning clothes and celebrate that women compete in beauty," Laurentine goes on.

"In any case, I was beautiful that afternoon and, when you are beautiful, you know it, you can feel it in your being," Anne-Marie says with a smile.

"Like royalty in her super-wax," Laurentine continues, "her makeup enhancing the glow of her velvety skin and accentuating the flawless beauty of her face, Anne-Marie made quite an entrance. As soon as she noticed Gustave's wife..."

"No, she noticed me first, which gave her a strategic advantage. I did not suspect at all that she would be there."

"Listen," Laurentine says, "you tell me to tell it and you keep interrupting me, so go ahead, tell it yourself."

"No, but it's true, I had no idea she would be there. It was only when I entered the room that I noticed her. I think it was the first time she was seeing me, even if she certainly suspected I existed. I knew her, of course. A mistress always knows her lover's wife whereas the opposite is rarely the case. Anyway, the women around her must have taken malicious pleasure in revealing who I was to her. I suddenly understood why Gustave went to so much trouble to find a reasonable excuse not to come with me to the party: he knew his wife would be there. Perhaps they were even invited together, and he gave her some equally convoluted excuse not to come with her. He didn't have the balls to choose between his girlfriend and his wife—oh, excuse my language, Méré, but it's hard for me to hold my tongue when I think of all that. Our eyes met, hers burning with hatred, mine feigning indifference. I walked by her table to join my friends, all of whom were single and waiting for me. As a sign of my disdain for her, I curled my lips slightly and changed my way of walking into small slow steps which made me bounce as if the soles of my Dior pumps were cushioned with air. As luck would have it, I happened to be wearing this super-wax *pagne* that we call 'My husband is successful,' a way of saying in this case that the successful husband, her old man, was also mine. She was incensed. When I finally reached their table and sat down, my friends started cheering for me at the top of their voices. A few minutes later, I saw her get up and walk out. Like my friends, I thought she could no longer bear the fact that I was there, withdrew from the competition and left the party. I was wrong.

"Fifteen minutes later, she came back. I saw right away that she went to change her outfit. As a response to my *pagne*, she was now dressed in a 'three-piece' super-wax that we call 'Kanga lopango,' which literally means 'lock your compound'; in other words, no one was capable of entering her house and stealing her husband, because she had barricaded him in. Her response to me could not have been clearer. The earrings and the dainty chain she was wearing were not knockoffs. They were made of real jewels from Anvers, very expensive... the same ones Gustave offered to me. A puny body in oversized clothes, she headed over to the disc jockey with jerky steps which seemed even more mechanical because of her flat buttocks—our grandmothers, at least, had the intelligence to wear thick strands of pearls around their hips under their *pagnes*, the famous *djiguidas*, to make up for the curves they lacked, and gave them style. She had barely left the disc jockey's booth when the speakers started vibrating to Rochereau's song *A Woman's Beauty*, sung by Mbilia Bel:

I heard a lot about my rival / But I've never seen her / Finally today I see her... and the song went on to say that she thought her rival would have the beauty of an angel, but instead, she was hideously ordinary. Holding her Chanel bag ostentatiously in her hand, she started to dance with her group of women repeating at the top of their voices, the song's refrains, *Finga, finga, tonga, tonga*, etc., which means insult me, speak ill of me, say whatever you like, my dear—meaning me, Anne-Marie Ossolo—, but no matter what you do, that man is mine, I'll hold on to him, he's not going anywhere. The message could not have been more explicit, right?

"Now it was my turn to be incensed.

"I immediately pulled out a thousand-franc bill. I called one of the waitresses and told her to give it to the disc jockey and ask him to play Lutumba Simarro's *Nalembi*, which he did right away. As soon as the song started playing, all the girls who were at my table got up and rushed onto the dance floor. I in turn got up. I was also donned in an assorted ensemble of jewels—about two hundred thousand francs-worth—, swinging my purse in my hand, not a Chanel, a Gucci, even more chic, and I started to dance, repeating along with my friends the key words of the song addressing the older woman, the '*mama kulutu*', which said that, if she wanted us, the youth, to respect her, she should start by respecting us and not by acting ridiculously as she was.

"When the song was over, rolling our hips and shouting with joy, we went back to our singles' table, loudly congratulating ourselves."

"You made a strategic error," Laurentine interrupts, "you should not have counterattacked with that song. You should have made her seem old-fashioned with an ancient song played by some old-fashioned band."

"I don't know any."

"*Les Bantous de la Capitale*, for example, that band of grandpas no one ever listens to anymore except old men."

"But wait, Laurentine. As soon as we sat down, what did I hear? The song *Mwana Bitendi* by Youlou Mabiala."

"And how does that song go?" you ask, you, seeming more and more out of it among these two women who are very much with it.

"*My rival? A worthless rag doll / The poor thing hides and sleeps outside / While I am in the man's house and share his bed.* Me, a rag doll? Me, hide? Well, she's going to find me! She's going to see me in the spotlight! And I immediately bombarded her with Franco's *Bomba bomba mabe*, that song where the rival defies the woman of the house by shouting from the rooftops: *No more sneaking around / I announce openly that I am your husband's mistress / The whole city knows it except for you, fool.*

"And then as soon as my song was over, she shot Mpongo Love's *Ndaya* at me like a missile. Through the lyrics, she was telling me that she and her husband were like a belt holding up a pair of pants. No rival could unsettle their marriage. His mistress could run the most perfumed baths for him, give him manicures and pedicures, pamper him as much as any woman could, he would still come back to her, his 'first lady'!"

"Your response?"

"I admit that for a moment there I panicked because nothing was coming to mind to counterattack. Luckily our fight had become a group battle, with each table supporting her leader. My table thus suggested responding with *Niekesse*, also by Mpongo Love: *God truly went to great lengths when he created me / He made me a beautiful woman / So beautiful that all men grovel to me and work for me*, implying: her husband included.

"We continued like that, insulting each other, competing against each other, scratching each other's eyes out with songs. At one point, she had the DJ replay the first song with which she had initiated the brawl, *A Woman's Beauty*. That showed that she was running out of resources, that she didn't have any more songs to throw into the fight. Defeat, in other words!

"The room, which until then had been entirely rapt as we ruthlessly tore each other to pieces, booed when she repeated her record. That was when everyone understood that she could not battle adequately with me. I delivered the fatal blow with *Bilei Ya Mobali*—her husband's favorite dish—by the young and handsome Karmapa, a song I had danced to with Gustave not too long before. Through those lyrics, I made that poor woman understand that her husband was her husband as long as he was in her house, but that, the moment he stepped outside, he was everyone's husband. Besides, if he was happier with me, it was because I cooked his favorite meals whereas she only gave him reheated leftovers, a monotonous routine.

"Out of songs, thus vanquished and humiliated, she got up and, in a rage, yelled in my direction: 'Filthy whore, don't think you're going to come out of this like that!', then rushed outside with her entourage of friends. We all burst out laughing and one of my girlfriends ordered a round to celebrate our victory."

"It's now that it gets ugly" Laurentine announces. "Go ahead, Anne-Marie, be brave, tell her!"

"That same evening, around seven o'clock, Gustave came to my place seething with anger. 'I have some things to say to you,' he shouted at me, before we got to the living room. 'First, where were you last night? I came by twice and you weren't here.'

'I went out to run some errands with my brother.'

'Why didn't you tell me? I'm going to ask your brother if you were really with him.'

I was a little taken aback since up to that point, we had established a sort of trust between us. Why, all of a sudden, this jealous fit? There had to be something else.

'Don't be jealous,' I said to him.

'I am not jealous. I pay your rent. I buy your food. I buy your clothes. Is it too much to ask you to be home when I want to see you? But that is not the reason I came. I am here on a much more serious matter. Why did you provoke my wife this afternoon at the end of mourning celebration? It is hell at home! Couldn't you be more discrete? What exactly do you want, you want me to leave you?'

'She is the one who provoked me,' I replied.

'It would be normal for her to attack you. She is the entitled one, you know that.

'So,' I say to him, 'I'm the spare tire, huh? Just because you pay my rent doesn't mean you have to treat me like an object.'

'I don't treat you like an object,' he objects. 'All I ask is for you to be discrete, and in addition, to respect my life and be grateful for what I do for you.'

'Because you think you're generous?' I snapped at him. 'Don't take me for an idiot. You come to me looking for what your old lady cannot give you.'

'Don't insult my wife!'

'Well then, go be with her and leave me alone. Go on, get out!' I yelled at him.

It was pathetic seeing him like that, a real caricature of those men who are all macho on the outside but who toe the line at home as soon as their missus raises her voice. He could tell I was really mad because his tone suddenly changed.

'No, no, don't be angry with me, I was only explaining to you that...'

'No, get out,' I screamed, throwing a pillow I was holding, and went into my bedroom. I came right back out wearing only my bra and slip, because of the heat.

'You're still here?' I screamed at him, 'Go home to your beanpole wife!' I took off my bra, again because of the heat, leaving my breasts totally bare. I spread my legs wide apart and bent over to pick up a towel to wipe off my sweat. Out of the corner of my eye, I noticed his eyes glued to my chest, then slide downward. The poor guy couldn't help himself. He came over to me, wanting to touch me. I pushed him away.

'It's over, my dear. Listen, Anne...'

'Get out,' I told him, 'Get out!' And I went back into my room and slammed the door. "He stayed in the living room for a while, thinking I was going to come back out, then I heard the door slam shut. He was gone."

"He came back two days later, unable to hold out any longer. Apparently, his shrew could not keep him in her supposedly sealed compound. He brought a pair of sixty thousand-franc shoes with him to ask for forgiveness. Since I know when not to go too far, after I let him beg and cajole me just enough, I was back to being nice. We agreed to finish making up at a nice restaurant. That was before... the drama that evening."

"Well," you say, "you know what you want, right, and you know how to get it."

"How can one survive in this jungle of a city, Méré, if one doesn't know how to defend herself?"

"No one bullshits Anne-Marie," Laurentine adds.

"So, you went out to a restaurant and once again to your place…"

"No, sadly, it was over at the restaurant," Laurentine says. "Sorry, Anne-Marie, I didn't mean to interrupt you. This is the most tragic part of the story."

"You can say that. We had an amazing meal at this great restaurant I had never been to. After all, he was Gustave Boko-la, the businessman and senator. I think that, if you add the bottle of champagne that we popped open for the occasion, the bill was close to one hundred thousand francs. We ate well and were happy and, when we left the restaurant, I was wondering if after all that food, he would be able to beat his three-minute record in bed.

"We were heading toward the car holding hands, two lov-ers back together, when we heard the word 'whore' as if it were coming from a screaming rabid animal! We jumped. A figure leapt out from the shadows and Gustave recognized his wife. He let go of my hand… and ran to his car. I did not have time to react before I felt something burning my face. I howled in pain and brought my hand to my cheek. Blood everywhere.

'That's for you, dirty whore!' were the last words I heard before that woman disappeared again into the shadows, nimble like a beast of prey. For a moment, I thought I had gone blind. I cried out: 'Gustave, Gustave,' but there was no sign of him. The coward tried neither to defend me nor to go get help. He skedaddled with his tail between his legs as soon as he saw his missus. Staggering through the darkness, crying from the pain, I managed to find the door to the restaurant. The customers shrieked in horror when they saw me. A horrid gash across my face from the top of my eyebrow to the bottom of my cheek, almost to my chin. The wound was deep. It was not from a thin Gillette blade. She probably used one of those handheld straight edge razors barbers and hairdressers use. They tried their best to stop the bleeding with towels and ice while they waited for Armando whom I asked them to call with my cell. That is how I got this hideous disfiguring scar."

"Did you file a complaint?" A stupid question on your part since you already know the answer.

"A complaint against whom?" Anne-Marie replies. "You know very well that 'the woman of the house' is always right. And then the mockery! I am not the first "second office" to be slashed with a razor. Besides, most women think it's only fair, just like they find it normal to necklace a burglar. No, I kept quiet, but I am preparing my revenge."

"There is no one meaner to a woman than another woman," Laurentine declares, sententious. Solidarity among women ends where jealousy begins."

"You could not have said it better! I heard the other day on the radio that an American astronaut drove over twelve hours and covered some nine hundred odd miles just to douse her rival with aerosol gas pepper spray because she was jealous of her. And what about Gustave in all that?"

"Oh, the honorable senator? You won't believe it, but he never came back to see me. He completely dropped off the grid. And that hurt me too, almost as much as the wound on my face, because in the end he mattered to me. I found myself alone and penniless. Obviously, I couldn't pay my rent anymore, even after I moved to a tiny studio apartment, nor could I pay for the *pagnes* I had bought on credit. I started selling some of my jewelry and at one time I was so broke I sold the cell phone that meant so much to me. It was after all that that I ended up at the stone quarry with you all."

"You know that *pagne* we call '*Boma libala*,' homewrecker? Well, there is a brand-new model that just came out. We'll buy it and we'll go show it off to that woman."

"I want to do more than show off, I want to give her a taste of her own medicine."

"In my opinion, it's not so much that woman you need to take your revenge on," you say. "From her point of view, she was defending herself as well as her source of revenue. You told me yourself that she had five or six children. Maybe, after all, she loved the old man too and didn't want to lose him, especially since the guy is rich. The biggest bastard in all of this is Gustave. We should take Moukiétou with us to beat him up."

"So, you think she was right to disfigure me?"

"No, not at all," you hurry to say, "there is no excuse for that kind of aggression. It's serious, drawing blood."

"For me, it's the equivalent of attempted murder," Laurentine says, indignant.

Digressing, Anne-Marie asks:

"Is plastic surgery expensive? Do you think plastic surgery can make this huge scar disappear? I'd like to have my old face back."

"Plastic surgery can do anything, but it's very expensive."

"How much? Two hundred thousand?"

"More like a million to start," you say.

Laurentine, her small mirror still in her hand, gazes at herself and says: "Luckily mine is starting to disappear."

"When all this is over, don't you have any other plan besides revenge for the money you are going to get?", you ask.

"I haven't thought about it yet. Revenge is my priority."

"Can I give you my opinion, Anne-Marie?"

"Of course, Méré."

"True revenge, successful revenge, is when you do not sink down to the level of the person who humiliated you. If you take your revenge right away squandering the two hundred or three hundred thousand that you're going to make when all your bags are sold, you will find yourself, once again, all alone and penniless, and you'll still need support from someone like Gustave Bokola to help you live. You're still young, Anne-Marie, younger than Laurentine and me. Invest that money, make it grow, then you will be a free and independent woman. Nobody will be able to brag about paying your rent and demand that you be home and wait for him like a slave. You will be able to buy anything you want, and you won't have to beg. You can even have your plastic surgery. Earlier, I said it was expensive, but it's not that expensive. You will be even more beautiful than you already are. You will be the girl from Ipanema. When you walk by, all the men will turn their heads, oohing and aahing in admiration."

She listens intently to what you are telling her and does not speak right away when you stop talking, as if she wants to wait for your words to sink into her brain. Then she says:

"No one has ever spoken to me like that before, Méré. My brother spends all his time telling me he disapproves of my behavior, but he has never told me what I should do. I still want revenge, but I do not want to fall back into misery and dependence."

"I have an idea," Laurentine says, "Let's partner up and open that beauty salon together."

"Now there's a good suggestion, Anne-Marie," you say.

"Yeah, that's not a bad idea. I'll think about it. Actually, I am a really good hair braider. I could open a hair salon right next to yours. I know how to do Fulani braids, Fulani braids with shells, and Senegalese twists. I also know how to braid a weave, updos, thread, not to mention loose braids, curly braids, twists, goddess braids. I'm sure I am missing some. I also know how to straighten."

"There you go! If you put your money together, you will be able to start out with at least five hundred thousand," you applaud.

"I prefer you say half a million, Méré," Laurentine corrects you.

That last comment makes all three of you laugh as the phone rings. Armando will be there in two or three minutes. You leave a big tip for the young waitress who thanks you gratefully. Armando is already waiting for you when you walk out. Laurentine and Anne-Marie head for the backseats. You stop them saying that you would prefer that one of them sit up front because you want to be in the back. "Oh no," they both say with a knowing smile, "go sit next to Armando." You smile back; they are mistaken. Fine, you let him kiss you yesterday, but that doesn't mean anything. Armando is not so important to you.

THIRTY-ONE

YOU ALL GATHER outside before entering, as a delegation, the waiting room of the airport where Zizina and her mother are waiting for you, after she checked in. You are all decked out as if it were a day of celebration. Well, it is a day of celebration! After all, one of your daughters, a stone breaker's daughter, has made it in life and is getting ready to take a plane to join the men and women who try to defend peace and order on this planet. That is no small thing.

When a protocol officer in charge of welcoming the invited First Ladies sees your well-dressed delegation, he quite naturally thinks that you are one of the group of women dispatched for the occasion, and orders you to head towards the VIP lounge. "We came for something much more important than that," Moyalo answers with her usual cheeky humor.

You walk in as a group. Bileko kept her word; she did not tell her daughter you were coming to the airport to send her off. The latter shrieks in surprise when she sees you, gets up and rushes over to you. You all begin to applaud. Anne-Marie hands her the gift you bought for her, a watch that tells both local and universal time. Your country's time being GMT+1, no matter where she is in the world, she will always know what time it is at home just by glancing at the watch face. That way, she will feel closer to you. She unwraps the box, takes the watch out and clasps the metal bracelet around her wrist. The watch band is itself a piece of jewelry, which does not surprise you since Anne-Marie, a woman with taste, was the one who picked it out. Zizina's misty eyes are glistening with emotion. She hugs you one by one as you all applaud. You look at Mâ Bileko. She has a big smile across her face, not because Zizina is her daughter, but because she offered her as a gift to all her colleagues from the quarry.

Once the emotional moment is over, Zizina asks you all to tell her about your future plans, now that you have gotten what you wanted. Laurentine goes first. She shares her desire to open a beauty salon with Anne-Marie, which will double as a hair salon. While she speaks, Anne-Marie nods enthusiastically in approval. Mâ Bileko, who is the next to speak, announces that she is considering taking out one of those low-interest loans offered by a local NGO, to restart her former business.

Iyissou, Bilala, Moukiétou and Asselam do not have specific plans to speak of, as if, used to living day-to-day, the sudden and unexpected influx of money far exceeding their monthly needs has stunted their imagination. Usually, it is a project looking for money, whereas in their case it is the money that is looking for a project. Bileko who understood that right away, suggests that the four of them open a tontine together with the money they received today. After four months, each of them would have gathered four hundred thousand francs, eight hundred thousand if they have the patience to do it for ten months. The only problem is that by putting that money aside, to survive, they will have to keep breaking stone until the tontine ends. The four women like the idea and reason that, since they have already been breaking stones over the past three or four years, ten more months would not be an unsurmountable obstacle. When she hears that, Moyalo decides to go in with them. "That's even better," Bileko goes on, "with five, each one of you will have five hundred thousand francs after five months and, after ten, you will be… millionaires!"

An announcement over the loudspeaker calling all passengers to board immediately interrupts you. Last hugs, and Zizina, her new watch on her wrist, her travel bag in hand, heads toward her gate. Before going in, she turns around, suddenly inspired:

"I ask one favor of you. I would like to have a photo of you all together, at the quarry. A group photo. I will keep it with me in my room."

"No problem, Zina, you can count on us. I'll see to it," you assure her.

Waving her free hand as a last good-bye, she turns around again and disappears through the gate.

When you see the plane with the UN colors take off and disappear into the horizon of the wide-open blue sky, you all have the impression that a part of you is leaving and, like that aircraft that tears itself from earth's gravity and hovers free in the air, you feel that you too, thanks to your hard labor and your tenacious struggle to demand a fair price for that labor, have emerged from the shroud of poverty and hopelessness which, until this moment, has ravaged your lives.

As you exit the airport, you cross groups of women wearing pagnes or uniforms with the effigy of the President of the Republic and his wife, some in busses rented for the occasion, others on foot. They have been commandeered to come and welcome Madam the First Lady's guests. Soon, she herself will be here, surrounded by security services no less important than her husband's. And, when she comes out of the VIP lounge accompanied by her guests, those women will start chanting, dancing, gyrating and sweating in the dust and heat. It is what they call "an African welcome"! Making men, women and children dance to the beat of drums under a blazing sun! You think of the mastermind behind all this, the Minister of the Interior. Apparently, he did not carry out his threat, stopping you from coming to the airport. But could he really do that? Even in an autocracy, you cannot just stop a group of fifteen women who will not hesitate to resist and make a scandal by rejecting the orders given by the President's wife. Now it is time to leave the premises, and preferably one by one rather than in a group, so you can go fairly unnoticed.

Before each of you goes off in her own direction, you make a plan to meet tomorrow at the quarry. Who knows if it will be the last time?

As your group disperses, Anne-Marie comes over to you, hugs you and says: "Thank you so much, Méré, you have opened up my future."

You look at her. Her face is saying something that is difficult to define, something new. That slightly mischievous look which gave you the impression that her only aspiration in life was to please is gone. Instead, it expresses a sense of freedom that has never been there before, and the determination of a being who is ready to take charge of her own life. You never would have suspected that your little lecture this morning would have such an impact on her. You are happy about that. You smile at her and run a finger along her scar. You cannot help but admire once again that bizarre East Asian look emanating from her prominent cheek bones and almond-shaped eyes. From the time the Congo-Ocean Railway was built early last century, hundreds of coolies were imported from what was called back then Conchinchina: could one of them have been her great-grandfather?

"You are young and determined, Anne-Marie," you say to her. "You will make it. And if the hair salon venture doesn't work out, come see me, and I'll ask Auntie Turia to take you on at her sewing and embroidery shop. As you know, she is a renowned seamstress."

"Thank you so much, Méré. I will not hesitate."

She takes a few steps to go but comes back hurriedly:

"Oh no, this is terrible, I almost forgot! Armando asked me to tell you to call him for a ride home from the airport."

"Why?" you ask.

"I think he's in love with you."

You were expecting anything but that. While in your confusion, you take some time to react, she quickly moves away into the growing crowd. You shrug your shoulders and start walking too.

Tomorrow you will assess the situation. For now, you are savoring the joy of accomplishment. First, you think about the others. Even if Iyissou, Bilala, Moukiétou, Asselam and Moyalo's tontine does not work out as planned and they throw in the towel before they make their million, at least they will have broadened their horizons: they now know that life offers other alternatives for food, clothing and healthcare, beyond breaking stone. As for you, you have more than you need to get started with your plans. Tomorrow, you will go register for those three months of software training with business internships, which, you hope, will be the first step toward opening that small training school you have dreamed so much about.

Suddenly you remember the offer the Minister of Women and Disabled Persons made to you, to be her adviser. How could you completely forget about that? She promised to call you if you didn't call her, and her call could come at any moment. What will you do then? Wouldn't that be odd to go from being a stone breaker to a member of a ministerial cabinet, overnight?

Last night, you shared with Armando that if you did not fill the two remaining bags out of the twelve you had committed to, it would bother you for the rest of your life that not only did you leave a job unfinished, but you also let down your friends from the quarry. You still bore the weight on your conscience of that hundred-franc coin you never gave back to that unknown woman who had come to claim it late one night, on behalf of her son. You do not want to carry the weight of any additional regret. So, you need to go to the quarry tomorrow. Besides, you also need to keep the promise you made to Zizina: take a group photo by the riverside.

July 2005–December 2009.

AUTHOR AND TRANSLATOR BIOGRAPHIES

EMMANUEL DONGALA

Born in the Republic of Congo in 1941, Emmanuel Dongala is a scientist and author who came to the United States in 1997 during the civil war in his native country and was offered a professorship at Bard College, and later Simon's Rock Preparatory School, where he taught until 2014. Dongala is the author most recently of the acclaimed novel *The Bridgetower Sonata*, as well as *Johnny Mad Dog*, *Little Boys Come from the Stars*, and *The Fire of Origins*. He is the recipient of the 2011 Prix Ahmada Kourouma Award and his most recent novel *The Bridgetower Sonata* was shortlisted for the Prix Albertine in 2022. In June 2023, Dongala was awarded the *Grand Prix Hervé Deluen* from L'Académie française, a lifetime award for contributing to the promotion of French as an international language. After a longtime residency in the US, he now lives in Paris, France.

SARA HANABURGH

Sara Hanaburgh is a scholar (French and Francophone African literature and cinema) and translator working between French, Portuguese, Spanish and English. Her literary translations include *Kaveena* by Boubacar Boris Diop (*Kaveena*, 2016), co-translated with Bhakti Shringarpure, and Angèle Rawiri's novel *Fureurs et cris de femmes* (*The Fury and Cries of Women*, 2014). Her articles and translations have appeared in africaisacountry.com, *The Savannah Review*, *Warscapes*, *The Dictionary of African Biography*, *Imagine Africa*, v. 3 and *C& América Latina*. She teaches at Fordham University and is currently editing a volume on the history of adaptation of African literature to the screen. She lives in New York.